ROOM 526

ESPIONAGE, INTRIGUE, AND CLANDESTINE BROTHERHOOD

**A COLD WAR NOVEL BY
GERHARDT B. THAMM**

**THE SALTMARSH PRESS
2015**

Printed and bound in the United States of America
The Saltmarsh Press
P. O. Box 21232
St. Simons Island, GA 31522

www.saltmarshpress.com

DEDICATION

I dedicate this work to Manfred "Fred" Hertz, my friend and mentor in the U.S. Army's clandestine service. Born in Germany, and shunned by his homeland because of his heritage, he fought as a U.S. Army rifleman from Normandy across France into his then former homeland. Thereafter, he became the consummate intelligence officer. He taught me everything I know about clandestine intelligence. I also learned from him how to stay alive in this, the world's second oldest profession.

Not forgotten are those who have lived and died in the murky shadows of the clandestine world; who worked under incredible conditions that most others, even those in the intelligence community, cannot imagine. These operatives must remain nameless to protect them and their work.

Last, but certainly not least, this book is also dedicated to the wives of intelligence operatives. They see their husbands depart from the safety of their homes never knowing when or whether they will return. Wives never receive the credit they deserve because in this shadowy profession credit is rarely, if ever, given publicly.

ROOM 526

A MAN FOR ALL SEASONS

ANONYMOUS

A case officer must be intelligent and possess high, but flexible, moral standards. He must be an after-dinner speaker, a before and after-dinner guzzler, a night owl—work all day, drink all night, and appear fresh the next day. He must learn to sleep while riding on trains and on non-pressurized cargo planes. He must exist on one meal a day to make up CIF (Confidential Intelligence Fund) losses.

He must be able to lie convincingly to everyone and in that respect accomplishes the impossible task of lying to his wife without being caught.

He must live his lies, never forgetting which ones he has told to whom, but also remember who he really is, and that he must NEVER lie to higher headquarters even when telling the truth may mean embarrassment to him.

He must be a man's man, a ladies' man, a good provider, a Plutocrat, a Democrat, a Republican, a New Dealer, an old dealer, a fast dealer—technician, electrician, politician, mechanic, polygamist, ambidextrous and a specialist on the black market and various shady dealings.

He must be an expert driver, talker, liar, dancer, bridge player, golfer, poker player, chess player, philanthropist, nudist, and an authority on palmistry, chemistry, archeology, psychology, physiology, meteorology, criminology, international business law, reading tea leaves and crystal balls, blondes, brunettes, and redheads. He must be able to take dictation and type 150 words per minute in English, German, French, Russian, Bulgarian, Chinese, Japanese and Sanskrit, as well as read American Indian sign language, Egyptian hieroglyphics and the deaf and dumb alphabet.

He must have a memory, which is capable of remembering all dates, places, names and other assorted information brought out during three-hour conversations during which no notes were taken.

He must be a naturally gregarious individual, but be capable of working alone for long periods of time.

He must be able to establish close personal relationships without becoming involved.

He must love people and be able to make them love him. He must always maintain the proper amount of cynicism and view those who love him in an objective manner, being ready to terminate a relationship without explanation if that relationship is no longer of value to him.

He must be the cosmopolitan type.

He must be comfortable sipping wine in the best restaurants, but also capable of inhaling dust, living outside at 10 degrees below zero, and working all summer without perspiring or acquiring B.O.

He must be able to maintain an expensive wardrobe on a meager salary. He must be methodical and have patience, tenacity, initiative, integrity, but he must not let these traits stand in the way of accomplishing his task in half the time it would take to do it right.

In addition to all of the qualifications, it helps if he is CRAZY.

****

Old Spooks never die, they ...

****

So many thoughts, so many memories, so much home life; all lost.
Thus says the Pointman

****

Espionage, the world's second oldest profession—
and one not quite as honorable as the oldest.
—From the coffers of an old Intelligence Officer.

ACKNOWLEDGEMENTS

First and foremost I must give thanks to Suanne Zuzel Thamm, my wife, for her patience, for enduring my many hours of questioning, and for her encouraging me to complete this manuscript.

Also many thanks to my publisher, Carlton A. Morrison, of The Saltmarsh Press, for his encouraging words and guidance, and to my editor, Emily Carmain, for her efforts to make this manuscript a readable book. She often found, and corrected, many little glitches that this author seemed to have overlooked.

GERHARDT THAMM
Fernandina Beach, Florida
August 2015

PROLOGUE

Although this is a work of fiction, much of it is based on fact, and on some forty years I spent in the intelligence services of the United States of America. The particular circumstance the book deals with, and expands upon, was the U.S. Navy's interest—in the 1950s—in developing a highly advantageous titanium submarine hull. In learned Navy-associated journals, expert submarine structural engineers, and metallurgists, praised the advantages of titanium hulls over the usual HY-80 (high yield) steel commonly used—but when it became apparent that the cost of a fleet of titanium submarines would exceed the entire Navy budget, articles on titanium became rare. In Soviet intelligence circles, this was taken to mean the U.S. Navy's interest in titanium had gone "black;" in other words, had become highly classified.

I first heard of titanium submarines when I became a submarine analyst at the Naval Intelligence Support Center (NISC) at Suitland, Maryland. "Old timers" told wonderful stories— folklore—about the U.S. Navy's interest in titanium. These stories encouraged me to write this fictional account of a highly classified clandestine operation, an operation ordered by the President of the United States, an operation intended to induce the Soviets to spend themselves into bankruptcy by themselves building titanium submarines. Actually, whether or not they could afford it, the Soviets did build six highly automated, modern, titanium submarines, but all were decommissioned after the Soviet Union's collapse.

At NISC, I eventually became the project officer for Soviet attack submarines. In 1993, I wrote an "After Action" account of an Intelligence collection—largely an effort by the Central Intelligence Agency—against Soviet Navy Projekt 705, the all-titanium nuclear-powered, fast attack submarine that carried the NATO designation ALFA Class SSN. The Agency accepted my report, and on 30 June 1994, James Woolsey, Director of Central Intelligence, awarded me "The Studies in Intelligence Award in Recognition of an Outstanding Contribution to the Literature of Intelligence." For more than a decade this treatise remained classified but can now be read online at the CIA website, in *Studies in Intelligence*, Vol. 52, No. 3, pp. 17- 24. The title: "The ALFA SSN: Challenging Paradigms, Finding New Truth, 1969-79."

Declassification gave me a needed "kick-start" to get on with this manuscript.

While this account is fiction, it is as close to fact as security rules permit.

CHAPTER 1

On this day, Hans Reiter, an American Special Intelligence Operations Officer in his mid-fifties, violated one of the cardinal rules of all intelligence services, a rule "carved in stone." *Never become friends with your asset.*

For much of the time during those tense days Reiter, of the highly secretive American counterintelligence element known only as Room 526, had dealt warily with his asset. Asset? Reiter had recruited a Soviet Intelligence officer to be a U.S. mole inside the GRU—*Glavnoye Razvedyvatelnoye Upravleniye*—Soviet General Staff Intelligence Unit. Reiter was the case officer, the Soviet his asset.

It was a beautiful summer day. Reiter and his asset were having another of their infrequent "Treffs," that is, another clandestine meeting, this one in the Kurpark, the park that surrounds the famous baths of Bad Homburg-vor-der-Höhe, a short drive from Frankfurt-on-Main. It was during this Treff that Reiter and his asset declared friendship for each other.

This violation of that cardinal rule of the clandestine world was not a sudden occurrence. Rather, it was the culmination of a succession of events that had started eleven years earlier. Acually, even earlier. Three decades earlier. A time of many dark secrets; the efforts of two nations both to keep them and to uncover them. The time of the Cold War.

CHAPTER 2

FRIDAY, MARCH 6, 1953
SOVIET MILITARY MISSION
BELMONT ROAD AND MASSACHUSETTS AVENUE, NW
WASHINGTON, D.C.

Shortly after the end of World War II the leaders of the Union of Soviet Socialist Republics were the first to recognize America's emergence from backwaters of espionage. As the Cold War pushed a reluctant United States onto the stage of world power and intrigue, Washington became the preeminent target for the world's second oldest profession, and the Soviets began to send their best intelligence operatives there.

Major Ivan Ivanovich Kasandroff arrived in Washington on a beautiful spring afternoon shortly after President Eisenhower's inauguration. Major Kasandroff of the GRU had an office in the Soviet Military Mission in the northwestern section of Washington. The facade of the early twentieth century mansion on Belmont Road concealed the Soviet Union's most proficient, most active espionage apparatus in America.

Kasandroff's basic mission was to report on American military intention, preparedness, and capability, including the quality and quantity of all existing and future weapons systems, as well as U.S. defense procurement and production capability. Success in the mission required answers to questions that only an insider, one working in the American military high command, could give.

Although the GRU had considered Kasandroff one of its best intelligence officers, he spent some twenty frustrating months trying to recruit an American government employee, without success. True, Kasandroff had arrived in Washington at a difficult time—an especially difficult time for a Soviet intelligence officer. The emerging Cold War, the hot war raging in Korea since June of 1950, and the not yet forgotten Berlin blockade of the late 1940s had embittered many Americans, making them shy away from contacts with anyone from a Communist Bloc nation. Yet, the Centre, GRU headquarters in Moscow, kept after him to recruit human sources with information on the Pentagon's ability to destroy the Soviet Union.

In late 1953, Kasandroff s starshina, the sergeant assigned to the major's office as an administrative assistant, handed him yet another message from the Centre. Kasandroff cringed. Even before he broke the seal, he knew it would be another of a never-ending string of messages demanding recruitment of U.S.

government officials, recruitment, always recruitment.

By the grave of my dear grandmother, he thought, *it's not as if I have not tried.* Kasandroff had searched for Americans, government employees, anyone with access to classified information, in telephone directories, even the Pentagon directory, all for naught. He glanced at the single-page message. As he read through the preamble he saw that it was indeed another reminder, "... request you apply urgency to all standard and special collection requirements. GRU London reports American military production nearing 1944 levels. Urgent: confirm veracity of this report. Centre sends."

Aside from being frustrated by his failure at recruiting, Kasandroff was comfortable in his Washington office. He occupied a tiny corner office in the old building conveniently located just a city block off Massachusetts Avenue, overlooking Washington's charming Rock Creek Park. From there Kasandroff and his colleagues were within easy driving distance of America's nerve center. Their mission: ferret out military, industrial, political and economic secrets. Their purpose: enhance the power and the prestige of Rodina, the Motherland—the Union of Soviet Socialist Republics.

From the two windows of his small office Kasandroff watched automobiles rushing along the parkway. During the morning rush hour they streamed westward toward the Pentagon and toward the CIA buildings on the mall near the Lincoln Memorial. In the afternoon the traffic flow reversed as all the government employees rushed home. *Everything is so comfortable here,* he thought, *except for the damned pressure from the Centre. If I could only recruit at least one of these government employees, I would be safe.* He shivered just thinking how his career would come to an end if he were to be recalled. *"Chert znayet—*the devil knows," he mumbled, "I might end up in the damned infantry with the rest of the peasants."

During his first year in Washington, Kasandroff had used every trick he had learned at Olympic Village, the GRU training center near Kirovograd in south central Ukraine, to recruit Americans—especially government employees—all to no avail. During the past six months he had become increasingly fearful that his Washington assignment might be terminated unless he found ways to increase his reporting. Kasandroff had wrestled with his conscience for weeks before surrendering, before violating one of the "carved in stone" GRU operating rules: never fake a source recruitment!

Kasandroff remembered the day he had first violated this rule. He had discovered this "recruiting" method purely by accident. While at the Library of Congress picking up recently published scientific data, he noticed that most desks had nameplates, many with impressive job titles. In a flash of brilliance, it occurred to him that he could list a few of the librarians as his sources. He knew it was an act of desperation, and totally against his better judgment. He also knew

3

that inventing sources was one of the GRU's cardinal sins, but in his own mind he tried to justify it: These librarians did provide him with information from their vast holdings. But deep down, he knew it was a flimsy excuse.

At first the thought of fabricating sources had terrified him, but following the old Russian proverb that "when in extremis the devil will eat flies," he soon attributed the information he had gleaned researching at the library to "casual" sources. Such nomenclature demanded less documentation than "numbered" sources. Many steps had to be negotiated before a source received a permanent number. To create his imaginary source dossiers and make them appear thoroughly authentic, he added physical descriptions and job titles of his "sources," as well as their habits. One dossier noted, "Mary eats doughnuts every morning at ten a.m.," another contained the more lengthy description, "John is a real lady's man. Flirts with all the girls. Seems to think women cannot live a happy life without him."

From the Library of Congress he expanded his "recruiting" to the libraries at the Patent Office and the Smithsonian Institution; he even ventured into the public libraries of the District of Columbia picking up bits of information. To cover his tracks—just in case a future replacement or internal security should inquire—he listed all these government employees as unwitting sources; informants who do not know what agency or country got the information. To make it all look proper and in accordance with the teachings at the Olympic Village he kept meticulous records of the supposed lunch and dinner expenses he had incurred to keep these sources happy. He intended to use these surplus funds to pay his informant, whenever he recruited a real source.

However, in the meantime, he had an unanticipated problem: where to stash the money? He could not spend it on himself without attracting embassy attention. As an interim measure, he had taped bundles of money inside the spring mattress of his bed, but as they grew in size, he realized that he would soon have to find a better hiding place.

Kasandroff knew that these casual sources were only a temporary measure. They were not as good as real, by-the-GRU-book, recruited sources, but it placated the Centre somewhat, until... well, until real tasking came along. The message his starshina had handed him this afternoon was real tasking, tasking that required insider information on war material and production figures—and he did not have an insider.

CHAPTER 3

It was a beautiful Friday in late 1953, but GRU Major Ivan Ivanovich Kasandroff felt all closed in; he needed fresh air; he had to get out of the office to breathe. He thought that maybe an afternoon breathing the rarefied air at the Library of Congress would ease his anxiety. He slipped his ready-tied necktie over his head and looked in the mirror to straighten it. He glanced at his reflection. He was twenty-nine years old, but looked older—somewhere in his middle thirties. Appearing older had always been to his advantage. "With age comes wisdom," assures another old Russian proverb. He was not exactly handsome; his appearance was more on the rugged side. He was nearly six feet tall, barrel-chested and muscular. Six mornings each and every week, between six and seven, he jogged and lifted weights in the embassy's gymnasium. It was part of his service's requirement to be, and appear to be, "lean and mean."

He picked up his notebook and ballpoint pens, walked downstairs to the guard desk and signed out: Major Kasandroff, Source contact, ETR 1900 hours.

On that particular Friday Kasandroff just wanted to get as far away from his office as he could. Centre Moscow had harassed him for months with not so subtle reminders that he had fallen down on his job. He drove quickly out of the garage, turned right on Belmont Road, and drove around the block watching for surveillance—he saw none. His car was an older model Chevrolet with a much-neglected paint job. Although it had diplomatic license plates, it did not look like a car driven by the average diplomat.

As he drove into Southeast Washington he decided to swing around the Washington Navy Yard to see if there was anything worthwhile reporting. Last summer, more or less by accident—while driving along the Anacostia River watching gorgeous, sunbathing American girls—he noticed a good location for intelligence photography of the yard. Early April, unfortunately, was still a bit too cool for sunbathing beauties, but he had his camera ready. He drove along the Anacostia River snapping photos of the yard and of a visiting U.S. Coast Guard cutter. *Well,* he smiled, *not as pretty as girls in skimpy clothing, but it will make for another report—not that it will placate Centre.*

He crossed back into Washington proper via the South Capitol Street Bridge and drove around Capitol Hill until he found a legal parking space. With the last urgent message from the Centre in mind, he entered the periodicals section of the Library of Congress. Kasandroff thought that the library should have some financial statements or stock information on aircraft manufacturers such as Boeing, and gun makers like Winchester or Colt. He located several sheets with financial information on stocks of weapons and weapons' systems production companies but could not quite grasp the complex numbers and graphs. He finally asked one of the librarians who explained them, finishing with, "I wish I had bought those stocks two years ago. I would be a rich woman today."

Kasandroff decided this statement was "confirmation," conclusive proof that the American arms business was on the upswing and that an increase in weapons production was an inevitable consequence. He decided to report that GRU London's assessment was correct. He even remembered the name of the librarian; she was one of his regular "sources." He returned all the papers to the librarian and thanked her for helping him.

It was already past six o'clock, and with Washington's afternoon rush hour nearly over, he decided to reward himself with a good dinner at Sam's Bar & Grill, his favorite Georgetown restaurant.

Kasandroff had discovered this bar-restaurant shortly after his arrival in Washington. He had been a total novice in a land for which the instructors in the Olympic Village had supposedly prepared him. It was all so different from what he had been taught. During a late afternoon more than a year ago, he had ventured from the Soviet military mission building on foot to familiarize himself with the area, to reconnoiter the terrain. For a newly arrived case officer, to acquire a thorough knowledge of the area, of the terrain, was one of the most important requirements. The old colonel at Olympic Village instructed his aspiring future case officers to know every alley, every public space that could be entered and left without arousing suspicion. Most important: "walk the land."

Kasandroff became fascinated with the well-kept houses and gardens. As he wandered along the tree-lined avenues and explored the wonderful old side streets of this section of Washington, he lost all sense of time and place. After several hours, his rumbling stomach reminded him that he was a long way from his Belmont Road office, and that he had not eaten since just before noon. He oriented himself with the aid of the street map he had fortunately stuck into his back pocket before he left the office. It was hunger as well as a bit of curiosity that led him to Sam's Bar & Grill. Finding this restaurant had been one of the luckier moments of his stay in America. As he wandered along M Street looking for a place to eat and ogling the girls in the pretty dresses, he noticed a partially blocked, handwritten sign that proclaimed "Happy Hour: 4-6." The sign intrigued him. He opened the door while wondering what "Happy Hour" meant; it was one of the many American colloquialisms the instructors at Olympic Village had failed to mention. Kasandroff thought, *By the beard of Father Lenin, I'll turn this into a training mission. Might as well enjoy it.*

He opened the door and peeked somewhat uncertainly into the establishment. A bar with dark wood and a polished brass rail ran along the entire left side of the restaurant. It was crowded with men—apparently office workers judging by their attire—and a few well-dressed women. Unsure what to do next Kasandroff stood staring into the smoke-filled room. A waitress approached him and asked, "Table for one?"

Kasandroff nodded, hoping he understood what that meant. He followed the waitress who seated him at a small table with two chairs. He ordered dinner and a beer, and while he waited for the waitress to return, he took in his surroundings. *There must be a thousand different bottles on the glass shelves behind the bar,* he thought. *How does anyone know what to order?*

Lights, hidden by a dark, wooden cowling hung from the ceiling, barely illuminated the bar. Numerous lamps with colored glass shades hung from the ceiling throughout the dining area, where each table held its own little lantern.

Rather cozy, he thought. *I must come here more often.* Just then the waitress returned and set two glasses of beer on the table.

He looked at her somewhat puzzled. "Two?"

The waitress smiled, "Sure, it's Happy Hour." Kasandroff watched as the shapely young waitress approached the next table. He thought, *This is a cozy place. Here I can be myself and enjoy my stay in America.*

He raised his glass and toasted himself, "To Happy Hour."

Shortly thereafter, the waitress brought his dinner. He was hungry and downed it before he started on his second beer. Then it dawned on him that this was the first time since his arrival in America that he was completely relaxed. It was simply wonderful. No one in the restaurant seemed to know, or care, who or what he was. Holding the half-empty beer glass close to his chest he leaned back and examined his surroundings. He admired the three bartenders rushing back and forth, laughing and talking nonstop to the drinkers standing or leaning on the bar. The bartenders seemed to know everyone, and everyone seemed to know everyone else. He was among a crowd of young professionals, including, it seemed from hearing them talk, a good assortment of government employees.

As he listened to their chitchat he heard familiar acronyms—acronyms he had learned at Olympic Village. Someone said, "DOD," another—"Pentagon," a third—"Agency." He knew that DOD was the American War Department, and that the Pentagon was the gigantic building that housed the War Department. And he had been told that the insiders, and those who wanted to appear to be insiders, always referred to the Central Intelligence Agency as "The Agency." Kasandroff realized that these late afternoon revelers must have come to the bar directly from their offices.

It was then that he knew that Sam's Bar & Grill was not only a comfortable place to spend a late afternoon or evening but, properly handled, it could be the ideal place to meet, and maybe even recruit, some of these government employees as GRU sources. In the meantime he listened to the chitchat between customers hoping to pick up some tidbits for his next message to Centre. In his mind this justified eating here at least every Friday. He wondered what his chances were to recruit at least one of these men—and a few women—who crowded around the bar.

When the waitress brought the bill Kasandroff noticed that she had charged him for only one beer. When he mentioned it, she smiled. "It's Happy Hour." Now he knew why Americans had given this time-period that name, it made him happy.

He made another discovery. Four young men sitting at a nearby table ordered something they called "bourbon on the rocks." The waitress brought them whiskey glasses filled with a brown liquid and ice cubes. Since Kasandroff actually preferred whiskey to American beer, he decided to make bourbon on the rocks his drink of choice during his next visit—although he wondered, *Why do Americans call ice cubes rocks?*

That seemed an eternity ago. Kasandroff had kept his promise to make this cozy place his hangout. He had dined here at least once each week; sometimes, when the mood struck him, even twice. Most of the customers came in groups of four or more. Only a very few, such as himself, came as singles. He never saw women dining alone, but there were two or three men, middle-aged ones, who did. He noticed one, a plainly dressed loner, who glanced sometimes in Kasandroff s direction. He wore clothes that were not especially well coordinated—browns and blues mixed. At first Kasandroff thought, *I hope he is not one of those homosexuals looking for a date.*

It no longer worried him. Today Kasandroff had far more pressing concerns. The last message from Centre bothered him; the tone seemed to imply that Centre had become increasingly unhappy with his performance. Thoughts of a career-killing recall to Moscow troubled him.

On that particular Friday afternoon Kasandroff must have arrived at just the right time. He managed to get the last "table for two." Being a good tipper may have helped. Just as he settled down, a new rush of customers crowded around the bar. The whole place was once again in perpetual motion. Bartenders rushed back and forth, waitresses scurried between tables, and happy drinkers talked loudly as they emptied their glasses. Smoke whirled toward the ceiling. "Ah, what a great place," said Kasandroff to no one in particular.

Four of the men at the next table were in a heated discussion—something about the Democrats and Republicans. Kasandroff heard one of them loudly blustering, "These assholes on the hill..." Kasandroff realized that this person most likely spoke ill of his national leaders on Capitol Hill. The first time he heard such talk he wondered whether there was not an FBI agent present who would arrest this loudmouth. But over time he had learned that such talk was strictly what was known as "the American way."

Kasandroff watched the familiar scene around him, when he was startled by a voice. "M ... m ... may I share your table?" He looked up to see the rather plainly dressed, unremarkable middle-aged man whom he had dubbed a "regular" standing at his table.

After a brief hesitation Kasandroff replied, "Of course! Please do."

"Thank you," replied the American. "This p ... place is p ... pretty crowded. I appreciate it. My name is Walter, Walter Waldmann."

Kasandroff introduced himself and agreed with the American. "This is a very popular place. The food and drink are outstanding."

Walter Waldmann replied, "Yes, I eat here often." He looked around as if to see if anyone paid any attention. "From your name and your accent I assume you must be Russian?" Before the shocked Kasandroff could answer, the harried waitress approached them and quickly took their drink orders. After she left their table, the American looked at Kasandroff and asked in a lowered voice, "S ... so? Are you with th ... the Russian embassy?"

Kasandroff, now taken completely off guard by such an unexpected opening question, stuttered, "Eh, yes, eh, I am."

The American pretended to busy himself with his napkin. He looked around as if checking to see whether anyone was watching—or listening. "Sssso, you must be with the intelligence. Are you KGB or GRU?"

Kasandroff flinched, as an alarm signal went off in his brain, and panic filled his thoughts. *What in hell is going on? What does this fellow want?* The arrival of the waitress with their drinks gave him an opportunity to gather his thoughts and recover his composure. After she left their table, he took a sip from his glass and calmly protested, "No, no, I am the economic attaché."

The American leaned back and smiled. "Ah, so you are GRU."

In rapid succession security warnings flashed through Kasandroff's mind: *Entrapment? No! Recruitment? No! Finally, what am I doing here sharing my table with that...? What the hell is going on?*

Before answering, he studied his table partner. Waldmann did not have the appearance of an FBI agent, at least not from what Kasandroff had seen of FBI agents in the training films at Olympic Village. In the films they were all very self-assured, moved confidently, and wore dark suits, white shirts, and plain, dark neckties. And, for reasons Kasandroff could never fathom, they always wore gray or black fedoras.

Kasandroff observed Waldmann watching him through old-fashioned, black-rimmed eyeglasses while playing with his drink. His patient waiting had given Kasandroff time to think over his options. Kasandroff decided to take a chance. He proceeded cautiously.

"Well, let's assume I am GRU. What is it to you? I mean, I am sitting here minding my own business. You come to my table, ask to share it with me because all the other tables are taken. I am nice enough to permit you to sit, and you ask all sorts of questions. What is it you want?"

The American smiled, still turning his drink one way then the other. "Just testing. The first time I saw you having dinner at this restaurant I thought you were Russian."

"And why was that?" asked Kasandroff warily.

"I don't know," the American shrugged. "I knew you were a foreigner from your accent when I heard you order your meals. And from the way you wear your hair. You must get your hair cut at your embassy. Right?"

Kasandroff was chagrined. He had been told that the embassy barber was American-trained. He made a mental note to report that to security. "What else?"

"As I said, I saw you dining a number of times—always alone. I thought you looked and sounded like a Russian. So, I sp ... spent several Saturdays at the park near Belmont Road, near your military mission building. I saw you coming out of that building once or twice." He paused and seemed to spend a few seconds collecting his thoughts before continuing. "This is my favorite restaurant. I come here often. I wanted to talk with you, but there were always empty tables and I had no goo ... good reason to sit at your t... table. Today is different."

Kasandroff was still puzzled. "So? I also have noticed you eating here, and also alone. I ask you once more: What is it you want?"

The American looked around again discreetly as if to see whether anyone was listening.

"I may have something of interest for you. Let me put my cards on the table. I am a ship design engineer, a naval architect, for the U.S. Navy."

"You work for NAVBUSHIPS?" Kasandroff asked. He wanted the American to know that he was not entirely ignorant of U.S. government organizations.

"Well, yeah, NAVBUSHIPS, but we call it BUSHIPS for short."

"Ah, that's good to know," replied Kasandroff. "You build navy ships and submarines, right?"

"Right. Well, we don't build them, we just design them. We are the U.S. Navy's design bureau." Waldmann glanced around the room before adding with a touch of urgency, "If you are GRU, say so."

Kasandroff stared at him for several seconds. He wondered, *Should I risk further contact with this strange man whose tongue darts in and out of his mouth like a snake?* Finally, as if to signal resignation to fate, he sighed and said, "All right. You are correct. I am GRU."

The American visibly relaxed. Hunching over his drink and lowering his voice, he said, "Okay. With that out of the way let me tell you what I have. You tell me if it is of interest to you, and how much it's worth to your country."

Waldmann took a brief sip from his glass. "I am a native of this area. I was born in Alexandria, Virginia, across the river from here. I am a graduate ship design engineer. I have worked at BUSHIPS since fo... forty... since 1944."

Kasandroff nodded, and Waldmann continued, "I live in the northwest section of Washington, on Irving Street, right off 16th Street. I rent a third-floor apartment in a row house. I've lived there since I came to work for the U.S. Navy in 1944. I was draft-exempt in World War II because of poor eyesight. It's a nice place, comfortable, except the landlady is an old ditty."

The waitress briefly interrupted this conversation. They ordered their dinner. Then Kasandroff asked, "Ditty? What is ditty?" He had not heard that term before.

"Yeah, d... ditty, old woman, and a nosy one at that," replied Waldmann with a nervous laugh. "When I first moved into the apartment house I noticed she read all my postcards, and looked at my magazines. I finally got myself a postal delivery box at the snack bar and newsstand nearby. I go there anyway after work to pick up *The Evening Star*, so for a few bucks I got one of about twenty mailboxes the owner keeps for his customers. At least that way the old ditty doesn't get to see my girlie magazines."

Kasandroff was becoming bored. He wondered whether this man was worth his time. He decided to cut off Waldmann's ramblings. "You still have not told me what you want from me." Waldmann looked up, "Oh, yeah. Well I am willing to provide you with certain information—for a price."

Kasandroff leaned over and spoke quietly, "Mister Waldmann. You must understand that this business I am in is just like any other business. The quality of the goods received drives the price. Tell me what you have and I can more or less give you ... what is the American term ... something to do with baseball?"

"B... ballpark figure?" Waldmann suggested helpfully.

"Yes, yes, ballpark figure," agreed Kasandroff.

"Okay. How about if I can bring you the naval ship's characteristics of, let's say, the next destroyer that will be launched maybe three years from now?"

"Ship's characteristics?" A thought shot through Kasandroff s mind. *Holy Madonna, if this fellow is for real, he is selling the store, the whole goddamned store.* He tried his best to hide his excitement, to appear not too impressed by Waldmann's offer. "Please, give me in detail what that would be."

Waldmann now seemed to be in his element. He was so engaged in his talk, he even seemed to have lost his stutter. "I could get you all sorts of information on the ship, like length overall, length between perpendiculars, beam at waterline, maximum beam, engine designs, horsepower output, auxiliary generators, fuel

11

load, range—I mean how far it can travel—nautical miles, electronics, weapons configuration, ammo load—you know, how many shells, depth charges, all that stuff. Also, I'll tell you how many officers and sailors it takes to run the ship. Those sorts of things." He paused to take a breath, along with another sip of his drink before adding in a low voice, "I might even be able to bring you the whole ship's plan, and blueprints of warships, but that would be more difficult."

"That," replied Kasandroff thoughtfully, trying not to betray his eagerness, "would bring a nice sum of money. Maybe, I don't know, maybe three, four thousand dollars. I think if you could bring me copies of blueprints that would be even better. I mean, more money—for you."

A grin flickered across Waldmann's face.

Kasandroff became serious. "But, before we go any further, I must know why you are doing this."

Waldmann turned red-faced. He seemed uncomfortable and embarrassed as he looked around the room. "A whole lot of reasons. I am as good an engineer as anyone in my off... office, better than some, but I don't participate in all the office bullshit, the parties, and that sort of stuff. In the office the big thing is briefing admirals. If you get to brief them, they get to know you."

Before he continued he briefly glanced around again. "P ... probably you noticed that I have a speech impediment. I don't get to brief the big shots. They don't know me; I don't know them. I am made to work in the back room like I have some kind of terrible disease. Guys, smooth talkers that worked half as long as I, guys whose drawings I have to check for errors, get promoted. I mean, others get promoted, b ... but I get passed over. Also, a lot of the guys are married and get together with the boss for picnics. Eh ... they don't think I fit in."

Waldmann swirled the liquor in his glass, then quickly downed his drink. "I am pissed off with them, b... because of office politics. I work as hard as the next man, better than some, but I don't get promoted."

The mention of "ships characteristics" had intrigued Kasandroff. He decided to play the role of sympathetic listener to his unhappy table companion. Kasandroff found it difficult to respect a man who seemed so pathetic. Yet, perhaps an investment of sympathy for this loser would yield high stakes results.

After relating several specific examples of poor treatment by his superiors and receiving several sympathetic clucks from Kasandroff, Waldmann appeared even more resolved. "Yes, yes, I am pissed-off enough to get even with those bastards. That's the real reason why I wanted to talk with you," he said, then signaled the waitress for another drink.

After the waitress left he continued, "I am single. I mean, I admit, I am not the best-looking guy around, but I enjoy the ladies of the night. That costs a bit of money. Money is important, but not the main reason."

Kasandroff had heard what he wanted to hear, what he needed for his initial contact report to the Centre. He would write, "Source is motivated by desire for revenge against the system and his boss." This was a motive much favored in the teachings at the Olympic Village. Now that they were partners of sorts Kasandroff felt he could ask Waldmann at least one additional question, not just out of curiosity. "Tell me, when I told you that I was the economic attaché, why did you say, 'So, you must be GRU?' I mean ..."

Waldmann smiled. "We just had our annual security briefing. That's where I heard that the economic attaché is always GRU, and the political attaché is always KGB." Kasandroff made a mental note. He would make this a topic for his next message to the Centre. "Casual source informed me..."

Although Kasandroff was in a euphoric mood following Waldmann's tantalizing offer to provide blueprints of warships and ships' characteristics, he knew that there was a problem; a serious problem as far as GRU recruiting procedure was concerned.

Waldmann was a walk-in—a person who had volunteered to betray his country—and GRU frowned upon walk-ins. Kasandroff was determined to circumvent GRU procedures. He remembered the old colonel's warning about walk-ins at Olympic Village, and he was not about to let this, his only U.S. government official, fall through the cracks because of a mere bureaucratic procedure. While Waldmann recited his litany of the mistreatments and injustices he had endured over the past many years, Kasandroff racked his brain trying to figure out a way to turn the walk-in into a genuinely recruited GRU HUMINT source. He had an idea. He had to convince Waldmann that their meeting was not as accidental as it might have seemed.

He impatiently held up his hand to stop Waldmann's seemingly endless tale of woe. "Mister Waldmann, just so you know, over the past months I too had noticed you eating here, and also alone. I have known for some time, from Department of Defense telephone books and some investigation conducted by my office, that you work at NAVBUSHIPS. As a diplomat I was somewhat reluctant— eh, you know, security procedures, et cetera—reluctant to approach you, hoping that the right moment may happen. Just as I had worked out a plan to approach you, you visited my table!"

Kasandroff chuckled and smiled at Waldmann. In a friendly voice, he added, "Of course, I am very, very happy that you did so. But let there be not one doubt in your mind, the Soviet Union chooses its friends very carefully. Had I not already been fully aware of your background and your potential usefulness as a friend to the Soviet Union, you would not be sitting here with me as my guest."

Waldmann looked puzzled, and then shrugged in resignation. "Well, okay. I guess that's how you fellows work."

Kasandroff s smile disappeared as suddenly as it had appeared. He peered closely at his "guest" as he added in a clipped tone. "Good. Just so we understand each other, should I ever be required to turn you over to one of my colleagues, you may have a need to recall our first meeting. It will be in both of our interests that you remember that only chance resulted in you making the first contact with me; that I had my eye on you for a long time." He glanced at his watch, as though he had something more important to do later this evening.

In a cold, clear voice he captured Waldmann's full attention. "Never doubt the resourcefulness of your new partners. We are always in control. Nothing happens in this business by chance. You would demonstrate your intelligence by keeping this thought constantly in mind should we decide to buy what you want to sell."

Waldmann stopped fiddling with his half-eaten dinner and looked thoughtfully at Kasandroff for several seconds. In contrast to his earlier, whining tone, he seemed to have lost his stutter, and appeared to be in complete control when he replied, "I understand. You will not be disappointed."

With this problem solved, Kasandroff's brain raced through the possibilities available with this well-placed source, the monies to be paid out, the entertainment allocations ... then a shocking thought flashed through his mind: *This newly found relationship could become profitable for both of us, me and my source.* That traitorous thought momentarily terrified him. He knocked a spoon from the table as he physically tried to wipe "profitable for both of us" from his mind. But, while he retrieved the spoon, he thought, *Why not? After all, I am working alone. Of course, it could be done; of course, it could be done!*

Now that he finally had a potential source Kasandroff wanted to be certain that both he and the American could work together undetected by the FBI. He also wanted to be sure that this, his last chance to rise in the eyes of his superiors, would not be lost because of some stupid slipup. "Mister Waldmann," he asked, "what would be the most convenient place for you to let me know when we should meet the next time?"

The American looked surprised as if he had not heard correctly.

"Mister Waldmann," continued Kasandroff, "there are procedures to operate securely, I mean without being detected. I will tell you more about this at our next meeting. These are tested and tried procedures to defeat counter-surveillance. For both of us, it is terribly important not to arouse the suspicions of the FBI, right?"

Waldmann appeared to contemplate the issue for some time. He played with his drink, took a sip or two and finally seemed to have come to a conclusion. He said, "I take a daily walk just to get some fresh air. Usually I leave the office right after lunch; walk along Jeff-Davis Highway. You know where that is, don't you?"

"Yes, yes," Kasandroff answered impatiently.

"Well," Waldmann continued, "I walk up to the Memorial Drive overpass and then back to the office. Get a little break from sitting at the drafting board too long."

"Mister Waldmann," Kasandroff said. "We have two ways of meeting—we call it Treff.

"What's a Treff?"

"It comes from the German word for meeting, but here it means 'time and location.' For a regular Treff we meet once each month, each time in a different place, but always at the same time. What time would be most convenient for you?"

Waldmann thought for a moment, "Well, I think during the week after work, maybe around seven. That's after the rush hour; makes for easy parking here in Washington."

"All right," agreed Kasandroff. "Seven p.m. it is." They agreed to meet next at the reflecting pool of the Lincoln Memorial. "Mister Waldmann, a tried and proven method goes like this: I will be at the reflecting pool on the side of the memorial. You will walk past me."

Waldmann again looked puzzled.

"I know this sounds complicated to you, but the procedure is good, has been tested many times. When you walk past me I will make sure no one is following you. I will also make sure no one has followed me. You walk on one side of the pool, I on the other. If everything is okay, I will turn right and walk toward the Potomac River where we will meet. If something is wrong I will go back to my office and we will meet at the alternate Treff." Kasandroff then explained that the alternate Treff would always be for seven p.m. at the entrance of Dumbarton Oaks Park, the corner of S Street and 28th Street. First there would be a visual recognition at the White Tower hamburger restaurant on Georgetown's M Street at exactly seven in the evening.

Kasandroff instructed Waldmann on what a walk-by encounter was, and that this would take place at the restaurant. "Mister Waldmann, when you see me there you walk out with your hamburger. Walk slowly, because I too will buy a hamburger. You will walk up M Street, turn left on Wisconsin Avenue, turn right on Reservoir Road."

He looked to see whether Waldmann seemed to understand his instruction. When Waldmann nodded, Kasandroff continued, "I think Reservoir Road is a quiet street with few people walking. There I can see if anyone follows you. I will also make sure no one follows me. You then turn left on 32nd Street and walk to the entrance of Dumbarton Oaks. There you stop as if looking at the gate of the park. If all is in order I will meet you there. If I suspect surveillance I will walk past you as if I do not know you."

Kasandroff again looked to see whether Waldmann had digested the instruction, and Waldmann once again nodded. "Good," Kasandroff smiled. "Now you repeat what I said. I want to make sure all is understood." To Kasandroff s surprise Waldmann managed to repeat the alternate Treff instructions almost verbatim with barely a stutter.

Kasandroff continued, "To meet urgently we must have a sort of bulletin board or mail box." After discussing plausible sites for a signal—Kasandroff mentioned chalk marks—they agreed to use one of the granite pillars at the Memorial Drive overpass as their "mailbox." They agreed that if either one placed a white chalk circle on the pillar it signaled a meeting for the same evening at a pre-arranged site, or Treff. The time would always be seven p.m., but they would agree on the location of the Treff at each previous meeting, just as for the monthly meeting.

"You are walking to this overpass every day," said Kasandroff. "I, or one of my officers, will check the granite pillar every afternoon for a sign. If I must see you I will mark the pillar in the morning."

Taking a deep drink Kasandroff wondered whether he should give Waldmann the emergency Treff procedure. Then he thought, *What the hell. Why not?*

"Mister Waldmann, there is a third Treff notification used only in dire emergencies. At our next meeting I will give you a telephone number you can call—but only in emergencies. Ask to speak to Sandman. Do not mention your name or mine. Give only a very short message like 'Sandman, corner Wisconsin and Q.' I will be there as soon as possible. Do you understand?"

Waldmann nodded again. Kasandroff knew he had given the well-tried and proven GRU mailbox and alternate Treff techniques. Time and location for the alternate Treff were never to change unless extraordinary circumstances necessitated a change in venue. "Mister Waldmann, just to be sure we will try what we call the alternate Treff just to see if it works. When would it be convenient for you? Is tomorrow evening fine?"

Waldmann said it was.

"With all that completed, here is what we will do today. After I pay the bill I will leave first. I will walk across the street and watch your departure. Just to make sure no one follows you. Is this agreeable to you?"

Waldmann nodded once more.

Kasandroff left the restaurant. A few minutes later the American departed. Kasandroff detected nothing unusual. After Waldmann disappeared from view Kasandroff walked up Wisconsin Avenue to his car. He had to force himself not to skip and dance for joy. That Friday in the middle of October 1954 had been his lucky day. With the American engineer from NAVBUSHIPS, he had finally come into his own. For a moment he thought he had shouted out loud, *Slava bogu—praise to God—Ivan Ivanovich has a source!* He looked around fearing he had actually shouted for joy; apparently not, because no one took notice of his exhilaration.

He arrived at his apartment on the fifth floor of the Soviet embassy complex

16

in a highly euphoric mood. He was almost one hundred percent certain he had the American naval architect working for Rodina, the Motherland of all Russians. He was also almost one hundred percent certain that the American Secret Service, the FBI, had not noticed his Treff with his first real HUMINT asset, Walter Waldmann. This occasion called for celebration, for a bourbon on the rocks celebration.

CHAPTER 4

Major Kasandroff may have thought that all he had learned about counter-surveillance had baffled the FBI, but a team of FBI agents, three cars, and five agents had seen his encounter with that funny-looking little fat fellow wearing old-fashioned glasses—soon identified as Walter Waldmann, employed at NAVBUSHIPS—as a possible GRU asset. A team of agents had covered Kasandroff ever since he had arrived in the United States. Kasandroff, operating out of the Soviet Military Mission on Belmont Road and Massachusetts Avenue, NW, was relatively easy to shadow; he seemed not to care who saw him or where.

In a note, one agent wrote that Major Kasandroff seemed a different person —happy, relaxed, almost bouncing.

Agent reports had Kasandroff driving all over the city—a sort of terrain reconnaissance—where he photographed Washington's historic Naval Yard, the Pentagon, and selected buildings in the District of Columbia and nearby Maryland and Virginia. He was also reported spending much time in the Reading Room of the Library of Congress. A report had him "acting strange, almost afraid of asking the reference ladies for assistance."

Later reports noted that he "seems" to be more relaxed; actually he had become a lady's man, asking the reference ladies whether he could bring them coffee from the cafeteria. Still later Kasandroff had his own research cubicle where he was observed using a miniature camera, a Minox, to photograph pages from military and scientific journals. He did the same at George Washington University Library.

Also reported were his regular Friday evening dinners at Sam's Bar & Grill, Georgetown, and his regular Friday noon luncheons at a pizza and beer joint on Silver Hill Road, Suitland, Maryland.

FBI Note: Silver Hill Road, Suitland, vicinity of a planned Naval Intelligence facility.

CHAPTER 5

JUNE 1970
OLD TOWN
ALEXANDRIA, VIRGINIA

The shrill ringing of his recently installed telephone caused Hans, Hank to his friends, Reiter to let the razor nick his chin.

"Susan," he called, "can you answer that?" He then remembered that Susan, his wife of many years, had just left for the nearby grocery store. "Who in hell can that be?" he grumbled, as he reached for the receiver. "Reiter, here."

"Hank?" an unfamiliar male voice asked and, without waiting for an answer, continued, "I am Hiram Smyth, Smyth with a 'y,' and I'm an old friend of Jack Heissinger, your old boss in Frankfurt. He told me you might be interested in a job that's right up your alley."

Reiter did not remember ever having met anyone named "Smyth with a 'y'," and he always resented strangers using the familiar "Hank"—only his family, and close friends in the clandestine service, called him Hank.

However, somewhat curious, he allowed he might be interested.

Hiram Smyth gave him his address, an apartment building in upper northwest Washington. "It's right on Wisconsin Avenue," Smyth said. "Think you can find it?"

Reiter said, "Yeah, it's just a few blocks from where my parents once owned a townhouse."

Smyth chuckled. "Yes, I know."

Reiter was puzzled, and rather annoyed with himself for having agreed so readily to consider starting a job just days after retiring from the U.S. Army. Susan and he had discussed at length future plans, and any involvement in what Susan called "travel into distant lands," had become off limits. It irked him for having even agreed to consider a job that was "right up his alley." *Damn,* he thought, *this would never have happened had Susan not gone shopping.* He looked around the house. Boxes, still unpacked, stacked two high along one of the walls of the living room.

He and Susan had just moved into their northern Virginia home; had not yet had enough time to unpack their belongings. "Well," Reiter mumbled, "I can always tell Smyth with a 'y' that I have other plans." Just then he heard Susan's car pulling into the driveway.

19

Both of them had wanted to get away from the gypsy life of overseas tours of duty, clandestine operations and the uncertainty of living on razor's edge. They wanted to stay on the East Coast, near their families, and finally live the comfortable life of suburban Americans. On their return from their last overseas assignment they had enrolled Phillip, their younger son, in Hans's alma mater, Georgetown University; Frank, the older son, had been in Department of State training since his return to the States the previous year.

Hans and Susan had selected this particular house in Alexandria's Old Town because it was near Washington's National Airport. Both their parents lived north of Washington, his in upper New York State, and Susan's in New England. Also, Hans's brother, Christian, and his wife, Kjerstine, lived in Manhattan. Christian was CEO of Quadrant Import-Export, the family business. Hans was his silent partner.

Master Sergeant Hans Reiter had spent twenty years and six months in army intelligence, most of that time in the clandestine service. In early June 1970 he had received his honorable discharge. Months before his retirement, as he and Susan debated their future, he had talked of either entering a graduate program at Georgetown University's Foreign Service School, or joining a private business as a security advisor.

Hans had been one of those "very unusual" enlisted men. He had remained in the enlisted ranks by choice. He had followed in the footsteps of his older brother—with one exception. Christian had served as a first lieutenant in the Office of Strategic Services, the world-famous OSS. Hans, eight years Christian's junior, had chosen to serve as an enlisted intelligence agent. Although he had attended fine private schools in New York state and Switzerland, although he spoke fluent German and a bit of French, and although he had a bachelor's degree in political science from Georgetown, he had rejected offers of a commission. As an enlisted agent Hans enjoyed unprecedented freedom, unencumbered by concerns for "command time," in other words, serving six months plus one day as commanding officer of some MI company or battalion to get promoted to the next highest rank. Furthermore, although only his closest friends knew it, Hans was financially independent. An annual dividend check from Quadrant Import-Export arrived in his bank account on the last day of every year.

Quadrant Import-Export—originally known as Reiter Haus—was an importer of fine European goods founded in 1900 by Erwin Reiter.

Now, the company's name appeared on an engraved bronze plaque near the glass doors of the cavernous entrance to a landmark Manhattan skyscraper. This had been the firm's address since the early 1930s, when it became the first occupant of the twenty-fifth floor. In January 1934 the *Manhattan Business Review* reported: "Quadrant Import-Export has moved into spacious quarters in Manhattan's business district. During opening ceremonies Harold Reiter, son of

20

founder Erwin Reiter, said, 'This is an important step for Quadrant Import-Export as well as for New York. President Roosevelt has brought hope into the hearts of all Americans. The future of business, and of the people of America, looks better than it has for many years.'"

The company had grown from a small import business in Brooklyn into an internationally known import and export enterprise. True to the sign over his small shop, Erwin Reiter had imported only the finest wines, gourmet foods, arts and quality furnishings favored by his Central European customers. Leaving his little Brooklyn ethnic enclave in 1917, he relocated to Manhattan and renamed his business Quadrant Import-Export, both to add a touch of class and to remove the Teutonic connection—an important business decision when America and Germany went to war.

Erwin Reiter spoke fluent German and had learned to speak passable French—and, since it was beneficial in the import-export world, he insisted that his son Harold and his grandsons study these languages. Harold inherited the company before the outbreak of World War II, and enlarged it further into a thriving concern with close connections to European markets. Along the way he became a wealthy man with important military and political contacts, the Eisenhower brothers, Milton and Dwight, among them. As part of the elder Reiter's work ethic, Harold's sons, Christian and Hans, apprenticed in the business while attending universities.

CHAPTER 6

On the morning after Smyth's telephone call, Hans Reiter waited for Washington's rush hour to subside and then drove to the Wisconsin Avenue address. He inquired of a suspiciously military-looking doorman how to get to Room 526.

The concierge pointed to the elevator and said, "Go up to the fifth floor and turn right."

In Room 526 Reiter told a young lady at the reception desk that he had an appointment with Mister Hiram Smyth. After she scrutinized Reiter's military ID card, she pushed a button on her desk console and waited. When a light on the console lit up she escorted Reiter to one of the doors leading from the foyer, knocked, opened it, and announced him.

Reiter entered a well-lit, but sparsely furnished, room. Three dark brown, government-type, combination-lock, file cabinets lined the side of one wall, a small wooden table with three chairs filled the corner under one of the room's two windows, and a dark-brown metal desk sat in the center of the room. Behind the desk, backlit by the windows, shades drawn, sat a man in his middle forties, broad face looking in need of a shave, curly gray hair, a bit on the corpulent side, his desk covered with paper, and a coffee mug sitting atop some document. Reiter assumed, correctly, it was Mister Smyth.

Smyth heaved himself up and walked around the desk to greet him, "Hello," he said, "Long time no see."

"We have met?" Reiter asked cautiously. He was sure he had never met Mister Smyth with a "y," ever.

"Well, sort of. I saw you in Frankfurt, a couple of years ago."

Smyth hesitated, but only for a moment, "Well, maybe more than a couple. Time flies when you're having fun. I am a friend of Jack Heissinger, and you were in his office on the sixth floor of the I.G. Farben Hochhaus when I visited Jack. You look a little older, but I remember you as if it were yesterday, a little over six feet tall, skinny," he chuckled. "You used to have dark-brown wavy hair, and I see you never got your nose fixed. Still looks as if it had been broken in a couple of places.

22

"Yep," he nodded, "it's you in the flesh."

Reiter did not remember ever having seen Smyth but thought to trip him up—just for the hell of it. He asked, "So, how is old Jack?"

Smyth laughed. "Testing me already? Jack said you were a sharp cookie. Jack is retired in Frankfurt-on-Main, and lives with his wife Eileen in one of those new condos on Eschersheimer Landstrasse."

"Okay, that'll do it for me. What can I do for you?"

"Hank, it ain't what you can do for me—well, maybe it is—but what I can do for you. We got an operation starting here in a couple of weeks, and you could become part of it."

Irritated again to be called "Hank," Reiter said, "Hiram, you don't mind if I call you that, since we are on a first-name basis?"

He nodded agreement.

"First of all, who is 'we'?"

Smyth chuckled again. "We here on the entire fifth floor of this building are a combination of special agents from Washington counterespionage agencies. Eh... and that's about all I'll tell you at this time." He then asked Reiter whether he was interested in the job, as a civilian government employee.

Reiter thought about this for just a few seconds, then agreed. *Counterintelligence, he thought, the opposite end of the intelligence sounded like a hell of an interesting job.*

Smyth slapped him on the shoulder. "I thought you'd take the job. Sit down at the table over there. You've got to fill out a couple of forms, look 'em over is more like it."

He walked over to one of the file cabinets and extracted a folder. "Here," he handed Hans the folder, "check them over. See if there are any changes, make them in pencil, and the secretary will do the rest."

The tab of the folder had Reiter's name, rank, Social Security number and, in parentheses, his old Army serial number. He opened the folder. He saw his old DD Form 398, his Personal History Statement, the security clearance form from a few years back, along with a bunch of privacy statements he'd forgotten he had signed way back when. There were only a few changes to be made, retirement date and place, change of address, age, color of hair—his, as Hiram had mentioned, was now a bit on the grayish side—and he had gained about ten pounds. Reiter handed Smyth the folder.

"Great," Smyth said, " I'll have this typed up in a jiffy. Grab a cup of coffee and we'll go to work." Carrying his half-full cup, he joined Reiter at the little side table. He took a sip from his cup. "Hank," he asked, "while we wait for the paperwork, I've got a question. When I asked Jack to suggest a helper, he said almost immediately, 'Get the Pointman.' I thought I had heard him wrong, but then he added 'Hank Reiter.' Now, if I remember correctly, you've never served in the infantry, have you?"

Reiter laughed. "Not in my wildest dreams. Fred Hertzwald, aka Herr Doktor Hermann, stuck me with that moniker. I bird-dogged Fred for almost a year; he was my mentor, taught me all the street smarts I did not learn at the spook school. Fred fought his way in the infantry across Europe from Normandy to the Alps in the Big Red One. He was infantry, and he had this thing ... well, he told me that I was like the pointman in the infantry. Before going into an op area he made me do first a map reconnaissance, then walk the area to learn every structure, every alley, every way to slip away from surveillance."

Reiter smiled in contemplation, "I remember him cautioning me with 'You are the pointman, but unlike in the infantry, you don't have a squad of heavily armed buddies behind you—you are always alone. You'll find that you are always in enemy territory, and that your gut will tighten like the catgut on a violin.' Fred was one hell of a teacher. I learned more from him than I ever learned at college or the spook school."

"Okay, that at least makes sense. I wish I'd had one like Fred when I started in this business. I had to learn by my own mistakes—not a good way to start out." He paused. "Now, why didn't Jack tell me about that?"

"Unfortunately, Jack and Fred did not get along together—totally different philosophies on how to approach clandestine operations. Fred did it like a surgeon with a scalpel; Jack, with a sledgehammer."

"Yep," Smyth agreed, "that's Jack, all right. He was that way when I worked for him in Austria."

The woman from the front desk returned the security form. Reiter reviewed and signed it; it was a different form, called "Security Investigation Data for Sensitive Position, Standard Form 86," but the information was almost the same as on the old DD 398. Smyth handed him a couple of other forms to sign, all engraved with fancy seals, and lots of cautions about "telling nothing to nobody."

"Okay," said Smyth, "now to the down and dirty." He explained that he had received a once-in-a-lifetime chance to "stick it to them Russkies and twisting it." It was a deception operation of the highest order. "Those of us here on the fifth floor," he said with a grin, "know it's a deception. The DNI will—"

Reiter interrupted, "What's DNI?"

"Oh, military parlance, the Director of Naval Intelligence. He's the guy who gave us a safe drawer full of stuff that he wants us to feed to the Russkies. It's a combination of real dates and data that looks real but isn't—we'll feed it to the Russians to screw up their intelligence analysts; make them draw false conclusions; make them start to distrust their own collectors; all that for a look inside the GRU. It's up to us get into the back door of the GRU. I think I know who has the key, but I need you to convince him to open the back door."

Smyth chuckled—he seemed to enjoy this job thoroughly. "All that others

24

in U.S. Counterintelligence will be told—and only if there is an official inquiry—is that it's an attempt to trace compromised information from its source to its destination."

"I don't know how all this started," he admitted. "Way before my time, but since them Russkies got the information about us building some kind of fancy submarine; the DNI wants us to feed information that confirms the accuracy of the data originally collected. Aside from that, I have no idea what this is all about." He paused, and then added, seeming reflectively, "You know how it is, Hank, 'Ours is not to reason why'... and all that shit."

Reiter, still not quite sure what the goal of this whole operation was, asked, "Hiram, to get into the other side's Intel network, we have to know more than just 'a drawer full of stuff.' There must be more background to all this, or we, I especially, will get sandbagged at some time in the future."

Smyth nodded in agreement. "That's what I told the DNI, and he said, 'The word is titanium.' I acted as if I knew what that meant, but I didn't fool him. He told me he would have one of his S&T guys brief us as soon as I had found a guy who could handle the job."

Smyth then walked Reiter around the fifth floor to meet the rest of the crew. Most of the people Reiter met were strangers; he remembered meeting only two of the men, one a former Army CIC agent from the 66th Counter Intelligence Corps he had met in Stuttgart, Germany; the other, Frank Milushkyi from Reiter's old 411th USASA Special Operations Unit.

Then Smyth sequestered him in the classified reading room where he went through volumes of dossiers, surveillance reports, mug shots, and a surveillance photo of a civilian identified by the FBI as a GRU Major Kasandroff, another of a funny-looking little fat fellow wearing old-fashioned glasses, and one of the two of them together. A note by the Naval Criminal Investigative Service, NCIS, identified the funny-looking fellow as having been recruited by Major Kasandroff. The note read, "He is a mole in NAVBUSHIPS." The folder also contained photographs of Washington, New York, and Moscow buildings.

A few days later, a dapper civilian, college professor type, appeared in Room 526 carrying a locked leather courier satchel. He identified himself as Lieutenant James Beringer. Smyth ushered him into his office and introduced Reiter as "the man who will do the job."

Beringer smiled as he and Reiter shook hands. He unlocked the satchel and neatly arranged several piles of paper on Smyth's desk.

"Gentlemen, I have here, arranged in chronological order, all the background information you will need for this deception operation." He coughed and apologized, then admitted that this was all the information that the DNI office had on the topic of titanium as it related to the deception operation. As background, Beringer explained, "We have to go way back into the early 1950s when submarine engineers recognized that titanium is far superior to the high-yield, HY-80 steels used by submarine builders worldwide."

"Briefly," he continued, "titanium has many advantages over steel. Titanium is stronger and weighs thirty-three percent less than steel; the pressure hull can be stronger without increasing displacement; its use gives a submarine a stronger hull for greater diving depth and increases resistance to explosives at lesser depths. And the submarine is essentially nonmagnetic, thus decreasing the likelihood of magnetic anomaly detection, known as MAD."

Beringer looked up to see if Smyth and Reiter understood the importance of MAD. When he realized that neither had any comprehension, he explained, "Magnetic anomaly detection is a vital anti-submarine technology—it's used to locate submerged submarines, Soviet or others, including ours."

"During the early 1950s," he continued, "there was a lot of talk about building titanium submarines. The advantages were overwhelming. Various technical papers, many articles, including in our Naval Proceedings, and other naval-related scientific and technical journals, praised titanium as the future metal for submarine construction. But a few years later all that died down. When it became clear that a totally different manufacturing process would be required; all shipyard workers would have to be retrained; construction halls would have to be reconfigured, and that bending and shaping of heavy plates of titanium alloy would be far more difficult compared to steel—when, with all that, it became clear that a titanium submarine would be at least three to five times more expensive than one of steel, the U.S. Navy concluded that a fleet of titanium submarines would bankrupt the United States."

Beringer paused and reached for the next pile of papers. "Now for a change of pace, and for the reason of your involvement. I have here some history that will make sense, that will convince you that what you will venture makes sense." He again glanced at Reiter, smiling. "As everyone knows, the Soviets are a paranoid bunch. I mentioned Naval Proceedings, but that was only one of many authoritative publications that wrote enthusiastically of the many advantages that titanium could contribute to submarines. Then suddenly there was a noticeable decrease in open-source articles on this topic. Apparently, our CI folks had noticed an increase in Soviet espionage regarding titanium.

"At the same time, the Eisenhower administration concluded that it could not compete with the Soviet Union regarding armament. The President's advisors cautioned Dwight Eisenhower that the United States would face bankruptcy in about five years if we continued our military spending as we had during the past years. The President and his advisors pondered this dilemma for some time. Finally, Eisenhower called a man, a former OSS agent, whom the then-General Eisenhower had ordered to land before D-day on the French coast to conduct a most delicate operation."

Beringer again looked at Reiter. "Mr. Reiter, you may have noticed my smile when we first met." He leaned back in his chair. "My grandpappy used to say, 'It's a small world,' and the other day when I looked at your Standard Form 86, I realized that I would meet the second 'Reiter,' and that my grandpappy was right."

Puzzled, Reiter shifted uncomfortably in his chair and looked at Smyth. Smyth shrugged, indicating that he was as perplexed as Reiter.

"You have no idea?" Beringer leaned forward. "Your father had close connections with the two Eisenhower brothers, right?"

Reiter nodded agreement.

"You knew that your brother Christian was OSS?"

Reiter nodded again.

"Well, President Eisenhower called on your brother to form a team of his old OSS comrades to, as he put it bluntly, 'Bleed the goddamned Commies white.' In the olden OSS days, your brother became 'the New Yorker,' one of a three-man team; two other, one called the 'Philosopher', and the other the 'Wizard' made up the team later designated the OMEGA Solution. And your brother and his crew did exactly that—I mean, they presented the President with an operational plan way back in 1954 that could bring financial ruin to the USSR. Initially, the only ones involved in this, the President's scheme, were the President and the three former OSS guys. Later a very reluctant Rear Admiral Carl Di Rovalleri, the Director of Naval Intelligence, became the prime mover of the President's plan." Beringer paused only briefly. "Mr. Reiter, have you ever met your brother's two close OSS comrades?"

"To tell the truth," Hans Reiter brushed away the question, "I know Christian had a few very close friends from the olden days, the OSS days, but I was not particularly interested... well, there was also the age difference, and because I was away at college."

Lieutenant Beringer leaned back and smiled, "This is how it all started; it started long ago, actually fourteen years ago, before the time I entered high school."

27

CHAPTER 7

Mrs. Clarke, Christian Reiter's long-time, usually unflappable secretary, rushed breathlessly into his office. "Mister Reiter, a call from the White House," she managed to gasp. Reiter had never seen his secretary so bewildered.

Christian Reiter had inherited the level-headed Mrs. Clarke when he took over the reins of Quadrant Import-Export four years earlier when his father retired. *Is this some kind of a joke?* he thought, as he lifted the receiver.

The operator came on the line. "Mister Reiter?"

He had barely time to reply.

"Mister Reiter, the President of the United States would like to speak with you."

The muscles in the back of Christian's neck stiffened. A few clicks on the line, and then he heard the cheerful voice of the Old General. "Christian, I hope this is not too early for you New York folks, or are you still an early riser?"

"I just got into the office a half-hour ago, General. We New Yorkers are night owls."

"Of course, Christian, of course. I wondered whether you might have the time to come to Washington to share a cup of coffee with me." He paused for just a moment, not long enough for Christian to reply. "Actually, I wondered whether you could drop by during the next few days. I need to talk with you, pick your brains." The Old General paused again, and then continued somewhat hesitantly, "I need to talk with you about old times— and more. I need your advice." He sighed and then added, "Bad."

"Well, sir," Christian began cautiously, as he motioned Mrs. Clarke to pick up the extension, "I plan to be in Washington next month, around the middle of the month, if my memory serves me correctly." Mrs. Clarke, glancing at his calendar, nodded in agreement.

"Not soon enough, I'm afraid," the President replied. "I was thinking more like day after tomorrow at ten a.m."

Christian could see Mrs. Clarke blink in surprise as she turned to his calendar once more. Yes, she signaled. Reiter could make it.

He paused briefly, torn between suspicion and curiosity. As a man who had carefully and successfully avoided the pitfalls of politics in his post-war business career, he was not eager to put himself in a position where he might be pressed into government service—again. Yet how could he turn down an invitation to meet with the President of the United States, who seemed to be seeking his advice?

"All right, sir, ten o'clock it is."

"Thanks, Christian," the President said, relief evident in his voice. "Have your secretary call mine with your flight arrangements and we'll make sure the Secret Service will be there to meet you when you arrive."

"Do I need to bring anything or prepare for this meeting in any way, sir?" Christian asked, hoping to elicit some additional information on the nature of this highly unusual meeting.

"Not at all, Christian, not at all. Let's just say that this Old Man will appreciate your time—and your brains. See you soon!" The President rang off before Reiter could say goodbye.

As he carefully returned the phone receiver to its cradle, Christian was aware that Mrs. Clarke was already on the phone to his travel agent, making arrangements for his trip.

What in hell is this all about? he mused as he sat doodling on his clipboard, the same clipboard he had taken with him to his first secret meeting with the then Supreme Allied Commander Eisenhower during his OSS days. *God!* He winced as the memories flooded back. *Surely, those days are over; he can't ask me to return to life in the shadows. Not again. Not now.* He was jarred from his thoughts by Mrs. Clarke's light knock on the door.

"Mr. Reiter, your flight has been confirmed, and I am making arrangements for a car to take you to La Guardia from home. Is a six-thirty pickup too early for you?"

"What? Oh no. That's fine," he replied, a slight frown crossing his brow.

"Is something wrong, sir?" Mrs. Clarke walked up to the desk, looking at him with that piercing stare that always made him feel he had no secrets.

He sighed and tried to smile, "No, Mrs. Clarke. It's just the thought of visiting Washington this time of year. Ugh!"

She broke into a rare smile, allowing him to believe that she bought his explanation. Already he was exercising his old ability to lie easily, and convincingly. As she left the room Christian felt the sharp stomach pain that had always preceded his wartime missions. Was this an omen? He was uncomfortable at the thought that somehow his painstakingly crafted postwar life of symmetry was about to collapse because of a phone call from the President of the United States.

Kjerstine Reiter greeted her husband with a hug and a kiss when he entered the first-floor living room of their fashionable upper Manhattan brownstone. The hot day had turned into an even worse evening. A steady drizzle had made

29

Manhattan's streets slick, and glaring lights reflecting from the wet streets made driving hazardous. Christian returned Kjerstine's kiss and hug with, "Sweetheart, I cannot tell you how good it is to be home. What a rotten drive. I am just glad for Casey's garage door opener. At least I didn't have to get wet parking the car in the garage."

Kjerstine laughed, "And I remember all the trouble you gave me about converting the basement into a garage."

"Well, I guess my thinking was old-fashioned. My dad had always parked his car in front of the house, and I thought, well...?"

Kjerstine smiled. Her husband had grudgingly agreed that since their house had access from the alley, the idea of turning the basement into a garage had merit. She was not too sure whether Casey Miller's still unpatented electronic garage door opener would ever make it on the open market. It had a few bugs, which Miller had promised to fix. Miller had told them, "It's still experimental. Unfortunately, I have no garage, so I'm just glad you agreed to serve as a guinea pig."

"Oh, sweetheart," Christian interrupted himself, "I almost forgot. Guess who called me today from Washington, D.C.?"

"Who?"

"Ike."

"You are kidding."

"No. He asked to see me day after tomorrow. Mrs. Clarke has already made all the arrangements. A car will pick me up at six-thirty Wednesday morning."

"What does he want? How long will you be gone?"

He shrugged. "I have no idea. All he said was something like 'this Old Man will appreciate your time—and your brains'."

"Well," kidded Kjerstine, "that shouldn't take too long."

This time it was Christian's time to chuckle. "Right, so I should be back by early Wednesday afternoon."

Christian and Kjerstine Reiter had developed this wonderful, fun-loving give-and-take during crisis times when Christian would periodically disappear during the war without warning, often breaking a carefully arranged London social engagement. But it helped them cope with disappointments and Kjerstine's persistent fear that someday her fiancé might never return.

CHAPTER 8

Two days after the call from the White House Christian Reiter caught the early morning flight. At National Airport, a Secret Service agent met him and discreetly escorted him to a waiting Ford sedan in the VIP parking lot. They drove over Fourteenth Street Bridge into Washington proper. The agent parked in a No Parking Zone across the street from the Executive Office building. The two men entered through the side entrance, walking through the building and out one of the rear doors that led to the White House gardens. They entered the White House via a door leading into the mezzanine.

As they rode the elevator to the second floor, Christian asked, "Am I getting the back-stage tour?"

"Yes, sir," replied the agent. "Something like that." He ushered Christian quickly into the President's private quarters. As they shook hands, the President said, "Sorry about the cloak-and-dagger atmosphere. I wanted this to be a very private meeting." They settled down in easy rocking chairs, and Ike offered him a cup of his "famous" Washington coffee. Over coffee he asked, "How are you and Kjerstine enjoying Manhattan?"

"General, New York is the greatest city in the world. Sometimes I think we both enjoy it too much; at least, judging by the American Express bills for restaurants and theaters."

The President chuckled. "Do you still get together with the boys from the old outfit?"

"Well, General, some of us do, occasionally. Two of my closest cronies, Harold McCurrill and Casey Miller, and I meet for lunch several times a year. We had promised to get together every month or so, but business often seems to get in the way."

There was a long pause in the conversation, and Christian watched Eisenhower, apparently deep in thought, silently tapping his fingers on the arms of his chair.

"Christian," the President finally said, "you must be wondering why I called you. I'll come right to the point..." The point was: The President wanted advice from qualified persons outside government about how to respond to the Soviet Union's increasing bellicosity. The Soviets had exploded their own atomic bomb,

31

blockaded Berlin, backed North Korea in an attack on South Korea, and were continuing an arms build-up.

The Pentagon was pushing hard for additional funding because "the Russians are upping the ante."

"Their words, not mine," the President said. "In many respects they are right, but my economic advisors have warned me we cannot match the Soviet arms build-up without destroying America's economic viability.

"Of course, our defense industries are in full agreement with the Pentagon; in fact, they're pushing the same message through their political pawns on Capitol Hill. The newspapers just repeat what industry and defense tell them in support of increased defense spending. Everyone clamors for tax dollars we don't have."

He shook his head and continued: "On the other hand, the Soviet threat is real. Make no mistake about that. It is real! The numbers don't lie. We saw in the last war how tough those Russian soldiers can be. What they don't have in quality they have in quantity."

The President told Christian he was having trouble getting good advice from Washington bureaucrats. "The OSS leftovers who love the spy game and the college boys from rich families just can't cut the mustard in today's world of Commie cutthroats. I'm getting nothing but crap from these college boys at CIA. They are all Ivy Leaguers who have never been near a battlefield."

Ike motioned for Christian to come to the window. "Take a look. See those temporary office buildings over there? They may just as well be on the moon. The guys who work there make a lot of promises, talk a good game, and use words even I don't understand. They make plenty of fancy moves, and create big smoke screens. I have grammatically correct staff studies coming out of my ears. The studies are chopped a dozen ways by scores of so-called experts who think they know what I want—baloney!"

As the President fumed Christian placed his hand on his arm. "General, I thought Harry Truman's big reorganization solved all these intelligence problems. What happened?"

"The way all these reorganizations happen: nothing. Now I have just another layer on top of all the others, one additional agency to deal with. I get their very polished early morning intelligence briefings that are full of possibles, probables, and potentials. Sometimes I get possible potentials, and even possible probable potentials. When I hear them I could just rip out my hair." He paused for a moment, and then gave Christian his million-dollar smile. "Or whatever little there is left."

Serious again, he said: "Christian, I need—well, actually, every president of the United States needs—well-grounded and well-rounded ideas from outside Washington, from outside government circles. I am not speaking of intelligence information, if that is what you think. I am talking about ideas from outside the government circles, unorthodox ideas. I'm convinced our career government employees are too close to the problem. Franklin Roosevelt had outside advisors he consulted whenever..." His voice trailed off, as he seemed to collect his thoughts. "A few trusted advisors who were not confused by government bureaucracy... private citizens who had nothing to gain from government contracts. I need something like that. That's why I called you."

The President stood up and turned to Christian, fixing him with a determined look. "What I want to know from you is this: Can you gather some folks from the private sector, from academia, smart, knowledgeable people outside the Washington circus tent, who might be able to come up with a practical way to ease the Soviet threat?"

Christian stared pokerfaced at the President, hoping not to appear as shocked as he felt. His first thought was, why me? He and the Old General were a generation apart. The Eisenhowers were his father's friends. During the years between the two world wars, Milton and Dwight, the Eisenhower brothers, had become, first, steady customers of Quadrant Import-Export and later good friends with Christian's father.

Christian recalled having spoken with Ike only three times; once before the war at West Point graduation exercises when the elder Reiter was the guest of the then Major Eisenhower, and Christian had accompanied his father to the event; then again, in 1944, under totally different circumstances. Eisenhower, then a four-star general and Supreme Commander, Allied Expeditionary Forces, had called the lowly First Lieutenant Christian Reiter to Supreme Headquarters, Allied Forces, Europe, London. The last time he talked with Eisenhower was in 1952 in New York during Ike's campaign for president.

The President continued, "I know that you are well connected in international circles. You have trusted friends in business, academia, industry, and banking—I need their advice, that kind of advice; ideas on how to get away from this ever-increasing cycle of spending, spending, spending being pushed by our military/industrial complex." He stared at his now empty coffee cup.

After a while he looked up at Reiter and said, "I'm sorry to have off-loaded on you but I need help. There seems to be something missing. I get all those highfalutin' briefings, but nothing beyond facts—no creative thoughts, no new ideas, no acceptable recommendation. There may be some people in this huge bureaucracy who have the answers, but I never hear from them. I want to have an unbiased assessment from someone outside the government; someone who does not have an ax to grind—or a pocket to fill."

Christian sat in stunned silence, unsure that the President had selected the right man for this conversation. He could not fathom what he could contribute, when apparently the best minds in government could not get a handle on this problem. He heard the Old General say in apparent frustration, "I can't believe that the Soviets can spend so much on defense without suffering elsewhere. If we can't continue to spend more and more on defense without risking terrible economic consequences, how can they?" Without waiting for Christian's answer he added, "That's what I need to find out."

The President paused again. "I want to know what it takes to bleed the Commies white; to bankrupt their whole system."

Ike gave Christian a quizzing glance, "What do you think? Do you think that someone from your wide range of business acquaintances could come up with something that has not been tried before?"

"General," Christian replied slowly and deliberately, "financial and economic experts in the business community have wondered how long the Soviet Union can continue this spending spree. Some economists believe that the Soviet economy is standing on knife's edge at this very moment, near the brink of collapse; that the entire system is so inefficient, that managers don't manage, and the workers don't produce. Other financial experts have predicted that the entire system will collapse on itself, by itself."

Ike agreed. "I've heard that theory for several years. It doesn't help me now; nothing is happening. I don't know, but maybe, just maybe, all it needs is a little nudge, a shove, to have the whole house of cards collapse. No one in this town seems to have even the faintest idea what leverage to use to tip the Soviets over the brink. I was hoping that some of your friends outside of government might be a bit more inventive in reviewing options."

"General," Christian asked carefully, "have you considered the ramifications of a total financial and economic collapse of the Soviet Union?"

"Yes, I have given it much thought, but I cannot see any other solution. I know the Russian people have long suffered, and they will continue to suffer. For the past thirty years their leaders have promised them a workers' paradise. They have survived famine, collectivization, political pogroms and purges and devastating war. How much can those Russian folks endure—for how long can they endure?" He rose from his chair and started to pace back and forth.

"Christian, I want to push them to the wall economically. There must be a way to push them over the brink. I want you and your learned friends to think of a way. Try. See if those bright people you rub shoulders with daily can think of an affordable solution."

Christian, without commenting on the enormity of the President's request, got down to business. "Let's assume that my friends and I can come up with some scheme that could work. What then?"

"For all practical purposes it must appear that the U.S. government is not involved. The removal of the Soviet threat, even the nonviolent removal, can only be done by an entity not associated with the U.S. government. When two world powers clash, it is by necessity a violent confrontation. Today that means a nuclear holocaust. Such a confrontation would be the complete opposite of what this President, this country, wants or can afford." Eisenhower looked at his watch, and Christian, taking this as a signal the Old General's time was limited, rose from his chair.

CHAPTER 9

The morning after his return from the White House, Christian Reiter sat deep in thought in his Manhattan office high above the streets of the city. He was still unsure how to approach the problem the President had dumped on him. He knew that his real fear, the one that caused him to hide in New York's safe society world, was that he believed he had lost the edge for clandestine activity. His OSS instructors had managed to reshape only the surface of his conscience. For God and country he had buried his deep love for humanity, but only for the duration. Open, lifeless eyes, twisted bodies of men he had killed, were forever pursuing him.

He reached for his Rolodex. The first card he turned to was that of McCurrill. Funny, Christian reflected, he always was my first choice for defining options. Guess that's why we called him the Philosopher.

Despite the vagaries of the university's switchboard, he got through to McCurrill relatively easily. "Harold? Don't tell me that you finally decided to put in some office hours. You're spoiling your students."

"Well, if it isn't the New Yorker!" McCurrill laughed. "What's the matter? Run out of champagne?"

"More like: run out of ideas." Christian leaned back in his desk chair. "You know, I think I could benefit from a long evening in the wilds of Princeton with a couple of clear-headed companions."

"You had me with you until you said 'clear-headed.' I was hoping you'd invite me to be your guest at a very expensive dinner with lots of expensive imported wine; imported by Quadrant Import-Export, of course."

"That can certainly be arranged." Christian chuckled. "But for now how about dinner Friday? At Henderson's Inn? My secretary will make a reservation for three, if you can get Casey to join us for this 'Gathering of Fools.' I'd like to talk to you both at the same time."

The light tone immediately left McCurrill's voice. "Christian, is something wrong?"

Christian hesitated briefly. "No, let's just say that this is not going to be like one of our usual get-togethers, where we rerun and analyze certain moments we shared during the war. This meeting is going to be about the future—and whether we want to ante up to join the game."

36

McCurrill replied, "I am both puzzled and excited at the same time, but count me in for Friday, my friend. This promises to be more stimulating than grading freshman philosophy papers."

CHAPTER 10

Christian Reiter's drive through the New Jersey countryside on that early Friday afternoon was thoroughly invigorating. Once he was away from the perpetual motion of Manhattan with its heavily polluted air, even his Mercedes seemed to run smoother. He arrived at the Historic Henderson Inn in time to shower and then go out to the verandah to relax with a glass of vintage Frankenwein. It was his favorite German wine, dry, with a taste of the rocky slopes of the Franconian hills just north of Nürnberg.

He spotted McCurrill as he was about to enter the lobby and mused, My friend, what am I getting you into?

The slightly stooped, pale professor with the wisp of blond hair broke into a wide grin when he recognized Christian, and quickly crossed the verandah to greet him. "Always good to see the New Yorker out here in the boondocks."

"Where's Casey?" Reiter asked.

"Your guess is as good as mine. I tried to contact him for two days. No answer at home or at work. I called you this afternoon to let you know that he seems to have disappeared, but your secretary said you had already left for Princeton."

McCurrill took a seat at the table and ordered a draft beer. "Looks like you're stuck with just me this evening."

They exchanged small talk until the waitress returned with McCurrill's brew. They were almost alone. One elderly couple sat quietly talking at a table on the opposite side of the verandah.

Christian poured himself another glass of wine, sighed and began. "So, Harold, what would you say if I told you that the President of the United States had invited me to visit him at the White House earlier this week to ask my help to keep this country out of bankruptcy?"

McCurrill blinked. "Old Ike? I'm not sure I follow you."

"Well," Christian said, "I warned you that this would be a long evening. I guess I might as well begin at the beginning. But before I start I must tell you that I'm just testing the waters, trying to ascertain if we, just the three of us, can do what Ike wants."

McCurrill settled back into his chair Buddha-like, asking no questions as his friend unfolded his tale.

38

Finally, Reiter summed up his impression of his White House meeting: "The general seems uncomfortable with the Washington insiders. He is not impressed with the play-it-safe advice he's been getting. He said he wants unconventional ideas, and he seems to think they might come from people like us. To quote him, 'Ivy Leaguers who have shit on the battlefield.'"

McCurrill smiled and nodded, "Yes, the old war-horse is right. It is indeed a rare combination. I mean, the combination is right. We have a considerable number of intellectuals in this country, hell, there is an ungodly number right here in this town, and we all know there are millions with wartime experience." He grinned. "But there are damn few who have both of these fine qualities." He took another deep swallow from his third nearly empty stein. "Of course there are the other qualifications, the OSS training, language familiarity and geographic area knowledge, et cetera, but philosophically speaking, the President summed it up correctly, in his very own, eh, colorful way."

Christian leaned forward. "I know, ours is a dying art; our experience..." He hesitated. "But... do you think ... I mean, are we physically and psychologically able to do the President justice? First of all, is it right? I want you to tell me whether it is right legally, ethically, and most important, is it right for us?" When he saw McCurrill contemplating his beer stein, he added, "You realize of course that if we agree to get involved we can never really go back to our normal lives until the President releases us."

For some time McCurrill sat viewing his beer stein from every angle. "I don't agree with your last statement," he said finally. "I think you're making a mountain out of a molehill. It, that is, our involvement, does not have to be extensive, timewise and otherwise. First of all, we have to come up with a plan. Then, we'll have to examine it from every angle. Like pre-mission reconnaissance."

Christian nodded, as McCurrill continued. "We examined every facet of the terrain, the weather, the enemy, every potential pitfall that could get us killed, until we, the guys who took all the chances, became convinced the mission was doable." Christian waited for him to continue but for some time his friend sat Buddha-like in his chair. Suddenly he raised his head. "Sorry, I just became lost in thought. But this is what we have to do first. No great gestures, no fanfares, all we must do is examine the issue, get inputs from Casey, from you and me, and then look at what we have."

He seemed to become increasingly lost in thought as he leaned further back in his chair. After a few moments, he resumed, "Casey will have some good thoughts on this matter. He and I can discuss the preliminaries."

McCurrill took a deep sip from his stein. "Hell, we may not be able to handle it. There's no need for a commitment until we know we have the assets." He looked up, startled. "Ye gads, I am already talking in the old terminology."

Reiter frowned at his old OSS comrade. "Harold, I think I should have told the general that he asked the wrong man. But he seemed so desperate, I couldn't refuse him."

"Bullshit," was McCurrill's reply as he took another deep sip from his recently refilled stein. He leaned across the table and stared intently at Reiter. "Listen. Uncle Sam pulled you, Casey and me out of mundane lives and stuck us into the OSS. We came into the organization as innocents. I don't know whether you remember, but one of the instructors, I forget his name, told us that we were joining 'the world's second oldest profession, one not quite as honorable as the oldest.' We cheated, lied, and killed for 'God and Country.' Those of us who survived were honored, decorated, and given the Ruptured Duck, that ugly pin I still proudly wear even though it looks like a dead bird." His hand brushed over his lapel.

As an aside he mumbled, "I can't think for the life of me who would ever design such an ugly symbol for those having served in the war." With his eyes closed he continued, "We went home to our loved ones and tried to do whatever we had done before Pearl Harbor. Some of us succeeded. Even Casey now lectures at MIT." He smiled, and then laughed. "Do you realize he starts each new class with the story of the electric toothpick?"

Reiter guffawed. It was their private joke. Miller had almost killed himself with that toothpick.

McCurrill, still laughing, said, "And he still invents kitchen gadgets; he is the savior of a million housewives." He became serious again. "And I read philosophy to a bunch of spoiled rich kids." He paused as if to gather his thoughts. "Let me ask you a couple of questions. Are you the same man who went into the service in 1942? Are you happy making money? I mean, does making money truly fulfill you?"

Darkness had slowly settled in. A cooling breeze had replaced the heat of the day. There was a sound of thunder in the distance. Christian squirmed uncomfortably in his chair. He had expected answers, not questions. This particular question disturbed him. He asked, "Am I happy in the import-export business?" He answered his own question. "Sure I am. It pays the bills. I am carrying on the family tradition. Quite successfully, too." He thought for a moment. "Does it fulfill me? I don't know. What does fulfilled really mean? I have more than I need. I could delegate most of my daily business routine to my managers. That would free up any time I might need to concentrate on the President's business, but I—"

"Why should you?" McCurrill interrupted.

"Because the President of the United States, who also happens to be an old friend, asked me—"

"Horse manure," interrupted McCurrill. "You are bored, Christian. You're bored to death. I don't know about Casey, but let me tell you this: life has been good to us. We are doing exactly what we always wanted to do after we got out

40

of the service. Some of us make more money than others, some get more publicity than others, some live happier lives than others, but personally—I am bored."

He emptied his stein and waved to the waitress for another refill. His eyes twinkled as he looked at Reiter. "By your thunderous silence, I take it you feel the same."

The hotel had turned on its muted lanterns. They barely illuminated the gravel walkways and seemed to accentuate the darkness of the towering trees and the sky. "We are both bored," McCurrill said. "In France I dreamed of nothing else but returning home to the university, getting my doctorate, and teaching eager students the fine points of logic, ethics, philosophy, and political theory. Imparting wisdom in the form of lessons based on what the world should have learned over the last twenty years. Letting the next generation know why we fought the war. But, Christian, that's not enough!"

He lowered his voice as if he suddenly recognized that the elderly couple across the verandah had stopped their conversation, seemingly more interested in staring at him. "Maybe the world has changed. I know I've changed. I have killed—reluctantly, but I have killed. I have felt true euphoria, because I survived—and at the same time utter shame because I did, and others did not. I prefer to think that I killed to wipe out evil; to make this a better world, but who the hell knows? Most of all, I know that I miss living on the razor's edge. I miss the exhilaration."

He looked somewhat puzzled about his own observation. "Until now I hadn't realized it. Or let's say that I wasn't ready to admit it to anyone-even myself. Now I know. The routine, the fairly predictable life is not my cup of tea. I crave some excitement—a greater goal, something other than teaching spoiled rich kids." He sat silent for a minute or more, his eyes dreamily staring into the trees and beyond.

Christian was afraid to interrupt the Philosopher.

After a long pause McCurrill continued, "I am ready. Ask Casey. I think he'll jump at it!" They sat there in silence enjoying each other's company as full darkness slowly enveloped the land, as the lights from the hotel's lanterns cast flickering shadows over the gardens that surrounded the verandah.

"Christian," lectured the Philosopher, "change is constant. Five hundred years before the birth of Christ, the Greek philosopher Heraclites told his students that the only constancy in life is change. He said, 'No man has ever stepped twice into the same river.' In 1944 we stepped into the river. Every experience thereafter has changed us. Not fundamentally. We are what we were, but we are also different. We are no longer totally satisfied with lecturing students, inventing kitchen gadgets, or managing exports and imports. Call Casey. Let's have lunch or whatever; talk it over. You don't have to carry the burden alone. If I know Casey as well as I think I do, he'll jump at the chance. I sure as hell am ready to

41

be reborn."

He leaned back in his chair again and looked into the evening darkness. "Reborn? Does that sound too philosophical?"

The two men seemed oblivious to the repeated interruptions of the waitress, asking them if they wanted to order additional drinks or perhaps move to the dining room for dinner. Christian finally turned to her with an exasperated sigh. "Look, Miss, just leave us, will you please? We won't be needing you anymore this evening. Here's enough to cover the tab plus a twenty for your trouble."

The startled waitress looked at the pile of bills in her hand and backed away quickly, apologizing for having interrupted the two men. "Now, Harold," Reiter resumed. "Where were we?"

McCurrill's earlier animation returned. "Tell me exactly what the Old General told you—in a sentence. I mean, what does he really need? Forget his frustrations with everyday life in the Oval Office. What is his real problem, his Gordian knot?"

"In essence, he wants to eliminate the Soviet Union as a world power. He wants to get rid of the threat, and he wants to get rid of the threat in a nonviolent way." Reiter then explained the President's reluctance to have anyone from the federal government involved in the activity out of fear that this could lead to a violent confrontation, even a nuclear confrontation between the two superpowers. He paused for only a moment recollecting the President's salient points. "The Old General cannot believe that the Soviets can spend so much on defense without suffering elsewhere. Instinctively he feels there's something missing in all the evaluations of Soviet capabilities he gets from his intelligence services. "

McCurrill smiled. "Just curious. What did the old man really say? Exactly?"

Christian laughed. "Well, actually he said, 'I want to know what it takes to bleed those goddamned Commies white; to get them off my back.' In one sentence, that's what he said. Then he added 'financially'."

"Well," McCurrill laughed, "that clears the deck. I think he wants us to construct a theoretical model to bankrupt the Soviet Bloc. That should not be too terribly difficult." He became thoughtful, silently pulling his lower lip as he stared at a point beyond Reiter's shoulder.

"Tell you what. Let me talk to some of my colleagues. Many of my scholarly friends complain about the needless spending of money for the military. I'm sure that some of them will be free with advice on how America should balance guns and butter. Some know Russia better than most Russians. Although they won't come out and say it, especially in light of that asshole Joe McCarthy and his shenanigans, many of them do believe in the need to keep the Red Menace at bay. Of course Casey and his colleagues are better positioned to speak to technological issues." He paused and smiled, "Bleeding the goddamned Commies white. I love it. I love it. That old war dog still has teeth."

42

Darkness had completely enveloped them by now. The candle in the lantern on their table was dying. The flickering light cast shadows over the two men who sat silently for long moments: the New Yorker and the Philosopher. A soft, cool evening breeze wafted through the verandah. The Philosopher tilted his stein; it was empty. He carefully set it down and slowly rose to bid his comrade good night, begging off dinner. McCurrill seemed to have some difficulty forming his words. "Get hold of Casey as soon as you can. He'd never forgive us if we left him out of this adventure. Who knows? It could be our last hurrah."

They shook hands, and McCurrill turned and walked somewhat unsteadily down the steps from the verandah, through the garden toward one of the few street lamps casting its splashes of light through the branches.

Christian continued to gaze into the dark garden long after the Philosopher had disappeared among the trees. Now he knew why he first called Harold Mc-Currill. McCurrill had given him the answer that had escaped him. He, Christian, was only the instrument. McCurrill and Miller would decide whether to answer the President's call, or not. He rose from his chair a little unsteadily. Had he really finished an entire bottle of wine by himself? No matter. Tonight he would sleep well for the first time since his sudden trip to Washington. Tomorrow he would rise early and return to Manhattan; Monday morning he would call Casey Miller, the Wizard.

CHAPTER 11

Christian Reiter was in his Manhattan office long before the start of New York's rush hour. The start of the business week found him facing mountains of phone messages and mail, his reward for having taken Friday off. He was able to dispense with the most urgent business by noon. He tried several times unsuccessfully to reach Casey Miller at MIT. There was no answer. Come on, Casey, he thought impatiently. *Don't disappear on me now!*

Toward six, Christian realized he was hungry. He had missed lunch in his attempt to catch up on work. Kjerstine would not be expecting him for dinner tonight, because she was visiting her aged parents in Connecticut. He left the office in search of a light supper at a small hole-in-the-wall around the corner from his building. He usually ate there when he had a meeting late in the afternoon or early evening. The three-man crew of the countertop diner, two skinny whites and a black giant, was quick. Their food was outstanding, typical of so many small Manhattan eateries.

He sat on the last stool away from the door and watched in fascination as the crew, in perpetual motion, cooked the food; a study of confidence and efficiency, of teamwork. Three minutes after his entry the black man placed the Spanish omelet and a glass of iced water on the counter. "Anything else, Mr. Reiter? Don't eat too fast. It's bad for your digestion."

And, Christian thought, *tourists say New York has no heart. Of course, it pays to be an old customer.* He finished his meal and paid his bill, waving to the three short-order cooks, as he stepped outside and merged into the pedestrian traffic.

Back in his office, he picked up the telephone receiver and dialed Miller's home once more. After two rings Miller came on the line. "Hello?"

Christian, anticipating yet one more unanswered call, could barely contain his relief.

"Casey, Christian here. How are you?"

"Just sitting here with a gin and tonic, looking into the flickering logs in the fireplace and admiring the fire, God's gift to civilization. Awaiting a visit from an extremely attractive librarian, who has promised to bring dinner. What are you up to, Christian? And although you are an old friend, I'd appreciate it if you told me quickly."

Christian laughed. Casey was one interesting son-of-a-bitch! He'd bet that this librarian was only one of several current girlfriends. "Well, in that case I'll come right to the point. I wondered if you could break away from whatever you are doing and come to New York. Harold tried to call you last week. We had tried to set up a meeting at Princeton, but he couldn't reach you. We thought you had gone AWOL."

"Not a chance. I went sailing in the Bay for a few days. Uh ... with a stunning undergraduate who wanted to learn the mechanics of sailing. But I digress. What's going on? Why the meeting?"

"It's too complicated to explain over the phone. But I need your help. Actually, it's the Old General who's asked for help. He called me a few days ago and invited me to Washington."

"You're kidding."

"Not a chance. I wanted the three of us to get together to talk about it. I still do. It's a pressing issue and I thought maybe we could get together over the weekend: you, Harold, and me. Harold already has the details. He'll call you about it, but both of us think we need you on this as well. I really don't know how to handle this thing with Ike. I can't say much more about it, but it is important. Can I count on you?"

"If you say it's important, it must be. I can break away almost anytime with a few days warning. I can always have one of my graduate assistants lecture. They already do most of my paperwork anyway. You have aroused my curiosity. It sounds like foreign intrigue, cloak and dagger, mystery... just like old times!" He laughed. "I'll be there, just tell me when."

"Saturday, here in Manhattan. As soon as I can firm up a time and place with Harold, I'll get back to you." Christian added with a note of exasperation, "That is, if I can ever get through. You are the hardest person to find."

Miller chuckled. "Sometimes one does not see the need to be found. But let me give you a new telephone number. This one rings through to a special line connected with a device I've been working on to record messages when the intended recipient is not available—or does not wish to be found. Just leave the place and the time for Saturday's rendezvous. Uh-oh," he broke off, "I hear the door bell. Dinner's arrived! Save your story for Saturday!"

Christian laughed. "Thanks for your cooperation ... and your confidence." He paused for a moment, smiled, and then asked, "Casey, just wondering. It's ninety frigging degrees here in Manhattan, so it can't be much cooler in Boston. Why the hell do you have a fire in the fireplace?"

Miller chuckled, "Why not? It's a perfect setting for an evening of romance, especially with air-conditioning on full blast. And besides, if you keep me on this phone much longer I'll need it to warm up my dinner."

"Hint given and received. No wonder we called you the Wizard. I'll call you as soon as I've talked to Harold. So long." Christian replaced the receiver and silently leaned back in his chair. His mind was racing over the details he would need to see about in preparing for their weekend meeting. Where should they meet? Did anyone else need to be brought into the circle? How would they handle communications? What about expenses?

The sound of the night watchman making his rounds reminded him that it was late and he needed to go home. He put away the last of his papers and turned off the office lights, then took the elevator to the underground garage. In just a few minutes he was weaving his way through the light evening traffic. His favorite radio station brought a re-broadcast of "Die Fledermaus" recorded in Salzburg, Austria. *Yes,* he thought, *it's beginning to feel like the old days. Harold was right: I'm alive once more.*

Arriving at his office the next morning Christian told Mrs. Clarke he had some calls to make and did not wish to be disturbed for half an hour. As he did so he noticed Mrs. Clarke's all-knowing look of concern. He had never withheld any business secrets from her. He would have to involve her. She would be handling all the calls should the trio ever devise a plan of action.

He started to go on to his desk but then turned and asked, "Mrs. Clarke, what is our schedule for this next hour? I would like to push everything back about one hour."

"You wanted to work on the Thyssen import proposal," she informed him with a slight chill in her voice.

That confirmed it. Now he knew she felt left out. He decided that this was as good a time as any to have his chat with her.

"Okay, we can delay that. Would you please come into my office?"

She gave him a look of concern, and did as she was asked, bringing along her steno pad and taking her usual place for receiving dictation. "Mrs. Clarke," Christian began, "we have been together for many years. You know me better than anyone but my wife. I can't keep secrets from such a trusted and loyal friend and staff member. But I hesitate to involve you in something that has absolutely nothing to do with the import-export business." He could tell that although Mrs. Clarke put up a brave front, concern was written in her eyes. He rose from his chair and moved to sit on the front corner of his desk, directly facing her.

"Remember a few weeks ago when the White House called? Well, it was all a con job, a Presidential con job." Then he told her the gist of what had transpired in Washington. She sat silently through the narrative, not moving a muscle as she perched on the edge of her chair.

"As you already know, during the last two years of World War II, I was with the Office of Strategic Services. I was called to London to do a special mission for General Eisenhower. But, long before the war, my father knew the Eisenhowers—Ike and Mamie, as well as Ike's brother, Milton. That's why he

46

felt comfortable calling on me. But to make a long story short, I have been asked to help the Old General—unofficially, of course. For the past few days I've been trying to get together with some of my friends from the old days to try to create a plan that might pass muster with Ike."

"You mean Mr. McCurrill and Mr. Miller," she added helpfully, the look of concern no longer apparent. Christian now realized the futility of trying to keep her in the dark on anything. Of course, he had often asked her to place calls to these men and set up their lunch get-togethers.

He smiled. "Right on the nose, as usual, Mrs. Clarke." His normal, relaxed manner of dealing with her quickly returned. "They will be coming to New York hopefully Saturday, so that we can begin having some meaningful discussions about the problem Ike identified."

"Mr. Reiter," she asked in her typically practical manner, "will you need me to help with meeting arrangements? Place? Food? Accommodations?"

"That would be very helpful indeed." Christian began to think that Mrs. Clarke was enjoying this break in routine. "Soon you will meet these two men..." Reiter stopped. "I should also warn you. If you get a call from someone who calls himself the Wizard, that will be Casey Miller calling from Cambridge or Boston."

"Wizard?"

"Oh yes, he was our special equipment designer. He designed everything from exploding chunks of coal to deadly darts shot from a fountain pen."

"I never knew—"

"Ask him about the electric toothpick. He'll tell you all about it. He is an inventor; had been one before OSS got hold of him, and has, I don't know how many, patents for kitchen gadgets. You'll love him. Just keep at arm's length. He's quite a ladies' man."

Blushing, Mrs. Clarke asked, "And the other gentleman?"

"Oh, that's Harold McCurrill. He is now a professor at Princeton. Because he was so brilliant we called him the Philosopher. In retrospect, we probably could have called him the 'Answer Man.' He seemed to be able to put logical order to any sort of problem-solving."

Christian paused and walked toward the window. He turned and looked at his secretary for several seconds before continuing.

"Mrs. Clarke, I want you to know that you have the right to opt out of this 'extracurricular' activity. I do not want to presume on our long acquaintance. If you would rather not be involved, you and I will continue our relationship as usual."

She no longer seemed worried or confused. "As I see it," she said, "in the foreseeable future nothing much will change—except for a few more telephone calls."

47

Christian agreed. He was not at all certain if it would even necessitate additional calls. But he wanted to reassure Mrs. Clarke that nothing would change as far as Quadrant Import-Export was concerned. That business would continue as usual.

CHAPTER 12

Thanks to Mrs. Clarke's efficiency, all three of the former OSS friends were enjoying a fine Saturday lunch at Antonio's Italian Ristorante. As soon as Christian arrived at the bustling ristorante, Antonio, the proprietor, greeted him, *"Buon giorno, Capitano."* He added, "Your friends are already here at the window table, as always." He escorted Reiter to the table where McCurrill and Miller were halfway into a bottle of Chianti.

After pouring a glass for Christian, McCurrill said, "I love it. Antonio greets anyone with a lapel pin as 'capitano.' The way I figure it, this place is always prepared for an attack with all these spaghetti-slopping 'captains' as customers."

Miller laughed. "And he makes us all feel like real Italians."

Christian broke in with, "Hard to believe that during the war he was an army mess sergeant. He cooked chow all over the Pacific Theater and has never been to Italy, but his cooking is superb. He told me he learned it all from his mother. It's authentic Italian, all right. I can attest to that."

They carried on the lighthearted conversation throughout dinner. Then, while enjoying Antonio's cappuccino, Reiter turned to Miller and said in a low voice, "Casey, I know Harold has already had some time to fill you in, more or less. Let me just briefly give you my take on where Ike's coming from." He then recapped the high points of his meeting with the President.

"So all he wants us to do is figure out a way to bankrupt the entire Soviet Union?" Miller asked, his eyebrows rising along with the pitch of his voice. "So what do we do for an encore? Cure cancer?"

Reiter hesitated. McCurrill, playing with his cappuccino spoon, said matter-of-factly, "Sure. Why not?" McCurrill smiled. "Just kidding. Christian and I talked about this at some length in Princeton while you were giving sailing lessons. At first I felt just like you. But, on reflection, this impossible task looks ... well, for now let's just say it looks less daunting."

"I can't wait to hear this one," Miller said sarcastically.

"Well, listen," McCurrill joked, "and even you might learn something." Miller had forgotten that McCurrill was unflappable, once he was on to something big. "Let me tell you," McCurrill continued, "I spent most of last week talking with ... I don't remember how many of my colleagues." He carefully placed his cappuccino spoon next to the cup. "Now, you all know that some of my colleagues are the greatest brains in this country."

He looked at Miller, who snorted derisively. "Okay," he continued, "I'll concede that there may be a great brain or two in one of those fancy New England universities, too." Then he became serious, lowered his voice and leaned into the table. "My people are pretty savvy on life in the glorious Soviet Workers' Paradise, but they told me things even I found difficult to believe ... well, anyway, here it is. Number one, corruption in the Commie homeland is far more widespread than anyone in the Soviet Union is willing to admit."

He waited for comments from his two friends. When none came he continued, "Number two, collectively the Russians are all underproducers. They don't know how to work and apparently they are not interested in learning—no incentives." He paused and looked first at Miller, then at Reiter. Reiter nodded, and McCurrill continued, "The super-purist Communist officials are as corrupt as were their czarist predecessors. An old Russian proverb says 'A Russian peasant's life is made bearable only by the corruptness of the czar's officials.' That was true then, and that is true now. It also dovetails right into the theory that every human being is a capitalist. The corrupt official doesn't buy Karl Marx's idea that the ideal state would have workers who produced as much as they could so that everyone's needs could be met."

Miller mused, "From each according to his ability, et cetera..." McCurrill nodded.

"That's right—The Communist Manifesto. Today's corrupt Soviet official wants more. In other words, the workers should work as hard as they can so that the wants of a select few can be fulfilled." When no one interrupted, he continued, "And here is where number one leads to number two. Corruption carries within itself inefficiency. Not only is the system inefficient, the entire labor force, from the top supervisor to the bottom echelon worker, is inefficient and corrupt." McCurrill explained that the Russians did not call it stealing; they thought of it as "organizing," as just being smart, that each and every one steals the state blind in his own fashion. The big guys steal big, and the little guys steal little, and inefficiency is everywhere. He closed by saying that if viewed with Western eyes, Soviet Communism was an economic basket case.

Christian chimed in. "So much for the glories of Communism. Are your friends suggesting we bring back the czar?"

McCurrill continued in his professorial mode. "Not at all, not at all. Not all the blame can be placed on Communism. Russia never had a competitive economy, not under the czars, nor under their Communist leaders. What my learned friends tell me is that the Russian peasant worked somewhat productively only when someone stood over him with a bullwhip; the threat of a beating was what made the peasant work. It's still true now."

"So, in other words," Miller interrupted, "you're suggesting that the whole Soviet economy resembles a Potemkin village—people working hard at not working. And if there is no real work, it follows that there is no real production."

McCurrill laughed. "Right on the money, Casey, they even joke, 'We pretend to work; they pretend to pay us.' A sort of gallows humor." He took another sip from his cappuccino cup, "If we look at a Russian's productivity from a purely capitalistic point of view, we would soon realize that, collectively, they are all idlers; they simply do not know how to work by Western standards. Thus, my learned friends suggest, the entire Soviet economy is ready to implode, fall into a bottomless pit. Only the strong hand of a harsh dictator prevents its total collapse."

The three men sat silently contemplating this idea. After a moment Casey asked how this condition could have been sustained for so many years. "Good question, Casey," McCurrill continued, "but here again, as unbelievable as this may sound, these are the opinions of researchers and academics who have watched this phenomenon develop for many years. Folks who know the Soviet system better than most Soviets.

"According to my friends, the economy is not balanced by supply and demand. Profit does not demand production efficiency. Instead, the bureaucracy defines efficiency, which does not necessarily relate to the marketability of goods or services."

"How can that be?" Christian interjected. "If your product cannot meet market needs at a reasonable price, you are out of business, my friend."

"Ah," McCurrill said. "Spoken like a true capitalist! But let me give you an example of how a typical Communist thinks. And just for your sake, Casey, I want you to know that I am not making this up." Grinning, Casey leaned back in his chair.

"The output of a Soviet furniture factory is not measured by quality and quantity of items produced, but by the weight of the furniture," McConnell said. "Thus, the factory that produces the heaviest, the clumsiest furniture, fulfills the norm quickly and gets praised. Of course they produce furniture nobody wants, but nothing else is available.

"Let me give you another example of socialist equality, this time in the military. You want to hear about Communist equality? Listen! The common soldier smokes Makhorka, cut-up tobacco stems with very little leaf tobacco. He wraps this coarse mixture in a strange kind of pipe made out of his army newspaper that he calls 'Goat Leg' because of its shape, I suppose. The company-grade officer smokes a Papirossa, a factory-made cigarette that is actually half a cigarette; the other half is a paper holder. Field-grade officers smoke factory-made cigarettes that are similar to those we know, only the quality of the tobacco is not as good as Western tobacco. High Communist party officials, and the foreign affairs and

51

secret police chaps, have far better cigarettes available to them, imported from Western Europe or the USA. Karl Marx's dictum 'From everyone according to his capability, for everyone according to his needs,' is total horse manure.

"Now, that's just one example of 'to everyone according to his needs.' This concept is spread throughout the Soviet Union. You'll find it at every level. I guess the high-ranking party folks need better smokes than the 'common' citizens—so much for their much-heralded equality. In other words, there ain't none. This is where the corruption comes in, and I mean total corruption; much worse than anything we have here in the West. The little guy steals small; some tools, some boards, nails, that sort of thing, to build a shed. The big guy steals big; on the sly acquires an automobile, gets free rides on aircraft, nylons for the wife, mistress, or girlfriend. Or fur coats for both the wife and the mistress. The big guy shops in a special store where the little guy cannot even get by the guard at the door. And when nobody is looking the guard steals from the store—little things for the girlfriend, the wife, and the mother, just to show that he too has influence. This is the system. It's all about power, about connections, about influence. The little guy envies the big guy, wishes he could do the same. Corruption is a way of life. In a strange way it works, but it hurts the economy something fierce."

Miller started to chuckle. McCurrill held up his hand. "Having given you just a couple of examples, I don't mean to suggest that the Soviet Union and the Warsaw Pact nations are merely cartoon adversaries. On the contrary, despite their inefficient and corrupt system, they still pose a considerable threat to the free world."

"How?" Miller asked sharply. "From what your 'learned friends' have said so far, I wouldn't think the Commies could produce a bicycle, much less a tank, or a submarine."

"Casey, for Westerners this is almost impossible to fathom. As one of my colleagues said, 'It's the enigma within the enigma.' The Communist system produces some of the world's finest mathematicians, scientists, physicians, and engineers, but they cannot mass-produce a decent car or a sewing machine. Their infrastructure is totally inadequate for the size of the country. Yet, the military threat comes only partially from the quantity of their deployed forces. The Soviets have always had good armored vehicles. Their World War II tank, the T-34, as well as their self-propelled guns, are legendary. Soviet aircraft, fighters as well as bombers, have undergone considerable improvement since World War II, and their navy is currently being converted from a coastal defense force into a true 'Blue Water' navy with a heavy reliance on submarines."

McCurrill paused, as if to make sure that his friends were paying attention after his long discourse. "However, my friends, all this is being done at horrendous cost. It costs the Soviets three to four times as much—by Western measures—to produce the average tank, aircraft, ship or submarine."

Miller interrupted, "Hold on there, Harold, hold on. Let me think. This is important."

"What?" asked McCurrill, somewhat thrown off his lecturing pace.

"Why, Harold," Miller said, "are you surprised that I thought you had something important to say? You said it costs the Soviets three to four times as much—by Western measures—to produce the average tank, aircraft, ship or submarine. Wouldn't that fit into Christian's thing of bankrupting the Soviets?"

Before McCurrill could answer, Christian whispered, pounding the table, "That's it, that's it. Harold, the combination of production inefficiency, costs of production, and corruption."

McCurrill, looking surprised, agreed, but then held up his hand. "True, but the quantity of equipment produced, the pure numbers, is precisely what gives our military-industrial faction reason to demand an increase in the U.S. defense budget. So, before we do bankrupt the Soviets, my colleagues at Princeton tell me that the chances of a Soviet attack will increase exponentially should the Soviet economy deteriorate significantly. Therein lies the dilemma."

Christian looked disappointedly at his two friends. "Are you saying that we're damned if we do and damned if we don't?"

McCurrill thought for some moments, and then shook his head. "Not if we are careful, not if we don't overdo it. I've spent long hours in theoretical discussions with colleagues and specialists about the military-industrial complex. They, especially my more liberal friends, believe the cost is not sustainable, that the Soviet Union needs just a little push to free-fall into the abyss."

"What do you think, Harold?" Christian questioned carefully.

"I'm not sure," McCurrill admitted, thoughtfully pulling on his lower lip. "I do know, however, that the people themselves are capable of enduring hardships the likes of which few Americans can even imagine. While we worry about choices between guns and butter, the average Russian wouldn't even ask the question if it came to defending what they term Rodina, the Motherland."

Christian seemed to think out loud. "So the real question is how to get the officials, the Soviet leaders, to understand that their system isn't really working, and that no matter how many resources they divert to military build-up, they can never overcome the inefficiencies of their own system to win a competition with the free market economies of the West?"

"Bingo! That's it!" announced a triumphant McCurrill.

Miller sat scowling. "I admit that there's logic to what you say. However—and it's a big however—I fail to see how the three of us fit into any of this. I'm afraid I'm more confused than ever."

Christian glanced sympathetically at his old friend. "Casey, this is the point where you come in. Think, man! What's the single biggest part of the Soviet budget?"

"Military spending," Miller replied without hesitation.

"Okay, so what we need is a vehicle, something that would make the Soviets spend even more than they are now spending, but the Soviets must believe that it is for their own good ... something like that."

The men sat silently as they waited for their bill to arrive. Gradually the tables around them had emptied. The waiters were clearing the lunch tables and setting up for the evening diners. Miller leaned slowly toward his companions. "Listen. Harold has had a crack at the social science aspect of this problem. I think the key might be weapons system development. But I'm not confident of my facts. I have a few learned friends, too, you know. I'd like a chance to pick their brains. One brain in particular, a retired Navy captain who teaches submarine technology. He has been doing some work in the area of what we call 'fancy metals.' Scuttlebutt around the lab is that there is talk of building submersibles out of titanium."

McCurrill asked, "Would this be a significant development?"

Miller looked at him as though he could not believe that a man as bright as Harold could ask such a naive question. "Significant? Are you kidding? Do you have any idea what it would cost to produce enough titanium to build one of today's submarines, much less a fleet of tomorrow's subs? A bloody fortune, that's what!"

Miller, still puzzled, shook his head. "Before we make any decision we still have to make damned sure we know that this is feasible. That's why I have to talk to the captain—the real one, not one of Antonio's."

"Great," McCurrill whispered. "Christian, Casey, if we can combine corruption and inefficiency with a product that shows great potential as a weapons system..." He looked up, "My God, I think we've got the answer to Ike's problem."

"Well," Christian interrupted, "well, that sounds almost too easy."

"Only in theory," said McCurrill, "only in theory. But before we even delve into that, let's first find out what Casey's sailor has to say. If he shoots it down we have to think of another way—or maybe just drop the whole thing."

Christian replied, "No, we can't quit now. We just got started. Too much is at stake. Casey, talk to your captain—pronto."

"Aye, aye, sir," said Miller, giving Christian a rather sloppy salute. They finished their cappuccino. As they rose from their chairs Antonio escorted them to the door. He held the door open and then shook everyone's hand in true Italian fashion.

The trio departed for their own destinations, having agreed to await "the sailor's" assessment on titanium.

Two days after the lunch at Antonio's, Christian was back at his desk at

54

Quadrant, when his intercom buzzed. "A man calling himself the Wizard wants to talk to you," Mrs. Clarke said.

"Oh, that's Casey. Thanks. Please put him through," said Christian as he picked up the receiver.

"Christian," said Miller, with what seemed to be barely controlled excitement in his voice, "the word is 'titanium.' My sailor tells me it has great potential. When can we get together?"

"I'll call Harold. We can meet either here or in Princeton."

"Let's meet in New York. That's halfway between my place and Harold's."

Mrs. Clarke made the arrangements for the trio's early Saturday morning meeting at the Plaza Hotel. She knew that her boss preferred the Plaza to the Waldorf-Astoria. She knew he enjoyed the Plaza's striking palatial presence with all the pomp of a French chateau. A small meeting room had been set aside for their use. She also made arrangement to have coffee and refreshments served. The hotel was conveniently located near Quadrant Import-Export's offices.

Mr. Reiter had given her a description of his to former OSS comrades and Mrs. Clarke was anxious to finally meet the Philosopher and the Wizard. Early Saturday morning Mrs. Clarke sat in the lobby waiting for the appearance of the duo; they arrived within ten minutes of each other. From her boss's description she recognized Harold McCurrill immediately. The Philosopher wore khaki trousers, an outdated narrow necktie, a tan shirt; he carried a brown, rumpled jacket with leather patches at the elbows loosely slung over his arm,

However, with all the comings and goings in the hotel lobby she almost missed "Casey" Miller. The Wizard, a slender man, wore a somber suit and well-matched shirt and tie. His curly red hair was in place, not an errant strand. He looked every part the Scot he was: tall, slender, and pale as if he had never been in the sun; not at all what Mrs. Clarke imagined an inventor to look like. Luckily, she had asked the desk clerk to give her a discreet signal. As Miller registered Mrs. Clarke rose and introduced herself, and then escorted him to the meeting room. She returned briefly to the hotel's catering desk to make a final check, to be sure her arrangements for food and drink were on track. Then she returned to the small, very comfortable suite where she encountered a tumultuous scene. The air was already full of cigar and cigarette smoke; there was excited talk and it seemed all three were talking at once.

When Christian spotted his secretary he said, "I know you've met Mrs. Clarke in the lobby, but allow me to formally introduce our chief of staff, Mrs. Clarke. She will be the one whose voice you will always hear first during this entire operation. That is, if we have an operation."

"Well, at least one person who knows what she is doing." Miller kidded. "So, let's go to work."

McCurrill busied himself at the breakfast bar, "I don't know about you,

Christian, but I have waited long enough for Casey's promised report. As a Princeton man, I am very capable of eating and listening at the same time. The only question I have is: Can MIT engineers eat and talk at the same time?"

"Watch me!" Casey announced. "Gentlemen, be seated, otherwise what I am about to tell you will knock you off your feet!" The other two obediently sank down into the deep leather conference room chairs.

"That's better," Casey said, as he rifled through some papers he retrieved from his suit jacket pocket. He had a habit of pausing for effect. "When we met last week, we talked about the possibility that 'fancy metals'—specifically titanium—might have application in weapons development." He checked his notes. "My sailor told me that titanium has its pluses and minuses. First the pluses: It's harder than steel, lighter than steel—very important for submarines. It not only is stronger, but it weighs thirty-three percent less than the HY-80 steel now used in submarines."

Christian interrupted, "HY-80?

"HY-80," Miller continued patiently, "is the abbreviation for high-yield steel that can withstand 80,000 pounds of pressure per square inch; HY-100 is steel that can withstand 100,000 pounds of pressure per square inch, and so on. But titanium would seem to be the ideal material for submarine pressure hulls. Titanium submarines would be stronger than high-yield steel ones without the corresponding increase in weight—an extremely important feature in the undersea world where everything is weight-dependent; where every ounce counts."

Again Miller paused, double-checking his notes. "But equally important for submarines, titanium is non-magnetic. And this, my friends, is another very important attribute."

"Why?" asked Christian impatiently.

"Why?" Miller repeated, as the pitch of his voice dropped. "Having a non-magnetic submarine completely throws off submarine detection."

"You've lost me, Casey, and I don't mind admitting it," McCurrill said. "I'm afraid my science education ended with high school physics."

"Sorry, lads. Let me try to explain it better," said Miller apologetically. "My Navy captain—let's just stick with Harold's nickname for him, the sailor, shall we? — mentioned a system known as MAD."

The Wizard chuckled. "As if I didn't know what that was until he explained it.

MAD is an acronym for 'magnetic anomaly detection.' My sailor told me that the world's navies heavily depend on MAD. With MAD the submarine does not even realize it has been detected. We, and our Western Allies, rely heavily on that type of submarine detection."

McCurrill interrupted excitedly, "So a titanium submarine can move without fear of detection by conventional methods!" He paused, looking somewhat puzzled. "But I have an extremely important question for you: If you can detect steel-hulled submarines by magnetic anomaly and you can't detect titanium submarines, why aren't we Americans building titanium submarines?"

"That's the clincher, Harold, that's the clincher. They are too damned expensive!"

"What do you mean?" Reiter asked. "How much more expensive could it be to build a submarine out of titanium?"

A broad smile broke across Miller's face. "Dream on, lad, dream on. According to the sailor, titanium—the metal alone—is three times as expensive as HY steel, not to mention the increased costs of working with the material and changing construction techniques."

Miller leaned back in his chair, watching the expressions of his friends, who now seemed to be racing to the inevitable conclusion.

McCurrill's eyes lit up as he carefully stated, "That means that it would cost the Soviets between six and twelve times what it would cost the U.S. to build a titanium sub, right? I mean, with their inefficiencies, their costs would race ahead of ours."

"Bingo!" Miller said.

"If we want the Russians to build outrageously expensive titanium submarines," McCurrill concluded, "there must be a payoff for them—a big payoff. MAD is it. The Silent Service does not ever want its boats detected." He turned to Miller with a mixture of awe and glee. "You are a genius, Casey, a bloody genius."

"I'm only grateful that you finally acknowledge that inescapable fact," Miller smiled, eyebrows raised in a comic attempt to appear haughty. "Of course there's another advantage to using titanium. The sailor said, 'Same weight, three times the depth.' That is also of great importance for submarines."

"Harold is right, Casey," Reiter said. "This is brilliant. There is only one rather large question remaining: How do we convince the Russians to build titanium subs?"

Their discussion was interrupted by a discreet knock on the door. Reiter glanced at his watch. "That must be lunch." McCurrill opened the door and accepted the cart. "Don't bother to uncork the wine," Reiter informed the waiter, sending him off quickly with a generous tip.

Using his own corkscrew, Reiter uncorked the dry Riesling and checked its clarity. He thought it would do. He poured. "I think that after this morning's work, we all deserve a drink."

"Hear, hear," the others quickly chimed in.

"But first a toast," Christian added. "Gentlemen, we are about to embark on a mission once again. We need a code name, just like in the old days."

Miller mumbled, "I must be getting rusty—can't think of one."

Christian suggested, "How about something that indicates a close-out, a final step?" He corrected himself immediately. "But not the word final; that leaves a sour taste in my throat."

"I've got it!" McCurrill announced. "How about OMEGA?" He looked at Christian. "Wasn't that the call sign the Old General gave you? Besides, most likely, it will be our last operation if we do pull this one off."

"Sounds good to me," Miller said. "How about if we add 'Solution' to that? After all, the Old General hopes that it will solve his problem, right?"

"That's it," Christian agreed. "So, gentlemen, let us lift our glasses and toast the OMEGA Solution."

They clinked glasses and drank. "Now," Christian said jovially, "let's do justice to this lunch then get back to work."

After the busboy had cleared away the debris of lunch, the members of the newly christened OMEGA Team debated options, many options, but the trio could not think of a convincing scenario that would lead the Soviets to spend their money faster than they already were. They debated a multitude of scenarios to force the Soviets into a large-scale titanium-submarine building program. Every suggestion hit a solid wall when one of the trio asked how they, as three private citizens, could build a deception program without some sort of solid governmental backing.

After a frustrating afternoon, they left for dinner, deciding to walk several blocks to a neighborhood restaurant so they could get some fresh air and clear their heads. Upon their return to the hotel, they resumed the debate into the late evening hours. Finally a frustrated Reiter said, "Look, we aren't getting anywhere. I'm not sure I even know where we are at this point. What do we have so far, Harold?"

McCurrill took up the conversation, "Okay. Let's look at it from the top: First, Ike wants a plan that will lead to Soviet bankruptcy. Second, the best one we have come up with so far is to get the Soviets to build titanium submarines. Third, we agree, more or less, that the only way to con the Soviets into building titanium submarines is to let them know the U.S. Navy is building them. Fourth, here are four civilians sitting in a hotel room with a plan—and that's about as far as we've gone." He looked around for agreement, and his two cohorts nodded.

"So," Miller put in, "we have come to a dead stop. I mean it's fine for the President to say 'nobody in government is to know about it.' It's another thing for a businessman and two college professors to overthrow the Soviet Union without force and violence. I mean, we aren't magicians or miracle workers. To me, that's totally unrealistic."

Christian leaned back, "Casey, the way you put it, it does seem impossible."

McCurrill agreed. "Yes, but only if we go by Ike's rules. But didn't he want an unorthodox solution? Well, he can't have one going by his rules; that's for sure."

During the silence that followed, Reiter studied Miller. "Casey, your research has been invaluable. But do you want to continue? I mean, no hard feelings if your job, or your personal life prohibits you from travel. You still could contribute in other ways—"

"Not on your life," Miller interrupted. "This is the best thing that has happened to me since I invented the electric toothpick. I haven't had that large a charge since the day I first plugged that thing into the light socket."

McCurrill and Reiter exploded in laughter. They knew that Miller had nearly killed himself testing the toothpick on himself. "After all that," Reiter said, still laughing, "let's call it a day. Maybe tomorrow we can think more clearly."

The men stretched themselves. McCurrill yawned. "I guess I'm more tired than I thought I was. When do we meet tomorrow?"

Christian said, "Nine o'clock, if that is okay with you?" They nodded. "All right then, until tomorrow." They slowly filed out of the room. Miller volunteered to escort Mrs. Clarke to the subway station.

Christian walked the few blocks to his office building and picked up his car from the garage. As he navigated his way home through the Saturday evening traffic, his favorite radio station brought classical music from Carnegie Hall. He had not realized how tense he was. The soft music of the string quartet started to relax him. He parked his Mercedes in the garage of his brownstone and walked upstairs.

Kjerstine looked at him quizzically as he opened the door. "If I didn't know you as well as I believe I do, I'd think you were having an affair."

He laughed. "Not with Harold and Casey, I hope."

Kjerstine hugged him, "Well, I hope not. But it's nice to have you here at least for the rest of the evening."

"I hope tomorrow will be a bit shorter than today. We're making progress, but Ike will go through the roof."

"Why?"

"Well, he wanted no one in government to be involved, and I think we will need to involve at least one official. Casey put the finger right on the problem when he asked how one businessman and two college professors could overthrow the Soviet Union without force and violence."

Kjerstine nodded. "That would take a miracle."

"That's just about what Casey's assessment was."

The next morning, after reassuring Kjerstine that he really would make an effort to spend the evening with her, Christian headed off to join the other members of the OMEGA team. He decided to have the valet park the car, and he slipped quietly into the lobby, arriving punctually at the appointed time. He greeted McCurrill, who had already discovered the breakfast tray that Mrs. Clarke had thoughtfully provided, along with several large carafes of various beverages. "Where's Casey?" Christian asked, as he poured himself a cup of coffee.

"Not sure," Harold mumbled, finishing the last of a messy Danish. "He said something about having to get copies made of something before this meeting."

"Well, at least he's here in New York. That's a relief."

Suddenly, a voice boomed, "Good morning, my friends!" Casey Miller had arrived. "I must thank you for your hospitality, Christian. I had a wonderful night in this fine establishment last night, and I am looking forward to an equally wonderful one tonight." He removed his jacket and carefully placed it on a hanger in the room's small closet, before moving toward the pastry tray.

"Not at all, Casey," replied Christian with a little note of sarcasm in his voice. "Anything to make sure that the allure of this meeting could compete with the allure of your Boston harem."

Casey laughed heartily. "Now, now, Christian. Those of us who don't have your money, or your fascinating Kjerstine, must be satisfied with our simple pleasures."

Mrs. Clarke seemed amused by the friendly banter between the two friends. Christian smiled. "Well, I can see that you are up and about. Don't know that I'd go so far as describing you as bright-eyed and bushy-tailed, though. You must have had as much trouble sleeping as I did."

McCurrill, who looked a bit more rumpled than usual, pointed to the empty chair. "Sit down, Christian. Mrs. Clarke has ordered a whole breakfast banquet for us—eggs, bacon, toast, coffee, and orange juice. I hope that's okay?"

"It will do today, although I usually don't eat this much. I have to watch my waistline; can't remain lean and mean on a heavy diet."

After the busboy had cleared away the dishes, McCurrill briefly reviewed yesterday's operational plan "At our initial meeting Christian asked me to engage my learned friends in conversations regarding comparisons between United States and Soviet infrastructure, economies, people, and all the factors that contribute to the well-being or the demise of a nation. I have written a report, almost a dissertation, on this topic that Christian can, if the need arises, present to the President. For the moment, think 'corruption.' Now, Casey, here, also did what we asked. Accepting his authorities to be as knowledgeable in their fields as mine are in theirs, his conclusions about the properties, value and cost of titanium are equally valid. Titanium is our baby. If we can make the Russians believe that we're building titanium submarines, they'll go nuts."

Christian agreed. He raised his cup in salute. "Harold, I congratulate you. You have made the scenario as simple as could be done. You have always had the skill to cut right to the bone." Then he turned to the Wizard, "Casey, when you have the numbers, call me. You, Harold, and I will meet either here or at Princeton, or up your way, to finalize the plan so I can present it to the Old General. So how about if we get together in two weeks from today? Casey, is that too soon for you?"

"Two weeks from today it is."

"Christian," said McCurrill, as he started gathering up his things, "when you report to the President, tell him this: Casey and I looked for a solution to his dilemma in two different ways, mine from the socioeconomic angle, Casey from the technological one. We agreed that if we combine Russian paranoia with technology—no, let me put that another way. If we make the Soviets think that they must build titanium submarines because we are building them, it could bankrupt the Soviet Union. And that is exactly what he wanted us to do. But remember, we must convince the Russians that we are indeed building those submarines."

After the others said their goodbyes and departed, Christian took one last look around the room before he also took his leave. He was happy that he would be able to keep his promise to Kjerstine, since it was only early afternoon. In the car, weaving past the tourists and Sunday drivers, he thought that all had gone well. He felt confident that he would be able to report to the man in the White House that it would take more than a mere suggestion.

CHAPTER 13

In late afternoon the day after the "Plaza Hotel Weekend," Christian Reiter flew to Basel as planned, to conclude a round of negotiations involving Quadrant Import-Export. During the two weeks he was gone, McCurrill and Miller finalized the conceptual plan for the OMEGA Solution. They had already set the date for their next meeting: two days following Reiter's return from Europe. This time it was in Reiter's offices.

Christian assumed his usual place at the head of the table with Mrs. Clarke next to him, notebook and pencils at the ready. McCurrill seemed most comfortable in his professorial stance, pacing back and forth along the side of the large conference table, while he both talked and listened. Miller, on the other hand, was happy leaning back in a deep leather conference chair, legs crossed with his feet on the table.

McCurrill reported that he and Miller believed they had finally hit upon a workable plan.

Miller, in the act of lighting one of his big cigars, said, "Hold it for a moment." He took a few puffs, and then said, "On the Soviet economy, Harold was right. His colleagues have assured him that the economy is in very bad shape. My guys at MIT agree. So: If we manage to con the Soviets into building titanium submarines on top of their regular construction program, it could very conceivably break their back. The question we now have to address is: How do we convince them to undertake this building program?"

McCurrill, still pacing back and forth, looked at Reiter. "Christian, we have sketched out a scenario of our plan. Here it is in a rough outline: The U.S. Navy designs a titanium attack submarine and then slips the plans for that submarine to the Soviets."

"Hold it, hold it," interrupted Christian. "Did I hear you correctly? How in hell are we going to do that?"

McCurrill smiled smugly. "We are not. The U.S. Navy is!"

"I'm confused," replied Christian. "The U.S. Navy? The Old General said specifically no government involvement."

"Well," McCurrill replied, "Ike can't have his cake and eat it. Let me just ask you one question. Have we not agreed that building titanium submarines is the best way to spend lots of rubles quickly to protect and preserve Rodina?"

Christian hesitated. "Yes."

"Don't forget, the general asked for something out of the ordinary. This is it! We have to use Russian paranoia to our advantage. How? By convincing them that the U.S. Navy is designing or building a super-submarine of titanium. When they hear the word titanium, they'll know exactly the capabilities that come with this type of sub. They will know precisely the threat level their fleet faces without having a countermeasure, or without at least a sub with similar capabilities."

"And," Miller triumphantly announced, as he flourished his cigar, "we do not necessarily have to build this submarine. We merely demonstrate a serious effort to design one, and then somehow slip the plans to the Soviets."

Reiter watched his two friends with a mixture of amusement and disbelief. They were as giddy as schoolboys. He said, with a note of sarcasm, "I would feel much better if I thought the whole point of this exercise was to write a novel. Both of you would be right up there with the best." Then he turned quickly serious. "Would you two kindly remember that I am the one who has to present this so-called plan to the President? I'm the one who is supposed to give him a plan that will be carried out outside normal government operations channels."

He sighed, "But you are right. There's no way that the three of us— or any other three outsiders—can pull off a plan like this."

"That's why we need to involve the DNI," Miller said.

"But remember the President said that he didn't want any inside involvement, that...."

Miller broke in, "Hold your horses, Christian. You haven't heard us out yet. Harold, drop the big one on Christian."

McCurrill rose. "Okay, here it goes." He again started to pace back and forth. "Christian, only this approach would make this a successful operation. First, to make the whole thing believable, the President needs the cooperation of the DNI."

"Wait a minute!" exclaimed Reiter.

This time Miller waved his hand, "Listen to him, Christian. It gets even better, or worse, depending on where you stand." He smiled, as though he was secretly pleased at having made the New Yorker so uncomfortable.

Ignoring the interchange, McCurrill continued, "Second, NAVBUSHIPS, the U.S. Navy's ship design bureau in Arlington must establish a super-secret design section with a few bright engineers and designers who actually work on plans to construct a titanium fast attack submarine."

"Actually," Miller broke in, "that's the easy part. This all sounds complicated, but it doesn't have to be. In the first place, the Navy does not actually need to build titanium submarines. On the other hand, there is absolutely nothing wrong with developing plans for a very advanced submarine for the future. That's not unreasonable or far-fetched. You could even argue that it is extremely prudent. You never really know when you might need something like this. Harold and I have played this out, back and forth."

"Right," McCurrill agreed, nodding at Christian, "but I'm sure by now you can see that the DNI must be privy to the deception. If Ike can get him on board, everything else will fall in place. Once the DNI is in, all Ike has to do at one of his meetings with the Chief of Naval Operations is maybe wonder out loud about innovative submarine construction: how to make his submarines superior to all others, blah, blah, blah. In the course of all this talk Ike would mention the word 'titanium.'

"Then maybe the DNI could suggest, mind you, just suggest, that he has heard rumors that the Russians are building titanium submarines; just rumors— or maybe Ike could suggest it. Then the DNI could mention the virtues of such a submarine—you will have a list with all the advantages in your hip pocket when you see Ike. I bet the CNO will have NAVBUSHIPS start a design section for titanium submarines in a New York minute. That in turn would, in my opinion, launch a request to the Office of Naval Intelligence to collect everything on titanium submarines. All that can be done overtly."

Christian shook his head. "But... eh—?"

Miller interrupted, "Now wait just a minute, I know exactly what you're thinking, but let Harold play out the entire scenario. After that, we have some additional shockers for you to consider. But, first just listen to the whole story."

McCurrill continued pacing. "Third, in response to NAVBUSHIPS' request for information, Naval Intelligence issues an urgent, all-source intelligence collection requirement. But let's concentrate on the first collection. Navy tasks all intelligence collectors, the U. S., the Brits—no, all the NATO guys—to gather information on submersibles and submarines made of titanium alloy. Both searches include construction methods and techniques for shaping and welding large submersible and submarine components, as well as reports of difficulties encountered, and how problems were solved."

McCurrill tried an analogy to reinforce his argument. "Remember the intelligence analysts at SHAFE? Those guys sometimes would not even believe what we brought them. They wanted double and triple confirmation. I'm sure the Soviets are just like us. They'll know that we are collecting on this topic. Once our level of interest seems sufficiently high, they will have to counter with their own titanium sub program. Can't you see that?"

Christian looked at him silently, skeptically.

McCurrill paused, taking a deep breath. He then outlined the rest of the plan.

By the end of a long afternoon, Miller and McCurrill had convinced Reiter that Navy involvement was indeed essential. To catch the Soviets' attention the Navy would have to launch massive information-gathering operation, partly as an open-source titanium research project, and partly as a not-too-well-disguised intelligence collection of major proportions.

They agreed that as part of the open-source research, NAVBUSHIPS would insert Miller, via a Massachusetts Institute of Technology project, into the operation as soon as possible. For all overt purposes Miller would be working on his Ph.D. dissertation, but with a partial government contract, all funneled and documented through MIT. Appropriate MIT officials would write letters of introduction to various institutes of higher learning, including the Leningrad State Library. As part of the contract, MIT would also arrange all the permits, pay all travel arrangements, hotels, visas, etc.

"I think the first tip-off for the Soviets," said McCurrill "will be when they realize what Casey is doing at the Leningrad Library."

"So since when," Christian asked, turning to Miller, "have you become a Russian linguist?"

McCurrill laughed. "Casey thought of that. He thinks we can create an even better red warning flag for the Soviets if the Defense Department details an Air Force or Navy officer studying at Syracuse University's Russian Studies Program to assist Casey in Leningrad."

"Imagine," Miller chuckled, "here are two men looking for titanium information at the Leningrad Library. One from MIT, who carries a letter of introduction stating unequivocally that he works under U.S. Navy auspices; the other, a young military-looking man who speaks damned good Russian, and who makes no secret that he is in the U.S. military, should anyone ask."

"Furthermore," McCurrill said, "we feel that for personal security it would be best if two persons were to do the research in Leningrad. And," he added with a devious smile, "that military-looking young fellow will make the GRU even more suspicious."

McCurrill explained that Miller would make a stopover in Berlin on his way back from Leningrad. A visit there to the Technische Universität, at Berlin-Charlottenburg, the Faculty for Maschinenwesen-Schiffstechnik, the Institute of Mechanical Science-Maritime Technology, would bring Miller's name even further into prominence. While in Berlin he would get the navy to introduce him to NATO military intelligence collectors. And of course, he'd mention titanium as a top collection target. All arrangements, courtesy of the DNI.

McCurrill and Miller both agreed that it was a good idea to spread the word in two places, Leningrad and Berlin. This approach would get the Soviets' attention and would thus become the first bait. But they argued that it was of the utmost importance to have second bait dangling somewhere; one totally independent from Miller and MIT; one with credible and substantive evidence of "official proof that the U.S. Navy had high interest in titanium submarines."

He looked at Miller as if for reassurance before proceeding. "Christian," McCurrill began gently, "Casey and I are of one mind that it would be best if the Soviets somehow could get hold of the actual U.S. Navy plans for the American titanium submarine."

Reiter shook his head.

"You've got to be kidding. How could we possibly do that?"

"Well, it's a pretty safe bet that the three of us can't do that," McCurrill acknowledged. "Casey and I have gone back and forth over this, but we haven't thought of a way to do it. We do both agree, however, that this is the most crucial aspect of the plan. We need a one-two punch. Casey's research is designed merely to bring titanium to their attention. The second bait must be presented in such a way, in a hard evidence way, that the Soviets think they've snared it on their own. This is one of the reasons why we really need the DNI to be a player in this game. And part of your job is to convince the President that this is the only way it can work"

"I don't know, boys," said Christian, running his fingers through his hair as though he were about to pull it out. "This all looks just about impossible to me."

"Yes, it does," replied the Philosopher. "But for a deception, for a ruse of this proportion to succeed, it must follow a logical sequence. Logic is the key. Everything must have the appearance of normality; everything must follow a logical path. If it doesn't, someone may wonder and question it; once questioned, the entire plan could become unraveled. A lie that must be explained falls apart. A lie that needs no explanation can very well become the truth. If we want to fool the always suspicious Russians this plan must make sense, or as you always said, 'it must have hand and foot.'"

McCurrill looked at Miller. Miller nodded. "Think!" McCurrill continued

66

animatedly, "Who produces the secret submarine design plans? NAVBUSHIPS. Who has access to the secret submarine design plans? NAVBUSHIPS employees. Who can leak secret submarine design plans? In our opinion: only NAVBU- SHIPS employees, or some sloppy courier dropping the case, or something like that. We just can't pull any of this off without the knowledge and assistance of the DNI."

"It's that simple," interrupted Miller. "The Navy has the plans. How in hell could we, a couple of civilians who don't even live in Washington, get hold of secret plans for a submarine?"

This time McCurrill nodded in agreement. "Christian, you have to at least agree to the logic. There's no way to make all the pieces fall into place without the cooperation of the rear admiral in charge of the Office of Naval Intelligence. We know Ike wants no government involvement, but logic dictates it. We have thought this through, and we like the idea. It is definitely feasible as long as the DNI is involved. He will be the linchpin in the deception."

Miller added with a note of urgency in his voice, "Christian, we played this through a hell of a lot of scenarios. We discarded them all. We must have a real leak, and the plans must come from inside NAVBUSHIPS, from people with access. Maybe the DNI can think of something. He has the inside track on naval affairs. We need him desperately. We don't just need his ideas; we need his full cooperation." He hesitated, then said, "To be quite frank, this is it. We have run out of ideas. I'm afraid that if you can't make Ike buy this plan ... well... I don't know how else to say it, but this is the best we have come up with. Sorry."

Reiter exclaimed, "Christ! So, what do I tell Ike? Get the Director of Naval Intelligence involved? Have the DNI leak the plans to the Soviets?"

The others answered in unison, "Exactly!" McCurrill added, "Ike wanted something out of the ordinary, something unorthodox, well, old buddy, this is it."

Christian sat quietly for several moments. "Okay. Let me walk through this one." He looked at his notes. As he repeated the points, he gave each bullet a check mark with his number two pencil. He went step by step through the entire scenario. At the end he said, "And after all that you want the Navy to pass the plans to the Soviets and make it look as if they had stolen the blueprints from NAVBUSHIPS? For crying out loud, fellows, Ike will think we are a bunch of loonies."

McCurrill stopped pacing directly opposite Christian and suddenly dropped into a chair. He leaned across the table and stared steadily into Christian's eyes. "Got any better ideas?" he asked tersely. He did not wait for an answer. "That's your job, convincing the Old General. We just made the plan. You gotta admit it's a good one. No, it's a great one. You drew the tough job of selling it to Ike. You have to convince him that in essence this is a simple plan; that is logical and that it makes good sense."

"Casey and I have sweated bullets to put this plan together. To be frank, we can't come up with any other options. I think Casey will agree with me that if the Old General cannot, or will not convince the DNI to cooperate, we're just about ready to throw in the towel."

Miller added, "Harold and I are of one mind: it will only work if we can convince the Old General to have the U.S. Navy build, or at least design, a titanium submarine—in complete secrecy, of course."

"And," Reiter interrupted caustically, "any suggestions on how I convince the Old General? Or how he would convince the Navy to build that submarine?"

McCurrill had a definite twinkle in his eyes. He seemed to enjoy this. He said, "Well, Christian, since we have been busting our brains on this problem while you were off enjoying the good life in Switzerland, we thought that it was only fair to leave this problem to you. And, to be frank, it's our 'Hail Mary Pass,' because we're out of ideas, Old Ike can take it, or leave it. That's what it really comes to."

"Yeah," Miller chimed in. "We were afraid you'd feel left out."

The two men enjoyed a hearty laugh at the expression on Christian's face. Miller finally said in a friendly tone, "Christian, if you can convince the Old General to get the DNI involved, this will work, and the payoff will be enormous. Just think, it will cost the Soviets untold billions of rubles. Believe me. Ike wants to bankrupt the Soviet Union, doesn't he? Well, it's not just that the titanium alloy itself is so much more expensive than steel." He explained that a totally different manufacturing process would be needed. Currently there were no shipyard workers in the entire world with the experience to do the work.

"In fact," suggested Miller, "you can tell Ike that there are no shipyards in the whole world with the infrastructure to build them. The Soviets would have to train a whole new crop of shipyard workers. They will need totally new construction halls or they'll need to totally refurbish their old ones. Bending, shaping, and welding heavy plates of titanium alloy is far more difficult, far harder, than shaping steel; titanium cannot be heated, shaped or welded when exposed to air—to oxygen." Titanium welds are usually shielded by an inert gas, most often argon gas, he explained, and if titanium gets a whiff of oxygen during processing it bubbles, it becomes brittle—useless, junk.

"Just think, Christian," McCurrill jumped into the conversation, "the Soviet navy will have to pour money into new research and development, and into manufacturing technology. I mean I'm talking big, big rubles. If we can pull it off—the deception, that is, the Russkies won't have a Chinaman's chance in hell to save their economy!"

Christian, still only half-convinced, smiled, "So, in other words, although it looks impossible, it's definitely doable. But only under your conditions, which run counter to the President's charge. He shook his head, and then laughed, "You two have done a tremendous job. The sequences of the events look real. I'll dump this on Ike and ask him to approve that little change you so strongly suggest. He may go through the roof at first. But I think he'll be forced to admit that three civilians alone cannot do what he wants."

The three men stood up and stretched. It had been a long, tense discussion. Miller and McCurrill congratulated one another on their successful selling of the plan to Reiter. They shook hands with him and started to leave the room, ready for a celebratory evening on the town. As they reached the door, he stopped them. "Not so fast, boys. How would the Navy create some sort of security breach so that the Soviets could get the plans?"

McCurrill and Miller looked at each other, then at Christian. "Let Ike ask the DNI. He's got to have some expert on security and counterintelligence in his organization.

CHAPTER 14

It was now Christian's mission to convince President Eisenhower that his trio's brilliant plan to bleed the goddamned Commies white, had one little fly in the ointment: it needed some surreptitious action by at least one knowing government official, the Director, Naval Intelligence. Christian arrived at the White House and after they had dispensed with preliminaries, the President said, "You told me that you had good news. From this I gather the Philosopher, the Wizard, and you have fabricated a plan. But first tell me about your musketeers."

Christian explained that his old OSS teammates had agreed to be of service, and briefly laid out the capabilities of the group. "General," he said, "you must also know that we have had a lot of help from folks who have no inkling what this is all about; folks at Princeton and MIT—Miller has a friend and colleague, a retired navy captain, a submarine pressure hull expert—who made a major contribution to this project. Now McCurrill, on the other hand, had his fellow professors at Princeton provide input on all sorts of stuff like Soviet economics, psychology, et cetera. This information made all three of us more confident in recommending this venture."

Ike nodded and smiled. "Okay, this brings us to the reason for this meeting. How does your illustrious team propose to help me?"

"General, as I mentioned before, we had expert help. McCurrill believes the essence of all successful deceptions is logic. Deception must have a logical base and follow a logical sequence to its conclusion. He had conversations with Soviet area experts at Princeton; he and his colleagues are of one mind: 'The Soviets are corrupt, have always been corrupt, and they are paranoid and will always be paranoid; it's part of their makeup'."

The President seemed to agree.

Christian continued, "Miller, after having long talks with a retired Navy captain working at MIT, came to the conclusion that the solution is titanium. Titanium has many advantages when used in submarines instead of the normal

70

HY-80 steels. Furthermore, it would seriously degrade U.S. Navy MAD, non-acoustic detection."

At the conclusion of the technical portion he paused briefly, and said, "Now to the actual deception. Let me warn you. There are a few wrinkles in this plan that only you can iron out."

Eisenhower sat poker-faced.

"In short, we believe that we must convince the Soviets that it is to their advantage to build titanium submarines."

The Old General looked puzzled. "How?"

Christian laid out the scenario concocted by the Philosopher and the Wizard: It would need the collaboration of the Navy, "If the deception is to succeed, sir, it is our consensus that you will need to involve at least one person who is currently on active duty: the Director of Naval Intelligence."

"The what?" the Old General sputtered.

"The DNI." Reiter began to perspire and talked quickly, as he explained that the OMEGA Solution required a three-pronged deception. First, the U.S. Navy must create a highly compartmented submarine design section; a real, highly acclaimed design team must draw up plans for such a submarine, and then the Navy must build or pretend to build a new, ultra-modern submarine entirely of a titanium alloy. Second, on completion, that plan must somehow get into the hands of Soviet Intelligence. Third, U.S. Intelligence must seem to have high interest in titanium for submarine pressure hulls and recruit a large net of informants on this topic.

Also, to make it seemingly official, the Navy must send Casey Miller, along with a military Russian language speaker, to research the titanium issue at Leningrad State Library and Berlin's Technische Universität, Maschinenwesen- Schiffstechnik—the Faculty for Propulsion Machinery and Maritime Technology.

"We went back and forth on that one but McCurrill insisted, and he convinced me. He said, 'Logic dictates it.'" Reiter explained that this whole operation depended on U.S. Navy cooperation—even if it would, as far as most are concerned, be an unwitting cooperation.

When he finished his presentation the President sat quietly, just looking at his hands. Finally he raised his head and asked, "Let me get this straight. Your plan calls for the U.S. Navy to design, in strict secrecy, a titanium submarine. Right?"

"Yes, General," Reiter nodded.

"Then," the President concluded, "you want the Navy somehow to let someone steal, or otherwise pass the secret plans to the Soviets?"

"Yes, General."

"Christian," said the President, "that's totally ludicrous—insane. Who dreamed up this thing?"

"General," answered Reiter, "the Philosopher and the Wizard." Eisenhower looked at him long and hard. It was obvious that he was in no mood for familiar jesting.

Finally he asked, "The DNI? The DNI? You know, I mean—just thinking about it... you know... damn you, Christian," the President slapped his thigh, "you know what? This might actually work. I mean it's crazy, but I think the approach your musketeers suggested makes a hell of a lot of sense. It might just do the trick."

"Okay, Christian," Ike rose from his chair, "give me your notes so I don't screw up my meetings, first with the DNI, and then with the Chief of Naval Operations."

"Yes, General. One other item, the rest of the Navy must not know about the titanium construction." Reiter heaved a sigh of relief. A great weight had been lifted from his shoulders. He passed Eisenhower his notebook

The President eased out of his chair and escorted Christian to the door. They warmly shook hands and Ike again thanked Christian. The same Secret Service agent who had brought Christian to the President's family quarters escorted him through the first floor offices and then through the gardens to the side gate. Christian leisurely made his way through the Washington tourist throngs; by late afternoon he was back in the Big Apple.

CHAPTER 15

On the first Wednesday of November 1954, Rear Admiral Carl Di Rovalleri, the Director of Naval Intelligence, was sitting at his desk in his fifth floor Pentagon office when he received a call summoning him to the White House. It was an unusual call. Even the President's military aide had no explanation. The aide told him that the President wanted to see the DNI alone—no aide, no escort. Alone.

Unprecedented, the DNI thought, *no horse-holders.* What worried him even more was the fact that no one in his office had received any advance notice. He wondered whether he had somehow antagonized the President during the last meeting, and what he could have possibly have said that might have singled him out as a scapegoat.

He felt the worried looks of his office personnel following his every move as his aide helped him into his coat. He tried to reassure the folks in his office with a confident smile and friendly wave of his hand. The DNI hoped he had convinced his staff that indeed there was nothing to worry about. But on his way through the long Pentagon corridors to the River Entrance where his driver would be waiting, he thought about his last visit to the White House. Then superiors and aides had comfortably surrounded him. He tried to recall what could have possibly occurred now. Was it the CIA complaining of Navy's shortcomings in HUMINT collections?

He acknowledged that there were problems in the HUMINT area, but he tried to reassure himself that the meager effort in that arena was not his fault, or that of his predecessors. It was the Chief of Naval Operations, and all the previous chiefs, who preferred to spend Navy dollars on aircraft carriers, not on spooks. The chiefs had never heeded his, or his predecessors' pleas for additional funding for HUMINT operations. The chiefs were unanimously opposed to the clandestine business because "It could get the Navy into deep trouble;" and the chiefs held the purse strings.

The staff car glided through the West Executive Avenue entrance to the White House and stopped just short of the mansion. A Secret Service officer opened the door and escorted the DNI through the maze of corridors. As he entered the Oval Office he saw the President silhouetted against the bright windows. When Eisenhower turned, the DNI's concerns were somewhat eased as he noticed the President's famous, broad smile.

"Come on in, Admiral, come in," the President said as he raised the coffee cup from which he had been sipping. "Come in and have a cup of the best coffee in Washington."

The DNI heaved a silent sigh of relief. He carefully laid his coat and cap on a nearby chair, and poured himself some coffee—straight, black.

"Cream and sugar are there if you want them."

"No, thank you, Mr. President. Aboard ship you learn to drink your coffee black—and like it."

"Whatever you prefer." Eisenhower remained standing while the DNI took a few careful sips of the hot brew.

As the President silently observed the DNI he realized that this was the first time he had seen Di Rovalleri without the presence of the other uniforms. *No wonder the poor fellow looks nervous,* the President mused. Ike saw before him a short man, although his well-tailored uniform, and the way he carried himself, made him look taller than he actually was. In civilian clothes he would probably disappear in a crowd. He noticed the DNI's paleness; the whiteness of a man who had worked too many months out of the fresh air, out of the sunshine.

Then he noticed the Admiral's light blue eyes; they had the hard look of a man who had made life-and-death decisions. He seemed to stand apart from the usual crowd of Pentagon Commandos. For the first time, the President realized that this was a man he could come to like. Instinctively, he noticed that Di Rovalleri felt uncomfortable facing the President of the United States. To ease the DNI's concerns, he guided him toward a pair of comfortable chairs.

"Admiral, just to let you know, I have been thinking about the Soviet buildup; what all of you talked about during our last meeting. As an old soldier, I ardently believe in a strong military force capable of protecting our country against all comers. As President, I know that America must be strong, both militarily as well as economically. Unfortunately, these two strong beliefs of mine are in conflict, because I know that our assets are finite. We cannot continue spending our tax dollars as we have since 1942. We are bankrupting this country. Even a rich country like ours has spending limits.

"Admiral, you well know," he explained, "that military and economic strengths are interrelated. I am not willing to tax the American people into bankruptcy in this zeal that we seem to have to match the Soviet arms spending spree."

Ike noticed Di Rovalleri shifting uncomfortably in his chair. He added to the DNI's discomfort intentionally by leaning toward him and punctuating his remarks with his right index finger. "The service chiefs may think that 'their money' will continue to flow to them as usual. It won't. My economic advisors tell me that we are at the outer limit of defense spending. That's why I have been determined to find another way to beat the Soviets at their own game, a way that will not involve a war or unlimited defense spending."

Ike stopped and studied the DNI, hoping to get a reaction. But the admiral sat ramrod straight and poker-faced. Ike wondered, *Am I making a mistake by drawing this man into this scheme? Should I stop now and go back to Reiter for another idea that doesn't involve the DNI?*

Then he remembered what he had told Christian Reiter at the end of their meeting: There are risks in everything you do. The President remembered another point in history where decisiveness was needed and he'd chosen his course of action accordingly. Damn the torpedoes! Full speed ahead!

"Admiral," Ike continued, "you will remember that I have repeatedly asked the chiefs for help in coming up with an unorthodox way to deal with this problem. What have I gotten? Old 'whines' in new bottles, nothing original, nothing risky. Just the same old answer: 'Give us more money.' Sometimes I get the feeling that they treat me like they would treat a revered grandfather in a nursing home: they nod their heads at what I ask because they don't want to upset me. But they pay no real attention to my demands, because they believe they know what's best for me."

Di Rovalleri looked miserable. Two red spots of color had appeared on his cheekbones, and he was perspiring profusely. He seemed to want to say something, but would not do so, without the President's permission.

"So," the President continued, "when I realized that I could not get help from my own people—or rather, the people whose salaries are paid by the American taxpayers—I decided to go on a fishing expedition outside the government. And I think I've hooked a big one. But I need your help to reel it in."

Ike saw the puzzled look on the DNI's face. "Admiral," he asked, "how much do you know of the intelligence game?"

The admiral stuttered, "I, eh, I... I am no expert by any means. My expertise is submarines. I served most of my career aboard diesels in the Pacific. And of course I had staff jobs both at Pearl and here in Washington."

"Precisely why I called you here this afternoon. I too am only vaguely acquainted with that black art. Of course, I used intelligence information extensively during the last war and thereafter, but even now I feel a bit uncomfortable dealing with 'the experts' down the street." He waved vaguely in the direction of the CIA Tempos, the temporary office buildings on the Mall between the Lincoln Memorial and the Washington Monument.

Now the admiral seemed to relax. Ike noticed that he even sipped the White House coffee. "Since you and I have confessed that we are both sort of new to this intelligence game," Ike resumed, this time in a more friendly manner, "I'd like to share with you some information that came to me from—well, for now let me just say that it came from outside government sources. I think you'll find this information as interesting as I did."

He proceeded to give the DNI a synopsis of Reiter's comparison of U.S. and Soviet economics, work habits, the strengths and weaknesses of a free economy and that of a state-directed one. He concluded with, "Thus, these economists are convinced that the entire Soviet system is as hollow as one of those pretty Ukrainian Easter eggs."

Di Rovalleri started to feel more comfortable with the President. Both of them were outsiders to the game of intelligence, yet locked into the game by their current positions. However, he still did not know why in hell he was summoned to the Oval Office, or why the President was spending so much of his valuable time delivering this lecture on Soviet economics. Still puzzled, he heard the President say, "Admiral, I have consulted with others I trust; they have given me a totally unorthodox solution to my dilemma. They said: Just let the Russians outspend themselves!"

The DNI thought, *What in hell does that mean?* Somewhat startled, he heard the President ask, "What do you think of that?"

He thought about this question before speaking. Then he decided he would risk making a statement that might land him in "the shallows."

"Sir," he said, after taking a deep breath, "I'm afraid that the person who gave you this advice is—" he wanted to say "a fool" but stopped himself and said, "a dreamer."

Eisenhower smiled. "A dreamer? Yes. Well, maybe. I might prefer the word thinker or even genius. My friends call him the Philosopher."

Ike rose and walked to his desk, where he pulled a notebook from beneath a pile of documents. He returned to his seat and laid the notebook on his lap. "Admiral, I am about to share with you the details of a plan that is known to only four people—three are former OSS agents—none of them in the government today—and the other is me. One of these men is a man I not only learned to trust implicitly during the war, but also as a family friend. He brought me this plan, which was developed by two men we'll call the Philosopher and the Wizard."

76

The DNI did not dare move a muscle. He was fascinated, but wary.

"The Philosopher, you may call him the dreamer, teaches philosophy at Princeton. The other one, the Wizard, is an MIT lecturer and an engineer with several successful patents to his credit."

The admiral listened as the President outlined the details of this so-called plan. According to the President, the "dreamer" believed that Russian paranoia would cause the Soviets to spend just about any amount of rubles to build a military force superior to that of the United States. Then the President hit him with, "Would you agree at least with that assessment, Admiral?"

"Without reservation, Mr. President," the DNI replied. "Without reservation. Absolutely."

Ike was convinced that he could bring the admiral on board. "All right then," he said. "The Wizard said that the most expensive material for military use is titanium. Not only is the raw material costly, but manufacturing is even more so. Would you agree with that?"

Di Rovalleri agreed. "Although I'm no metallurgist, I know that the Navy has looked at titanium as a possible material for submarines, but rejected it as too expensive, too difficult to manufacture in a shipyard environment. Mr. President, we have the capability to build small deep-diving research vessels out of titanium, but submarines? I think not."

"Absolutely," Ike smiled. "That's exactly what the Wizard said. He also believes that titanium alloy is the metal of the future. It's light, as strong as steel, and essentially nonmagnetic. He claims it's the perfect material for submarine pressure hulls."

"Only if one does not consider the practical aspects of submarine construction, and the cost, Mr. President," the DNI interjected tersely.

"Precisely! This is where you come in. That is, if you think the Navy can pull it off."

The DNI's eyes went wide.

"Admiral, you know that before and during World War II, President Roosevelt depended heavily on the Navy to bring him information that others were reluctant, or unable, to give, and he and the Navy fared well. If we can make the Russians believe we are building titanium submarines, we believe they'll start building titanium submarines. If they do, they'll spend a good chunk of their national treasury, far above and beyond what they are now spending, on defense. Eventually they'll go broke."

He then outlined the OMEGA Solution as contained in the notebook that Reiter had left with him. He concluded his presentation by mentioning the down-

77

side should the Soviets succeed in building titanium submarines. The admiral sat without saying a word.

Ike asked, "Can we pull it off?" When the admiral did not answer, he continued, "During the last war we confused the Germans rather successfully with such a deception exercise. We had General Patton race across the Dover landscape to fool the Germans into thinking that the real invasion would come across the Channel, that we would hit the beach at Pas de Calais. It worked. But," he cautioned, "that was a short-term deception. Here we're talking long-term, possibly five to ten years, or more."

The President briefly looked at Reiter's notes, "There is one more item. The fellows who dreamed up this plot think it's essential that the Soviets know that we have serious plans for building titanium submarines. That means we leak the official plans to the Soviets." Ike placed the notebook on a side table and turned his full attention to the DNI, and continued gently, "They think you, and only you, could accomplish that."

Di Rovalleri sat up suddenly. "What? Eh ... Mr. President? Leaking classified plans to the Soviets. How?"

"Yes, Admiral, plans classified Top Secret, but made Top Secret only for this deception operation. We're talking about a deception operation of grand proportions. For it to succeed the Navy will have to plan, then design, and possibly even start, or appear to be building a super-secret submarine. The plan's authors say that super-secrecy is the lure, and titanium is the bait. They named the plan the OMEGA Solution. With your help, and that of the Wizard, we can let the Soviets know of our high interest in titanium. But the deception can succeed only if the other party, the one we are deceiving, learns of the secret plans. Thus, they must be leaked by the Navy to the Soviets."

The DNI sat as if stunned without uttering a word. Ike continued, "Crazy, right? One problem remains: My friends have not thought of a foolproof way to leak the plans. The Philosopher quoted Sun Tzu: 'The enemy is deceived by creating shapes.' We can create the shapes, but how do we get the Soviets to see them? The Philosopher insists that the deception must follow a logical sequence, one that is never questioned. My friends are of one mind: Leaking the actual plans would clinch the deal. And they want that to happen as soon as possible."

Di Rovalleri still seemed to be in shock as the President said, "Think about it, Admiral. I don't need an answer today or even next week. However, for the plan to work the information must be closely held, very close. At this time you and I are the only ones in the military complex—no, in the entire government— who know about it. For the present time, tell no one. Should anyone ask, say you were called to the White House to review plans for future naval intelligence operations. And that is the truth. Later we will convince the Chief of Naval Operations that the Navy needs to build, or at least have plans to build, titanium submarines." He raised his voice slightly to give his next statement added emphasis, "Admiral, for this to work, I need your help."

The DNI looked uncomfortable. Indeed, the President noticed that he had been squirming in his seat for some time. "Sir," the DNI said apologetically, "would you permit me to use your restroom?"

Of all the questions Ike had been expecting, this was not one of them. But, after all that coffee, he could certainly understand the DNI's plight. "Of course," Ike replied, pointing to the left," it's right down that corridor. Matter of fact, I'll use another one while you're gone."

Di Rovalleri heard Eisenhower chuckling as he left the Oval Office. *Well, the admiral thought, what else was I supposed to do? A DNI with wet drawers is not going to inspire presidential confidence.* Besides, he needed some time, however little, to think.

So what are my options? He wondered, as he stood at the urinal. *I can say yes, and keep my boss, the CNO, completely in the dark; or I can say no, this is nuts, Mr. President. Some choice.*

He walked to the sink to wash his hands, and caught a glimpse of himself in the mirror. He was a man with a singularly undistinguished career looking at retirement within two years. There were probably no more promotions on the horizon. *Screw it. Go for broke. What do I have to lose?*

Furthermore, he thought as he dried his hands, *Ike is right: there are no interesting or inspiring ideas coming from the military with respect to beating the Commies. Every year at budget time, it's the same old stew warmed over. Maybe this idea isn't so harebrained after all.*

Returning to the Oval Office a few minutes before the President, he picked up the notebook and started reading intensely. He did not hear the President return a few minutes later. "Well?" he heard Ike ask, as the startled DNI dropped the notebook. "Do I take it from your reading the plan that you have made your decision?"

"Sir," Di Rovalleri said firmly, "Count me in."

"Well spoken, Admiral," said the smiling President, shaking his hand. "I was hoping I could count on you. When you've constructed a model for this deception, call my secretary and just mention 'the OMEGA Solution is ready.' She will set up our next meeting." He paused a moment as if a thought had just occurred to him.

"Admiral, it may be wise not to make your visits to the White House too public. I suggest that when you have reason to come here the next time I will send a Secret Service agent to pick you up at the Pentagon. That is, if you don't mind?"

When Di Rovalleri agreed, the President asked, "Where would you want him to wait for you, the Mall or the River Entrance?"

"Mr. President," the DNI answered, "the River Entrance is best for me."

The President shook his hand again and escorted him to the door. With a new spring in his step the DNI followed the Secret Service agent to the Navy car waiting at the side entrance. He had not been in such high spirits since his graduation from the academy.

When he returned to the Pentagon from his appointment with the President, his aide met him as he entered the office. As he accompanied him into the inner sanctum, he announced with some urgency, "Admiral, the CNO wants to see you as soon as possible. His aide has called several times requesting your presence."

"John, does the CNO know I went to the White House?"

"No, Admiral, I am sure he does not. At least, Admiral Norton didn't mention anything, or ask questions."

"Well, if Admiral Norton didn't know, I'll have to tell the Old Man. By the way, John, tell the crew there's nothing to worry about. The President just wanted to run some new ideas past me about naval intelligence collections. You know CIA has complained that we're not carrying our load. That's all. I'll tell the CNO what the President wants. Maybe it will shake his money tree a little, and we'll get better funding for the next year."

The aide wasted no time in leaving the room. The DNI smiled. He knew word would pass like wildfire.

He was still smiling when he returned from a half-hour session with the CNO. This time, he had gotten twice the time allotted by the CNO's aide, Admiral Bobby "Brown Nose" Norton. Bobby Norton was one of the DNI's old academy classmates and a real ass kisser. Any day the DNI could piss off Bobby Norton was a good day. Today felt almost like Christmas.

On the way from the CNO's office Norton hissed, "Carl, you ruined my entire day's schedule."

"Bobby, what could I do? The Old Man loves me," the DNI replied. Back in his office Di Rovalleri drank a cup of coffee that had been sitting in a percolator since God was a young man. Then he summoned his car for another outing.

At the Pentagon's River Entrance he told his driver, "Naval Observatory." The DNI enjoyed these visits to his naval intelligence domain. Here he was absolute king. He would have loved to have his office and his entire staff at Observatory Circle. It was so much more civilized here, compared to the Pentagon. To the technical director at the Naval Scientific and Technical Intelligence Center—known in the business as NAVSTIC—he said, "Charley, make me smart on the latest submarine construction worldwide. New materials, high-yield steels, other suitable alloys, new ideas, whatever you have, the whole nine yards."

After a flurry of activity, including briefings by the lead submarine analyst, the head of the engineering analysis department, and the only metallurgist at Observatory Circle, the DNI received a small information package that the analysts had quickly assembled from readily available references. They apologized for the cut-and-paste method of the package. Di Rovalleri quickly glanced through the stack of papers. He noticed several items that mentioned titanium, including an additional message sheet. It was a response to a request levied on one of the DNI's reporting elements. It read:

```
220015ZSEP51
FROM:    NAVAL RECONNAISSANCE ELEMENT 163
TO:      ONI, WASHINGTON, D.C.
SECRET/NOFORN/WINTEL//2433/51//
SUBJ. IIR 2 334 32034 51
REF. A.  CIR-36887-51 REF. B.   A-00078
```

(S/NOFORN) In response to ref a, source ref b reports following:

A. (S) Metallic titanium was first isolated in various forms in the late nineteenth and the early twentieth century. It started to see use as a structural material starting in the late 1940s. Titanium occurs chiefly as an oxide ore; it is one of the most abundant metallic elements in the earth's crust.

B. (S) Because of the high strength-to-weight ratio of its alloys and their resistance to corrosion, titanium metal is important strategically and critical in its application in high-performance military equipment. However, even considering all the favorable attributes, the high cost and complexity of mining and manufacturing of titanium has limited the use of the metal. Thus only about five percent of the world's annual production of titanium minerals is turned into metal. The rest is used predominantly as white pigment for paints, paper, and various other materials.

C.(S) All reactive gases, including oxygen and nitrogen, must be excluded from the air when welding and shaping titanium; impurities in the atmosphere surrounding the weld make the welded material brittle. The exclusion of all impurities adds considerably to the cost of shaping and welding titanium alloys. Large-scale welding of plates, such as submarine hull sections, increases the manufacturing cost exponentially.

(S) The trade-off, especially in naval application, is the most favorable strength-to-weight ratio of titanium compared to high-yield steels. Another attribute is the non-magnetic property of titanium. Since most anti-submarine warfare detection depends on magnetic anomaly detection (MAD), the lack of a magnetic signature would make titanium a most favorable material—were it not for the enormous cost.

2. (S/NOFORN) Above information is closely held. Request: sensitive handling to protect source and method of collection.

(U) Request evaluation of report (agent payment involved).

(U) Navy Recon Element One Six Three sends.

Di Rovalleri smiled and thought, *That sly fox, the President, must have gotten some pretty smart advice from the Philosopher and the Wizard.* As he departed he said, "Charley, that's exactly what I wanted." Pointing at the message, he asked, "Is this the only info you have on titanium?"

The TD looked at his metallurgist, "Bert?"

The metallurgist replied, "No, we have some other information, mainly theoretical discussions."

The DNI thought that was interesting. He knew that his question, without a doubt, would generate some activity at Observatory Circle. It was now up to him to develop the plan, and he would have to do it at home, alone, after hours, so as not to have his aides trying to help.

After more than a week of working late into the night he had the essence of a plan. He reviewed several pages of notes. He condensed these notes, along with the cut-and-paste references from Observatory Circle, into a point paper. In longhand, on a page of yellow legal-size paper, he finalized the background information he would carry "in his hip pocket" for his next meeting with the President. In it he had outlined the process for designing ships, the mechanics that drive a ship design, Navy and national priorities, etc. He would make sure the President would suggest and push the CNO into believing that the titanium submarine program was a priority not only of the Navy, but also of the nation.

In addition, from information he had received from his S&T Intelligence staff, he quickly wrote a paper on titanium that he could hand the CNO when he made his usual, "Carl, make me smart on..." request. Back at his Pentagon office Di Rovalleri asked his yeoman to type a Memorandum for the Record on the topic of titanium. He handed him a part of what he had written during the past few nights.

Now, with the paperwork done, the DNI felt better. However, the most important element of the deception had as yet eluded him: how best to leak a Top Secret submarine construction project to the Soviets? How to facilitate a leak without raising suspicions from both U.S. and the Soviet counterintelligence? The President had cautioned him not to consult with anyone. The DNI was accustomed to having his assistants, his staff and his analysts, brainstorm ideas. This time he had to work alone. He thought long and hard. In his mind he screened through the many briefings his staff, and the staffs of subordinate elements had presented.

One morning, days later, while he was shaving, he suddenly remembered. He became so excited that he nicked himself with the razor when the thought occurred: *NAVBUSHIPS*. He recalled a long-ago counterintelligence briefing about an engineer, or someone at NAVBUSHIPS suspected of being a Soviet agent. That very morning he called the director of NCIS, the Naval Criminal Investigative Service, and asked for the chief investigator to give him an update on Soviet spying on the United States Navy.

After enduring almost an hour of the chief's eloquent waxing on the virtues of the NCIS, Di Rovalleri finally heard the word NAVBUSHIPS. "Wait a minute!" he acted surprised. "Do you mean to tell me that we have a Soviet spy in NAVBUSHIPS?"

"Well, sir, Admiral, well... uh," stuttered the chief investigator, "a man some folks suspect, sir, merely suspect of being a spy. We have nothing concrete; nothing that could get a conviction." The director of NCIS explained that his boys and agents of the Federal Bureau of Investigations, the FBI, had observed a man code-named NAVBUSHIPS-0001 for some time, but that the Bureau did not have enough evidence for conviction.

"Tell me about that NAVBUSHIPS man, and the Soviet," the DNI ordered.

After the investigator painstakingly explained every detail of NAVBU-SHIPS-0001, and then described Major Kasandroff of the GRU, who, according to FBI files, operated out of the Soviet Military Mission in Washington.

Di Rovalleri thanked him for his observations, adding, "I commend you for your prudence. We must always be careful not to overreact to accusations. There are too many possibilities for lawsuits. We have had some trouble in the past... eh ... been accused of knee-jerk reaction, and the Navy does not need any more unfavorable publicity."

The chief investigator departed a happy man.

CHAPTER 16

NOVEMBER 1954
THE OVAL OFFICE, THE WHITE HOUSE
WASHINGTON, D.C.

Per agreement, the DNI telephoned the White House with the information that the OMEGA Solution was ready. Within a day, the President's secretary had arranged the next meeting between Di Rovalleri and the President. This time a Secret Service agent picked up the DNI at the Pentagon's River Entrance, drove his car directly through the Pennsylvania Avenue gate of the White House and deposited the DNI near the entrance of the West Wing, where another agent stood waiting to escort him.

In the Oval Office, after they had once again sampled some of the "best coffee in Washington," the President motioned the DNI to the settee. "So, Admiral, tell me about your plan."

"It could be done, Mr. President, it could be done," he said as he opened his briefcase. "I went on a fishing expedition at Observatory Circle to ask my S&T folks about HY-80 and HY-100 steels, as well as new and exotic structural material for submarines. Casually I mentioned titanium. They reacted in horror. 'Can't be done, Admiral, can't be done,' they said repeatedly. 'Not large-scale manufacturing in a shipyard atmosphere, too expensive.'" He chuckled, "Mr. President, all the reasons you mentioned and more. The Wizard was right."

The President smiled. "Good. Now what's your plan?"

"As your friends recommended, the CNO must order preliminary designs for a titanium submarine, and Navy, or the Defense Department, must slowly begin purchasing titanium sponge. Preferably the Defense Department, so the CNO won't have a heart attack. There is no way I can operate alone, Mr. President, you must be aware of that."

The President nodded.

"With the CNO's approval," the admiral continued, "we can set up a research and design section—outwardly very hush-hush—at NAVBUSHIPS, our ship design office, down here near the Pentagon, on the road past Arlington Farms. We'll need maybe three or four engineers, a metallurgist, one or two draftsmen, and a rotating Marine security detail out of Henderson Hall, just up the road from NAVBUSHIPS."

"Fine," replied the President, "but with all that security, how do we let the Russians know what we are doing?"

"Mr. President," the admiral began carefully, "we have a man in NAVBU-SHIPS, an engineer, whom we believe to have been working for the Soviets for some time; perhaps several years."

"What!" Eisenhower exclaimed, as he sat bolt upright. "Admiral, how can you expect me to believe or accept that a Soviet spy has been privy to American defense secrets, and that we have done nothing about it?"

Soothingly the DNI continued, "Sir, we have had our suspicions. He has a dossier about a foot tall. But we have never been able to get enough evidence to convict him. He is careful, pretty damned cagey." Di Rovalleri watched the President as he massaged his forehead. He had feared that he would get a reaction like this. *Hell,* he thought, *how would you expect him to react to the idea that we know we have a spy on the payroll?* The DNI resumed his briefing quickly, fearing that Eisenhower's reaction might prevent him from explaining the rest of his plan.

"Sir," he said matter-of-factly, "it's not as bad as it might seem. First of all, he is not working in a Top Secret area. All of NAVBUSHIPS operates under a low-level Confidential clearance. So, although he has access to classified materials, he does not have access to anything above Confidential. Secondly, in the course of their investigations, NCIS has been in regular contact with the FBI. Some of the folks there have discouraged my boys from transferring him to an unclassified position. I think you will find their reasoning very interesting."

The DNI paused and looked at Eisenhower, hoping to see the storm clouds dissipate with his last sentence. It seemed to work. The President had stopped scowling. His interest seemed to have been piqued. "This had better be good," Eisenhower said.

"Sir, I think it is better than good, almost providential. Over the years the FBI has wanted to initiate some kind of a disinformation operation. By that I mean, developing some credible means to pass bad intelligence on to the Russians. As you might imagine, something like this is easier said than done. It's both risky and costly. Think back to some of the points the Philosopher made about the nature of deception. For a disinformation operation to work, it must be carefully thought out, with little room for error."

"So, what you are about to tell me," interrupted the President, "is that you have found the means to leak the titanium sub building plans to the Russians."

"I think so, Mr. President, but we aren't quite ready to go yet." The DNI glanced over his notes. "It would take a hell of a lot to convince our suspected spy that we are building titanium submarines, even though he would be the logical one to funnel the information to Moscow."

"Admiral, I congratulate you," the President beamed. "I think you've solved our problem."

"Not so fast, sir," the DNI cautioned. "The next problem that needs solving is to devise a plan that will allow that engineer to have access to the information we want passed without arousing his suspicion. Don't forget, our people have been watching this guy pretty closely, and we've never been able to catch him— if you'll pardon the expression—'Red'-handed."

Ike winced, but then chuckled. The DNI added, "We will have to think more about that. I'm not afraid to say that I could use some help in that. Mr. President, maybe ... could your friends ... maybe The Philosopher? Could you ask him for some suggestions?"

"Absolutely!" the President exclaimed, "Admiral, your plan has possibilities." He halted, shaking his head as if even he could not believe what he had been told. "I still can't believe that I'm happy to learn that we have a ready-made Russian spy in place." He continued, "Admiral, let me ask you, do we have a chance of carrying off this deception over maybe a decade or more?"

"It all depends," the DNI replied carefully, "on how many people I can involve."

The President seemed uncomfortable. "Let me ask you, why involve anyone else? I don't want anybody else involved, only you, at least for the time being. The CNO does not need to know about the deception. All we have to do is convince him to build—no, not even that, just to design the titanium submarine. At our next meeting I'll just casually mention that I heard from friends that the Russians are building titanium submarines. Let's see what his reaction will be. Why wouldn't he want to design a future titanium submarine, especially if it were an opportunity to enhance his budget at the direction of the President?

"As for the design team, they can actually work on designing the submarine. They can make a detailed feasibility study, total specifications, testing which titanium alloys are most suitable for deep-diving submarines, everything ... and who knows, maybe, some day we will actually build a titanium sub based on their work."

The President seemed to lapse into thought. Di Rovalleri apparently took this as a signal that the meeting was over and began gathering up his things. The President stood up and walked him to the door. He held out his hand. "Thanks for visiting, Admiral. At my next meeting with you and the CNO, be prepared when I casually mention titanium submarines."

The President gave him his famous broad smile. "When you leave this office, and when you return to the Pentagon, look a little miffed, as if this had been an unpleasant meeting with some ass-chewing. Otherwise those who observe these things will smell a rat."

"Yes, Mr. President," the DNI smiled as he snapped his briefcase shut. "Mr. President?" he asked carefully.

"Yes?"

"When do we meet with the CNO?"

"Soon. I'll let you know as soon as possible. Between you and me, and I mean that, strictly between you and me, from now on we will plan on having the best-designed titanium submarine in the world. But first I have to consult with the Philosopher and the Wizard."

The admiral departed from the Oval Office trying his best to look as if, as the President had put it, there had been some ass-chewing.

CHAPTER 17

A little over a month after the Director of Naval Intelligence had suggested it, Karl Cedric Miller , known to most of his friends as K.C. "Casey" Miller, of MIT and U.S. Air Force Captain Alois Howard, detached from his advanced Russian language course at Syracuse University, left for Leningrad's State Library. Several weeks earlier, MIT had mailed letters of introduction to both the Leningrad State Library and Berlin's Technische Universität, Maschinenwesen-Schiffstechnik—the Faculty for Propulsion Machinery and Maritime Technology. The letters requested permission for Mr. Karl Cedric Miller of MIT to conduct research on the property of various titanium alloys and their reaction to seawater. The letters advised that Mr. Miller was conducting this research for a doctorate in metallurgy under U.S. Navy auspices. Permission was also requested for Miller's research assistant, Alois Howard, to be accorded the same privileges.

The researcher and the USAF captain arrived in Leningrad on February 22, 1956, a freezing cold Wednesday. The city was covered with a blanket of freshly fallen, crystal white snow, making the city look deceptively clean. Miller and Howard immediately endeared themselves to the librarians at the State Library. They had brought along small souvenirs from America. Howard passed out several dozen ballpoint pens emblazoned with the logo "Property of the United States Government."

They searched the files for the elusive word titanium. Then they made sure that each written document request contained that word as well. For the first few days the librarians brought stacks of hard-cover and loose-leaf documents to a large table that served as the researchers' desk. They smiled and even joked, especially with the handsome Howard. Every librarian sported at least one of Howard's ballpoint pens in a breast pocket, behind an ear, or as a hair ornament. However, when several very curt, officious-looking bureaucrats arrived, the ballpoint pens disappeared; the librarians stopped smiling; additional documents were slow in arriving at the Americans' research table.

The sudden change in behavior of the librarians amused the Americans. The librarians appeared embarrassed. Suddenly they were unable to produce many of the items listed in their card files. Most often the excuse was "book not on shelf." The bureaucrats did nothing but stand at the back of the research area; they watched and perused every item Miller requested.

Howard whispered to Miller, "These guys must be KGB. Take a look how they shuffled through the items, setting aside some books. I don't think we'll get to see any more of those handwritten, loose-leaf folders." Later Howard, gesturing toward the librarians, said, "Look at those poor women, they're scared shitless."

Miller and Howard watched in amusement as the bureaucrats sorted the books into two piles. One pile was returned the bowels of the library; the other came to Miller's table. After Miller returned the books to the service counter the surly bureaucrat and several of his helpers scrutinized them minutely.

At times young men, who called themselves graduate students, gathered around Miller and Howard's table. They asked questions, wanted to know about Washington and the Cambridge-Boston area, and asked whether Howard had any ballpoint pens left. The generous Howard gave each one a government-issued pen. Most of the young men spoke almost fluent English. Miller especially enjoyed bantering with these so-called graduate students. They were mainly interested in the connection between MIT and the U.S. Navy. One of the students asked what "under navy auspices" meant. Miller explained that it meant the U.S. Navy financed a part of his studies and received the results. He informed them that in America universities conduct much of the government research into technology, and that the U.S. Navy happened to be interested in titanium technology.

"In my case," Miller said with his Cheshire cat smile, "I am researching for my Ph.D. dissertation. I don't have personal funds to travel and visit your beautiful Russia. I am very grateful to have gotten some government funds to help me."

From the questioning it appeared they knew that already.

Upon leaving the Soviet Union, Captain Howard returned to Syracuse University to complete his Russian studies program, and Miller flew into Berlin to continue his titanium research and to create ripples in the West Berlin intelligence community. He arrived at the Technische Universität in West Berlin on March 2, 1956. His first stop in West Berlin was at the office of Navy Task Force Unit 168.1.4. The DNI had already prepared the groundwork there. The Navy received Casey Miller with open arms. A Navy agent met Miller at Tempelhof Airport. They rode to Berlin-Dahlem where the agent had rented a room for him in a private residence. From there Miller was within walking distance of Onkel Toms Hütte subway station. His quarters were also conveniently located near the offices of all the other Allied intelligence units.

During the first afternoon Miller and the Navy agent toured Berlin. The agent taught Miller how to negotiate buying tickets and to ride the U-Bahn—the Berlin subway—to Berlin's Technische Universität; he also advised Miller never to ride the S-Bahn, the elevated train, because the tracks and the stations were East German territory—even in West Berlin. At the Technische Universität, Miller presented his letter of introduction to one of the reference librarians, a lady in her early thirties.

After she scanned the letter she looked at Miller. "Ah, Mr. Miller," she smiled. Miller noticed that her English had only the slightest touch of a German accent. "We have been expecting you. My assistant, Fräulein Anneliese, will situate you in a reference alcove. As you probably know, no one, aside from employees of this institute, is allowed into the book stacks. However, Fräulein Anneliese will be at your disposal."

Miller saw the librarian glance once again at the letter of introduction. "Mr. Miller, since you are here doing research on a Navy-related subject... eh, if you wish ... we have here, almost on a permanent assignment, a Herr Wolfgang Schutter. He works for the distinguished West German submarine designer Doktor Ulrich Gabler. He does research somewhat similar to what you are doing. If you wish, I could introduce you to Herr Schutter."

Miller could hardly believe his good fortune. "Miss..?" he groped for the librarian's name.

"Fräulein Hermann, Ursula Hermann," she introduced herself.

Smiling, Miller shook her hand as he replied, "Fraulein Hermann, I would be delighted to meet Herr Schutter, I am sure he can point me in the right direction and save me a lot of time."

For the next few days Miller combed the library's holdings for information on titanium. He talked to the librarians, professors, and graduate students at the faculty for Maschinenwesen. He found a good number of people interested in titanium, and even more in his "under U.S. Navy auspices" interest in titanium. One of those most interested in Miller's work was Herr Schutter. Fräulein Hermann had introduced him the day after Miller had arrived, and Herr Schutter readily offered his assistance. He spoke English hesitantly, however, since Miller spoke almost flawless German, they soon were spending their mid-morning and mid-afternoon coffee breaks together in the institute's cafeteria. Miller told Herr Schutter that he had just recently visited the Leningrad State Library, where he had conducted similar research into titanium, and that he had MIT graduate students checking the patent offices in Washington and London.

"Herr Miller," Schutter asked," are you telling me that the U.S. Navy is planning to build submarines made of titanium?"

"Well," replied Miller, "I am not sure of that, but I think so. I do not think the Navy would spend all that money for my research just so I can get a Ph.D. There must be serious plans in the works."

"But why?" asked Herr Schutter. "The expense of such a building program must be horrendous."

"You are entirely correct," replied Miller. "But my research shows that the large initial expense is worth the effort—long-range. Once all the problems of bending and welding are solved, the cost of building titanium submarine hulls is somewhere close to the cost of building high-yield HY-100 or HY-130 hulls."

"That's interesting," replied Herr Schutter as he scribbled a few notes, "because there had been some talk at Doktor Gabler's institute about titanium, but I have never gotten a request to do research. I might have to suggest research along that line to my bosses."

"Don't forget, Herr Schutter," added Miller, "the payoff, the end result, could be a submarine far, far superior to anything afloat today." Schutter nodded as he observed Miller transferring many copies of written material from his desk into his briefcase.

After Miller completed his work at the university, the Navy agent introduced him to the interrogators at the Berlin Refugee Center. There he "spread the word" to as many German, American, French and British interrogators of the U.S. Navy's high interest in titanium so that titanium was of high interest to the U.S. Navy and any information on that topic would be highly appreciated. He was quickly, quietly covering all the intended bases.

Miller's last stop in his European odyssey was Frankfurt-on-Main, West Germany, to visit the unit the G-2 had selected for the "exotic metals" task. There he met and briefed the members of the U.S. Army Special Operations Team Three.

CHAPTER 18

Casey Miller had already notified his two OSS buddies of his scheduled return flight from Frankfurt to New York. Christian Reiter and Harold McCurrill greeted Casey enthusiastically. Christian drove, and the OMEGA Team sequestered in the inner sanctorum of the Quadrant Import-Export office. Mrs., Clarke joined them as they listened to Casey's European exploits. In anticipation of Casey's arrival, Mrs. Clarke had ordered lunch and dessert. As always, Mrs. Clarke took copious notes so that her boss could properly brief the President. Casey joked about the wonderful, ever so helpful librarians at Leningrad, and how their attitude so suddenly changed when the KGB team arrived to see what these Americans were doing in Leningrad.

"Well," Christian laughed, "was this not the real reason you came to Leningrad?"

"Naturally," chuckled Casey, "my U.S. Air Force major and I had the greatest time pulling the KGB's chain." He paused for a moment, "Oh, you ought to know that Captain Howard has half of Leningrad supplied with ballpoint pens emblazoned with the logo 'Property of the United States Government'; even the Leningrad office of the KGB."

Christian guffawed, "How in hell did that happen?"

Casey laughed. "He brought maybe fifty or so pens just for his 'good will' purpose, and everyone loved him for that, even the KGB guys."

Finally, Mrs. Clarke mentioned the luncheon she had in her office, and with that the four walked into the conference room to celebrate.

Over drinks, Christian thanked all for their contribution to the OMEGA Team's mission, "You all realize that this was our last hurrah. Tomorrow Mrs. Clarke will make the appointment for me to brief the President that our mission is completed, and that we will all returned to our normal life." He added, "If that is even possible."

* * * * * *

It would be the last meeting between President Eisenhower and Christian Reiter. After Ike and Christian had their usual cup of coffee, Christian told him about Casey's Leningrad visit and the attention Casey and Captain Alois Howard received from what appeared to be a whole contingent of KGB agents. "Mr. President," Christian told, "the Soviets kept trying to understand why a university professor escorted by what seemed to be a military person, was interested in titanium, and why this professor was doing the work for the U.S. Navy?"

The President chuckled. "Of course, that was completely alien to the Soviets."

"Yes, and furthermore," added Christian, "Casey made no secret that he was indeed doing his Ph.D. research while the Navy paid all his expenses."

The President nodded. Then Christian related the story about all the ball-point pens embossed with "Property of the U.S. Government" now in Leningrad, including in the offices of the KGB. The President thought the comment was hilarious.

Then Ike rose from his chair and thanked Christian for his contribution. "Be sure to tell the Philosopher and the Wizard how much their President appreciate their contribution. Unfortunately, I cannot acknowledge any of it. Now we just have to wait and see if it will bankrupt the Soviets."

Christian took this as his signal to depart.

The President then decided to write instructions for the serving DNI, and those who would follow him. On White House stationery he composed a brief handwritten instruction. He thought that his instructions should be brief and to the point so that there could be no misunderstanding or misinterpretation of his words. He placed the instruction into a security envelope and wrote in large letters "To the Directors of Naval Intelligence – FOR YOUR EYES ONLY." Then his secretary called the soon-to-retire Admiral Carl Di Rovalleri for just one more meeting. Over the past year or so there had become a closeness between the two conspirators. Both realized that this would most probably be their last, at least official, meeting. They had a long and friendly conversation, which further cemented their friendship.

Admiral Di Rovalleri would visit the retired President periodically at his farm in Pennsylvania to bring him updates of the OMEGA Solution.

CHAPTER 19

On Monday, July 8, three years after the plan to bring the Soviet Union to its knees was hatched, NCIS Special Agent, nicknamed Little Albert, the man inserted into the top secret NAVBUSHIPS office, informed Senior NCIS Special Agent John Bradford that on the next Friday, he would cast the bait near the end of the working day. He would signal if NAVBUSHIPS had taken the bait. He would do it by shaking the window curtain that was visible from the BUSHIP's parking lot.

On the drafting tables were drawings for the construction of a titanium attack submarine. This extremely streamlined boat had an overall length of 280 feet, would displace some 4,000 tons submerged; about 3,000 tons surfaced. After the engineers had completed the design drawings, Little Albert put the final touches to them, labeled them, and added the nomenclature: "[Experimental] Titanium Fast Attack Nuclear Submarine (SSN-X)" to each of the drawings. Then he placed large red "Top Secret" stamps on the upper left-hand and the lower right-hand corner of each drawing. The plan was for him to "carelessly" stick a couple of seemingly poorly reproduced drawings into one of the burn bags near the Ozalid machines.

Little Albert carried the rolled-up drawings to the reproduction room. Apparently, the two Ozalids were acting up again. After muttering a disgusted "Aw shit," Little Albert loudly crumpled three bad copies and stuck them, just a bit hastily it seemed, into one of two paper burn bags. He purposely left a corner of one of the copies with the "Top Secret" stamp sticking out invitingly from the bag.

He returned the finished blueprints to his office, rolled them carefully but firmly, and put them into cardboard tubes.

The discarded Ozalid sheets remained stuffed in the burn bag until just before closing time when NCIS's suspected Soviet agent Walter Waldmann volunteered to clean up the reproduction room. He wiped the Ozalid machines meticulously clean, threw all unclassified papers into the trashcan and carried the burn bags to the rear of the office where several large safes waited to be locked and secured.

Alone in the room, Waldmann saw the blueprints with the prominent red "Top Secret" protruding from the burn bag. He looked around to be certain no one was near the Ozalid room to observe him pulling two of the blueprints out. He quickly folded them, flattened them, unbuttoned his shirt, and stuffed the blueprints under his belt. He patted them down so they would conform to the shape of his body, buttoned his shirt, patted it down once more, and continued his cleaning of the room. He left the third blueprint in the burn bag. Three folded blueprints would have made a bulky package, possibly drawing notice from others in the office.

Satisfied that the room was clean, he threw the burn bags into the safe, locked it, and signed the checklist that certified that he had locked the classified containers in compliance with Navy security regulations.

Via that strategically placed mirror, Little Albert saw that the suspect his security detail had been watching the past several months had moved the burn bags to the rear of the room, and that he had somewhat furtively unbuttoned his trousers and then had tucked in his shirt. Although he was not certain that Waldmann had taken all or even one of the blueprints, he suspected that his out-of-the-ordinary activities in the rear of the room were sufficient evidence to signal the surveillance team in the parking lot.

Little Albert busied himself with one of the bright, colorful curtains that covered the window.

John Bradford and his partner Mike Holland waiting on the parking lot had concentrated their attention on a specific NAVBUSHIPS window. Holland suddenly turned to Bradford, "Did you see that? John, I think Little Albert is shaking that damned curtain. NAVBUSHIPS must have hit the bait."

"Yep," Bradford confirmed, "I see it. This is it." Now both agents concentrated their eyes on the only NAVBUSHIPS exit. Bradford snickered, "Just think, Mike, you could have gotten Little Albert's assignment and been stuck in the draftsman's job for the past six months."

"Not me. I can't even draw a straight line."

"Lucky Little Albert," Bradford said, not taking his eyes off the NAVBU-SHIPS entrance. "He was always a little wise guy, bragging about his college engineering courses. Our little college boy got called up for active duty, though, just like you and me."

"So, that's how he got that job," Holland snickered. "But at least he's sitting in an air-conditioned office while we're sweating our asses off here in this stinkin' car."

"Good point, Mike. Good point," Bradford said with a sigh as he wiped his forehead with his already soaking wet handkerchief. Suddenly he became all business. "Look, they're letting out. Watch for BUSHIPS Number One. Do we have his car covered?"

"Yeah, Bill Kirkland is watching it. He'll come around our car with his motorbike to let us know."

"Let's hope everyone remembers the orders. The Old Man said, 'loose surveillance.' Christ, I hope nobody gets too eager. That'll really piss him off."

"Not to worry, they all got the word," Holland said quietly, as both men trained their eyes on the nondescript figure of Walter Waldmann scurrying through the parking lot toward his car.

Minutes later, Special Agent Bill Kirkland's motorcycle pulled up to the senior agent's vehicle. Over the roar of his motorcycle he shouted, "It's in the trunk of the car!" then sped away.

Bradford started his vehicle and drove slowly out of the parking lot. He hesitated at the exit wondering whether he should take the road over Memorial Bridge into Washington or not, when the suspect passed the surveillance vehicle; Washington it was. One of the three surveillance vehicles eased its way through the traffic and passed both Bradford's and the suspect's cars. They had followed their man from afar a number of times in the past. Then it was a surveillance to establish a pattern; today it was the real thing.

Waldmann usually drove across Memorial Bridge, around the Lincoln Memorial, along the Rock Creek Parkway into Georgetown. More often than not he parked his car in one of the side streets just off Wisconsin Avenue and stopped in one of the less expensive eateries either on Wisconsin or on M Street. He held true to his normal routine today. He drove west along M Street, turned north on Wisconsin Avenue, and then right on N Street. The agents saw the suspect find an empty spot and park his car.

During the pre-surveillance briefing Bradford had ordered Kirkland, the motorcyclist, to stay put and watch the suspect's car from afar. Bradford and his partner followed Waldmann into the eatery and found seats near the entrance from which they could observe him.

Occupants of the second car remained inside their vehicle after parking, while those in the third car parked their car and then deployed up-street and down-street from the eatery. They wanted to be certain they could follow anyone who made contact with the suspect without raising his suspicions, or those of the one he was expected to meet. All seven agents were positioned and in place.

John Bradford and Mike Holland watched Waldmann, who seemed to be in no hurry. He ordered his beer, and then walked over to the only pay phone in the restaurant and made a very brief call. Then he sat down and leisurely ate his meal. The two NCIS agents observed no one approaching his table, and Waldmann made no signs of recognition—he seemed to concentrate all his attention on his supper.

To the two NCIS agents it seemed as if Waldmann had no concern at all. He finished his meal, lit a cigarette and nursed a second beer. Bradford and his partner had already paid their bill and lingered nervously over their coffees. Finally, Waldmann paid his bill and left the restaurant. Bradford and Holland waited a good thirty seconds before following him. As the two agents exited the restaurant, Bradford saw two of his other agents following Waldmann up Wisconsin Avenue, one walking on either side of the street. The two agents who had waited in their vehicle watched as the suspect turned into the side street where he had parked his car. As his car emerged, they followed it at a distance.

When John Bradford and his partner reached their vehicle, they could not see Kirkland or his motorcycle. Holland asked, "What in hell happened to Bill?"

Before Bradford could answer their car radio crackled, "Toby, this is Toby Seven. Over."

Holland picked up the microphone, "Toby Seven, this is Toby. Over."

"Toby, this is Toby Seven. Remain at original location. Repeat. Remain at original location. Out."

Bradford slammed on his brakes and backed up into his old parking space. He turned to Holland, "What in hell is that all about? Where the hell is he?" Holland just shrugged. Their long silence finally was interrupted by another difficult to hear call.

"Toby, this is Toby Three. We put item to bed. Toby Two will maintain surveillance. Relay from Toby Seven. Toby Seven will return to original location. Toby Three will meet you there. Out."

Bradford turned to his partner and said, "These radio transmissions are so shitty. Even here in town you can hardly understand them with all that static. I wonder when the hell we'll ever get better radios. I hear that the Army CI guys have those new ultra-high-frequency radios with relays and booster stations all over town. They're supposed to be a hell of a lot better than that crap we have in our cars."

"I still can't understand why Bill left his post. And where is he calling from?" Holland said. Several minutes later the two agents heard the roar of a motorcycle in the empty streets of Georgetown.

Kirkland pulled directly behind the surveillance vehicle, jumped off and ran excitedly to the vehicle. He opened the rear door and climbed in. Even before slamming the door he almost shouted, "You won't believe what happened. I parked my bike on the goddamned sidewalk. I sat there tinkering, or at least pretending to tinker with the motor, wondering what the two of you were having for dinner. Along comes some guy—good suit and tie—stops behind our man's car, pulls a goddamned key from his pocket and opens the goddamned trunk. Can you believe that? He had a key and he opened the NAVBUSHIPS guy's trunk!"

He didn't wait for a reply. "I didn't see it at first, but the guy had a small flashlight. He pokes around the trunk with the light and comes up with a neatly folded bunch of papers. I'd say about fifteen-by-fifteen, or twenty-by-twenty inches square."

Bradford and Holland looked at each other and then back at Kirkland.

"Okay, okay," said Kirkland, slowing down as he realized that the two senior agents probably wanted to hear the whole story. He stopped briefly, and then continued, "Okay, let me back up. When NAVBUSHIPS got to his car in the parking lot after he left work, the first thing he did was to open all the doors, like he was venting the hot air. Then he laid his jacket on the back seat. Next he opened the trunk, took off his necktie, unbuttoned his shirt and pulled a little package from under his belt. He placed the package in the trunk. I'm guessing it was the blueprints."

He took a deep breath. "Anyway, back to the guy who opens the trunk, the guy with the key and the flashlight. He slips the packet into his briefcase, shuts the trunk, and walks off toward Wisconsin Avenue. Man, I am in a dilemma. Should I follow the guy or stay here as planned? I decide to follow. While he walks to the end of the block, I pull my dark blue shirt over the dirty T-shirt—just in case. I start my bike and just as I come to the corner of Wisconsin I see the guy get into a black Chevy. I decide to follow, can't see his license plate, don't want to get too close. The Chevy heads up toward Q Street, real quiet street, you know? Gets on Dumbarton, around Sheridan Circle. Man, I am sweating blood. I almost lost him heading up Mass. Avenue. He picks up speed, but I stay almost a block behind him. Suddenly he turns right into Belmont Road. I slow down, real slow, and cruise passed Belmont. What do I see? Two guys get out of the car. My guy is one of them. The car takes off. The two run into the mansion on Belmont. You know what that is?"

"Sure," interrupted Holland excitedly, "that's the goddamned Military Mission. Sonofabitch, that's the goddamn Soviet Military Mission."

Kirkland sputtered, "You know who that was? That Sonofabitch was GRU Major Kasandroff. I should have recognized him when he searched Waldmann's car, but the light was bad, but when he jumped out of the car and ran into to the

Mission, I saw him clear as day.

"Pay dirt!" shouted Bradford. This time even he almost lost his cool. Just then the second car, Toby Three, arrived. Toby Three's driver agent leaned out the window and asked, "What gives?" After Kirkland repeated the whole story, the two special agents in Toby Three exploded together "Sonofabitch! Sonofabitch!"

Finally Bradford got everyone quieted down. "Listen, guys, I told you that this is a special job commissioned by the Old Man. I don't know, but I have the feeling that it is something big, very big. He said 'national level.' I suggest we all keep this quiet for the time being. No report gets written without his approval. I'll give the Old Man a verbal report as ordered."

Bradford told them to go home. "We don't want to make too big a hoopla over this." He told Toby Three to report back to him by noon the next day. "I'm taking Bill and Mike with me to brief the DNI tonight—but this time without the goddamned profanities, understood?" He looked at the two agents, who laughed nervously. "Let's go, boys."

John Bradford drove the car, and Kirkland followed on his motorcycle. They arrived at the Washington Navy Yard. From the guard shack Bradford called the DNI at his quarters. When he returned to the car, he said, "The Old Man wants to see us. Now!"

Rear Admiral Frederick Van Sollen, Rear Admiral Carl Di Rovalleri's replacement as the Director of Naval Intelligence, was waiting for them on his front porch. He greeted them warmly. "Come in, boys, come in," he said as he ushered them into his library. "No need to stand on ceremony," he said with a twinkle in his eyes. "My wife is out of town visiting family."

They removed their jackets and loosened their ties as they settled into easy chairs. "Now, what do you have for me?" the DNI asked expectantly. At a nod from Bradford, Kirkland launched into his account.

There were several moments of dead silence when Kirkland wrapped up his report. When the Old Man heard the name Major Kasandroff he slapped his thigh and shouted "Sonofabitch, Sonofabitch, the curtain has fluttered, the bait has been taken. We're right on track. Kasandroff, we got you by the balls."

CHAPTER 20

SUMMER 1970
ROOM 526
WISCONSIN AVENUE, NW
WASHINGTON, D.C.

This was Lieutenant Beringer's second visit to Room 526. Beringer, Hans Reiter and Hiram Smyth sat in Hiram's office. Beringer's boss had instructed him to prepare Hans Reiter for his mission, and for Hans's insertion into the Naval Intelligence Support Center (NISC) in Suitland, Maryland.

"This deception has stumbled along for more than fifteen years," Beringer said, "and my boss wants to be sure it is still on track, and if not to give it a kickstart." He looked at Hans, "You have seen the photos of GRU Major Kasandroff. He is your target. The DNI wants the Soviets to b convinced that we are building, or at least have plans to build titanium submarines. Actually, I have the feeling that the DNI thinks it's time for you here in Room 526 to bring it to its conclusion."

He looked at Hans, "Mr. Smyth had convinced us that you are the right person to do the job. My boss wants you to apply for an analyst job at NISC, in Suitland. Take any job offered. In time you will end up in NISC-32, the submarine job. There you will learn all about the navy and learn to talk navy. In the meantime you have the reference books here to give you an overall view of this organization. If you need to come here, or if I need to talk to you and Mr. Smyth, let us know. My office will call your boss and tell him you are needed at Room 526." He paused briefly, "I thought this might explain some of these activities that involved your brother Christian." After briefly looking at his notes, Beringer continued, "Actually, your brother and his two OSS comrades had that operation well planned. It was maybe a bit risky, but they had decided to send the man known to us as the Wizard, but to the Soviets by his real name, Karl Cedric "Casey" Miller— to visit the Leningrad State Library as a fully documented PhD researcher working in support of a U.S. Navy project, and later to Berlin and Frankfurt-on-Main.

When Beringer mentioned Karl Cedric Miller, along with Frankfurt-on-Main, he had not noticed that Hans Reiter had suddenly risen from his chair.

"Are you telling me that Miller's tasking was nothing but crap?" Hans demanded.

Hiram Smyth and Lieutenant Beringer looked up in surprise. They had not seen Hans in such an upset state.

"What's the matter?" Smyth managed to say.

"What's the matter? I'll tell you what's the matter. We—I and my team," Hans sputtered, "spent a whole goddamned year back in the 1950s hunting all over East Germany for titanium-- for nothing."

* * * * * *

In February 1955, the U.S. Army clandestine unit in the I. G. Farben Hochhaus had received an Intelligence Collection Requirement, an ICR, from "way up" in the Pentagon; it was prepared by the technical director of NAVSTIC, the Naval Intelligence Scientific and Technical Intelligence Center, and issued to all military intelligence elements worldwide. This ICR directed Hans Reiter's Army clandestine element to recruit as many East Germans as possible to collect information on titanium manufacturing and research in East Germany. It included the term "spread a wide net of informants"—in total contradiction to clandestine collection modus operandi, which dictated strict compartmentation to assure a certain degree of survivability for U.S. agents and their sources.

Shortly after the ICR was received, Karl Cedric Miller arrived. Although a civilian, he had the Army G-2's "blessings." The Old Man, the Chief Agent, introducing Miller to Hans Reiter, informed Hans that Miller was there to brief them on a new collection target called Exotic Metals, and that he had placed Reiter and the entire team at Miller's disposal.

Initially, Miller had seemed somewhat confused when he met Reiter but only for a moment.

With Miller's help, Hans Reiter's unit became titanium "experts." When Fred Hertzwald, Reiter's old mentor, heard of the exotic metals assignment, he immediately volunteered one of his East German sources, a metallurgist named Heinz Schwertfeger. Schwertfeger became the first of Reiter's sources of high potential. Hans assured Fred Hertzwald that for Schwertfeger's personal security he would retain him as a "singleton"—a lone operative.

Hertzwald, an experienced recruiter, activated additional sources working on metallurgy research in East Germany and transferred them to Reiter's team. The informant net grew rapidly. Within a few months, Hans and his team had covered every one of East Germany's metallurgy institutions.

However, the change in modus operandi led to extensive discussions between case officers and the operations department. With the informant net considerably enlarged—with the numbers of recruited informants rising to forty-five and beyond—handling agent security became a serious concern. They selected the Treff areas now even more carefully than before. The operations department also decided that the agents should receive additional firearms training.

* * * * * *

After hearing all that from Hans, Lieutenant Beringer could only say, "This is really interesting; two brothers working, unwittingly, on the same project. This I've got to tell my boss."

Smyth laughed. "Want to hear some more news about good old Cedric?" He paused for emphasis. "Tell the admiral that good old Cedric had just about ruined Hans's clandestine operation with that damned titanium info collection."

Now Hans looked surprised.

"Hank, my friend Jack, Jack Heissinger, had some pretty colorful words to say about Miller—'Casey' Miller, to him."

Hans cut in, "I remember the special titanium tasking, and all the shit that Washington put on us. Your buddy Jack Heissinger tried to fight it tooth and nail, but this guy, Karl Cedric Miller of MIT, had Washington Army G-2's 'blessings' from way up high, I think. Our Old Man even introduced him to us personally. My guess, to make sure we did not fuck up this operation.

"This was a totally wasted effort. For just about a year we ran all over East Germany looking for titanium—where there was none; a total failure. But, not only a failure, this massive recruitment issue was in violation of our asset and agent security measures."

"If I recall," replied Beringer, "I knew that Miller had also stopped over in Frankfurt, but I didn't know at which office." He added, "In retrospect, that is, Monday-morning-quarterbacking, your so-called 'wasted effort' was in fact a highly successful operation. It was part of the triad of deception, the Russian paranoia, the spreading of false leads, and the stealing of the titanium submarine blueprints."

He then suggested that he could just casually mention to the DNI that he had a two-brother team working the project. "Maybe I can pull the Old Man's chain for you. Very carefully of course."

Hans said, "I sure did not know that Miller was one of my brother Christian's OSS cohorts."

To this, Lieutenant Beringer added, "You must remember, that all was planned and executed in 1954. I will have much more to tell you once I get to dig through the DNI's files. I believe that President Eisenhower had much confidence in your brother Christian, and in the Philosopher and the Wizard. Beringer paused only briefly to look at his notes, "I've not seen it in a report, but I've read some handwritten notes by one of the DNIs that your brother must have had a brainstorming session with his guys, because the DNI received a suggestion from the President that he should make it appear to the agents at NCIS that this was a typical, large-scale, national-level, counterintelligence operation. The DNI was to slip one of the Navy spy-catchers, a man with all the proper clearances and all that, into the BUSHIP engineering office."

Beringer mentioned having seen cryptic notes about burn bags and Ozalid machines, and seemingly poor copies of technical drawings slipped into burn bags.

Hans asked, "Ozalid?"

Beringer chuckled. "Yes, they copied blueprints on those old, smelly machines. The machines are pretty large and smell of ammonia."

He continued, "NAVBUSHIPS had installed a single-room 'secure' office at the office on Jefferson-Davis Highway in Arlington 8, Virginia. Early on, rumors circulated through NAVBUSHIPS. What project? No one knew, and the four guys behind the closed door weren't talking. "That was the bait," Beringer smiled, "secrecy." He added that all the insiders of NAVBUSHIPS knew that three of these guys on the far end of the building, behind a security locked door, were long-time employees of NAVBUSHIPS, and one, "a new kid," was a recently hired apprentice nicknamed "Little Albert"—and that all four were working on a special Top Secret project.

"Actually, the new kid was an NCIS counterintelligence agent. But, neither the design engineers, nor the NCIS agent, had any idea what was really going on; they were pawns in the game played by the President of the United States.

"The DNI told the NCIS agents involved that the FBI needed Navy's cooperation in tracing messages from a suspected mole within NAVBUSHIPS."

Beringer reminded Reiter and Smyth of the photos of GRU Major Kasandroff and the funny-looking little fat fellow wearing old-fashioned glasses. Beringer pointed at Kasandroff's photo, "Remember him well," he cautioned Hans, Kasandroff is our target. He is the guy we want you to recruit. The other fellow, Waldmann, is not important to us."

Beringer paused only briefly, "We will follow Kasandroff, and once you are fully trained in navy technology and navy speak, and when Kasandroff is in the right location where you will be able to approach him safely, you will try to recruit him." Then he explained how Kasandroff obtained the blue prints, the bait, from Waldmann. Beringer added, "later, when the time is ripe, I, or my replacement, will brief you thoroughly on the submarine's characteristics that Kasandroff delivered to GRU Centre.

Beringer explained that eventually he would have to deal with the now

Colonel Kasandroff. "All in good time," Beringer suggested.

Then Hiram Smyth and Beringer finalized the plan for Hans's insertion into Naval Intelligence Support Centers, and the contact procedure between the DNI's office and Room 526.

After Beringer's departure, Smyth agreed that now the entire operation made more sense.

For Hans's final training, Smyth produced a red, plastic-covered book titled "SECRET/NOFORN-Naval Ship Characteristics." "Read this, learn it by heart, you'll need it," he advised, "you're gonna be our new Naval Intelligence analyst."

"Hiram, I am a grunt, not a goddamned swabbie."

"You heard Beringer's explanation. You have to become familiar with Navy talk, or how could you persuade that Russkie that you know all about the U.S. Navy? You've got to become a ship or submarine analyst. The DNI thinks, and I agree, that if you're gonna be a Navy guy, you ought to be able to talk and walk Navy, and a year or so in Naval Intelligence will do that."

"Christ, what next?"

"Well, that's your daytime job. The rest of the time you work for me."

More kidding than anything else, Hans asked, "Does that mean I get two paychecks?"

"Dream on," Smyth said over his shoulder and left the room laughing, as if he had heard the best joke of the day.

Naval Intelligence, Hans thought. *Naval Intelligence?* He chuckled, remembering how he had tried the join the U.S. Navy at the Army/Navy recruiting office in Long Island, but the U.S. Army's Armored Center seemed to be of more interest—driving heavy vehicles had always interested him, and tanks were the heaviest. Thus, he'd ended up driving tanks through the Kentucky sand at the Armored Division training center. This used to be one of his party jokes. Now he would be, if not a sailor, at least a Navy civilian employee.

He started to page through the book. The surface combatant section looked confusingly complicated; it listed everything imaginable, including all the communications antennae. *What a bunch of crap,* he thought. *Who would list all these antennas, when a couple of sailors can change them in a jiffy? Besides, some of these photos are four or five years old.*

After he had read all about surface ships, from cruisers to ocean tugs, Reiter started on submarines, specifically Soviet submarines. He found these entries far less cluttered with extraneous details and a lot easier to absorb. He thought to tell Smyth that if he had to become a Naval analyst, it should be for submarines.

The following week Smyth told Hans to drive out to the Naval Intelligence Support Center in Suitland and get interviewed for a job. "Look concerned," he advised, "as if you really need that job, but not to worry, the fix is in. I was told they'd start you off with merchant ships. Once your old Top Secret Code Word clearance is confirmed, they'll transfer you to editing the analytical inputs, then to submarines. You stay with submarines a couple of years. Then ... who knows what?" He then told Reiter he would get to keep the GS-12 salary of a counterespionage agent and whatever the Navy thought he was worth would be funneled back in a convoluted way to the Navy.

"Not to worry," it seemed to be Smyth's favorite expression, "it's in the bag."

CHAPTER 21

Per Smyth's instructions, Hans Reiter drove from Alexandria over the Wilson Bridge into Maryland to Suitland. There he was interviewed and, just as Smyth had predicted, hired by the NISC's Merchant Marine Intelligence Section. This time he had to type his own security clearance forms; after all, at Navy he was just a lowly GS-7 trainee. Just as Smyth had foretold, as time went on, Reiter worked his way from merchant ships to editing war ship characteristics books, with a promotion to GS-9.

With another promotion to GS-11, Hans arrived at NISC-32, the foreign submarine intelligence shop, where he became the assistant to the senior submarine analyst. NISC-32 turned out to be a great place to work. His fellow submarine analysts were congenial folks, the work was relatively interesting and it was something he thoroughly enjoyed. It was a small office. The boss was a Navy lieutenant who had served on attack submarines operating in the Barents Sea. His deputy was a ships engineer. There was a second naval engineer, a submarine hull expert. Then there was one analyst for missile submarines, both ballistic and cruise missiles, and Hans himself handled all attack submarines—worldwide— both diesel and nuclear powered. Assisting all was another civilian, a former Navy officer and nuclear engineer, who correlated all-source information for the analysts.

This office produced the final submarine intelligence product for the Navy, to which the entire NISC organization contributed.

The all-important acoustic intelligence collected by surface ships and submarines, and photo interpretation— both hand-held from ships and attaches—and satellite imaging were included. A superb drafting and art department, as well as the editing section, gave the final product its "sellable" look.

NISC was a highly professional organization manned by about ten percent active Navy personnel; the rest were civilian government employees; many had been at NISC for decades. They knew where "all the bones were buried." Hans would get to know most of them; it would be his job to "undig" many bones, so that Room 526 could do the DNI's bidding.

When the captain of the unit learned that Reiter had been an Army Intelligence collector, he asked him to handle HUMINT collection tasking in addition to his submarine analysis work. It was not long thereafter that the captain detailed him to interface with collectors in the entire intelligence community. Hans was not sure, but thought the DNI might have suggested it.

When the senior submarine analyst retired, Hans became NISC-32's attack submarine analyst. Later he began to wonder whether interfacing with collectors was another one of Hiram Smyth's plans, because, whenever Smyth needed him, the DNI's aide called to tell Hans's boss that he was needed in Room 526. Instead of going to the Pentagon, Hans went to Room 526 at the Wisconsin Avenue address.

Whenever he was asked what was going on, he would say he had ironed out another HUMINT collection glitch—that always did the trick.

In late 1972, Hans started to integrate all the information he received on Soviet Projekt 705, NATO designation: Soviet ALFA Class SSN, nuclear fast-attack submarine. Reportedly, this submarine was made entirely of a titanium alloy; it displaced 3,700 metric tons while submerged and 2,400 metric tons when surfaced. It had a length from bow to stern of 80 meters.

One of Navy's assets in Leningrad's Special Design Bureau 143, or SDB 143—the place that designed the titanium submarine—called her the "Golden Fish," because it had cost the Soviet Navy a capitalist fortune to build.

The U.S. Navy, actually "the Rickover People," the highly visible, finely tuned organization at Crystal City, had offices just a stone's throw from the Pentagon; Admiral Hyman Rickover was the man in charge. Rickover, the father of the United States Navy's nuclear submarine development, would not accept as fact that the Soviets had made a quantum jump in submarine technology by building titanium submarines, or that they had the capability to do so. One of the arguments he threw on the table whenever he could was, "I know Russians. I was born a Russian. They have an old proverb, 'Never hang all your clothes on a single nail.' That's what they believe, and that's what I believe."

To anyone who disagreed with his assessment, he would bolster his argument with, "Admiral Gorshkov has a plaque on his desk inscribed with 'Better is the Enemy of Good Enough.' Just another great Russian proverb; but one he lives by."

However, NISC submarine analysts predicted that this submarine would become the world's first in many things; the world's first all-titanium attack submarine; the world's smallest nuclear-powered submarine; the world's deepest diving submarine; the world's most automated submarine, with the world's smallest crew; and most importantly, and most difficult for Admiral Rickover and his people to accept, the world's fastest submarine. It especially galled the "Rickover People" when Navy Intelligence analysts tried to tell the submarine community that Magnetic Anomaly Detection, also called MAD, could not detect this submarine. Hearing this, Rickover blocked publication of this assessment, because MAD was one of the U.S. Navy's primary ways of fixing the location of a submerged submarine.

The only fly in the ointment, as Rickover loved to point out, was that ten years earlier, Naval Intelligence had predicted the launch of a titanium submarine, and that submarine was yet to be launched; ten years after NISC-32 had predicted the imminent launch of this super-submarine.

Hans Reiter and his colleagues had watched the development and the construction of this titanium submarine through many "eyes." Informants from the inner circle of the Soviet Naval staff reported that Admiral Gorshkov was building a "super" titanium submarine. Finally, the "eyes in the sky," the imaging and electronic sensing satellites that circle the globe 67.3 miles above the earth, produced an image of Gorshkov's titanium submarine. Daring U.S. Naval attaches who periodically observed Leningrad's Sudomekh shipyard, provided a ground-level photo of this submarine as it sat in the launch basin—it looked much like the submarine built in the NISC model shop based on observations by Navy photo analysts.

* * * * * *

During one of their periodic meetings at Room 526, Wisconsin Avenue, Lieutenant Beringer mentioned to Hans that the DNI believed that all indications were that the Soviets had built the submarine from the U.S. Navy plans the then-Major Kasandroff had "procured." Beringer said, "The DNI believes that the ALFA is actually a much improved copy of U.S. Navy plans."

Hans, and his predecessor at NISC-32, had waited more than a decade to prove that NISC's assessment of this revolutionary titanium submarine was correct. Originally they had predicted that the Golden Fish would be ready for trials five years earlier—they lost a bit of credibility with that prediction. Problems with welding large titanium plates in a shipyard atmosphere had delayed the launch of the first unit for some twelve years.

NISC-32's credibility may have suffered somewhat in the eyes of superiors, but the analysts had based their assessment on information from highly credible Soviet academicians and engineers at SDB 143; Special Design Bureau 143

109

was the Soviet Union's finest, and most prestigious, submarine design bureau. Of course, SDB 143's errors did not particularly help NISC-32 in the eyes of the directors of Naval Intelligence—three of them had cycled through that office during the time the Soviets had tried to solve the complexities of welding titanium in a shipyard atmosphere.

Some things that had initially confused both Smyth and Hans were rumors, suggestions and reports from a multitude of sources, not only from Hans Reiter's own assets, of arguments for and against building titanium-hull submarines. U.S. Naval Intelligence analysts could not quite understand the rush to build these submarines. Also puzzling to the Naval attaches and intelligence analysts were statements from several, otherwise reliable sources from within the Soviet naval hierarchy, who continued to justify the construction of titanium submarines, "because Americans are secretly building deep-diving titanium submarines." Even those within U.S. Navy circles who prided themselves on having "special access," could not confirm the existence of such a U.S. program. The intelligence analysts at the Suitland complex surmised that it must be one of those super-secret programs at the "Skunk Works," whatever and wherever that was.

Of course, for the folks of Room 526, it was not a puzzle. Beringer had briefed Smyth that the U.S. Navy had indeed designed a titanium submarine on the orders of the President of the United States. And that it was Hans Reiter's mission to assure the Soviets of the U.S. Navy's continuing interest in building such a submarine.

"I think you're ready for your first mission," Smyth explained. "You know all the Navy stuff, you've learned all the lingo. I'm sure you can pass as a Naval officer." Smyth smiled. "Just don't forget to return the enlisted folks' salutes—and don't make it a smart Army salute. You know, them Navy guys ain't too good at that military stuff.

"Well, with that out of the way," Smyth continued, "The DNI wants you to meet Kasandroff, talk to him about the great Soviet stuff you saw at Paris, and, when you feel ready to drop the big one on him, be kind."

Smyth reminded Hans that Kasandroff had been in the U.S. during the middle to late 1950s for one and a half tours of duty—an extraordinary five years; that he had recently become the Soviet's senior military attaché in Bonn, Germany, and that he had, after a rocky start in Washington, been rewarded with an early promotion to light colonel for his excellent work in the United States.

The Agency reported that Kasandroff had already selected his favorite hangout, a restaurant in Königswinter, a small town on the Rhine River just south of Bonn. According to Smyth, Kasandroff had gotten greedy. He had stashed a lot of money, the military mission's money, in a secret "no-name" account in George

Town, Grand Cayman's branch of Barclays Bank. One of the FBI's assets at Barclays reported that Kasandroff had "several hundred thousands" in the account. Smyth opined that Kasandroff might have plans to retire to one of the many small Caribbean islands.

"Now, as you well know," Smyth gave Hans his devilish smile, "them Russkies don't look kindly on their own that screw them; especially when it comes to money. Has something to do with capitalist yearnings."

He seemed to enjoy this; he leaned back in his chair and added, "That'll play right into our hands." He then explained that when the time was ripe Reiter was to request, and the DNI would approve, a four-week sabbatical, an unpaid leave, to settle a family trust deposition.

CHAPTER 22

Hans Reiter, documented as George Trenker, Lieutenant Commander, USN, arrived in Germany on one of those rare sunny autumn days. An embassy car picked him up at the Cologne airport. At the embassy he presented his temporary duty orders to the Marine on duty. The Marine called the naval attaché who escorted him into his inner sanctum, the security zone.

"Commander Trenker," explained the Naval attaché, "the DNI wrote that you have a mission that requires no input from us, except light personnel security, and to acknowledge to anyone asking, that you are my assistant. Is that correct?"

Reiter agreed.

"I have waiting to meet you," the attaché continued, "a Marine security who speaks some German."

"Okay, let's get the introduction over with." The attaché called his front office and his Marine security man entered. Hans saw a young, redheaded, freckled-faced man, slender with a thick neck and broad shoulders. They shook hands, and Hans explained to the Marine that he just needed standoff security.

"Sir, what's that?" he asked.

"No big deal, actually. I assume you can dress like a German?"

"Yes, sir."

"Okay. Here it is. I will meet certain people in Königswinter and I would like for you to be there when I do, but only in the background. Never show that you know me. Never make eye contact with me. Interfere only if my life is threatened. Whatever you have at the restaurant will go on my expense account. Okay?"

At the Lorelei Restaurant, Hans saw his Marine dressed like a German workman, while casually keeping an eye on him.

Hans made his way through the restaurant moving back and forth as if looking for an empty table—there was none. He walked up to Kasandroff's table. Kasandroff looked up and noticed him. Hans smiled, "Excuse me please, if I am not mistaken you are Colonel Kasandroff, are you not?"

Kasandroff looked startled; he frowned.

"May I share this table with you? There is hardly any room elsewhere." Kasandroff nodded seemingly by reflex.

As Hans sat down he thanked him and introduced himself, "I am George Trenker, here on temporary duty with the U.S. Embassy."

Kasandroff, still appearing to be in shock, stuttered, "Kasandroff... Kasandroff."

Hans made small talk, commented on the surprisingly good weather for this time of year, the scenic location of the hotel, and the friendly people in this restaurant. He mentioned that he had just been to the Paris Air Show.

Kasandroff finally managed to agree. He mentioned that he also had attended the air show. Reiter, exploiting this bit of conversation, remarked, "I see where your people had an eye-opener with that new fighter aircraft. That was quite a show."

Kasandroff nodded, "Yes, this has been good for sales. I almost thought some of your people, eh, Lockheed for example, would try to buy one of them

Hans laughed, "They wouldn't dare. They'd be admitting that your fighters are better than ours."

Kasandroff appeared to like this comment, but then commented on the good quality of food and the good prices at the Lorelei; he used the German word, *Preiswert*—reasonably priced, of good value.

Hans hooked onto this word, switching over to German. "Oh, you speak German? If you are more comfortable speaking German, we ...?"

"Oh, no," Kasandroff replied hastily, "it's good for me to practice my English. I have not used it for some time." He seemed to relax a bit, although he continued scanning the room in a typical counter-surveillance mode. When the waitress approached their table he seemed to relax just a little; they ordered beer—Hans asked for Warsteiner—and dinner.

He asked Kasandroff, "Have you tried Warsteiner?" He had not. "It's my favorite German beer," Hans said. Over dinner, the Russian started to question Hans about his duties at the embassy, and how long these TDYs—using the abbreviation TDY probably to impress Hans with his knowledge of American English—usually last.

"It all depends on the work," Hans replied. "Sometimes it's weeks, other times it is months. But TDY is rarely longer than three months."

"And how long will you be here in Germany?"

"I should be going home in about two weeks, and glad to go. I spent a week at the Paris Air Show, and have been here for about a week. I can't stand the cold northern European climate. I prefer it warm all year 'round. Preferably with palm trees and warm breezes." Kasandroff leaned back and smiled; it looked as if Hans had struck a pleasant chord.

Hans mentioned that he had just recently taken up snorkeling, and how much he enjoyed the crystal clear waters of the Caribbean. "I have snorkeled in waters where I could see down maybe a hundred feet. Ah, the white sandy bottom, the colorful tropical fish. I just love the Caribbean islands."

Kasandroff smiled, "I have never done that but I have been to the islands. I have bathed in the waters, and, oh, yes, the palms ... what a wonderful area."

Hans agreed, "Yes, and I would like to live on one of these islands after I retire."

"Yes, that would be nice, but also expensive."

Hans thought this would be a good time to pull in the reason he was here, "Well, some people have more money than others, but I think with proper planning I could live there on my Navy retirement."

Kasandroff nodded, and added, "Ah yes, that would be the life."

Hans leaned over and whispered, "Colonel, that shouldn't be a problem for you, should it?"

"What?" Kasandroff appeared startled.

"Money!"

"What are you talking about?"

Hans continued to whisper, "Colonel, I know all about the little no-name account at Barclays."

Kasandroff stopped breathing. He turned purple. Reiter tried to calm him, "Colonel, no one else outside my office knows about this."

Kasandroff looked at him angrily. He started to rise as if to walk out, then thought better of it, and sat down again. "Who in hell are you? And what do you want from me?"

"Colonel," Reiter was still whispering trying to reassure him, "we do not care about the Grand Caymans. But we would like to make a deal with you."

"Who are you? And don't tell me you are a Naval attaché."

"No, Colonel, I am just lieutenant commander, an assistant to the Naval attaché."

"Bullshit, Mister Trenker. I don't believe you."

"Okay, Colonel, if you don't believe me, check me out with the embassy. They'll confirm it."

Kasandroff rose, threw a large bill on the table and walked out. For a moment Hans thought he had overreached himself. The waitress came over and cleared off Kasandroff's plates and the half-finished glass of beer. She picked up the bill and asked, "What happened?"

Hans told her that the gentleman had suddenly felt ill and wanted to go home. Then he ordered another glass of Warsteiner. While he waited for the waitress to return with his beer he thought about Kasandroff's sudden departure. He had anticipated that the Russian would be terribly upset by that disclosure, but had not expected that he would make a run for it. *After all*, he thought, *we know something that could end his GRU colonel career, if not his life.* Hans planned to wait it out.

CHAPTER 23

The encounter with the man who called himself "Trenker" had destroyed Kasandroff s wellbeing, his feeling secure in the Soviet embassy. At first he contemplated making a run for it, defecting, asking the U.S. Embassy for asylum. However, he quickly discarded that notion. He concluded that Soviet counterintelligence would have arrested him and shipped him to Siberia—or worse—as soon as they had discovered his Barclay account. He also had to consider Tamara Ivanova, his lovely bride. Tamara Ivanova came from a large family and had strong ties that would not allow her to leave Ukraine, and if he left without her, her life would be a living hell.

No, he thought, *I must act now.* He recalled his mother's proverb, "Walk fast and you can overtake misfortune; walk slow and it will overtake you." He poured himself a glass of bourbon over ice. *First things first,* he thought.

He had to make sure that this Lieutenant Commander Trenker— Kasandroff was sure that was not his real name—actually worked in the U.S. Embassy. "Trenker," he sneered. "No one on the clandestine side ever goes by his real name."

Kasandroff was sure that the man also was not a Naval attaché. He had to be sure, damned sure, that that Sonofabitch was actually working for the U.S. embassy. That he was not some German surrogate working for some private security gang.

He knew exactly what he had to do. He carefully wrapped one of his prized possessions, one of the wooden spoons his mother had presented him when he graduated from Olympic Village, the GRU "finishing school" near Kirovograd in south central Ukraine. *Tomorrow,* he thought, *I will get a German messenger service to carry the spoon to the embassy. I will describe Mr. So-called Trenker to the messenger, and I will insist that he hand the package to no one except that Mr. Trenker at the U.S. Embassy.*

He sat still for a moment remembering that now he would have to be doubly careful so as not to endanger Tamara Ivanova. He had met Tamara Ivanova, a fellow GRU agent operating under Tass news reporter cover, several years previously while on assignment to Yemen. They married a short time later. At the time they were both lonely, living in a country totally alien to their tastes. Furthermore, for intelligence operatives, sexual relations with "outsiders" was always dicey—and looked upon by the counterintelligence folks as undesirable. Tamara Ivanova was a few years Kasandroff's junior, tall, blond, and of Ukrainian birth. It had made Kasandroff's mother, a fellow Ukrainian, happy to have someone in her family who spoke Russian with the familiar soft Ukrainian inflection. Kasandroff s mother only regretted that no children had come from this union.

Of course, Tamara Ivanova knew nothing, did not even have the slightest idea, of Kasandroff s traitorous activities, or of his dormant secret Barclays offshore bank account. It was something that a Soviet intelligence agent could never reveal—not even to a loved one, not even to his mother. Kasandroff hoped someday—whenever the proper time arrived—that he and Tamara Ivanova could enjoy the fruits of his activity in the sunny Caribbean, far away from drab and shabby Dnepropetrovsk.

Now, Kasandroff thought, *somehow some bastard found out, and I will have to be twice as careful as before.* He decided that if this Trenker fellow actually worked at the embassy, even just temporarily, exposing his little scheme would not benefit the Americans. Once again, as he had done long ago when he recruited Mr. Walter Waldmann from the U.S. Navy's NAVBUSHIPS, Kasandroff planned to profit from his encounter with Mr. Trenker. Judging from the initial contact, not only would his secret stash in Grand Cayman be safe, but he would also recruit the man who called himself Trenker, and have another source of income, one with considerable potential. To be sure, and to play the GRU recruiting game, he would once again, as he had done so well in Washington, create a source recruitment totally in compliance with GRU guidelines.

Only this time, thought Kasandroff, *I can speed it up considerably. After all, I now have seniority.*

Indeed, he thought as he refilled his glass once more with his favorite bourbon on the rocks, *why not?* He raised his glass and whispered, "Ah, what would my dear old mother in Dnepropetrovsk say if she could see her son sitting in an apartment overlooking the Rhine River sipping an American whiskey—on ice?" Holding his glass Kasandroff walked exultantly to the window of his apartment. He stood there transfixed by the ever-changing scene. It was a view he never tired of seeing. It was a far cry from what he had seen during his prior assignments in Southeast Asia, the Middle East and Africa.

As the evening wore on, the level of the bourbon in Kasandroff s bottle lowered, along with his spirits. He became melancholy. Good fortune had brought him to various places in this world, far from his birthplace, the small village in the Caucasus Mountains. He was almost ten years old when his father died—he had broken his neck when his horse stumbled over some rocks. Shortly thereafter his mother moved to Dnepropetrovsk to be near her family. His pockmarked face added a certain ruggedness to his overall appearance. Kasandroff s swarthy appearance had made him unpopular, and caused many a scuffle with the blond, blue-eyed Ukrainian boys. A black mustache hid his scarred upper lip now, a souvenir from one of the scuffles.

For many years he had longed to leave the flatlands of Ukraine. As a boy he yearned for the mountains of the Caucasus and the rugged people who lived on the steep mountainside huts and in the deep, green valleys. He had left Ukraine without a moment's hesitation just after his seventeenth birthday when an army recruiter selected him to attend the military academy. It had never occurred to him that anyone would consider him to be overly smart—but the academy did—and so did a GRU spotter who convinced Kasandroff to join this elite military intelligence organization.

And so it happened. After three years of intensive schooling and tough practical training he became a GRU intelligence officer. Kasandroff was proud to be a part of the most influential element of the Soviet Army officer corps. He had never looked back. Once each year, during his annual home leave, he visited his mother in Dnepropetrovsk, in full uniform. Each time he brought her gifts from faraway places where he had served Rodina, the motherland. With his mother proudly at his side, he walked past those who had antagonized him during his boyhood days. He ignored them, but he loved seeing his former tormentors uncomfortable, cringing, and embarrassed as he sneered at their rough clothes and dirty hands.

Not a bad life, he thought. *It beats shoveling donkey shit in Dnepropetrovsk.*

CHAPTER 24

OCTOBER 1972
U.S. EMBASSY
BONN/BAD GODESBERG, GERMANY

With not much else to do following his first meeting with Kasandroff, Hans Reiter sat in the Naval attaché's office in the late morning reading the attaché's *Naval Proceedings* magazine. Shortly before lunch, a Marine on duty at the main entrance telephoned him—Hans had a visitor. He walked downstairs. The Marine pointed to a uniformed German messenger service person, "He has a package for you and insists to give it only to you, personally." He whispered, "We scanned it, and it looks like a wooden spoon."

Hans walked over to the messenger who looked at him searchingly. From his demeanor Hans assumed that someone had described him to the messenger. As soon as he recognized Hans, he handed him a small package. Hans signed his receipt and the messenger departed.

Back at the office, he opened the package. The Marine was right; it contained a beautiful hand-carved wooden spoon with the traditional heavy lacquer over dark golden birch tree leaves painted on a red and black background. Russians had told Reiter you could eat the hottest soups with these wooden spoons without ever burning your lips. A little note under the spoon read, "Sorry about my rapid departure. K."

From long ago, Reiter recalled the days when he was a U.S. Army clandestine case officer. His Soviet assets often spoke glowingly of Rodina, Mother Russia, and their connection to the Russian earth. Soviet politics, Communism, always seemed to be a mere side issue. All his assets exibited this real, this down to earth love for the Taiga, the wide Russian plains, and the high mountains of the southern part of Russia. They saw no conflict working for Trenker, the American. Most, if not all, cherished the wooden spoon given to them by their families when they had joined the Red Army.

Wooden spoons have existed in Russia for 1,000 years. The wooden spoon was widely used all across Rodina, the Motherland, and was quite indispensable, since Russian peasants ate a lot of soups and porridges. The best spoons were made in the Trans-Volga region. The traditional wooden spoon had always been a personal tool. A Russian carried his spoon wherever he went. Although the wood spoon is no longer used as an eating utensil, it has maintained its significance in the Russian mind; a symbol of the "good old days."

Over the many centuries, the wooden spoon has become a beautifully decorated, personal treasure—one must have at least one in one's possession—or so it is said. To present one of these personal treasures to another person is a sign of trust and friendship.

Reiter now felt assured that Kasadroff's wooden spoon signaled tacit agreement to a long time working relationship.

Before they left for the Lorelei, Hans wanted to talk to the Marine corporal. During their first meeting he either had not caught the Marine's name, or the attaché had forgotten to mention it. Hans thought, *typical officer. Probably, to him the enlisted ranks are just there to do whatever. I don't want to become one of those.* When the Marine entered, Reiter apologized that he had not gotten his name. He said, "In the rush of things, either we did not get introduced, or I somehow missed it. Sorry."

The Marine looked sort of startled, somewhat awkward; he did not seem to know what to say.

"Well, first of all, what is your name?"

"Sir, I am Corporal Johannes 'John' Dreier." Hans asked where he had learned to speak German. Dreier said he spoke it at home in Wisconsin. "Sir, I spoke only German the first five or six years of my life. The whole neighborhood—all the kids spoke German. Aside from that, I have distant family here, just south of Bonn in Bad Krip, near Remagen."

Reiter switched into German and asked whether he had visited his relatives, and Dreier answered in almost fluent German that he had, and that his mother and father had come to visit Germany for the first time.

Reiter laughed. "I guess the Navy does not know that you speak far more than just 'some German.'"

Corporal Dreier shrugged. "Sir, nobody ever asked. But my folks finally got up enough nerve to visit when I transferred to the Marine Security Detail. They had a wonderful time, sir."

"I'm surprised," replied Reiter, "that the DNI had not gotten you into his intelligence organization. Does the Navy know that you speak fluent German?" Dreier said he was not sure.

"Let me ask you. Would you like to transfer into the Office of Naval Intelligence? I'm not sure, but I think I can convince the DNI to have you transferred."

"Well, sir, the Corps' embassy security is especially trained to protect the diplomatic personnel and installations. I think a transfer would be difficult. But, to answer your question, yes, I would be interested."

"I'll see what I can do; no promises, but I will try."

119

When Hans arrived at the Lorelei, Corporal Dreier was already on guard at the bar. This time Hans lucked out; he found an empty table for two. He nursed his Warsteiner beer for almost half an hour before Kasandroff appeared. From what Hans could see, he was without a keeper. Without asking Kasandroff took the other chair. Hans could see that he was still angry.

"Okay," the Russian asked in a gruff tone, "what is it you want?"

"Colonel," Reiter again tried to be reassuring, "I would like to make a deal with you. Nothing threatening, mind you. I have assurances from my superiors that if you do not wish to cooperate we will forget having known of the no-name account."

"How could I possibly trust you to keep your word?"

"Because it is most important that we trust each other. We have nothing to gain from revealing your secret—nothing. However, and I should not tell you this, but we are desperate for information from the inner circle of the GRU. We know nothing of what goes on at GRU Centre, and would like to have someone we could ask, long-range I might add, who could answer a few very important questions." Hans then went on to explain that in return his organization was willing to supply Kasandroff with some information GRU deemed pertinent to its collection. Furthermore, that Hans was willing to guarantee a "bolthole," a place where Kasandroff could disappear, if needed, if his life was in danger, in any country, at a moment's notice.

For seemingly a long time Kasandroff just looked at Hans. His piercing eyes seemed to bore into Hans's brain. After what seemed like an eternity, he spoke in a quiet, very controlled voice, "So you have it all figured out, have you? What if I say no, and to hell with you?"

"Then our deal is off, and you will never see me again. You go your way, I go mine and it will be as if we had never met—ever."

Kasandroff rose, and said, "No, and to hell with you."

Reiter rose and bid him farewell in Russian, *"Do svedaniia, Tovarish Polkovnik"*— Goodbye, Comrade Colonel.

Kasandroff looked startled, then turned and walked away. The waitress saw Hans's empty glass and returned with one filled to the brim. He took a long drag and settled back in his chair. He was almost relieved that Kasandroff had turned down his offer, yet... a nagging feeling told him that it was not over. He looked around to see whether anyone in the restaurant had found Kasandroff's brief visit strange, but it seemed as if the business at hand, the eating, the drinking, and conversation, the gossip, was far more important to the guests than some guy angrily stalking out of the restaurant.

He waved to his waitress and ordered supper and nursed his beer in the meantime. Just as his meal was served Kasandroff reappeared as if nothing had happened between them. He took the empty chair and grinned. "You did not order for me?"

This time it was Hans who was startled. He stuttered, "Well, eh... no, I did not know what you wanted."

He laughed, smiled at the waitress and then said in German, "Bring me the same as my friend here has." He paused. "Oh, yes, and also bring me a Warsteiner." After the waitress had disappeared he grinned at Hans. "Just testing, Tovarish Trenker ... or whatever your real name is; just testing."

Hans was speechless.

"So, tell me what is going on."

"Well," Hans replied, "I thought we would first see what you can tell us of the inner workings of your organization, and then what we can do for you."

"The information I will need is guaranteed genuine?"

"And verifiable," Hans added. "We are interested in your well-being; your long-term employment. That is of utmost importance to us. As you well know, we will not be able to provide you with everything you want, but what you get will be verifiable—or as intelligence analysts will say, 'confirmed.'"

Over supper they arranged for future Treffs—contact times and places—and emergency bolthole procedures. Kasandroff wanted an emergency telephone contact number. It was one item Smyth had not anticipated, so Hans gave Kasandroff his telephone number at Room 526. Hans would message Smyth to isolate this number, have it added to the twenty-four-hour watch officer's list, so that it would be used exclusively for Kasandroff's emergencies.

"Just in the event," Reiter instructed, "... any event, call this number and say, 'This is Iron Horse, I need your help.' Give date, time and location and wait to be picked up. Or, if you should need immediate contact or relay critical information, always identify yourself as Iron Horse."

Kasandroff smiled, "Iron Horse? I like the sound of that name ... Iron Horse, great."   Hans also told him that he would be his primary contact, and that he would make visual contact, just for recognition purposes, with one additional person. "I'll let you know the time and place for that." Kasandroff appeared to be satisfied with the arrangement. After dinner and another beer he left, and Reiter followed shortly thereafter—just to make sure that Kasandroff did not have any "keepers."

Holy shit, thought Hans, *Kasandroff took the hook.*

With the adrenaline pumping, he had not realized how stressful these past weeks had been; he slept all the way on the aircraft that carried him back to Washington's Dulles International.

CHAPTER 25

Hiram Smyth was happy to see Hans, he told Hans, "Phase One, Mission Completed." Hans had already prepared a simple cover story regarding the family trust deposition should anyone at NISC ask—to Hans's great relief, no one did. "Hiram, before we do anything else: As I stated in my report, I gave Kasandroff, as a normal bolthole procedure, my telephone number here at Room 526—and I asked that this number be isolated and added to the twenty-four-hour watch officer's list, so that he could use it in emergencies."

"Bolthole?" Smyth exploded, "We don't have one." A long silence followed. Then Smyth nodded, "Yes, yes, of course. We should have more than one bolthole. Why in hell did I not think of that?" He rubbed his forehead, "Shit, let me think." He started his regular pacing back and forth; he claimed he did his best thinking walking in circles. A few minutes passed, then, "Okay, screwed up on that one. In most friendly countries a blown asset can walk into a U.S. Embassy and ask for asylum, but not in East Germany and the Soviet Union ... or other Commie satellites. Most important is East Germany."

He paused again, then returned to pacing. "East Germany is a 'passing through' country. I've got one Polish guy, long-time asset, and a couple of Russians. If they can make it into East Germany, having a bolthole would be extremely important."

"Okay," Hans interrupted, "but first things first. I didn't know that we had a bolthole problem. I don't want Kasandroff walking into any embassy, not even in West Germany. We've got Frank Mackenzie in Frankfurt. Why not let him rent a small walk-up in Frankfurt and call it your first bolthole?"

"Great idea." Smyth grabbed that suggestion and built on it. "Frank has been in the area for almost a decade. He has great connections with the local police Oberinspektor, and with some auto rental outfit."

Frank Mackenzie, aka "Mack," was a retired U.S. Army master sergeant who had decided to stay in Germany and gotten a job, again via Jack Heissinger, Smyth's old friend, with Room 526. He lived in a small house in the Frankfurt/ Bockenheim area and was known locally as an antique clocks buyer, repairer, and exporter.

Hans, not wanting Smyth to get carried away with other bolthole plans, continued. "Hiram, I told Kasandroff that in extremis he should call this number and say 'This is Iron Horse, I need your help.' He will give date, time and location and wait to be picked up." Hans also mentioned that he himself would be Kasandroff s primary contact, and that he would make visual contact with one other person, just for recognition purposes.

Smyth agreed, "Frank's the guy. Let's get this done."

"Okay," Hans agreed, "That settles our Kasandroff problem. He has the emergency number; he has the code word 'Iron Horse'; in the near future I'll have a walk-by recognition between him and Frank."

"Now," Hans continued, "if you are interested in at least one bolthole in East Germany, I may have a suitable bolthole operator for there. But the IC, or DIA, will have to encourage the Army case officers to relinquish one of their assets. You know well, that this will piss off some people, but..."

Smyth agreed to that, and promised to get the Intelligence Community Staff or DIA involved in the asset transfer.

CHAPTER 26

A fter his last encounter with the American Trenker, Kasandroff sat once again at his favorite perch, the chair near his apartment window overlooking the Rhine, sipping an American whiskey. Day or night, there was life—the lights of the river barges and the cruise boats traveling up and down the Rhine. He never tired of this view. It was something so real, so stimulating. From his window the river looked clean, sparkling and so full of activity— not like the drab, slow-moving Dnepr River of his mother's hometown.

With the leftover whiskey still in his glass, the ice cubes clinking, he walked to the small table near his bed and retrieved a large leather-covered notebook. For some time he sat near the window, staring into the night. Then he opened the book and turned the pages to his last entry. There, in his neat Cyrillic writing, he recorded having met the American Mr. George Trenker during the last Paris Air Show, and that Trenker, working for the U.S. Navy, seemed to be a person of great potential.

Kasandroff had it all figured out. Over the next few months Moscow Centre would receive continuous updates of Kasandroff's recruiting efforts. He would fabricate Trenker's entire recruiting scenario to make it fit standard GRU recruiting procedures.

He drained the remainder of his drink and once again sank into his favorite chair. He smiled as he recalled the old colonel's lectures at Olympic Village. One of his favorite topics was "source recruiting." He warned his students especially on walk-ins. According to the old colonel, a walk-in could be the best, but was most often the worst thing that could ever happen to an intelligence officer.

"Comrades," the colonel would shout, waving his wooden pointer like a saber, "a walk-in could become your worst nightmare; the worst that ever happens to you and to our organization."

This seemed to be his favorite theme. He explained that a walk-in could be a "dangle," a false defector from the other side's counterintelligence service. He mentioned the British intelligence service—he always called them the "Britischers"—as being the most proficient in dangling a false defector. They had used dangles for centuries. The old colonel seemed to get a charge out of the way the

Britischers had fooled the Spanish, the French and even the Americans during colonial days.

Whenever he mentioned the no-good Germans he would chuckle, and then say, "They really shoved it up the Germans' asses during the last debacle." Then he would raise his "saber" and shout, "Comrades, they are doing it to us now if we are not careful. The Americans are not far behind the Britischers; the Americans are quick learners. Beware!"

Following the GRU-approved recruiting procedure, Kasandroff started Trenker's long recruiting process in his notebook. First he listed the four main topics of recruitment: Spotting, Assessing, Vetting and Recruiting. Between each topic he left four blank pages. Since spotting was the easiest part of the process Kasandroff described how, always in search of potential sources, he had found Mr. George Trenker twice in listings in the Paris Air Show; one in the visitors' register, and again in the hotel registry, and once in the registry of the U.S. Embassy at Bad Godesberg, Germany. He added one comment, "Trenker complained to another American about the shortage of funds for visiting the Air Show." Then he left a blank page.

That, thought Kasandroff, *is more than enough for tomorrow's first message to Moscow Centre.* He knew that this message would raise Centre's interest. He expected the operations officer to request additional information about this new U.S. Navy source, including Trenker's position. That in turn would lead to Kasandroff's next spotting report portion in this lengthy recruiting process.

Six days after having submitted his spotting report Kasandroff received Centre's response; it contained little additional information, and one additional question: Is this the George Trenker reported to have been working in Berlin during the middle 1960s?

Kasandroff thought, *I will surprise Trenker with this Centre query.* He smiled. "This," he mumbled, "ought to tell Trenker that GRU is not entirely helpless and dumb."

According to procedures, Kasandroff dutifully recorded Centre's assessment in his notebook. And, since Centre's message included Trenker's name, and since Centre had no derogatory information on him, Kasandroff knew he now had approval to proceed with the vetting process. Kasandroff decided to write Trenker a letter to have him confirm or deny that he was the one mentioned in Centre's query.

A few days later he picked up mail from his DLD, the dead letter drop, in Königswinter, including Trenker's confirmation that GRU Centre's information was correct. He wrote, "Bravo Zulu to Centre. I have worked in Berlin and in Frankfurt-on-Main during the middle/late 1960s. Feel free to let Centre know that the information is correct. See you soon."

In message number two Kasandroff reported that the Trenker on record at Centre was the Trenker in his spotting report, and that Trenker appeared to be a potential source of value. Thus, he laid the groundwork for a lengthy recruiting process that Kasandroff would, based on his seniority, speed up to completion within a few months, instead of the usual year that GRU officers with less seniority were required to take.

He knew that based on the additional information regarding Trenker's expertise, habits and weaknesses he had submitted, Centre would make a very careful assessment as to how to proceed. The following day Kasandroff received permission to start vetting Trenker. Along with permission came advice on how best to recruit him.

Kasandroff laughed. *If those smart fellows in Moscow only knew.* However, he dutifully recorded the "recommendation" in his book, and sent a message expressing his gratitude. Kasandroff knew it was best to let the recruiting process rest for several weeks before his next transmission. He did not want Centre to think that recruiting this American was too easy. He also wanted Centre to know that he was not rushing the process; that he was following GRU rules.

Anticipating the next Treff, Kasandroff prepared his first "vetting" report in advance. He confirmed that he had overheard Trenker complaining about the high living expenses at the air shows and how little per diem the U.S. Navy allocated. He added that in a follow-up he had observed Trenker at the U.S. Embassy in Bonn, Germany, and dining at a restaurant at Königswinter. Kasandroff also gave a brief physical description, highlighting Trenker's spending habits and his love for Warsteiner beer.

Several weeks later Kasandroff s starshina, his administrative sergeant, delivered a message from Centre requesting a progress report on Trenker's vetting. Kasandroff responded by making this particular vetting appear dangerous. He described suspected surveillance, long waits in dark neighborhoods and drives through the heavily wooded Westerwald, the mountain range along the right bank of the Rhine River. In a follow-on message Kasandroff reported that he had met Trenker at an inn just south of Bonn, and that Trenker had once again voiced his need for money, as well as his "unhappiness" with his bosses. Kasandroff described the circumstances of the meeting, concluding that money, as well as revenge, seem to be Trenker's primary concerns.

In response to the latest message, Centre gave the go-ahead to continue the vetting of the source. Kasandroff waited patiently to again make the vetting look authentic. Some two months into the process, Centre prodded Kasandroff for another progress report on Trenker. Kasandroff reported that he had expended some funds known as "care and feeding of source." To the message he appended the outline of his final recruitment scenario—again asking for Centre's approval.

He took into consideration all he had learned at the GRU training facility,

126

especially the old colonel's two favorite explanations for treason: revenge and money. "Revenge is a great motivator," the old colonel explained. "Those who think the bosses are against them feel the need for revenge—no doubt about that. And," he spat out the words in disgust, "there are those Judases who betray their country strictly for money."

Six months after Kasandroff had first met Trenker, Centre gave permission to recruit him. Kasandroff was fully aware that his plan required many avenues, all designed to anticipate twists and turns inherent in the recruiting phase. Deep in thought, he stared fixedly out of the window contemplating his options. He discarded all the fancy recruiting approaches; they did not fit this scenario. "No, Ivan Ivanovich," he cautioned himself, "don't risk failure!"

This was another great opportunity to increase his "retirement fund." Trenker had assured him that this was to be a long-term association. Thus the recruitment had to be uncomplicated. Any unforeseen complication, he knew, and the entire spotting, vetting, recruiting scenario could turn into donkey shit.

Also, since this was another personal moneymaker, his entire career, even his life would not be worth a rusty *Kopek* should his scheme become unraveled. He had no intention of spending his retirement years in Lyubyanka Prison—if he was lucky.

Kasandroff shuddered just thinking of the dire consequences should Centre ever discover the duplicity. He remembered the security training film at Olympic Village. Horror upon horror, as a twisting and screaming GRU or a KGB traitor was slowly lowered into a blast furnace. The recurring theme was "Death to Traitors."

He decided that for pure simplicity the "straight punch" was still the best recruitment method. "Yes, yes," he muttered to himself as if to confirm the correctness of that thought, "Centre always admires those who use that approach; it shows courage, daring." And, Kasandroff recalled that he followed the old Cossack proverb: Simplicity has a charm of its very own.

He prepared a message suggesting that he was using straight punch, and sat back to await Centre's decision. Kasandroff contemplated this future action. He knew that recruiting would entail expenses such as a monthly stipend, entertainment bills to cultural events, concerts. Based on his Washington experience, he no longer worried about hiding the recruitment moneys headquarters had allocated. He already had a safe deposit box at the Dresdner Bank on Gallusanlage 7, in Frankfurt-on-Main—one that even the Americans had not found, or at least had not mentioned. As always, he carefully documented all the entertainment he supposedly had spent on Trenker—a tidy sum, all things considered. Again he recalled the old colonel's admonition, "Remember the money trail!"

Hiding money had always been the most difficult aspect in this spy business—for informants as well as spymasters. In several training exercises Kasandroff and his fellow students had examined old case studies of several spies—and rogue case officers—big spenders, caught by alert auditors who had followed "the money trail." In the counterintelligence portion of his training at Olympic Village he was told that most spies, as well as rogue case officers, were caught spending more money than they earned legitimately—Kasandroff had never spent a single Kopek of the allocated funds; every bit had been deposited in his hidden bank accounts.

He could never forget that he had been a rogue case officer for many years, and since he was still a case officer, he must have done most things right—no one had traced his money, except for the Americans. Somehow they found out about his Barclays account.

He had underestimated the Americans; he now knew that they must have at least one good source working for Barclays in the Grand Caymans. He recalled how careful he had been in selecting that bank when, during the middle 1950s, it had been in his area of responsibility; it included Mexico, and all the Caribbean islands. He had tested the bona fides of his forged U.S. passport during his first "inspection trip" of the islands of Barbados, Puerto Rico—where he photographed naval vessels at the American Roosevelt Roads Naval Base—and a wonderful place called the Cayman Islands, specifically Grand Cayman.

Kasandroff discovered that setting up the account was remarkably simple. All he needed for a numbered account, also called a "no name account," was money, a five-digit number and a password. It was a simple procedure, strictly a cash transaction. No one at Barclays cared about him or his story. They did not even ask for any personal identification; their game was making money—"no name" accounts paid no interest.

He had selected Barclays of George Town as the best bank for his retirement fund. Although Barclays had just recently opened its George Town facility, the Barclays Bank itself had been in business since 1837. This fact, and the impressive eagle logo, had inspired Kasandroff s confidence in the bank. The Grand Cayman branch was a dedicated offshore banking centre well regarded in the community with strong connections to local law firms, management and trust companies, as well as key individuals on the Islands. Almost immediately after he had opened his account Kasandroff decided that, years hence, he might become one of those key individuals—living the good life.

The "no name" account added another step in obscuring the money trail from Moscow Centre. With that account he had the almost perfect set-up: one with many trap doors, each one difficult to penetrate. Although the Americans had penetrated his security screen, the money was still safe. Since he now worked for the Americans he hoped the money would continue to multiply. With his other account at Dresdner—this one paid a modest amount of interest—he had another source for his retirement, this one with money from the U.S. Treasury.

CHAPTER 27

MAY 1973
THE LORELEY
KÖNIGSWINTER, GERMANY

Kasandroff met Hans, but just briefly, at their favorite restaurant in König-swinter.   "I told you a while ago I wanted you to see another contact just in case I'm unable to make a Treff," Hans said. He indicated that the tall man at the end of the bar would meet him if Hans were unavailable.

Kasandroff saw a man in his late thirties. He appeared to be very European in dress as well as in his behavior—he was deeply involved in conversation with an elderly German man Kasandroff had seen often, a regular at the bar.

"We'll call him Frank," Reiter continued, "and he can meet you almost any time, especially if you have an emergency."

"So," commented Kasandroff, "he is my lifeboat, just in case?"

"Yes, and he can provide you with security, also a bolthole."

"How do I contact him?"

"One telephone call to my number, and if you are in a hurry he can meet you either here or between here and Frankfurt within an hour or so."

"Sounds okay." Kasandroff leaned back in his chair and smiled, "I thought I'd tell you that Centre has given permission to recruit you."

Reiter laughed. "What took them so long?"

Now Kasandroff laughed. "Procedures, procedures, you know that in this business you can't be too careful; it's all a damned bureaucracy. And, by the way, Centre had lost track of you some time ago and was happy to hear that you have finally seen the light."

He paused. "Oh, I have almost forgotten to tell you. I thought of a counter-intelligence measure that would make our meetings look official— at least in the eyes of my counterintelligence people."

"Colonel, what do you suggest?"

"Well, since this is now a two-way street... I mean our meetings. I thought it would be good cover if you had on your person an envelope stuffed with some-thing that looks classified. Should my security guys check up on me, it would look as if you are supplying me with information—which in most cases is true. However, when I give you an envelope, I thought it would look great if you open it, look into the envelope as if there is money in it, sort of smile, nod and thank me. What do you think?"

"Colonel, I think that would give you a lot of leeway should you be questioned. I think it's a great idea," Hans said, smiling.

Kasandroff leaned back and laughed. "Let this be your instructions from your GRU case officer."

Hans nodded. "So be it. Next meeting I will have the envelope securely tucked in my jacket pocket. But for now, I just wanted to get this recognition procedure over with ... I mean the identification with the bolthole operator. I'll see you in a few months; when it gets warm again in Germany."

Kasandroff laughed. "For the cold German winters I still have my old fur cap made with real fur—badger fur; not that cheap rabbit stuff you get to buy here in Germany."

"You'll be glad to know, that I have one of those myself. I bought it in Berlin a long time ago." Hans left the restaurant, and Kasandroff had another Warsteiner before he returned to his embassy.

CHAPTER 28

A few days after Hans Reiter returned from Germany, Smyth called him at NISC and asked him to "stick around" for a mid-morning meeting at Room 526, because the recently promoted Lieutenant Commander Beringer had some additional information to be passed on to Kasandroff. This time Beringer, in lieu of his usual courier satchel, had only a notebook. He informed Smyth and Reiter that the DNI had found another little tidbit that would enhance Kasandroff's image at GRU headquarters. "Nothing earthshaking," he said, "but there is some information the Soviets already have that can be accredited to Kasandroff's asset."

Looking at Hans, he continued: "It seems that during the early days, after your brother had dreamt up the scheme to make the Soviets believe we were indeed building titanium submarines, one of his OSS comrades known to us as the Wizard, but to the Soviets by his real name, Karl Cedric 'Casey' Miller—this OSS comrade visited the Leningrad State Library, and also Berlin, fully documented as working in support of a U.S. Navy project.

"What the DNI wants to pass on to the Soviets, via Kasandroff, is that U.S. counterintelligence services had identified a German named Wolfgang Schutter at Berlin's Technische Universität, as a Soviet agent who had infiltrated the offices of Ulrich Gabler, the distinguished West German submarine designer—and that Miller, the Wizard, had reportedly seen Herr Wolfgang Schutter copying the design of a submarine rescue sphere."

On the way out of Smyth's office Beringer added, "That ought to finish Herr Wolfgang Schutter's usefulness as a KGB agent. I'll let you know if Herr Wolfgang Schutter pulls a disappearing act."

From Smyth's chemical laboratory Hans selected one of the secret inks and wrote a letter telling his Georgetown University "college friend" studying in Moscow the hot news about Karl Cedric "Casey" Miller, who had been an OSS agent who operated under the cover name the Wizard. Hans also mentioned that U.S. counterintelligence services had placed a German named Wolfgang Schutter at Berlin's Technische Universität, on the KGB/GRU asset list, who had infiltrated the offices of Ulrich Gabler, the distinguished West German submarine designer. Reiter added that the CI information had been passed to West German counterintelligence.

* * * * * *

For several years Smyth and the fellows at Room 526 had attempted, with little success, to recruit members of Soviet trade delegations and others at the Soviet embassy and the Soviet Military Mission on Belmont Road. But, while Hans Reiter was in Germany, Frank Milushkyi, one of Smyth's agents, hit pay dirt.

Milushkyi looked the Russian he was, short and stocky, dark, straight hair framing a swarthy face. He was a first-generation American who spoke almost fluent Russian. His family had been slave laborers in Germany during World War II; they had chosen not to return to the "workers paradise." From a refugee camp in northern Germany they had immigrated to the United States. The U.S. Army had drafted Milushkyi, and after one tour of duty in Korea, and to everyone's surprise, had actually assigned him to a Russian interrogator unit in Army Intelligence. Thereafter, Smyth had hired him to work at Room 526.

On a May afternoon in 1973 Milushkyi had rushed into Smyth's office and told him he had met and talked with a Soviet navy officer, Misha Kovlosky, who worked out of the Soviet Military Mission on Belmont Road. A short, wiry fellow, Kovlosky roamed the Washington area servicing his organization's "mailboxes." These supposedly clandestine letter-drops were already well known to Room 526.

Kovlosky seemed happy in his job that allowed him almost free movement without too much restraint by the Military Mission. He enjoyed eating out in inexpensive local restaurants—and he ate with gusto. His metabolism was the envy of many a CI agent who kept tab of him. Although he ate as if there were no tomorrow, Kovlosky never seemed to gain an ounce.

Milushkyi had approached Kovlosky while they both ate in a hole-in-the-wall restaurant on Kalorama Circle. Kovlosky spoke English with a heavy Russian accent, but Milushkyi got the impression that Kovlosky's outlook seemed to be different from those of the regular members of the Military Mission. Kovlosky told Milushkyi that he was on detached duty at the Military Mission; that he normally served on submarines, and that he had several shore leaves while his boat visited Yugoslavia. He told Milushkyi that he got to know the area around Dubrovnik well and enjoyed listening to the opinions of non-Russians because they had an entirely different outlook on life.

Kovlosky also let Milushkyi know that he knew Milushkyi was part of the surveillance team, and that it did not bother him one bit. He understood that it was Milushkyi job to do what he had to do.

Smyth instructed Milushkyi to have lunch with Kovlosky whenever possible, and to put both bills, his and the Soviet's, on his expense account. Milushkyi needed almost six months to convince Kovlosky to become his informant—his asset. Milushkyi let Kovlosky know that his office was interested in a long-term arrangement, and that a monthly stipend would be deposited in an off-shore bank account to be paid out only upon Kovlosky's retirement—or if he had to escape prematurely. They also agreed on a Treff procedure, using a one-way communication initiated by the asset. The procedure called for the asset to mail a picture postcard of a city, and write a brief personal message such as "just had dinner (meaning 6 p.m.), or lunch (meaning 12 noon) at location (restaurant, museum, etc.)." The picture on the postcard indicated the city; the text indicated the specific Treff time and location. In Kovlosky's case the date was always fourteen days added to the date he had written on the postcard.

Before Kovlosky returned to the Soviet Union and service on his next submarine, Milushkyi arranged for several "dead letter drops," places to exchange information without physical contact between the asset and "the mailman" who serviced the drop. One of the DLDs was in Leningrad, the other one way up north, in Severodvinsk, near the Barents Sea. Embassy personnel serviced the Leningrad drop; Gregory Orloff, an academician serviced the Barents Sea drop.

Gregory Orloff was a trusted and often tried asset, lived and worked in the outskirts of Severodvinsk. Smyth had recruited Orloff a decade ago in Vienna, Austria. At that time Smyth was an Army master sergeant. He worked in Vienna screening Russian Jews leaving the Soviet Union. Their first stop in the Free World was the refugee-screening center in Vienna, where many of these "escapees" from the workers' paradise, changed their minds and decided to immigrate to the United States.

Screening these refugees for foreign intelligence, Master Sergeant Hiram Smyth found himself in an intelligence agent's dreamland. He talked to thousands of the escapees, and interviewed hundreds of engineers and academics. A skilled interrogator, Smyth produced voluminous intelligence reports that headquarters in Washington appraised as "High Value." Aside from people knowledgeable on scientific and technical details, he also found some who knew of a friend who wanted to, but was unable to leave the USSR. Gregory Orloff fell into this category.

Master Sergeant Smyth wrote a "Contact Proposal" regarding "Stay Behinds." His proposal was of such high quality that the G-2 personally detailed Smyth to lead this operation. Thus, Smyth became one of the few enlisted "commanding officers" of an Army Intelligence operation. He and three other enlisted ranks received TDY orders that attached them to the Army attaché in the U.S. Embassy in Moscow. His three enlisted ranks spoke fluent Russians—they were "Lodge Act" products—native Russians who came to the United States in 1950 under that act and served in combat in Korea; earned their U.S. citizenship that

133

way, and became professional soldiers.

Master Sergeant Smyth and his three "other ranks" came to the U.S. embassy with clandestine orders and cover names. Neither the Army attaché nor the ambassador knew the real purpose of this operation. Smyth stayed in the embassy, but his three "other ranks" lived in private apartments that Smyth had rented to accommodate his operation. They disappeared periodically and contacted those named during the Vienna interviews; Orloff was one of those "Stay Behinds."

Smyth's "other ranks" had no difficulty recruiting Orloff; they arranged a contact procedure for whenever Orloff departed for an "S&T" intelligence collection under the cloak of "scientific and technical exchange."

Some eight month after the initial contact Smyth met Orloff at Narita International Airport in Tokyo. Smyth had arrived a few days before the scheduled meeting. He stayed overnight at the apartment of one of his old Army buddies who gave him a grand tour of Tokyo and its transportation system. Smyth rode the bus to Narita International Airport located forty miles outside of Tokyo, an hour's ride from downtown Tokyo, and Smyth found it one of the most modern, most comfortable buses he had ever been on. He arrived about three hours before the scheduled meeting; surveyed the area; checked for quick exits from the restaurant where he was to meet Orloff, and then ate a surprisingly well-prepared, tasty airport dinner.

Since he still had some time to spend, he walked along the gallery that had a commanding view of the entrance to the restaurant. At the agreed time he noticed a slender European carrying a narrow briefcase walking several times past the restaurant. Smyth double- and triple-checked the Orloff photo; it was him—and he seemed to be alone.

For the next five minutes Smyth surveyed the wide expanse of the hall in front of the restaurant watching for "keepers." After he was sure Orloff was alone, Smyth quickly walked down the stairs toward him. As he was within three feet he gave the recognition signal, *"Guten Morgen."* Momentarily Orloff looked as if he had received an electric shock, then he walked, as arranged, into the restaurant—Smyth followed.

The waiter asked in unaccented English, "Table for two?" Smyth nodded, "Yes, and could we have one in the rear of the restaurant?"

"Of course, sir," he replied and guided them to the far corner near a bamboo cove and an artistically arranged waterfall.

Orloff was noticeably nervous. Smyth asked, "You have been careful coming here?"

"Oh, yes, sir. I made sure I was alone before I even mounted the bus to come here. I am sure I was not followed."

"Great. As my friend in Leningrad told you, I would like to meet you periodically in a place of your convenience—outside of Russia."

134

Orloff tilted his head. "And?"

"Well, I am interested in a long-range arrangement that does not endanger you or me. I understand you live in Severodvinsk?" Orloff nodded agreement.

"I'm interested in a message drop in your hometown. We call it a dead letter drop. Based on your recommendation ... eh, some place where you pass almost every day, where you can pass without arousing suspicion. A place public, but also hidden ... maybe a bush or a boulder ... where someone can drop a can or a waterproof box that others will not notice. But, a place that you can approach, bend down, tie your shoelace and pick up the box... that kind of place."

Orloff looked worried. "Is this safe? I mean, the person dropping the can will know the place, right?" Smyth nodded.

"So? Could that entrap me?"

"Yes, it could. Be there no doubt about it. Yes, it is not without danger. But most often not by the one dropping the can, but by someone inadvertently finding the can and reporting it to the KGB."

Orloff looked unconvinced.

"Let me put it this way: the person dropping the message is in as much danger as the one picking it up. I will have only those I trust use the dead letter drop. It will be used infrequently, and you will be notified that the drop has occurred." Smyth described the notification procedure, a place he would have to check every day while in Severodvinsk. Orloff described the area where he lived and the streets he walked on his way to his institute. They finally agreed on a spot near the institute that met all the requirements. Then Smyth made the financial arrangements—Orloff must have thought about this for some time, because he wanted his no-name account in San Jose, the capital of Costa Rica.

"I have been there only once," he remarked, "but fell in love with the people living in the highlands of that country. Let's make it San Jose, okay?"

"Mr. Orloff," Smyth warned, "the banks in Costa Rica are not the best for long-term holdings. There have been a number of scandals ... banking fraud cases. I would suggest as a much safer alternative, and one easier to reach, the Kantonbank in Basel, Switzerland. That is, if you agree."

"I did not know about the bank scandals. All the banks in San Jose looked so prosperous."

"Well, looks are deceiving, especially in our business. We like something long-term that can operate on its own. Swiss banks have this reputation." Orloff agreed.

That was long ago. Now Smyth, as head of the counterintelligence bureau, had too many balls in the air, he could not afford to drop everything at a moment's notice to meet Orloff. Someone else had to take over the DLD service. In 1973 Smyth transferred the handling of Orloff to Hans Reiter. Thereafter, Hans met the academician whenever he attended one of the scientific and technical conferences outside the Soviet Union.

CHAPTER 29

S tarting in September of 1973, Hans Reiter's HUMINT assets, supported by intercepted radio traffic, indicated that Admiral Ivan Petrovitch and Admiral Yegorov would be in Severodvinsk and would spend the night on a rescue ship, not out of "mere curiosity" but to witness an important event. Admiral Serge Georgiyevich Gorshkov, the Admiral of the Fleet of the Soviet Union, along with Admirals Petrovitch and Yegorov, had put their reputations on the line to make this event come true. Now, on a cold morning in late October that year, Rodina—the Motherland of all the Russians, the Union of Soviet Socialist Republics—would take a quantum leap ahead of all the other maritime nations with a titanium submarine, the Golden Fish.

Some months previously, U.S. Naval attaches reported that Admiral Petrovitch bragged to anyone within the inner circle of the Soviet navy that the Golden Fish would make others, especially the Americans, turn green with envy.

During a conversation at one of the U.S. Embassy's Fourth of July parties, a slightly tipsy Soviet admiral told the U.S. Navy attaché that the Americans had practically forced Admiral Gorshkov to build titanium submarines by building their own. "You are sneaky fellows," he babbled. "I have personally seen the blueprints of your titanium submarine." As he wiped the sweat off his brow he added, "You fellows can never fool Rodina. We know everything. We know you are secretly building deep-diving titanium submarines." After slugging down another Scotch, he acknowledged that the Soviet Union had no choice but to build a counter-weapon: the Golden Fish.

Through some "sleight of hand," one U.S. Navy collector had obtained a copy of Admiral Gorshkov's book, *Sea Power of the State*. In this study the admiral asserted that submarine warfare would play an increasingly important role in naval operations. He reasoned that his surface fleet might have difficulty departing their Far Eastern Siberian naval bases, and that in a total war even departure from bases on the Barents Sea would be hazardous. However, he insisted, his submarine force could circumvent any blockade—thus the Soviet submarine force would become the combat bulwark of their navy. The Golden Fish was destined to be a pillar of Rodina's naval strength.

From intercepted signals traffic, and through conversations reported by

Western attaches, Hans learned of arguments within Soviet navy circles for and against building a titanium-hull submarine; of assertions that the high cost of these units would take away funding for other, equally important, projects. He had heard the same debates from U.S. Navy authorities.

From the signals agency Hans received a report of an intercepted telephone conversation between the Soviet CINC Pacific Fleet and naval headquarters Moscow. It seemed to indicate that the Soviet navy had serious fiscal problems. Soviet Fleet Command had to shift additional funds to support the titanium submarine program. An irate Pacific Fleet admiral, requesting release of his already allocated funds, was told that at the present time the Soviet navy had put all its resources into building a highly superior submarine to combat the American titanium threat, and that the Pacific Fleet would have do with what it had—and no more.

The U.S. Navy attaché, Moscow, requested background information from the Pentagon regarding the U.S. Navy's titanium submarine program; no reply was forthcoming. Hans, curious by this attaché message traffic, asked some of the old-timers at the NISC submarine shop whether they had ever heard of such a project.

"Oh, yeah," one of them said. "There was a lot of talk about building titanium subs during the early 1950s, but a few years later all that died down. Nobody knows what happened to it." Others opined that the titanium project had such a high classification that Naval Intelligence did not have "the need to know." One old analyst made a finite assessment regarding the U.S. titanium submarine, "All bullshit."

But Bert, an in-house engineer who at one time had worked for Admiral Rickover, had his own thoughts. "Guys, you don't know Hyman. He works so hard to preserve his little submarine empire. Do you just for one second think he'd risk spending all that money on a few titanium submarines when he can build dozens of his top-of-the-line subs for the same amount? I think not."

One of the foreign aircraft analysts disagreed. "No way, Bert, not Rickover. Remember, every CNO is an Airedale. Airedales don't like submarines. Them titanium ones would cost the CNO a couple of aircraft carriers. He'd never allow that. He'd torpedo the project in a New York minute, because it would threaten his favorite toys."

Hans thought this information might be useful for Smyth to give to Kasandroff.

Aside from that, the NISC people were far more interested in foreign navies than their own, so, for them, all this guesswork was nonproductive.

HUMINT sources reported on the progress, as well as the problems Soviet shipbuilders had encountered building this submarine; electronic intercepts—electronic probing by satellites—confirmed the HUMINT intake; and photo analysts, interpreting the images coming from spy satellites, produced visual evidence supporting the two other disciplines. U.S. and Allied attaches added to that "take." Daring agents even placed electronic "bugs" in foreign embassies; others recruited just plain old-fashioned spies, "insiders" inside Soviet Navy GHQ. NISC analyzed every bit of this information for Soviet capability, feasibility and possibility.

Thus, at least for Hans, it came as no great surprise when NISC received an intelligence report from a clandestine element that reported the time and place of the Golden Fish's trial run. Of course the report did not identify the source of the information, but as a Room 526 "insider," Reiter knew it was Warrant Officer Kovlosky's information; he was now at Soviet Northern Fleet. Kovlosky had deposited the information in the DLD at Severodvinsk just before he reported aboard the trial submarine at Polyarnyy submarine base. Reiter's contact, Gregory Orloff, the academician, mailed the report while he was at a gathering of fellow scientists at Rome, in sunny Italy.

Several weeks earlier Hans had tasked the Top Secret National Reconnaissance Office, the NRO, to give maximum coverage of the Polyarnyy Fjord on Russia's Kola Peninsula. From the last "take" of the satellites, NISC photo analysts had assured Hans that Kapitan Pushkin's boat would depart as scheduled, during the early morning hours, Moscow time, of October 23, 1973.

Kapitan First Rank A.S. Pushkin's name and rank had, for some time, been featured prominently in various HUMINT reports and in intercepted communications traffic. From these "takes" NISC assessed Pushkin to be a highly competent officer, one well liked by everyone in his all-officer and warrant officer crew. Warrant Officer Kovlosky, now aboard the Golden Fish, had reported that the plain-spoken Pushkin, a man of the Taiga, the Siberian plains, had previously commanded a Victor-II Class SSN fast attack submarine, and had made several highly successful runs into the Mediterranean and along the eastern coast of the United States.

Naval Intelligence photo analysts had noted much activity in the quay area at Polyarnyy where the Golden Fish lay securely moored. Initially they had observed many footprints in the snow on the pier; then they noticed that the pier was cleared of snow. Other photos showed naval stores stacked near the boat; in later photographs the stores had disappeared.

The Director of Naval Intelligence decided to have USS Lapsong depart Holy Loch, Scotland, and enter the Barents Sea. Lapsong was a 637-Class nuclear-powered fast attack submarine specially outfitted to conduct acoustic intelligence in the waters off the Siberian coast. With a casehardened sail, she could hide under the icecap and, if necessary, surface by punching through light arctic ice.

In early October, Lapsong transmitted a coded "burst" transmission reporting that she had passed through the Northcape-Spitsbergen Gap into the Barents Sea and would be quietly hovering at 20 meters just off the bottom near the mouth of the Polyarnyy Fjord.

Hans was in his glory. The time had now come to make believers out of all of those who thought the Soviets would never put all their eggs in one basket or, to use the Russian proverb, "Hang all their clothes on a single nail."

CHAPTER 30

OCTOBER 22, 1973
NAVAL INTELLIGENCE SUPPORT CENTER
SUITLAND, MARYLAND

On the 22nd of October, Hans Reiter stayed in the office long after quitting time. The eight-hour time difference between Kola Peninsula and Washington made him work overtime—of course—in the intelligence services there was no such a thing as overtime or compensatory time. Hans slept on his desk in spurts. He checked for incoming messages whenever he awoke.

The 23rd day in October 1973 was the day Reiter would always remember—and remember it twofold. His intelligence assets inside the Soviet Union had informed him that in the early morning hours, at 0700 hours Moscow daylight savings time of that day, Soviet Navy Kapitan First Rank A.S. Pushkin would cast off the lines of Projekt 705, the Soviet Union's most advanced nuclear-powered attack submarine; the one Soviet insiders called Zolotaya Ryba, the "Golden Fish." Signals intercepts indicated that on that day, at that hour, Projekt 705 would start her trial run in the icy waters of the Barents Sea.

A little after two a.m. Eastern Standard Time a message from the National Reconnaissance Office's photo interpretation center read, "ALFA departed pier four, Polyarnyy." It felt great to have predicted the correct departure time. Hans queried NSA, Fort Meade, Maryland, but the signals agency had nothing of interest to report.

He must have napped for a while, because just before four a.m. the buzzer on his computer sounded. Four almost identical messages from NSA and NRO reported high volume of coded signal traffic between Admiral Petrovitch aboard a submarine rescue ship, and naval headquarters in Moscow.

At six a.m. NSA reported that a Norwegian signals station at Kirkenes, near the North Cape, had intercepted a voice communication between the captain of the submarine rescue ship and the commander, Zvezdochka shipyard; it had the shipyard commander saying, "Comrade Ivanov, you are not dumping that fucking hot potato in my yard. Try dumping that bastard way out in the deep waters off Novaya Zemlya, but not in my goddamn yard."

Ten minutes later the commander, Zvezdochka, acknowledged receipt of a coded message from the rescue ship that had a high priority "handle"; NSA believed it came from Admiral Petrovitch.

Hans was in a dilemma. Neither NSA nor NRO could explain the reason for this high priority signals traffic. He wondered how he could explain to the DNI what had transpired. He knew the DNI would call at 0700 hours requesting an update—and he did not have one that would make any sense at all.

Too excited to go back to sleep, he decided to make a pot of coffee and to await further developments. He might have been on his second cup when a transmission via relay from Holy Loch submarine base, appeared on his computer screen:

```
From: USS Lapsong
To: DIRNAVINTEL
Top Secret/Cluster Lord//2433/73//
Subj. Siberian Wolf
Ref. A. Special Tasking DIRNAVINTEL 3521/73
    1. (TS/Cluster Lord) In response to ref. a.
exclusive sonar detection (tapes conclusive).
Target dived to exactly 100 meters.  Target ac-
celerated to forty knots going into her first
turn.  Target came out of first turn having slowed
down to thirty-nine knots.  Target accelerated
again and reached forty-four knots—repeat for-
ty-four knots. Throughout the run target main-
tained her depth at exactly 100 meters.  Tar-
get went into her second turn on the racetrack
course under the service flotilla and came again
on course—accelerating.  Suddenly target shud-
dered and slowed.  All engine noises stopped.
Sonar department's assessment is: catastrophic
engineering failure; estimate reactor failure.
USS Lapsong departed collection area after target
surfaced, and rescue operation had commenced.
    2.  (U) USS Lapsong sends.
    BT
```

Hans leaned back, rubbed his eyes and reread the message. At last, he had something to tell the DNI. He had proof that his original assessment was correct, and that his assets had been right on the money—at least as far as the extraordinary high speed was concerned. He started to laugh wondering what Admiral Rickover and his minions would say when they read USS Lapsong's report.

Punctual as always, the DNI called on the Gray phone, the secure communications link, at exactly 0700 hours and asked for an update. Reiter was sure the DNI had already seen USS Lapsong's report, so he gave him his assessment of the trial run. The DNI, an old submariner, mumbled a few words of agreement that keeping a boat at exactly 100 meters right off the bottom of the Barents Sea at such a high speed could mean that the unit had to be on automatic or computer-assisted navigation.

Finally Hans said, "Admiral, this seems to confirm what my assets had reported years ago. I mean, the 44 knots submerged speed."

The DNI chuckled. "That'll really piss off Hyman and his boys, eh?"

"Yes, Admiral, but Admiral Rickover had also predicted that the mixture of lead and bismuth to archive the reactor's high boiling point to get this speed was risky. And he was right. It seems that it was the reactor, not automation, that caused the interruption of the test."

"Oh, sure, but we'll still have a thoroughly pissed-off fellow at Crystal City." He paused for a moment, and then said, "I think you ought to get to Holy Loch and meet Captain Johnson when he gets there. I don't want anyone ... and you know who I mean ... to contaminate the report. Get a copy of the sonar tape, and a voice tape of the event, and debrief Captain Johnson. Tell Jon Johnson hello for me. He served on one of my boats as a young lieutenant."

"Aye, aye, admiral. I'll go home right after I write my report and get on a plane."

"No, no, forget about the report. Get your ass on the plane, now."

143

CHAPTER 31

Hans Reiter arrived at Holy Loch the next afternoon. His office had passed all the necessary clearances, along with the BOQ reservations. He dropped off his bag at the bachelor officer quarters and reported to the base security officer, who then escorted and introduced Hans to some of the operating crews. He knew a few of the lads from Washington area briefings he had given to tell what information the DNI needed.

USS Lapsong arrived at Holy Loch a few days later. Jon Johnson and Reiter sequestered themselves in what they laughingly called the security officer's "Cone of Silence." Over cups of coffee they shared some gossip. Reiter relayed the DNI's greetings.

Johnson asked, "How is the old man?"

"A real charger, tough as nails," Reiter replied.

"I guess he hasn't changed a bit?"

"Well, I guess not, except he now has almost white hair."

"What? Old Curly has white hair? I hope the job isn't getting to him."

Reiter laughed. "And he ain't 'old curly' either. He has grown a large forehead."

"You're kidding?"

"No. Not on that one. But he does work long hours."

"Okay," Johnson smiled, "let me ask you something else. You know, every time I get one of those hairy missions, the order always starts with 'Collateral intelligence indicates that...' et cetera, et cetera. I have some idea, but what in hell does collateral intelligence really mean?"

"Well," Hans tried to collect his thoughts, "it means that a lot of people report on an item of high interest. Insiders. In this case I mean some of my highly vulnerable folks inside the Soviet apparatus, the Soviet navy. Also intercepted signals, decoded messages, voice communications, and more. You know the old man would never send you on a wild goose chase to prove what comes from a single asset, right? Collateral comes from all sorts of sources, some people call it 'all source.'"

"Yeah, I thought it was something like that, but I just wanted to be sure."

Jon Johnson then reported, in great detail, the submarine surveillance mission.

Hans told him that the sub he had monitored was an all-titanium submarine that cannot be detected by MAD.

Johnson interjected, "Who cares? You can hear that baby coming. She sounds like an express train. I bet the SOSUS boys in Iceland could hear her loud and clear."

Hans then explained that the unit Johnson detected was just the beginning, maybe the prototype of a totally new and revolutionary kind of submarine. "Think of the top speed you recorded."

Johnson looked somewhat chagrined. "You mean there was nothing wrong with my sonar?"

"Not a thing, Jon, my assets told me years ago that Gorshkov's goal was fifty knots submerged."

"Shit, man. You must be kidding. You mean this boat could outrun my torpedoes?"

"Yep. And you reported that she was cruising at that high speed at exactly 100 meters right off the bottom. My assets tell me that means total automation with not a single soul in the engineering spaces; in fact, no one aft of the sail."

"That's lunatic," Johnson exploded.

"No," Hans laughed at his surprise, "that's the future for submarines; small, fast, deep-diving—my guys tell me 3,000 feet."

"Three thousand feet?" Johnson had another one of his explosions. "That's almost three times what we can do, my man. Why hasn't anyone told us about that?"

"Jon, I'm trying, but your buddy Rickover does not believe me, and he convinced Navy that if he can't do it, nobody can, especially not the Russians. The Navy won't let me get the info on the street."

"How sure are you of your stuff?"

"About as sure as I am sitting here talking with you. My assets told me years ago what's coming down the pike, and your reports and your sonar tapes are going to prove me right. Just don't let anyone convince you there's something wrong with your sonar."

"Wait a minute, wait a minute." Johnson gave Reiter a puzzled look. "I got a message from Crystal City requesting recalibration of my sonars. That came right after my 44 knots message. I'm gonna have to watch these guys with a jaundiced eye. But don't worry; my sonar chief is convinced there's nothing wrong with his sensors."

"Well, Jon, I might as well tell you the rest of the story. That boat you tracked ... I am sure ... had a reactor failure. However, if they can fix that they'll have one hell of an attack submarine. With total automation comes a small crew. My assets tell me around sixteen to twenty, all officers and warrant officers. Plus, it has a built-in rescue capsule in the sail that can take care of the whole crew."

Johnson just shook his head. Hans went on to explain that the Soviets had probably copied the rescue system from plans that Doctor Gabler, Germany's submarine builder, had designed.

Johnson gave Hans a copy of all his sonar tapes and the voice tape of the event—the conversation between the sonar chief and Lapsong's control center.

The abridged transcript read:

    1700 hours XX October 1973. USS Lapsong holding at 20 meters off the bottom of the Barents Sea at coordinates XXXXN-XXXXE, fifteen nm north off Polyarnyy Fjord, Kola Peninsula.
    Acoustic reports large contingent of the Soviet fleet.
    Sonar tapes USS Lapsong, # 273-73, #274-73, #275-73.
    Sonar operator transcript:
    Diesels and gas turbines idling.
    Identified racing diesels and cavitating screws of numerous KGB border patrol.
    0800 hours XX October 1973. Senior sonar petty officer notifies captain heavy steam turbine and screw cavitation out of Polyarnyy Fjord in northerly direction.
    Dialogue: senior sonar: "Captain, we have a new sub. Sir, 'waterfall,' a totally new display. She is only doing about six knots, but she sounds as if she is going balls to the wall."
    Captain: "Well, chief, I guess that's why we are here. Good job. Keep it up. Let me know if anything unusual happens."
    (Pause)
    Sonar chief to sonar officer: "Lieutenant, they are getting ready to dive."

Sonar officer: "Sonar to bridge, captain, target commencing dive."

Sonar chief: "Bridge, target going down slowly; now at about 50 meters."

(Pause)

Sonar chief: "She is leveling off at 100 meters, sir, heading north at about ten knots."

(Pause)

Sonar chief: "Ejection noise, sounds as if it came from the sub's signal ejector. Gaining speed. Heavy vibration. Speed now at twenty knots; going on twenty-five. "

(Pause)

Sonar officer: "Something wrong here, chief."

Sonar chief: "I checked second and the third displays. They all recorded thirty knots, then above thirty."

Sonar chief to bridge: "Captain, sonar here, our displays all gone bonkers."

Captain (in sonar shack): "Chief, they can't all have gone wild at the same time. What is it?"

Sonar chief: "Captain, that baby is going as fast as a destroyer."

Sonar officer (in background) "Forty knots."

Sonar chief: "Forty knots going into her first turn. She is banking into a turn at forty knots,
sir!"

Captain: "I see it, but I can't believe it. Christ, I can hear the cavitation without a headset. I think that sucker is actually breaking the sound barrier."

Sonar chief: "She is coming out of the turn. She's slowed down to 39 knots, sir."

Sonar chief: "Sir, she is accelerating again. I have a reading of 44 knots at exactly 100 meters."

(Pause)

Sonar chief: "She is going into her second turn. She is on a racetrack course right under the service flotilla. Coming out of the turn." (Pause)

Sonar chief: "Captain, sounds as if the whole damned engine room conked out. The hissing is probably steam from the secondary loop." (Pause)

Sonar chief: "Captain, sounds to me like a reactor malfunction. I've never heard this before, except on a training tape."

Captain: "Well, just keep the tapes running, so we have something to give to the boys in Suitland." (Pause)

Sonar chief: "Captain, I hear four watertight doors closing. Now, sharp exploding noise, sounds like high-pressure air expelling the ballast water, then flow noises."

Sonar chief: "Captain, I hear the rushing sound of water flowing across the hull."

Sonar chief: "Now, Signal ejector noise. The boat is rising, slight crackling of the hull minutely expanding." (Pause)

Sonar chief: "Captain, she is rising. She is at 50 meters; now at 25 meters. I can hear her; she breached the surface." (Pause)

Sonar chief: "Multiple engine noises. Cruiser, other combatants, submarine rescue ship. Captain, heavy cavitation from KGB patrol boats."

Captain's log: I decided to depart target area immediately to avoid detection. Proceeding on a westerly course out of area. After passing Spitsbergen-Nordkapp line I transmitted SITREP to DIRNAVINTEL.

Hans read Jon Johnson's report, and then had the security section wrap the tapes and the copy of the transcript for transmittal to NISC by Armed Forces Courier Service. He was now fully convinced that his original assessment of the Golden Fish had been correct. He knew that the DNI would concur; he also knew that they would still have to battle the "Rickover Boys." No matter what, those fellows were not about to throw in the towel; at least not until their boss admitted that the Soviets now had a super-submarine; that is, after they have fixed that little flaw of a busted nuclear reactor.

CHAPTER 32

Navy photo interpreters confirmed that Admiral Petrovitch must have convinced the commander of the Zvezdochka shipyard to receive the "fucking hot potato" in his yard. There they first cut off the forward half of the disabled boat, including the sail area, and towed only the aft half to the outer reaches of the Zvezdochka yard, to Yagry Island, to what analysts called the "nuclear dump."

While awaiting the arrival of the courier package Hans made his report to the DNI.

"You have only half a loaf," the DNI said, shaking his head. "Rickover will use this failure to prove his point... that Gorshkov has failed. Hyman is still king."

"But, Admiral, he will have to admit that our assets were right when they told us Gorshkov could make forty-five knots."

"Sure, but he failed, and Rickover will use that argument against us."

"Admiral, we still have an ace in the hole. I'm expecting a note dropped off in the DLD for one of the warrant officers who rode the boat."

The DNI interrupted, "Don't talk riddles, what in hell is that DLD stuff?"

"Sorry, Admiral, dead letter drop. He's one of the guys at Severodvinsk who retrieves the messages left in the DLD by one of the ALFA's crewmembers. I hope he can tell us what really happened. The contact is coming to Stockholm for a long-ago scheduled conference."

"Go for it," was the DNI's reply, but he appeared not all that happy with the outcome of the trial run.

* * * * * *

Hans arrived in Stockholm, "The City between the Bridges," two days before the scheduled meeting with Gregory Orloff, the academician. Room 526 had a safe house in Stockholm only a city block from the Treff area. Olle Thomson, the support agent, the keeper of the safe house, was a semi-retired case officer—a "Minnesota Swede." He made Reiter welcome in Stockholm. To make the stakeout bearable in this cold climate, Thomson volunteered to do the daylight stakeout, watching for Orloff.

The Treff was to be in "Old Town," which the natives called "the city between the bridges." The exact location was the foot of Vasterlanggaten, a long and curving street with many side alleys. It was the best place to avoid surveillance and, with all those narrow alleys, an easy place from which to escape. Time of the Treff was undetermined—opportunity time, it was called, the source's opportunity to leave the hotel undetected. One problem Reiter had not considered: winter in Stockholm is not only frightfully cold, but it also gets dark around four in the afternoon.

Orloff had a hard time getting away from his "keepers." For three nights Reiter waited at the foot of Vasterlanggaten freezing his butt off, and at the same time trying to look inconspicuous—very difficult any time after seven p.m. when he was the only one on that freezing-cold street.

Toward the end of his conference, just before midnight, Orloff slipped out of the hotel; they finally made contact. Orloff had read the note left in the DLD that confirmed that the Golden Fish had suffered a catastrophic failure when the lead-bismuth liquid metal coolant spilled from the reactor containment vessel into the bilge. He also said that aside from that failure, according to Admiral Petrovitch's talk to the crew, the trial run was a great success. The high speed attained, the flawless workings of the computer controlling speed, course, and depth, these were highly encouraging achievements.

"The whole scientific community in Severodvinsk is excited," Orloff reported. "One of my colleagues told me that SDB 143 could fix the problem with ease. All that is needed is to redesign the container vessel, making it at least thirty percent stronger."

Orloff gave Hans Warrant Officer Kovlosky's handwritten notes, then left.

Hans watched as Orloff walked rather carefully along the snow-covered sidewalk, stopping here and there to look into store windows. That was an agreed-upon security screening measure.

Hans and Orloff were the only pedestrians on the street with the exception of the occasional police patrol car. Hans gave a friendly wave to the police because the Swedes, always concerned that one of their inebriated citizens could stumble, fall, and freeze to death, would stop and offer anyone a ride should there be a need.

After watching Orloff enter his hotel, Hans stopped at one of the store windows, made a quick U-turn and checked for surveillance. Seeing none, he then walked hurriedly back into '"the city between the bridges" to his safe house.

Olle Thomson was fully dressed and waiting. "I was getting worried," he announced. "I got dressed and just now got ready to look for you. Everything

151

okay?"

"Yeah, sure, aside from freezing my ass off in that goddamned alley. I have not been this cold in a long time. But the meeting went okay. You can message Hiram that I am coming home."

"Well, that's good to hear. I made some hot chocolate, and I have a quart of high-powered rum to jazz it up—if you like."

Hans smiled, "That's the best offer I had all night." And they both laughed; it released the tension that builds during extended clandestine rendezvous.

CHAPTER 33

H ans Reiter turned Warrant Officer Kovlosky's notes over to the Russian language specialists at Room 526 without expecting Admiral Rickover and his boys to be swayed by their translation. *The DNI was probably right,* he thought. *Admiral Rickover would use the failed trial run as proof there would be no super Soviet submarine in the foreseeable future—if at all.*

Several weeks later Reiter received the translation with a cautionary note: the translators had had some trouble reading some small parts of the asset's hastily handwritten notes. The translation read:

```
October 1973 Polyarnyy
OIC: Kapitan First Rank A. S. Pushkin
Heavy, white mist, temperature minus 25 degree
Centigrade.
     Polyarnyy Fjord deep inside Kola Peninsu-
la
     (Translator note: Soviet Northern Fleet
Area).
     XWG (unknown number of words garbled)
     The whole world shrouded in darkish gray.
     Shore power already disconnected.
     Departure preparation completed.
     We cast off bow/stern lines and follow KGB
boat.
     We follow escort through 15 nm of fjord, no
visibility, XWG (translator note: believe the
word is "white-out.")
     Reach operating area (XWG).
     Observers: Admiral Ivan Petrovitch, CINC
Northern Fleet and Admiral Yegorov aboard subma-
rine rescue ship.
     Kapitan exchange signals with flotilla.
     Receive good wishes, permission to dive to
```

100 meters and proceed on a racetrack course programmed into the on-board computer.

No crew aft.

Reactor compartment, engineering spaces
sealed off.

Diving, gauges show boat slowly approaching
the 100-meter mark.

Eerily, the no hands-on dive planes return to
zero marker.

Depth gauge exactly at 100 meters.

Boat maintains ten knots at 100 meters.
XWG.

Diving officer and engineering officer report
everything on schedule.

Boat gains speed—slowly by computer, then
faster, twenty knots, twenty-five knots, thirty
knots, forty knots.

Engineer, "Forty-three knots going into first
turn."

Boat reaches forty-four knots. Depth gauge
exactly 100 meters.

Boat makes second turn of racetrack under
service flotilla.

Returns on course.

Heavy vibrations, boat shudders and slows.
Kapitan Pushkin orders crew into rescue
sphere.

Engineer shuts compartments, pulls emergency
blow lever.

Kapitan hits emergency signal ejector button.

Boat rises to 50 meters, then breaches surface. Crew transfers to rescue boats.

Nuclear team checks aftership with detection instruments—Geiger counters ticking wild.
Severodvinsk boat towed away.

Hans knew the DNI would appreciate reading Kovlosky's notes, but only as
background information. Reiter could not leave the translation in the DNI's office, because this type of HUMINT information could compromise the source; it
narrowed the list of informants to the few men aboard the Golden Fish.

The DNI remarked, "This has been a long time coming, I mean this revolutionary submarine. Wasn't Ivan Petrovitch originally scheduled to command this boat?"

"Yes, Admiral, I believe he was."

"I bet it was not mere curiosity that made the admirals spend the night on the rescue ship."

Hans knew the DNI had a mind like a steel trap. He relished dragging up data that most others had forgotten.

"I think," the DNI continued, "all of them, Serge Georgiyevich Gorshkov, Ivan Petrovitch and Vladimir Yegorov had put their reputations on the line to make this event come true."

He rose and went over to one of his bookshelves. He pulled out a grayish, soft-cover booklet. Reiter knew it was Admiral Gorshkov's Sea Power of the State that Gorshkov, as Admiral of the Fleet of the Soviet Union, had written for his command, outlining the course of the future Soviet navy. The DNI held up his dog-eared copy, "Right in here," he pointed at a page, "Gorshkov promised to turn his coastal navy into a blue water one, and, by God he has." He closed the booklet and smiled, "It's your job to make a believer out of the Rickovers of this world."

"Aye, aye, Admiral," Reiter replied. "I think we're well on the way. My academician assured me that SDB 143 is redesigning the container vessel, making it at least thirty percent stronger, to do the job. The next unit, I am sure, will not have a reactor failure."

"Well," the DNI grumbled, "We'll just have to wait for the next trial run."

CHAPTER 34

A postcard with the photo of Berlin's Kaiser Wilhelm Gedächtniskirche confirmed that the arrangement for the next Treff with Kasandroff was on track. This time Hans Reiter requested NISC to grant him leave to visit a close relative in Istrup, a village in northern Germany. He actually stopped by for a day in this quaint little place and took a series of photos—just in case—then he flew from Hanover to Berlin.

Whenever Hans landed in Berlin, he could not shake the feeling that someone was watching. Paranoia? Maybe, but Berlin in 1975 was a far cry from the dangerous Cold War days. Now the infamous Berlin Wall actually lent a certain safety factor to U.S. agents working in that city. During the early Cold War days, Soviets and the East German surrogates roamed West Berlin. For them, as well as for West and East Berliners, access was easy. Even the subway—the U-Bahn— and the elevated trains—the S-Bahn—crossed through both parts of Berlin. Only West Berlin transit buses did not.

It was in those days, that is, in 1955, that an "unpleasantness" had occurred that partly justified Hans's feeling of unease. At that time the streets of Berlin were indeed dangerous, at least for U.S. intelligence agents. According to U.S. Army clandestine assets, the STASI had offered $10,000 in gold for any U.S. agent delivered to East Berlin. In the mid-1950s that was a whole lot of money for any German—East or West.

By far the most dangerous ride was by taxi. When traveling from Hans's normal operation base in Charlottenburg to Tempelhof airport, the taxi passed one city block away from Potsdamer Platz and East Berlin territory. Potsdamer Platz jutted out into West Berlin territory and the main road to Tempelhof air base passed it only one wide-open block away. Hans preferred riding the city bus along that stretch, but when he had to catch the early morning courier flight he had to use the Berlin taxi service.

Thus, he checked the taxi route to Tempelhof very carefully. He always had his .38 caliber Colt in his coat pocket ready to use should the driver make an unscheduled left turn on the road leading past Potsdamer Platz— East Berlin. Long ago he had promised himself never to be captured by the Red Army or her surrogates. Mentally, as well as physically, Reiter was well prepared, and in ex-

156

tremis he would shoot the driver in the head and roll out of the rolling taxi before it reached East Berlin. Quick action was necessary.

On one particular morning, Hans, late leaving the Pension, had to hail a taxi to make it to Tempelhof and the U.S. Air Force courier flight. He did it the usual way: hailing a cruising taxi just as he was taught, not one waiting at the street corner. He had the .38 caliber colt in his trench coat pocket and carried just a small travel bag—one the Brit who sold it to him called a "grip."

The taxi driver appeared to be friendly—talked a blue streak. Eventually his chatter became just a bit too much, and Hans grew increasingly uneasy. He did not know that in a split second on that nasty cold-wet early morning in February 1955 the .38 caliber Colt and the six copper-coated rounds of ball ammunition stood between him and a Communist East German dungeon—or worse. Hans had been trained to expect danger, and to react to it in the most violent way. But he also knew that taxi drivers routinely took the shortest routes to Tempelhof Airbase. The shortest way between Berlin-Charlottenburg and Tempelhof led past East Berlin's Potsdamer Platz.

Already a bit leery, he watched the taxi driver closely as he entered Schöne-berger Ufer, a shortcut from Charlottenburg to Tempelhof. The street led one city block from East Berlin's Potsdamer Platz. Riding along this section of roadway was always an adrenaline-pumping event. Reiter knew that if the driver made a sudden left turn at Potsdamer Platz he planned to collect his $10,000 "in gold."

The taxi driver still talked a mile a minute.

Strange, Hans thought, *why is that guy so nervous?*

The entrance to Potsdamer Platz came up at his left. Suddenly the taxi driver pulled hard to the left turn.

Hans screamed, "Halt, halt."

The driver glanced around quickly; he sneered.

By the time Hans had managed to clear the .38 from the trench coat pocket they had already crossed the Landwehr Kanal and were two city blocks from the East German checkpoint. Instinctively, as trained, he fired two shots. The first seemed to graze the driver's head; he dropped out of sight, the second shot hit the non-safety-glass windshield; it shattered. With the driver seemingly incapacitated, the taxi slowed down.

Clutching the grip in one hand and his .38 in the other, Hans somehow managed to open the door and to roll out of the still-moving taxi, hit the ground hard, rolling, flipping on the roadway and finally coming to a skidding halt. The impact with the hard surface had loosened the hold on the revolver and it slid across the sidewalk, stopping just short of the grass-covered area beyond. The taxi rolled toward the East German checkpoint. Just a hundred yards or so short of it—still in West Berlin territory—the taxi lightly bumped into a Litfassäule, an old concrete advertising pillar and stopped.

All was quiet.

Hans looked toward the East German checkpoint. Two VOPOs stood at their posts with raised PPSh, their Soviet-made submachine-guns, frozen, seemingly uncertain as to what was happening. Hans glanced toward Schöneberger Ufer; there was no one there either to witness the event or come to his assistance. He recovered the revolver and the grip, and then ran, limping and zigzagging, toward Schöneberger Ufer, expecting shortly a burst of East German submachinegun fire. Still clutching his gear he made it, breathing heavily, his right hand and right leg throbbing, into the West Berlin street. There, he took cover leaning against the wall of one of the leftover World War II ruins. After a few seconds, maybe a minute, he realized that he was still clutching the .38. Quickly he shoved it into the pocket of his trench coat and forced himself to think rationally once again.

He had incapacitated—maybe worse—that taxi driver. But no one except the two East German VOPOs had observed the incident. No crowds assembled, no police, no ambulances converged, no sirens wailed.

Nothing.

All was quiet except for the occasional truck or car rumbling past Hans on Schöneberger Ufer. Finally he rose, still in pain, and managed, just barely, to stand erect. He brushed the dirt from the coat; there was a rip in the right sleeve. His right arm must have hit the dirty road first; that's how he had lost the grip on his .38. He looked around. Seeing nothing that indicated commotion, he decided to walk, slowly at first, along Schöneberger Ufer toward Tempelhof.

His initial goal was to get out of the immediate area as quickly as possible; he also wanted to ease, or at least get used to, the shooting pains in his right arm and leg. Finally, he reached the environmental cover of a bus stop and checked the posted bus route list; Tempelhof was on the scheduled bus run. He remembered having bought a weekly bus fare ticket the previous day. With the still throbbing hand he carefully pulled it from his wallet—and waited.

The sun started peeking through the clouds. To his right a few sparrows fought on the sidewalk for a morsel. A seagull—it must have gotten lost from the Wannsee—joined the fight for the crumb, and won. A slight breeze bent the grasses on the strip between the sidewalk and the street. Far to the west he heard the sounds of a vibrant city.

Hans looked around. He was alive. *Damn it*, he thought, *life is good.*

The screeching brakes of the bus brought him back to reality. The sign blinking brightly above the driver announced "Tempelhof." Reiter entered, the driver greeted him with a friendly "Good morning," and the nearly empty bus roared on its way.

He arrived just in time to board the C-47 transport for Frankfurt-on-

Main.

* * *

Now, once again Hans walked along Kurfürstendamm. The city had changed much. Every building in this large city had been rebuilt, newly built—all much improved, except the Kaiser Wilhelm Gedächtniskirche, the only visibly large ruin on the Ku'damm. Kasandroff and Hans had arranged to meet in Cafe Einstein, an elegant Viennese-style coffee house on Kurfürstenstrasse. Hans waited about a half a block from the Cafe for Kasandroff to enter. He wanted to make a detailed security sweep to be certain that Kasandroff had not picked up any "keepers."

When Reiter joined Kasandroff at his table, the first thing he asked was, "You made sure I had no tail?"

"Yes."

"Good. I was very careful. I walked through the Kaufhof and watched. I mean, we are both experts in this business, right?"

"Well, we can never be too careful, but we do have double cover, since your guys believe I am your asset."

Kasandroff agreed. It was in both their interests to keep this operation going as long as possible.

Kasandroff placed a copy of the *Berliner Kurier*, a thick local newspaper, on the table. They ordered cafe royal and Kirschtorte mit Schlag, a cherry tart covered with a mountain of whipped cream. Kasandroff motioned toward the newspaper. "Got you some reading material. I think you will like it." He also mentioned that among the "reading material" was a note that had a number of questions, one concerning the status of the U.S. titanium submarine program.

"What is all that with the titanium submarine?" Hans asked.

Kasandroff replied, "I don't know anything about submarines, but this seems to be a high priority collection—from high up at Navy—been so for years, ever since I delivered the plans for the U.S. Navy titanium submarine. We are constantly tasked for information on it. It could help me a lot to report on that."

"Okay, give me a few days. I'll see what I can find out. My boss has fantastic contacts."

Hans opened the Berliner Kurier as if to read it. Some pages were glued together, but on page three Kasandroff had glued a list of his requirements.

Hans perused the list. "Okay, this one here I know, the reorganization of Defense Intelligence Agency. How much detail do you need?"

"For the time being just the organization chart. I may get more requests later."

"Tell you what. I'll send you the chart and the information on the submarine to your DLD."

Kasandroff, the good intelligence officer, came prepared. He gave Reiter a file card with a post office box address in Königswinter. "This is a new one. Better for security."

Kasandroff paused. "Now, what can I do for you?"

"Nothing right now, but thanks for asking."

But then Reiter remembered that the DNI was always asking about Soviet navy collection requirements. He thought it would not only make the DNI happy, it would also be better if there were a standing quid pro quo on the table.

"Tell you what," he said, "Bring us the ten top collection requirements on Navy collections that GRU has. What does Admiral Gorshkov want to know about the U.S. Navy—besides the titanium stuff?"

A little later Hans left the cozy atmosphere of Cafe Einstein and emerged into a cool, misty Berlin.

CHAPTER 35

DECEMBER 1975
ROOM 526
WISCONSIN AVENUE, NW
WASHINGTON, D.C.

A few weeks before Christmas of 1975, Hans Reiter received Kasandroff s first long-distance request for information. It had the appearance of a letter, handwritten, supposedly from one of Reiter's college classmates visiting the Soviet Union on a studies project. The return address read: John McAnerary, Graduate Student, c/o Moscow University, PO Box 1347, Moscow, USSR. Actually, all the other addresses Kasandroff would use in Moscow were GRU dead letter drops.

From the letter Hans learned that Kasandroff was at GRU Centre for a three-year tour of duty. Kasandroff had told Hans at their last meeting that from old secret writing technology, Centre had developed a typewriter ribbon saturated with silver nitrate that they now used to write secret messages between the lines of handwritten letters.

Anticipating Kasandroff s request for information, Smyth had a virtual chemical laboratory on one of his office shelves; among the chemicals were sulfur ammonium, iron-chloride, hydrochloric acid and copper nitrate. A star in the upper corner of Kasandroff s letter, after the date, indicated that it would react to a developer of sulfur water concentrate.

When the letter was developed the secret writing appeared in easy readable black.

Centre wanted to know the status of the U.S. Navy titanium submarine.

"Christ," complained Smyth, "won't they ever quit asking about that stupid submarine?" He scratched his head. "I'm gonna run over to talk to the director of the IC Staff just to make sure we're on the right track. He paused for just a moment. "I think, if we had been building that titanium sub, by now the goddamned thing would be in the water; it would be big news in industrial circles as well as written up all over those Navy publications."

With much solid intelligence available on the Soviet Navy's building titanium submarines, Smyth and Reiter tried to convince Lieutenant Commander Beringer, and via him the DNI, that the time had arrived to inform Colonel Kasandroff of "the U.S. Navy's failure building titanium submarines," and thus converting Kasandroff into a straight GRU source. Their efforts fell on deaf ears. But Smyth, being Smyth, took the bull by the horns and went directly to an old friend in the Intelligence Community Staff.

The following morning Smyth called Hans into his office. "Well, I talked to the IC Staff boss. He was scratching his ass when I asked him about the sub. He called the DNI, and they concocted a story that we'll feed Centre. Beringer will come over tomorrow to give us the text. I hope it'll look real, and, who knows, it may be real."

Beringer arrived at Room 526 early the next morning. After the usual cup of coffee in Smyth's office he said with a grin, "Well, finally, someone convinced the boss to quit this titanium feeding of the Soviets. I was afraid that we dragged this out too long. But here's what the IC Staff and the boss have concocted. I think it will do the job."

He handed Smyth a typewritten page.

"Finally," Smyth said. "I was afraid we might have encountered a problem by stretching it out too long. Kasandroff is far too valuable an asset to lose because we fucked it up. He will keep reporting what's going on at Centre, and that's of real value for days to come."

"Oh, by the way, that Karl Cedric Miller of MIT thing?" Beringer said. "All I could get out of the DNI was, 'Oh, the Wizard.' Then he clammed up. Don't know what in hell that means."

"He is cagey all right, but we know who he is. Hans remembers him from Frankfurt," shrugged Smyth.

Hans spent the next hour copying the information. He had two handwritten pages. He reread his handiwork:

Queried numerous U.S. Navy employees.

Was able to ascertain the following regarding your request:

U.S. Navy has developed conceptual design of titanium submarine, including studies of operational advantages and disadvantageous.

Big conflict among Navy brass.

Chief of Naval Operations denied request to start construction because cost would impact on aircraft carrier construction.

Admiral Rickover sided with CNO because the cost of titanium submarines would impact on the number of submarines he would have in the fleet.

Some Navy officials are still pushing to have titanium submarine built—citing the many advantages of titanium vs. HY-80 hulls.

To understand the complex structure: CNO is always an aircraft carrier pilot. No submariner in line for CNO. Surface navy dominates rank and file of Navy. Navy planners agree that titanium submarine has many advantages over HY-80 hull, but cannot get financial backing for titanium.

Struggle is between Pentagon/White House advisors and Navy leadership.

The Navy has sufficient titanium sponge in strategic reserve, but not ear-marked for submarine construction.

Will notify you if there is change in priorities.

Hans typed a letter telling his "college friend" studying in Moscow the latest news coming out of Georgetown University—he used much from the last university newsletter—along with some personal items about the growth and the terrible traffic in northern Virginia. Between the typewritten lines, he laboriously copied the DNI's handout using an old-fashioned pen and the silver nitrate solution. He sealed the envelope an addressed it to "John McAnerary."

He mailed the letter to Kasandroff s new DLD.

On a late afternoon in March 1976 Smyth called Hans into his office. He looked sad. Without a word he handed Reiter a message; it was from their mutual friend, Reiter's former boss, Jack Heissinger in Frankfurt. Fred Hertzwald, Reiter's old mentor, had passed into the great beyond. The former special agent, known to those on the other side as Herr Doktor Hermann, had died of natural causes in Frankfurt-on-Main, Germany, the hometown that had once tried to deny him his very existence. In his last will and testament Manfred Hertzwald had requested to be buried in America, his adopted country, the land that had accepted him as an orphan, the land for which he had fought in battle to free the other land, the one in which he was born. He wanted to rest in the land he had served for many years as a secret agent. The wounds he had incurred during that war had earned him a place in the hallowed grounds, where other warriors already assigned to their Final Posts would surround him.

Hans stood wrapped in his well-worn trench coat on a slight knoll above a field of white grave markers. For him it was a familiar place. He had been here many years ago as a young soldier. This time he came to pay his last respects to his mentor of bygone days who had received his final assignment: to be laid to rest at Arlington National Cemetery in the grave where he had buried his wife a decade earlier. Hans was the sole mourner attending the burial. He stood lost in thought in the slight drizzle of a March morning. He remembered the good and the bad days he and Fred had shared during the times when the Cold War was dangerously close to becoming a hot one.

Hans remembered some of the best advice Fred had ever given him, his young protégé, "In this business," he had told Hans, "you have to develop a feel, a nose for danger." He also thought of Fred's old saying, "It's a small world".

The sharp report of the first of three rifle volleys shocked Hans back to reality. There followed the haunting notes of "Taps" as the team from the First

Platoon, 1st Battalion of the 3rd U.S. Army Infantry Regiment, lowered the secret agent's casket into the earth. Hans stood with tears flowing over his cheeks as the burial team folded the flag that had covered the casket, as a member of the team handed the folded flag to its lone mourner.

So, Hans thought as the burial team marched back up the hill to Fort Myer, *at last he is at peace, resting in the land he had loved.* Hans needed time for reflection. It had been so many years since he walked through this cemetery. He stood among the endless rows of identical white headstones that marked the graves of warriors. There were more than 16,000 Union soldiers who had died during the War Between the States; there were the remains of 2,111 unknowns from that war. A total of over 200,000 soldiers lay buried here, and Hans wondered whether there would be room left for him in the 612 acres of this home of the brave when his time came.

Smyth had told him to take the day off and just meditate. He walked up to the old chapel just outside the cemetery gates and stood looking at the parade ground on which he had so often "passed in review" eons ago. He turned and walked into the chapel, sat down in one of the pews and just thought about life and death.

For some time he sat in the coolness of the chapel. Then a voice startled him, "Sir, may I be of assistance?" Hans looked up into the face of a young corporal. "No, thank you," he replied, "I have just buried an old friend and I thought about him and all that had gone by."

"I understand, sir," the corporal said. "If you need anything ... I'll be waiting outside."

The young man turned, and a little later Reiter rose from the bench and followed him. The sky had cleared, the sun peeked through the clouds and the world seemed all well again. He thanked the corporal for his thoughtfulness, and then walked back to his car in the parking lot.

Back at the office, Smyth gave him a questioning look. "It's okay," Hans said. "Fred is in the place of honor he deserves, and I am fine."

Smyth poured two cups of coffee, and they went into his office.

164

CHAPTER 36

Some months earlier, Smyth had received clearance from the IC Staff for the Army clandestine service headquarters in Frankfurt/Main to transfer one of their assets, Heinz Schwertfeger, to Room 526. Since the asset had once, long ago, worked for him, Hans Reiter would negotiate the transfer.

Hans Reiter knew that the Army guys would not look kindly at "the big shots in Washington" interfering with their operation—during the Cold War days, he had been in their boat several times when CIA demanded some of his difficultly recruited assets.

Shortly after he landed at Rhine-Main International, he rented a Mercedes 220 and drove out of the airport toward the Kassel Autobahn. He wanted to make a nostalgic visit to the former Army intelligence base he knew as Camp King, Oberursel, on the second to the last streetcar stop north of Frankfurt. He left the Autobahn at the Eschbach-to-Bad Homburg exit and turned west driving on a quiet country lane to Oberursel. Everything had changed since he was there in the early 1960s— he nearly missed the actual site where Camp King had once been.

Disappointed, he made a U-turn and headed toward Frankfurt and the I.G. Farben Hochhaus. The folks on the sixth floor were not exactly happy to see him, one especially, Dieter Steinmaier, Schwertfeger's case officer. After all, Hans had come to "steal" one of his assets.

Hans wanted to be in the good graces of this unit and apologized for the inconvenience he was causing. He mentioned that, long ago, while most of the guys were still in kindergarten, he had worked out of this very office, and knew exactly how they felt, because it happened to him a few times.

"You know," Hans sympathized, "it seemed that whenever I had recruited a fairly decent source, some guy from CIA would come up here and take him away—really pissed me off. They always claimed my source was of strategic intelligence interest—total bullshit."

He went with a few of the agents downstairs to the cafeteria for coffee and doughnuts and talked about the situation since the Berlin Wall went up, and the difficulties they encountered infiltrating and exfiltrating agents because of it. Once they were back upstairs in their secure offices, he told them a few war stories from the old days, and how dangerous it was at that time for U.S. agents operating in Berlin.

"I don't know about you," Hans said, "but I have been to Berlin a few times recently, and I feel a lot safer now than in the early Cold War days. I mean, in those days you never knew when some East or West German shithead wanted to make it big and collect a bounty. Even today $10,000 is a hell of a lot of money, and in those days it was a fortune for any German, not just an East German."

Steinmaier looked at him questioningly. "When the boss heard that you were coming to Frankfurt, he mentioned that rumor had it you were the one who knocked off the taxi driver who tried to deliver you to the Soviets."

Chagrined, Hans tried to dismiss it with, "Well, there are always rumors flying around."

"Well, yeah, but your example—if it was you—is taught at the spook school as one of quick reaction and survival."

Hans laughed. "Well, survival, yes, but that bastard taxi driver bought the farm."

With that castaway remark they seemed to be getting on the same track.

However, orders are orders and G-2 in the Pentagon had ordered the Army intelligence unit in the I.G. Farben Hochhaus to contact Schwertfeger and negotiate a turnover to the "special Washington unit."

Hans told Steinmaier that he once knew Schwertfeger, that he had inherited Schwertfeger from Herr Doktor Hermann for a special operation's job; that it was one of those crummy jobs without a single payoff; and that, after a few years of fruitless collection attempts, he had returned Schwertfeger to Doktor Hermann.

Since it had been impossible to meet in Berlin, Steinmaier had arranged for Heinz Schwertfeger and Lieselotte, "Liesschen," his wife, to vacation in Czechoslovakia. Steinmaier said, "They can get into Czechoslovakia, and from there, into Austria, without too much trouble. I always take along a few bottles of Scotch. Schwertfeger can give them to the Czech border guards when he goes back. They all think it's a black-market deal. That's what makes the world go 'round."

Schwertfeger had agreed to drive his Trabant, an offspring of the pre-World War 2 DKW—a mini-car still produced in West Germany. The Trabant was Heinz Schwertfeger's "dream car." The Schwertfegers had made reservations at a hotel in Ceske Budejovice, some miles north of the Austrian town of Freistadt, the Treff location.

* * *

Steinmaier had arranged for the recognition meeting in Freistadt on the city's main square in front of the Rathaus—the city hall.

Thus, on a misty day in late March, Hans and Steinmaier "toured" Freistadt, Austria. They had driven the previous day from Frankfurt to Linz, on the Danube River. It would have been more comfortable to fly from Frankfurt to Linz, but because of the closeness of the Czech border they thought it best to be heavily armed. In 1976, because the Bader-Mainhof Gang and other terrorist cells in Central Europe were raising hell, German airline security restricted armed air travel to law enforcement personnel.

They overnighted in Linz and arrived in Freistadt at midmorning. Freistadt, a charming medieval town, was watched over by the Alte Burg, the Old Castle. The town was still surrounded by a green space, the Stadtgraben, the original moat before the city wall. They parked the car behind the Stadtpfarrkirche, a church adjacent to the city square, and made themselves comfortable at a sidewalk cafe from which they had a commanding view of city hall and the square. Reading the local newspaper, still fastened in the old-fashioned way on a wooden rod, courtesy of the cafe, and sipping their coffees, Hans and Steinmaier conversed in German, commenting on the beauty of this idyllic place, the weather, and politics. Others around them, all seemingly locals—they seemed to know each other—were also conversing between reading their newspapers.

A little before noon Steinmaier motioned to a Trabant entering the city square. Everyone seemed to know it was an East German car—it rattled, it coughed, and trailed a plume of smoke worse than any diesel truck.

Steinmaier called over the waiter and paid the bill. The two agents then walked toward the Stadtpfarrkirche and their car. The Trabant apparently took this as a signal to follow. When Heinz Schwertfeger exited the Trabant he smiled; he had already spotted Reiter. They had not seen each other for more than ten years. While his wife climbed out of their car, Schwertfeger walked toward Hans with outreached hands.

"Herr Trenker," he managed to gasp, "Not in my wildest dreams would I have ever expected to see you again." He introduced Hans to his wife, Liesschen. They all decided to stretch their legs a bit before eating lunch. Schwertfeger and Hans walked toward the Stadtgraben, Steinmaier and Liesschen followed. Schwertfeger wanted to know what Reiter had been doing and whatever had happened to Herr Doktor Hermann.

Hans told Schwertfeger that the Herr Doktor had died just recently, and that he himself was now in a new organization that was mainly concerned with protecting endangered East German informants.

He thought that this was the right time to broach the topic of converting Schwertfeger from a railroad watcher, who reported on Soviet troop and equip-

167

ment movements from and to Germany, to that of a bolt-hole operator.

Schwertfeger wanted to know what that would entail, and Hans told him that only highly trusted agents in extremis were told to go to a certain location where they would be met be a trusted person—no names—to get temporary asylum. Then he told him that Schwertfeger's wife should be totally briefed into this operation, because she would become the "keeper" of the asylum-seeker.

"Not to worry about Liesschen," the German replied. "She knows all about my activities and has watched trains for me while I was at work."

"Yes, Herr Schwertfeger," Hans said, "but this is a little different than just watching and reporting. This means hiding a person."

Schwertfeger thought about this a while and then said, "Look, let me talk to her. See what she thinks about this."

They changed places, with Liesschen and her husband walking in front, and Steinmaier and Reiter following.

The mist had lifted and walking in the shade of trees along the Stadtgraben was invigorating. The Schwertfegers debated for some time.

Finally, they stopped and Liesschen told Hans that if only highly trusted agents would be allowed to find a secure place, she felt obliged to grant them safe haven. Hans warned her that there always was the possibility that the asylum seeker had been tailed by the STASI.

Liesschen Schwertfeger's reply was, "Mister Trenker, life is a gamble. Sometimes you win, sometimes you lose but if the odds are in your favor, you win more often than you lose."

Reiter agreed. He thought, *This is one short speech I must remember; keep for future references.*

After a wonderful lunch, Steinmaier excused himself. "While you all conduct your business, I'll enjoy another walk through town. I don't very often get a chance to be just a tourist on Uncle Sam's dollar."

Hans appreciated his thoughtfulness. Then he and Schwertfeger arranged the details, the must-do's and the absolutely must-not-do's—all associated with the security of the bolthole and its operators. He also reminded Schwertfeger of his no-name account in Liechtenstein, and that his organization would pay a monthly stipend into this account.

Just then they spotted Steinmaier coming into the city square. Reiter waved him to come over.

"All squared away?" Steinmaier inquired.

"Everything," Hans replied, "except for the Scotch you have in the car. I think Herr Schwertfeger can be generous, and the border guards will love him."

Steinmaier laughed. Together they walked to the Stadtpfarrkirche parking lot and, after a long goodbye, the Trabant departed in a cloud of oily smoke.

* * * * * *

Back in Washington, Hans reported the details of their newly established bolthole to Smyth, who was overjoyed. "Hank," he said, "I haven't told you, but this is only our first Bolthole in all of East Germany. Good job."

Reiter suggested that during his next attendance of the Staff meeting Smyth ought to have the director send a letter of commendation to the unit, along with a special letter of appreciation for Special Agent Dieter Steinmaier.

"Hiram, you know how it is when another, a higher office, takes away one of your sources. It always pissed me off when some of those green case officers from CIA did that to me, and those bastards never even said 'thank you.' I gotta say that your buddy Jack fought them tooth and nail."

"Yeah," Smyth chimed in, "and he usually lost."

A few days after this conversation, Smyth had completed all the details arranging the deposits in Heinz Schwertfeger's no-name account at the Zentral-Bank in the Principality of Liechtenstein. Smyth directed Hans to make the initial cash payment into this account during his next European venture. Later payments would be made by a "proprietary," a shadow business Smyth had established long ago in West Berlin.

CHAPTER 37

In early 1977 the DNI had found it proper to promote Hans to GS-13 and transfer him to Commander, Task Force 168, as HUMINT operations coordinator. The task force had sub-elements in Munich, Germany, the Panama Canal Zone, and Yokosuka, Japan.

A few months earlier, Frank Milushkyi's asset, Soviet Navy Warrant Officer Misha Kovlosky, reported that he had received orders to report for duty to the Soviet embassy in Tokyo. To keep Milushkyi in close contact with Kovlosky, Smyth wanted to send him on an extended TDY to Japan. The director of the IC Staff suggested Milushkyi be assigned to the U.S. Embassy in Tokyo, but Hiram Smyth wanted him to be less observable. After several months of debate between IC Staff, Navy and Smyth, Hans suggested that Milushkyi be attached to U.S. Navy Station, Yokosuka, where Task Force 168 had a sub-element where, as Hans told Smyth, Milushkyi could easily become a non-person.

Hans's suggestion was accepted, and Milushkyi went to Yokosuka.

Milushkyi met with Kovlosky periodically. Through Kovlosky the folks in Room 526 gained considerable "grass roots" insight not only into the Soviet submarine force, but also into collection activity of the Soviet embassy in Japan.

In June 1977 the night duty agent at Room 526 received a very brief telephone call—later traced to a pay telephone in Helsinki, Finland. The tape-recorded message was, "This is Iron Horse, I repeat, this is Iron Horse. If you have anyone working in the Soviet embassy in Tokyo, get him out fast. I think he has been compromised."

The response was immediate.

The message was relayed to Milushkyi, who gave Kovlosky the emergency signal that he was in danger—and Smyth informed Hans that the DNI was sending him to Japan, leaving that very afternoon, to assist Milushkyi in exfiltrating Kovlosky to bring him to the U.S.

Officially, this was to be an inspection tour to the TF 168 detachment at Yokosuka Naval Station.

Japan was new territory for Hans. Yokosuka, a former Imperial Navy base, is located on the southern tip of Tokyo Bay. The information package Hans received described Yokosuka as a place "ideally located in close proximity to the cosmopolitan Yokohama/Tokyo area as well as many colorful historical sites for shopping and touring pleasures." Yokosuka was also the largest (280 acres) U.S. Naval Shore Facility in the Far East. Yokosuka had a historical association with the U.S. Navy. Japan saw its first American Naval officer when Commodore Perry arrived there in 1853.

As soon as Reiter arrived he met with Milushkyi at his—Reiter's—hotel, which was near the main gate of the base.

Milushkyi had arranged a Treff with Kovlosky near the Great Buddha in the Holy City of Kamakura.

Japan fascinated Hans. It was indeed a land of immense scenic beauty. Riding the train to Kamakura was an adventure in itself. It was the greenness and the mountains that most surprised him. He had not realized that Japan was a land of many mountains; he always thought that Mount Fuji was Japan's only mountain. It was the only one he ever saw in travel brochures.

Shortly after the train departed Yokosuka it entered the first tunnel. Emerging from the tunnel, the train entered a lush green valley with several waterfalls, then another tunnel and another valley, and another tunnel, until it finally arrived in Kamakura.

Hans and Milushkyi searched for Kovlosky in the area around the Great Buddha—unsuccessfully. Milushkyi suggested, "Mr. K is probably watching to see if anyone has followed us. Let's just act like tourists, take a few photos and maybe burn a couple of incense sticks for good luck."

Since this was Hans's first time in Japan he had come well equipped with camera gear. He followed Milushkyi's suggestion. He had taken some twenty shots of the Buddha and the surrounding gardens when Milushkyi nudged him, "He is here," he said, indicating that he had spotted his Mr. K. "He's looking at the incense burner."

The two started walking in the opposite direction, away from the Great Buddha. Milushkyi said, "Let's make a final check for surveillance. He will follow, then he'll pass us, and we will follow him at a distance ... just to make sure. I don't want this one turning sour on us."

Fifteen minutes later, after they were sure no one had paid even the slightest attention, they overtook Kovlosky. As they continued walking Kovlosky told them GRU counterintelligence had been snooping around the embassy, asking all sorts of questions of everyone except himself. It did seem strange, but it did not occur to him that this was a bad sign. Even after it began to seem his fellow warrant officers were avoiding him he did not get suspicious. Then he received Milushkyi's signal to get out fast—so, here he was.

Kovlosky said he had brought some "stuff" for Milushkyi as his last "take," and that he wanted to leave Japan clandestinely.

"I just want to disappear, fade away, as if I had committed suicide." That, he said, was for the sake of his family.

Kovlosky's desire to fake a suicide changed Reiter's entire plan for the exfiltration. Originally, the plan called for taking him to the U.S. Embassy in Tokyo where he would ask for political asylum. After being interviewed by Soviet officials, who would want to make sure he had not been kidnapped, he would then be flown to the U.S. for resettlement. Now that that procedure was out, they had to devise a new plan.

Milushkyi's first concern of course was Kovlosky's safety. Both Milushkyi and Hans were armed, Milushkyi with a Walther P-38, and Hans with his trusty .38 caliber Colt police special. After a lengthy discussion they decided to first plant clues for the "suicide." They walked, Milushkyi and Hans leading, Kovlosky following at a distance—they did not want some taxi driver to link the Americans with the Soviet before or after the "suicide." From the Great Buddha the trio walked downhill; they passed the Gongoro Shrine and walked toward Sagami Bay. After what seemed an eternity, they finally arrived at the bay. Fortunately, the beach was not overly crowded. They searched left and right for a secluded spot and walked for what seemed to be miles before finding one on Yuigahama Beach, some distance, and out of view of Japanese sun-worshippers.

At a secluded area Kovlosky emptied his pockets of the "stuff" he had brought for Milushkyi. Then he took off his jacket, folded it neatly and stuck it under a bush at the upper edge of the beach. He then proceeded to take off his shirt and trousers. The crafty Kovlosky wore another shirt and a pair of shorts under his clothing. He again carefully folded and stuck the discarded clothes under the jacket. Finally, in his heavily accented English, he said, "Okie-dokie let us leave the place and go to America."

Hans thought *easier said than done* but made some agreeable gestures.

While they walked up the slight incline along Wakamiya Oji toward the rail station, Hans and Milushkyi discussed their next move. Hans suggested temporarily stashing Kovlosky in Hans's hotel room. Milushkyi would stand guard, and Hans would contact the lieutenant in charge of his Task Force 168 detachment.

Hans found the lieutenant in the Chain Locker Bar of the Admiral Arleigh A. Burke Commissioned Officers Club and pulled him away from his drinking buddies. He explained the situation to him and asked him to locate the base security/intelligence officer. The lieutenant left the Task Force 168 office to find the security officer, and Hans sent a "flash" message to the DNI updating him on the situation and telling him he needed his okay to get Kovlosky and Milushkyi aboard a U.S. Navy vessel or aircraft leaving Japan. Then he called Smyth on the Gray phone, updating him too, and telling him of the need to get the DNI's help. Smyth agreed to get it all arranged.

Then Hans waited.

About an hour later the lieutenant arrived with the security officer, a lieutenant commander, in tow. After brief introductions and after having shown his credentials, Hans informed the lieutenant commander that he needed accommodations for Counterintelligence Special Agent Frank Milushkyi and a clandestine asset to be housed, for security reasons, in a single room of the BOQ until further notice. Hans also told him that he expected momentarily a message from the DNI solving the other problem, the exfiltration of the asset.

The lieutenant commander's reply was, "Not a problem."

Hans was surprised. He had expected a lot of questions and the usual Navy double-talk, but the officer acted as if he had done this many times. Apparently seeing Hans's puzzled look the lieutenant commander said, "I'm a SEAL." Instant relief was what Reiter felt. He now was certain Misha Kovlosky was in good hands.

Two "flash" messages arrived from the DNI, one addressed to the base commander and base security, with a copy to Task Force 168 detachment, the other addressed to the detachment with copies to the base commander and base security. The first message validated Reiter's request; the second included notification that transportation to Washington had been arranged for Special Agent Frank Milushkyi and an unnamed individual called a "Way Bill"—via a U.S. Navy supply ship from Yokosuka to Pearl Harbor, Hawaii, and from Hawaii via Military Air Transport Service to Washington, DC. The supply ship was scheduled to depart two days later.

The second message also instructed Hans to continue his review of the detachment's administrative procedures. This, of course, was Hans's "real" job in Naval Intelligence. He was at Task Force 168 Yokosuka to check Intelligence Collection Requirements—also called ICRs, —for timeliness. There had been complaints that the detachment used old, outdated requirements to increase the unit's annual number of reports—to "pad their books." Hans culled the old ICRs and told the Navy chief to destroy them. He was reluctant until Hans explained the importance of reporting only information covered by the most recent ICRs.

"Look," Hans explained, "your reports may be the best thing since sliced bread but if the ICR was canceled a year ago, that report counts for nothing. All reports based on canceled ICRs receive either poor or no evaluations."

The chief and others in the office agreed that poor evaluations were worse than insufficient report numbers if the analyst cannot match the report with an ICR requirement.

Hans also advised them that it was to the detachment's advantage to separate the reports by specific issues and topics, even if they came from a single individual.

"It not only makes for better distribution to the right customer," he told them, "but it also encourages better report evaluation. Besides all that, it makes for easier filing for the analysts—and they like that."

Hans hinted that it would also increase the number of reports considerably. He also encouraged them to write IRs identified as "Collector Initiative."

"In initiative reporting," Hans advised, "you can include information and photography you deem important to Navy needs, even if it's not covered by an ICR."

That seemed to make them all happy.

CHAPTER 38

A week after Hans returned to Washington, Smyth called him at CTF 168 on the Gray Phone, the secure phone, to report that Milushkyi and his charge had arrived—and that he and his group of counterintelligence experts had tried to reconstruct the events before Misha Kovlosky's forced defection. Smyth and his crew in Room 526 read voluminous signals intelligence transcripts and defector and émigré reports, but never found a single clue that would reveal who or what betrayed this asset.

After one of those lengthy sessions with CIA and FBI, Smyth returned to his office; he was fuming. "These goddamned stuffed shirts," he thundered as he walked back and forth like a caged tiger, "don't want to admit that there is a skunk in one or even both of those organizations."

He pounded his desk.

"Hank, I'm telling you, there is a mole in there ... somewhere."

Before Smyth turned Kovlosky over to another agency for debriefing and resettlement, he had interviewed him and recorded it all on tape. Then he and Hans made an appointment with the new Director, Naval Intelligence. Smyth wanted to beat the other agencies to the punch with this information. Milushkyi served as the interpreter.

Former Warrant Officer Misha Kovlosky sat, nervously fiddling, looking at the tape recorder. Milushkyi tried to reassure him, "Misha, you are here, safe, among friends."

Kovlosky looked up, smiled. "Yes, I forgot."

"Okay," Kovlosky began, "as you know, we had been at Polyarnyy Fjord, Kola Peninsula, since early October 1973. Kapitan 1st Rank A. S. Pushkin stood with me and two other warrant officers in the sail of Rodina's finest, most advanced, titanium, fast-attack submarine, awaiting the signal to follow a KGB border patrol boat through the narrow, curving Polyarnyy Fjord.

"A heavy, white mist rose as the minus 25-degree Centigrade air touched the waters of the fjord deep inside Russia's Kola Peninsula. It was exciting, and almost romantic." Kovlosky smiled wistfully.

"The fjord, the ice, the warm air rising from the open hatch, and our highly respected captain in charge of Rodina's most modern submarine... By the way,

Kapitan Pushkin is one of the finest officers I have ever served under."

He paused deep in thought, then: "I think we suddenly realized how small this submarine really was, in comparison to the other attack submarines. We heard only the humming of the turbines. Only the low rumblings of the KGB boats' diesel engines broke the stillness of the early morning hour.

"On this cold 23rd October morning in 1973 the whole world appeared to be covered in a darkish gray shroud. Infrequently black shadows and flashes from hand-held signal lamps broke through the darkness. The small, teardrop-shaped submarine seemed to slightly tremble, pulling on the lines holding it securely to the floating pier; she appeared alive, anxious to get under way. Shore power lines had been disconnected during departure preparation. Kapitan Pushkin, I, and two others clad in heavy cold weather gear stood in the sail. We strained to see the shadow of the border patrol escort boat, listening for the signal letter J, for 'Am going ahead, follow me.'

"I reported, 'Comrade Kapitan, there it goes: one short, three long.'

"We cast off the bowline. Then the captain ordered 'Left rudder, ahead very slow.' Men on the pier retrieved the frozen bowline, then rushed toward the stern—they were in a hurry to get the stern lines in and themselves into the warm comfort of the shack at the end of the pier where the samovar with steaming black tea was waiting for them.

"With the submarine straining against the stern lines, the bow swung slowly to port pointing toward the escort boat. Kapitan Pushkin waited patiently until there was just enough clearance between his boat and the pier, then he turned toward the stern, and ordered, 'Cast off stern lines.'

"The captain told the boys on the pier, 'Thank you, Comrades, for being so patient. Have a glass of hot tea on me'."

"The men saluted the departing boat, and Kapitan Pushkin solemnly returned their salute. Then, through the increased whining of the turbine, we heard laughter and retreating footsteps."

"Kapitan Pushkin pushed the communications button, 'Helmsman, steady as she goes. Comrade Engineer, increase speed to slow ahead.'"

Kovlosky paused and sipped from a steaming cup of tea. "The captain turned and cautioned me, and the two other lookouts: 'Keep your eyes on the beacon of the escort. Let me know any variation in course or distance. I want everything double-checked on the radar repeater.' He turned to look at the rotating radar atop the telescoping mast. It was new, and the best Rodina had produced, but on a new boat you could never be too sure. We had to closely follow the KGB boat to get to the operating area. It was some fifteen nautical miles of twisting fjord with practically no visibility because of the white-out."

Kovlosky looked at Milushkyi. "As an aside may I say that it had been a long time coming to test this revolutionary submarine. We had waited years.

In fact, so long that Ivan Petrovitch, the captain originally scheduled to command her, became Admiral Petrovitch, CINC Northern Fleet. Admiral Petrovitch had personally selected the then-Kapitan 2nd Rank Pushkin to command this boat.

"Captain Pushkin told us that Rodina had put all its resources into play to build this highly complex submarine; the world's smallest, the world's fastest, the world's deepest diving submarine. He assured us that this submarine was by far superior to any other in the world."

Kovlosky then said that a small flotilla of surface ships, a submarine rescue ship, a diving tender, three high-speed patrol boats, and two additional border patrol boats lay waiting to observe the trials of this, Projekt 705.

Milushkyi urged Kovlosky to tell how the political officer had briefed the crew.

"He told us that Fleet Admiral George Mikhailovich Yegorov and his staff had departed Murmansk the previous evening, and that SOVNORFLT—Soviet Northern Fleet Headquarters—had issued an international notification announcing a live firing exercise being conducted on the Barents Sea off Murmansk; the off-limits firing sector ranged from the Norwegian border eastward to Kharlovka.

"I suppose," Kovlosky laughed, "should any foreign aircraft appear: 'So sorry, it was mistaken for a target drone.' The same would hold true for any NATO reconnaissance submarine. All through the previous night ASW escorts and helicopters with dipping sonar had searched the area and its fringes for foreign intruders known to frequent the test site area. As soon as visibility permitted naval aircraft would cover the test site and block any foreign surveillance aircraft trying to enter the area."

Kovlosky thought that the KGB Border Guard escorts must have given the admiral the "All Clear" signal even before Pushkin's boat had cast off its mooring lines.

Several hours into the morning the lookout aboard the Golden Fish announced, "Comrade Kapitan, we are nearing the test site."

Kapitan Pushkin exchanged signals with the assembled flotilla, in return received good wishes; then the boat prepared to dive to 100 meters and proceed on the racetrack course already programmed into the on-board computer. The captain had posted his small crew in strategic positions to report. Should any anomalies occur during the trial run he had two warrant officers in the torpedo room, two each in the passageway between the torpedo room and the control room. The rest hovered over, but never touched the rudder, the dive planes and the reactor controls—ready, instantly, just in case the computers malfunctioned.

"Everyone aboard knew the aft section of the boat, the reactor compartment and the entire engineering spaces—all the spaces aft the sail, were sealed and unmanned," Kovlosky said. Never before, never in any submarine, nuclear or diesel, were the engineering spaces ever left without crew—another first, but it made the crew feel just a bit uneasy.

"As everyone in the control room watched the gauges the boat slowly approached the 100-meter mark, the crew felt the eerie presence of the computer, with the controls automatically moving, adjusting the dive planes until the needle of the depth gauge stood at exactly 100 meters. The boat maintained ten knots speed at 100 meters until the diving and the engineering officers were satisfied that everything was according to schedule."

"Before Kapitan Pushkin gave the engineering officer the command to increase speed, he ordered Kovlosky, as the senior Warrant Officer, to fire a smoke grenade from the signal launch tube. They had been through these drills in the ashore simulator more than one hundred times, but now it was for real.

"Kapitan Pushkin turned to his engineering officer, 'Comrade Engineer, execute test run.' The engineering officer turned the switch to 'Full Automatic.' Those in the control room watched as the boat, without anyone touching the controls, gained speed; slowly at first as programmed, then increasingly faster. The boat vibrated, almost lifelike, as speed increased to twenty knots, to twenty-five knots, to thirty knots. 'We are going as fast as a destroyer,' the captain whispered, and the men around him nodded silently, holding their breaths.

'Forty knots,' whispered one of the officers."

"'Forty-three knots going into the first turn,' the engineer announced. Still accelerating, the boat sliced through the ice-cold arctic waters like a fighter-bomber roaming the sky. She leaned into the first turn and came out having slowed to thirty-nine knots, then automatically accelerated to the programmed maximum speed of 44 knots. The depth gauge indicated exactly 100 meters. Directly under the service flotilla she went into her second turn on the racetrack course—slowed, then, coming out of the turn, regained speed."

"Suddenly every dial in the control room went wild. The boat shuddered and slowed. All engine noises stopped. The rushing sound of water flow across the hull became audible as never before."

Kovlosky seemed to relive that moment. "We did not know what had happened; we looked around to see, panicked. But nothing else happened. It was eerily quiet. Then we heard the calm reassuring voice of our captain, 'All stations: report.' And, almost as if this were just another training exercise, we heard: 'Comrade Kapitan, torpedo room reporting: watertight integrity confirmed.'

'Comrade Kapitan, amidships compartment reporting: watertight integrity confirmed.'

'Comrade Kapitan, Chief Engineering reporting: propulsion compartment sensors confirm watertight integrity.'

The engineer checked the other sensor dials. Suddenly his head snapped back and forth, "Comrade Kapitan, Geiger sensor shows contamination ... high levels of contamination. Comrade Kapitan, the indicator is off the mark."

Kapitan Pushkin calmly ordered all non-essential personnel into the rescue sphere.

"Comrade XO headcount!'

"Aye, aye," the executive officer said, then rushed to the ladder and ordered the first man to open the bottom hatch, and then to file in all the way to the top. Then the executive officer ordered everyone to be quiet, and to await further orders. Then he stood at the bottom of the ladder and counted those entering it. With watertight integrity confirmed the disciplined crew calmly climbed into the rescue sphere. With the closed-down reactor all life support systems were now battery-powered—the submarine was unnervingly quiet.

Kapitan Pushkin ordered the chief engineer to shut the watertight doors. The chief engineer turned to the control panel and pushed several buttons. The computer reacted instantly; a klaxon broke the stillness, then four watertight doors closed with resounding clanks. He reported that all was secure.

"'Misha," Kapitan Pushkin ordered, calling the engineer by his first name, "Blow all ballast!" After the engineer had turned several switches the hull reverberated from the enormous hissing of high-pressure air expelling the ballast water. Shortly thereafter the engineer reported, "Rising, Comrade Kapitan, rising."

Kapitan Pushkin slapped his engineering officer on the shoulder and said, 'Misha, you had better get into the sphere.'

"Comrade Kapitan, if you don't mind, I'll stand by here with you in case you need help."

A sudden rush of warmth seemed to surge through the crew.

Kovlosky remarked, "What loyalty, what great comradeship. What a great crew. No panic. We were one crew. Our captain was one of the very few I had ever met in the Soviet Navy who actually cared about his men. They would have gone through fire for him; a true man of the Taiga."

Kovlosky continued his story with, "Kapitan Pushkin told his chief engineer, 'Otchim Khorosho'—very well, only one other thing to do. He pushed the emergency signal ejector and fired a red star rocket. Then he turned toward the engineer, 'Let's go, Misha,' and he and his engineer quickly climbed into the rescue sphere."

In a much less stressful voice the executive officer reported, "Now, all present and accounted for, Comrade Kapitan."

The chief engineer slammed shut the hatch and secured it. Then all waited and watched the auxiliary gauges in the sphere. They sat crowded on benches barely daring to breathe, and heard the water flow noises of the boat rising and the slight crackling of the minutely expanding hull as pressure decreased. "'Seventy-five meters," whispered the chief engineer, then "50 meters." Finally the boat breached the surface; they felt more than heard the boat surfacing; it started to heave and pitch ever so slightly in the waves. The chief engineer climbed the ladder to the top of the sphere and first opened the pressure release valve, then he carefully popped open the top hatch. First the engineer, then Kapitan Pushkin and his executive officer, climbed onto the sail. Almost immediately two rescue boats, the diving tender, and two huge ocean tugs came along side. The crew quickly transferred to the rescue boats as four men clad in heavy rubber suits and protective masks descended onto the aftership with detection instruments—Geiger counters. Similarly clad men climbed from the ocean tugs onto the foreship and fastened cables to the submarine's rescue shackles and the towing cleat. The rubber-clad men remained on the submarine only a brief time before returning to their ships.

Kovlosky said that Kapitan Pushkin and his crew transferred to the submarine rescue ship where a concerned Admiral George Mikhailovich Yegorov awaited them. Kapitan Pushkin made his report, giving the admiral a detailed description of what he and others had observed on the gauges and the computer screen.

Later, after they arrived at Severodvinsk, Kapitan Pushkin's boat was towed to the most distant northeastern corner of the salvage yard and secured to mooring points.

Former Warrant Officer Kovlosky said that he learned later that the boat had suffered a catastrophic failure when the lead-bismuth liquid metal coolant spilled from the reactor containment vessel into the bilge. Aside from the reactor containment vessel failure the trial run was a success. The high speed attained, the flawless workings of the computer controlling speed, course and depth were highly encouraging achievements. SDB 143 redesigned the container vessel; they made it at least thirty percent stronger.

A catastrophic failure? Yes. But, according to Warrant Officer Kovlosky, also a gigantic achievement. Success.

Smyth glanced at the DNI. For a minute or two the DNI looked serious, then smiled, "Yes, and it is a success not only for the Soviet Navy, but also for the tenacious Naval Intelligence. No matter what Admiral Rickover will say, we were right on the money."

Within the intelligence circles, especially in Naval Intelligence, Kovlosky became a celebrity. After all, he had been a member of Soviet Navy Kapitan First Rank A.S. Pushkin's crew that rode the titanium submarine on a fast racetrack course submerged at exactly 100 meters, at speeds in excess of forty knots, in a totally computerized submarine that was also the world's smallest one, et cetera, et cetera. The submarine that Admiral Rickover said the Russians could not build.

Hans felt vindicated. The DNI laughed, "Reiter, now that you have really pissed off Hyman. Tell Milushkyi I love him."

"Aye, aye, Admiral," he replied.

And Hans thought, *Admiral Rickover, eat your heart out.*

CHAPTER 39

"Mission accomplished!" Hiram Smyth declared. "Congratulations," messaged the DNI, who also suggested this triumph was a good time for Hans Reiter to step down—that is, leave Naval Intelligence.

For some time Smyth and Reiter had talked of retirement. Both were now in their early and middle fifties. They had roamed the world, often to the distress of their families. For Hans, just the travel was becoming ever more difficult—and the hazard of operating outside the diplomatic immunity envelope had become stressful.

But the chief, Intelligence Community Staff, had been unsuccessful in a search for Smyth's replacement, and Smyth did not want to lose Reiter, so talk of retirement, at least for the being, was just that, talk.

Anyway, Smyth and Reiter had spoken of what they would do after Room 526; whether they could even survive being cut off from all the classified "stuff" to which they had access. And then there was Kasandroff.

Hans felt responsible for his main asset, and neither he nor Smyth felt they could hand over Kasandroff to a junior agent in Room 526.

The upshot of it all was, Smyth arranged for the Defense Intelligence Agency (DIA) to offer Hans a job with a promotion he could not possibly refuse—and to hide his continued connection with Naval Intelligence Smyth had him placed on "Special Assignment—DIA."

CHAPTER 40

MARCH 1978
KÜSTRIN-ON-ODER RIVER
FORMERLY GERMANY

___

Several years earlier Smyth had cautioned Reiter that, "Ours was not to reason why..." On a freezing cold night in March of 1978 Smyth had no time to tell him why, not that he wanted to. Shortly after midnight Smyth called Hans at home and told him get to Andrews Air Force Base immediately. "I got you a seat on the courier plane to Frankfurt. They are waiting for you."

"What the hell is this all about?"

"You'll read it before you get on the plane. You'll get a briefing envelope. Just get going! Hurry! Dress warmly, look like a Russkie—fur cap and all. There is, or soon will be, a USAF Military Police car in your driveway."

Susan asked, "What is this all about?"

"I have not the slightest idea. Hiram didn't have time to explain. Take a look out to the driveway. See if there is an MP vehicle, my ride."

"I thought we had gotten away from this uncertainty, all these sudden operations. This looks like trouble to me. I'm really worried." But she helped him dress in his warmest garb, long johns. Susan dug out his old Russian fur cap from a trunk that they had kept from the olden days. Then she produced boots, a scarf and heavy gloves.

When he had finished dressing he looked like a stuffed toy. Hidden beneath all that was Hans's .38-caliber sub-nosed Colt in a shoulder holster. He hugged her; she held on to him for what seemed an eternity. As he kissed her goodbye, she turned her face away hiding her tears.

From the passenger seat of the MP vehicle, he saw Susan watching from the window, standing in her nightgown, a blanket wrapped around her shoulders—he had seen that look on her face before—in the bad old days. *Damn*, he thought, *this is like the olden days ... and I promised Susan that this would never happen again.*

The Air Police officer drove fast over slippery winter roads to Andrews Air Force Base, just to the south of Suitland, Maryland. A military escort vehicle with an illuminated sign, "Follow Me," escorted them to the airbase operations building. Another air policeman waved Hans into Visitors' Parking. In the terminal lobby the base security officer checked his badge and ID card, then handed him a thin envelope.

"I don't know what this is all about," the officer appeared chagrined, "but I am to tell you to read this. Then I am to destroy it in your presence; I need your signature as a witness."

Hans ripped open the envelope. The first line read, "Rescue Orloff." An emergency call from Kasandroff had been the tip-off. Either Hans's meeting with Orloff, or a careless move by Orloff, had apparently compromised him. He was on his way to Moscow, a premature departure from a Paris meeting of academicians—a bad sign. Smyth had arranged for one of his Polish assets, a secret police officer, to pull Orloff off the train somewhere between Poznan and Warsaw.

Since Hans was the only one who could recognize Orloff, he was to meet him at the Oder River crossing to the former German city of Küstrin. A VOPO colonel, an East German police officer named Heinz Gerstmann, was to escort Hans to the meeting and return Orloff and Hans to West Berlin. Smyth listed the contact information for his meeting with the colonel, as well as reservations for the connecting courier flight from Frankfurt-on-Main to Berlin.

At the bottom of the instructions Smyth had handwritten, THERE IS NO BACK-UP, SORRY OLD BUDDY. YOU ARE ON YOUR OWN.

Hans tried unsuccessfully to keep his hand from shaking as he returned the envelope to the security officer, who motioned Hans to follow him. They walked to a small office where he cross-shredded the envelope with its contents. Then they walked out on the tarmac where a huge four-engine courier plane sat waiting.

Hans's stopover at Frankfurt-on-Main Air Base was the briefest he had ever made there. A Jeep with the red-and-white checkerboard flag picked him up and drove him directly to the small twin-engine Berlin courier aircraft sitting on the tarmac with engines idling. He had barely time to tighten his seatbelt before the pilot gunned the engines for takeoff.

At Tegel Airport, Hans saw a young, redheaded, freckled man, slender with a thick neck and broad shoulders.

"Corporal Dreier," Hans almost shouted in surprise. "What in hell are you doing here?"

"Gunner," Dreier corrected him, smiling. "I am the man who will drive you to within two city blocks of the checkpoint. That, at least, is what I was told to do."

"God, it's good to see you. Did my talk with the DNI get you into Naval Intelligence?"

"Yes, sir, and, sir, many thanks. Your recommendation to the DNI has landed me in a great, interesting job."

As they walked out of the airbase to a parked car, Dreier asked, "Sir, if you can tell me, what is this all about?"

"I wish I knew. I have instructions to meet a German VOPO colonel and go into East Germany."

"Shit," Dreier cursed, "I can't even get into East Berlin to go shopping, and you're going into East Germany?" He told Hans that he had instructions to drop him off at Karl Marx Strasse, about two blocks from the East German checkpoint. On the way to the drop-off point they conversed in German.

Dreier told Hans that shortly after he had returned to the U.S. in October 1971, he had received orders to attend a USMC intelligence course at Quantico, Virginia, and then an Army advanced intelligence course at Fort Huachuca, Arizona. This one was for clandestine case officers. The Fort Huachuca training had brought him into contact with a number of Army agents, some were now here in Berlin.

"Sir, I cannot tell you how this has helped me and my Navy chief. We're the only Navy representatives here in Berlin."

"However," Dreier said, "this mission is one of the more unusual ones I have ever had."

"You're not the only one. I am scared shitless but up to now everything has worked like clockwork." He expressed his hope that it would continue to go well. "Or else, I'll have to kiss my ass goodbye."

Dreier laughed. "I'll see you here tonight. I'll be waiting at the drop-off point from four a.m. till whenever you get back, no matter how late."

The two men parted like long-lost brothers— Dreier's bravado—and Hans's—had slipped a few notches as they hugged a goodbye. At that moment Dreier was Hans's last link to the Free World.

Walking the two blocks to the East German checkpoint, Hans wondered whether the six copper-coated rounds of ball ammunition in his .38-caliber revolver would suffice to hold down the entire East German police force. Getting ever closer to the checkpoint he felt like a condemned man must feel walking his last mile to the gallows.

At the checkpoint an East German colonel, narrow-faced, hawk-nosed, tall—around six feet two inches tall, ramrod straight, in a field-gray greatcoat with a fur collar, reminiscent of the Hollywood version of a World War II Wehrmacht officer, approached Hans. The greatcoat hid parts of his spit-shined boots.

The colonel asked, "Herr Trenker?"

"Jawohl."

"Please follow me!" Then he whispered, "Try to look like a Russian."

To Hans's utter astonishment, the two East German VOPO guards saluted him, and he returned their salute in typical Soviet fashion: he raised the clenched fist that then unfolded it into a hand salute. He had seen this Soviet salute numerous times at the change of the guard of the Soviet monument that had been mistakenly built on the wrong side of the Brandenburger Tor in West Berlin.

The East German guards seemed to brace themselves ever more erect seeing this important "Russian's" salute.

A strange world we live in, Hans reminded himself. As they walked toward the car the colonel looked back and whispered, "They think you are a high-ranking Soviet passing clandestinely through Germany."

Understandably, Hans was still in shock as he climbed into the colonel's official car; there the colonel introduced himself. "Gerstmann, Heinz Gerstmann." Gerstmann drove through East Berlin like a man possessed; he sped straight north on Route 112. The cars in those days had no seat belts, and Hans braced his feet against the floorboards, and desperately held onto the door and the seat with his hands; it was a white-knuckle ride.

Gerstmann drove fast, but Hans had to admit it, he was an excellent driver. Whenever they came near a town Gerstmann turned on his flashing strobe blue light and wailing siren.

Gerstmann instructed Hans that he would handle the turnover between the Poles and the Germans, but that Hans first had to identify the person passing through the line. They talked about life in general and life in East Germany. Gerstmann noticed Hans's Silesian-accented German dialect and asked whether he was from Silesia. Hans told him his grandparents came from that part of Germany.

"Former Germany," Gerstmann replied seemingly very bitterly, "former..." He cursed, then muttered, "My parents also come from Lower Silesia—they were deported in 1946, by God, deported from their own home like goddamned cattle."

"My family, my grandfather, came from a small town in Lower Silesia, from Jauer."

"Oh, my God," gasped the colonel. He smiled. His whole demeanor suddenly changed as he patted Hans's shoulder, "Mine are from Striegau. We are *Landsmänner.*" With Gerstmann's acknowledgment that they were fellow countrymen, Hans somehow, suddenly, felt much safer than he had felt just moments earlier.

When they arrived at the border crossing, Gerstmann assumed his official face. He snarled at the East German border guard, "Are these Polaks ready, or late as usual?"

The guard snapped to attention. "Comrade Colonel, they are late as usual. I think they run on Polish time."

The colonel seemed to relax. He smiled at the guard. "Well said, Comrade, well said. I expected it."

The guard relaxed; he seemed to like the colonel's comment.

They waited in silence, and waited. Finally they saw movement on the Polish side of the border. As the Poles raised the barrier, Gerstmann motioned for

Hans to accompany him across the Oder River bridge.

"We'll walk as if we do this every day." Gerstmann suggested, "Check out the person ... I think I see a civilian there, just so we don't buy a pig in the poke."

The Polish officer walked toward Hans. "You Trenker?" he asked in good German.

"Yes, I am."

"Your man is a bit shook up, but he'll be all right once he gets to West Berlin, I think."

Orloff walked hesitantly toward him as if he suspected he would be thrown into the icy Oder River. Hans removed his fur cap. Orloff recognized him immediately and started to run toward him. "Trenker? Trenker!" he sputtered, and then hugged him.

Hans shook the Polish agent's hand. *"Dziekuja, pan."* He was saying, "Thank you, sir."

The Pole waved his hand, turned, and walked back to his car. Colonel Gerstmann hustled Orloff into the back seat, and they were off on another wild ride. This time Gerstmann drove right up to the barrier at Karl Marx Strasse, flashed his very impressive-looking red-and-gold credentials and, barely waiting for the barrier to be raised, gunned the engine and shot through the border crossing. At the first side street he made a sharp left turn and slammed on the brakes. "This is it, Herr Trenker. Good luck, *Landsmann.*"

They shook hands like old friends—then the colonel slammed his gearshift into reverse, gunned his engine once more, backed out of the road, skidded around the corner and raced back into East Berlin.

For a long time Hans just stood in total amazement. He was back in West Berlin. *That was one hell of a ride,* he thought. *I hope someday I'll be able to thank that East German colonel, my Landsmann,* for what he did. Hans felt someone tapping him on his back. Like a coiled spring he whirled around—he had totally forgotten where he was.

It was Orloff. Hans hugged him, and Orloff stammered in German, *"Danke, danke."*

"Let's go, my friend. We have a car waiting."

Two blocks from the checkpoint, the black Opel sedan sat waiting. Dreier saw the two men walking toward his vehicle. He jumped out and ran toward Hans. "I told you it was a piece of cake," he shouted, sounding overjoyed.

Hans laughed. "Not exactly a piece of cake, but it turned out better than I had expected." They climbed aboard and rode from Karl Marx Strasse to Tegel Airport and climbed into the waiting courier aircraft for Frankfurt— this time they were the only ones in the aircraft. Since they arrived in Frankfurt with time to spare, Hans thought he would introduce Orloff to a typical "American Air

Force" breakfast at the airbase cafeteria: freshly made glazed doughnuts and a steaming cup of American coffee.

They waited in the serving line conversing in German. One of two young Air Force captains standing behind the two "foreigners" became irritated. Hans heard the captain muttering something to his cohort about foreigners not being authorized to eat in the Air Force cafeteria. He finally tapped Hans on the shoulder and asked, "Are you authorized to eat here?"

Hans looked at him in wonderment and asked, "Who are you, are you the exchange officer?"

The captain became furious and called for the manager.

The German manager viewed the two foreign-looking men with seeming distaste. Hans assumed the manager routinely permitted German employees to eat in the snack bar, but these two looked more like Russians than Germans. Both Hans and Orloff wore fur caps, heavy, quilted jackets, and boots that looked like out of the Stone Age. As the manager came closer he sniffed. Hans wondered, and then realized that both he and Orloff gave off an offensive odor, a combination of stale sweat and the sour smell of fear.

Hans started to smile. *I wonder what is on his mind,* he thought.

The manager hesitated slightly. Apparently he did not quite know how to handle this situation. He spoke very apologetically in German, asking to see Hans's identification. Hans dug out his fancy, blue etui with the golden badge of the counterintelligence service. The manager's eyes widened. He bowed and scraped and apologized, walking backward as if he had encountered royalty.

The complaining officer, who had peeked over the manager's shoulder, said to his companion, "You never know who you meet here."

Hans turned around and snarled, "And don't you ever forget it."

Orloff, who understood a fair amount of English, appeared suitably impressed that his "protector" had stared down not only two "high-ranking" American officers, but also the German manager.

Hans and his charge got the last two seats on an Air Force transport, loaded with returning troops and dependents, scheduled for Dover Air Force Base, Delaware. The other passengers looked at them in amazement, seeing two civilians in heavy winter gear, wearing Russian-looking fur caps, conversing in German, and giving off an odious smell.

Hans dozed off right after takeoff and awoke when he detected the aroma of food. He suddenly remembered that, aside from the coffee and doughnut, he had not eaten a decent meal since two evenings ago in Virginia. When the stewards brought trays, Orloff said, "Hunger. Food?"

Hans nodded and asked one of the stewards whether they could have double rations. The steward looked at the two as if to tell them that there were no exceptions. Hans leaned over and whispered, "Sergeant, we come from the other side and we have not eaten anything for the last thirty hours," as he discreetly flashed his golden badge.

The man nodded, his demeanor suddenly changed. "I'll give you one meal now, and when you finished, you'll get seconds." He smiled. "Even thirds."

He motioned to his colleague and said, "Hey, Mike, give these guys an extra big cup of coffee; they look as if they could use it."

After Hans had finished off the double rations and the additional cups of coffee, he felt alive again. The coffee had warmed him and his companion up enough to take off their outer garments.

Orloff asked to go to the toilet. Hans thought it best to explain the procedures on a military aircraft; besides, he too felt the need to use the facilities. He walked Orloff to the front of the aircraft. He noticed the other passengers murmuring and pointing at him and Orloff. Hans had forgotten that he still had his .38 caliber revolver in his shoulder holster. He was embarrassed, but the steward waved "okay" to the others.

Suddenly the passengers smiled and waved. Hans thought that they would now have a story to tell when they got home.

As the aircraft neared the coast of the United States, the pilot announced that mission control had diverted the aircraft to Andrews Air Force Base, Maryland, but that there would be only a brief stop, and then off again to their final destination.

After a smooth landing the aircraft taxied toward the terminal; it stopped just a few hundred yards short of the terminal building. A debarkation ladder rolled up to the aircraft. A man in his late forties or early fifties, broad-faced, looking in need of a shave, curly gray hair, a bit on the corpulent side, opened the door; Hiram Smyth. He waved for Hans and Orloff to get off the aircraft. Then he thanked the other passengers for their patience, and slammed shut the door. Hans wondered what stories the passengers now had to tell when they reached their homes. After a thirty-minute drive Smyth, Hans and Orloff arrived at Room 526.

CHAPTER 41

Orloff's wife and five-year-old daughter were waiting for him in Smyth's office. When Orloff spotted them he seemed close to falling. He turned pale; his hands trembled, he stuttered, took a few steps toward his family, and hesitated as if he had seen a mirage. Smyth and Hans grabbed his arms; it looked as if he was on the verge of collapse. Then Orloff suddenly ran, pulling his two helpers along, toward his wife; they hugged and kissed—both of them cried.

In the meantime his little girl stood behind her mother, shy, hugging her doll, appearing totally confused by the events that had occurred in the past two days.

Hans turned toward Smyth. "How in hell did you make this happen?"

"Never underestimate me, Hank," Smyth said, laughing. "Never underestimate me."

He sniffed.

"Oh, by the way, you stink. You both stink. Why don't you go home, take a good shower and come back tomorrow. Then I'll tell you what happened."

Apparently Smyth had called Susan. She stood in the door crying. She hugged Hans and pulled him into the house. "Hiram said you would have an unpleasant odor." Between tears she laughed, "He did not tell me you stink."

"Is this the way to greet a returning hero?" Hans kidded her.

The ever-irreverent Susan responded, "Hero, hell. You probably sat in some Berlin bar waiting for some schnook from the East to whisper secrets into your ear."

He shook his head. "Sweetheart, not this time; not this time."

He made her promise not to scold Hiram Smyth, and then he told her the story of the rescue of the academician.

"You went into East Germany? Are you out of your mind?"

"Into East Germany, and I even met a *Landsmann*."

"East Germany? Who cares about a *Landsmann?* Why? Oh God, we are getting too old for this. Remember, you had promised to lead a decent, safe life after all that crap in the Army. You promised."

"I'm sorry, but it was for a good cause."

190

He told her the story of the rescue and his fellow countryman Heinz Gerstmann.

"Interesting fellow. Looked like a Hollywood Nazi officer, but this one was a VOPO. His folks came from the area where my grandfather was born. I didn't realize that I spoke German with a Silesian dialect. But this made the day for the colonel."

He hesitated. "And for me, if truth be told. I was scared as hell, until he called me *'Landsmann.'* Then, for some reason, I felt safe. Unbelievable."

Susan hugged him again. "Promise that you will never do this again."

He squirmed. "Not if I can help it. Believe me."

Susan smiled. "I wonder."

After a long shower Hans felt like he was newly born. Susan had prepared his favorite brunch: two soft-boiled eggs, toast, butter and strawberry preserves. She sat waiting for him, sipping from a cup of a freshly brewed pot of French-roast Melita coffee.

"So, tell me about your *Landsmann*," she said. "You never were high on East Germans, and cops in particular."

"Well, this was the first time with an asset that I had this strange feeling of being completely safe."

Susan cocked her head, questioning.

"I know, I know, sweetheart. All that crap they taught us at the spook school was, 'Never get close to your asset, never become friends, but when we spoke, when I told him that my grandparents came from that part of Germany, and when he said in a very bitter tone of voice, 'Former Germany, former...' I felt a great simpatico. I remembered Grandpa Reiter ... or was it my Dad? I forgot... talking with that same bitterness of losing his homeland to the Poles. I suppose, somehow this made the colonel and me friends ... Funny, I could never have conceived the thought of being the friend of an East German VOPO colonel."

Susan smiled. "We do live in a strange world."

"Yes, and when he told me that his parents were deported from their own home like cattle I remembered—I was at an age when family history was of little interest—but I remember ... sometime around 1945-46 ... my father trying to find the whereabouts of his uncle Reiter who had remained in Germany, in Silesia. He tried everything, the Red Cross and God knows what else. Never found out what happened to that branch of the family. They simply disappeared."

He looked at Susan seriously. "I don't know, but somehow, all this came back to me and suddenly I felt as if I was in good hands with the East German colonel. Strange."

* * *

Mid-morning the next day Hiram Smyth told the story.

He had received a call from Iron Horse that an academician named Orloff was on his way by train from Paris to Moscow, and that in Moscow he would be arrested for spying for the CIA. Orloff, oblivious of any danger facing him, had already gone through West and East Germany—Poland was Smyth's last chance for a rescue.

Smyth used an emergency notification to tell one of his assets, a Polish intelligence officer in Poznan, to pull Orloff off the train and to bring him to Küstrin-on-Oder River. Then, he notified Colonel Gerstmann of the East German People's Police to take a Mr. Trenker from the Karl Marx Strasse checkpoint to Küstrin-on-Oder River to pick up a Russian. He told Gerstmann that Trenker was the only one who could identify the Russian.

Then, he had a team from the U.S. Embassy in Moscow pick up Gregory Orloff's wife and daughter to bring them, hidden in the trunk of an embassy car, to the U.S. Embassy in Helsinki, Finland. From there a military attaché aircraft flew them to London, where a member of the Room 526 team escorted wife and daughter on a commercial flight to Dulles-International, and from there to Room 526.

"All in a day's work, Hank," said Smyth, "all in a day's work."

"Hiram, do you know what you did telling me to go into East Germany? You scared the living daylight out of me."

Smyth laughed. "I figured that much, but I had no time to explain. I had too many balls in the air. Besides, I knew you were in good hands with Heinz Gerstmann. He's an old trusted friend. He has worked for me since he was a VOPO captain. Always reliable, always a straight shooter."

"Hiram, you will be pleased to know that Heinz and I are *Landsmänner.*"

"Are what? How come?"

"Well, both of our families come from Lower Silesia; they lived maybe a half-hour's drive from each other."

"Great. I'll tell you, 'It's a small world.' Maybe you and Heinz can work together next time."

CHAPTER 42

AUGUST 1978
HERZOGENAURACH, WEST GERMANY

Hans Reiter had had only a single communication from Kasandroff since he'd reported to GRU Centre, Moscow in 1975. Aside from that one request and the two brief warnings that saved the lives of Gregory Orloff and Warrant Officer Misha Kovlosky, Hans had heard nothing at all from him. Finally, near the end of summer of 1978, he received a picture postcard of Herzogenaurach. On the back Kasandroff had written that he'd had a wonderful supper at the Hotel Herzog-Park.

So Kasandroff wanted to have a Treff, and, of special interest to Hans, in a location where he—Hans—had served while in Army intelligence. During the late 1960s he had been stationed at Herzogenaurach as a member of the 411th U.S. Army Security Agency Special Operations Unit, aka 411th USASA SPEC OPS. He could not remember Hotel HerzogPark, but he had wonderful memories of the town and surroundings.

Herzogenaurach was a little town some distance from Nurnberg. It was an old town, some 1,000 years old. The core of the town had retained its picturesque historic look. It was also the hometown of the world-famous Adidas and Puma athletic shoes.

"Maybe he wants to buy a pair of Adidas," Smyth joked when Hans told him about Kasandroff's postcard.

Hans's last Army assignment with the 411th at Herzo Base, a former Luftwaffe fighter base north of Nürnberg, had been an especially pleasant one. It was one of those assignments everyone called "great," one of the best Reiter had ever experienced. He had a team of communications interceptors—German, Russian and Polish linguists working three shifts around the clock—and he could choose rotating into any of them. Often, especially during East German / Soviet autumn maneuvers, he worked twelve to fifteen hours straight, but the camaraderie between the men was of such caliber that the hours just flew by. Aside from that, this base also served the best Army chow Hans had ever eaten.

Although Hans did not play golf, those who did had an outstanding facility among the huge antennae masts. It was, appropriately, called the Steel Trees Golf Course. During periodic thunderstorms the station would shut down, and the crew would stand in the open hangar door watching as lightning repeatedly hit their "bedspread" antenna; a huge wire mesh looking eastward, it was suspended between two of the tall steel masts. Each time the lightning hit the wire mesh it would light up like Chinese fireworks.

Two other delightful memories: local beer delivered right to the apartment door (his and Susan's apartment, which was in an American apartment house in Herzogenaurach), and the early morning freshly backed Brötchen, hard-crusted buns, from a bakery just a short walk from the apartment.

According to their Treff arrangement, Hans was to meet Kasandroff on the 15th of August. Hans arrived in Germany on the 13th, rented a car in Frankfurt-on-Main and leisurely drove to Erlangen, a city about a half-hour's drive from Herzogenaurach. From a hotel directory he found a hotel with an unusual name, Nh Erlangen, a three-star hotel on Beethovenstrasse, near the center of Erlangen. He dropped off his bag, showered, and then drove the short way to Herzo—by force of habit he still called it that—to reconnoiter the town.

Apparently, before the U.S. Army abandoned old Herzo Base, it had removed the huge transmission intercept towers. The Steel Trees Golf Course was now the nine-hole Herzo Base Golf Anlage.

Herzogenaurach looked even better than Hans remembered. The inner city was exceptionally clean. All the ancient framework houses sported fresh coats of paint. From various advertisements it seemed as if it had become a party town with a succession of festivals, one after another.

After some searching, he found the Hotel HerzogPark. It was on a Beethovenstrasse just as the hotel in Nh Erlangen was. The hotel had three rather interesting food and beverage facilities. The main restaurant, the Mondial, served international dinners and had an impressive wine list. Guests were given the impression they were dining at an elegant country estate. The Weinkeller was a charming cellar serving the finest Frankenwein, Franconian wines, local Franconian breads and sausages, and other hearty meals. Frankenwein was Hans's brother Christian's favorite German wine; it was the only German wine, dry enough for his taste. Then there was the Stüberl, or little room, a place for a light meal, all fresh vegetables and fruits. Hans decided to have an early supper there before returning to Erlangen.

Back at the Nh Erlangen, he crawled into bed early and awoke early the next day—he was still on Washington time. He went on a brisk three-mile walk. Since he had the whole day to himself, he decided to explore Nürnberg and the Main-Danube Canal, the waterway that connected the two rivers. It was an engineering marvel, and the only trans-European ship and barge connection between the North Sea and the Black Sea. "Crazy Ludwig," the last King of Bavaria, had started the construction during the late nineteenth century, but, lacking today's heavy construction equipment, the project died. Making his weekly run from Herzo Base to the U.S. Army Commissary in Nürnberg, Hans had observed the construction of the viaduct across the road between Herzogenaurach and Nürnberg. The Danube-Main River Canal would not be finally completed until 1992. The canal itself is only 106 miles long; it runs from Bamberg on the Main River to Kelheim on the Danube River through geographically difficult terrain—the Danube at Kelheim is 565 feet above the level of the Main at Bamberg. Sixteen locks, each some 623 feet long, manage to overcome the height difference. The highest lock is 1,332 feet above sea level; according to published data, it is the highest point on earth that can be reached by watercraft from the sea. The canal connects 2,200 miles of waterway between the North and the Black Seas. It took thirty-two years to build it, at a cost of 250 million Euros.

He parked his car on one the guest parking lots overlooking the canal, and stood watching in amazement as tourist boats and cargo barges passed over, not under, the road between Erlangen and Nürnberg.

That evening he found a local hole-in-the-wall eatery with a big sign in the window advertising Warsteiner beer. It was a good choice. He sat at a table with locals talking about the weather, politics, and politics, and politics again. The food was simple, and good. He savored his Warsteiner; he had not had such a good beer since he had last visited Germany. After supper he went for another long walk. He must have gotten used to the local time, because he slept well into the late morning; a good feeling.

He left Erlangen around four in the afternoon. After parking his car near the Hotel HerzogPark he scouted around Herzogenaurach. He remembered a small newspaper vendor near the old city hall—he, or his replacement, was still there and Hans bought the *Fränkischer Tag* newspaper to read while sitting on a bench across from the hotel watching and waiting for the GRU colonel.

After nearly half an hour of reading, watching and waiting he saw Kasandroff walking toward the hotel. Kasandroff stopped every so often looking into shop windows. He spotted Hans, nodded and walked past the hotel entrance. He turned the corner, and after several minutes reappeared from the same street; he then leisurely entered the hotel.

Hans waited a few minutes, then rose, crossed the street and walked into the hotel.

Kasandroff stood near the entrance to the Mondial restaurant. Hans walked over and extended his hand in greeting. Instead, Kasandroff gave him a big bear hug and said, "God, it's good to see you."

The concierge guided them to a table. "It's like old times," Kasandroff said, smiling.

They ordered Warsteiner and perused the menu. After ordering, Hans asked, "Whatever made you pick this little burg for a meeting?"

Kasandroff laughed. "When I tell you, you must promise not to make fun of me."

Reiter promised.

"I am here to purchase Adidas shoes for the Centre."

"What are they going to do with Adidas, run?"

"No, no, no." He was still laughing as he told of the wishes and the whims of the GRU hierarchy. Apparently, Adidas were the hit of Moscow, and everyone knew that those who wore these shoes, no matter whether they were runners or not, were people of influence.

"I had several running pairs, and when I wore them in the GRU gym in Moscow, everyone wanted to know where I had gotten those shoes. Before I was reassigned—oh, by the way, I am now in Vienna—the director of my department gave me a shopping list. I will buy several hundred pairs of Adidas and have the factory send them to a GRU dead letter drop in Moscow."

He joked, "Strictly a clandestine operation."

While they downed a sumptuous meal he mentioned that he had a brief-case full of information and two additional shopping lists. "One for intelligence information, the other is a real shopping list. I need your help on the second one," he pleaded. "It is from the wife of the deputy director. I have no clue what in hell some of that stuff is."

"How much time do you have?"

"Tomorrow and the day after. I think I need one day for the shoes—I think."

"Colonel, I'll look over the list, tonight, at my hotel. Meet me tomorrow for breakfast here at the hotel. Then we go shopping. Okay?"

"Mr. Trenker, that is a large load off my back—or do you say chest?"

"Chest, chest is better."

Back at the Nh Erlangen, Hans laughed when he read the list. Apparently the deputy director's wife was an avid embroideress. Fortunately, the list was in German. She wanted Kasandroff to buy all colors of *Perlgarn*—mercerized yarn—plus sewing machine threads of many colors, embroidering needles, knitting needles, sewing needles, sewing machine needles, scissors, and all sorts of other sewing, embroidering, and knitting tools.

When they met for breakfast Hans chuckled. "Colonel, you are going to be the darling of Centre. I know just where to get all that stuff for the ladies at GHQ. Everything. One-place shopping"

Kasandroff was relieved. "I thought this would take me many days. I am glad you know your way around this area."

"Colonel, I lived here for almost three years during the 1960s."

In Erlangen they went into the largest *Kaufhaus*—department store— of that city. More than two hours later Kasandroff was about to walk out of the store with a bundle he could barely carry.

Hans asked, "Do you have the address with you, the Moscow address?"

"Yes, why?"

"The store here has a department that will wrap and send that pile right from here. That'll save you lugging it around with you."

"What will they think of next?" was his reply. And the Kaufhaus mailed the hefty package without further ado.

They agreed to meet the next time in Austria, and Reiter drove to Frankfurt-on-Main for his flight to Washington's Dulles-International.

CHAPTER 43

H ans Reiter arrived at Dulles-International in the early morning hours; Susan had agreed to pick him up at the airport. She suggested a little mom-and-pop restaurant in the center of Fairfax City's Old Town that served early breakfast. Even before they entered, the aroma of freshly brewed coffee stimulated Hans's ravenous appetite. Early risers, some seemingly retirees, several workmen in rough clothing, and a couple of police officers crowded the small dining area.

In the rear a huge black man hovered over a large sizzling grill. "Come in, come in, there is still room." He pointed to his left, "Right over there. Mammy will be right with you." Then, almost as a second thought, he asked, "Coffee?" Hans nodded.

"Right over here," the man pointed again, "get yourself a mug. Mammy just brewed it."

Hans smiled. He turned to look at Susan. "Now I feel that I am home again. That's so totally different from Europe."

They walked to the coffee machine and poured two giant mugs. "This is comfortable, Susan. How did you ever find this place?"

"Never been here before. My friend Hellene mentioned it. It got a great write-up in the *Fairfax Journal.*"

Indeed, it must have been a popular place; they occupied the last available table. As they savored their coffee Hans spoke in a low voice, "Susan, you have heard me mention that 'crazy Russian' I meet every once in awhile?"

Susan agreed

"Well, I've worked with him now for some eight years. However, the craziest thing happened when I saw him this week. Maybe I should first tell you he just returned from Moscow. We had not seen each other for almost three years. When he saw me this time he gave me a big bear hug and said, 'God, it's good to see you.' I mean..."

He paused, not quite knowing how to end this story. "But right then it seemed as if everything had just changed. He seemed genuinely glad to see me ... and actually, I too was happy to see him again. We were not quite sure whether he would ever make it back to Western Europe."

"So? What's the problem?"

"Well, not a problem. I mean this guy is one hell of a great fellow, but all that shit we were taught at the spook school... you know, never become friends with your asset. I sometimes think some of these instructors had never worked the street. You can't help getting to know the guy you work with over the years, even if he is from the other side."

"You mean like your *Landsmann?*"

"Exactly. This is the second time that I somehow felt safer being with an asset. Hard to tell, but..."

Back in Room 526, Hans and Smyth opened Kasandroff's package; they found a gold mine. In the first envelope they had lists with names and positions of GRU personnel stationed at Moscow GRU Centre. After each name Kasandroff had inserted remarks, such as "womanizer," "boozer," "straight arrow." The next envelope contained a listing of GRU personnel stationed abroad, again with a remarks column. Then, each envelope had information by certain categories. One had a list of six GRU "sleepers" in the United States, with detailed descriptions; three of these names had "last known addresses."

In GRU parlance, sleepers were known as "illegal *Residentura*." For security reasons these intelligence agents worked completely divorced from any Soviet embassy or military attaché. Sleepers came under the direct control of Moscow Centre. They lived in their country of residence "underground," disguised either as citizens of that particular country, or as citizens of a friendly nation. They worked as legitimate businessmen or as gainfully employed craftsmen, teachers, or professors at universities; actually, they tried to gain access to strategically important institutions without being directly involved so that they did not need to fill out any type of security form that invited a background investigation. They had sufficient background documentation to withstand any credit research. Only a thorough counterintelligence background investigation, or the leak by an "insider," could endanger their "solid" standing as good citizens of the community.

Smyth slapped his thigh and exclaimed, "Hank, this is pure gold." He made several copies of the reports, then cut and pasted them by category, divided into geographic areas, and had his secretary type the lists with the Room 526 letterhead.

"I'll again pass the names, one by one, and very slowly, so that it looks as if the information came from different sources," he explained. "Somehow, I don't know why, but somehow I think, there is a skunk at FBI or CIA... or maybe both. I still don't know how Misha Kovlosky and Gregory Orloff were compromised."

Then he hand-carried one of the pages to FBI Washington headquarters, and a copy to the CIA in Langley, Virginia. Both the FBI and the CIA were over-joyed.

"Hank," Smyth slapped Hans's back when he came back from his outing, "we have these guys eating out of our hand. They wanted to know where that info came from, but I just told them to be happy and not to ask any questions." He laughed. "I love telling these guys that they don't have the need to know."

Kasandroff had contributed enough "stuff" to keep the translation depart-ment busy for weeks. Smyth was overjoyed that all went well; he especially enjoyed the little tidbits Kasandroff had contributed from inside GRU Centre. He laughed when Hans told him Kasandroff's main job was shopping for the deputy director's wife.

"You know, I was only kidding about buying Adidas shoes when you told me that you were meeting him in Herzo. But I gotta admit that I almost feel sorry for these assholes in Moscow if they can't even buy embroidery needles. Now, granted, Adidas shoes? That's different. Not everybody can make them. How many pairs did he buy?"

"I don't know. He bought them after I left, but I tell you, he bought at least one whole shipping crate full; big order."

Smyth checked Kasandroff's other shopping list. The GRU wanted ad-ditional information on titanium production, welding techniques, and progress reports on the U.S. Navy titanium submarine; also details on current fighter air-craft production, future USAF aircraft designs, current light and heavy armored vehicle production and future designs, and what the GRU termed "insider infor-mation" on the actual gross national product of the United States.

"Well," suggested Smyth, "looks as if we have to break out some more of the DNI's files, and then see if we can't get some 'fluff stuff' from the Air Force that we can slightly modify using Aviation Week, and some 'flying' magazines to make it look good and verifiable. I think we can have one of our guys look at the latest GNP figures, make lists from as many of the inputs we can get. We'll make good use of publications from the Congressional Budget Office. Then, we'll reduce, or increase, some of the official figures just a little bit to make it look good." Smyth opined that he thought the Russkies did not believe the published figures, and that they would compare the ones from his office with the published ones, and, he concluded, "That'll make it seem as if Kasandroff has the insider's dope."

Hans produced several GRU personality reports, each separately, and under different asset numbers, supposedly "to facilitate filing." These reports symbol-ized the inner workings at GRU's Moscow Centre. He told Smyth about Kasan-droff's two favorites—whom he called "the best two ass-kissers at GRU"—a General Fedoroff and his sidekick Colonel Shobkovskyi. Colonel Alexyi

200

Mikhailovich Shobkovskyi was the chief of GRU's Navy Interest Section and an expert in visual displays. His visual display was a gigantic map of the world with a large red pin signifying GRU Centre and various colored pins for all locations where GRU had intelligence collectors and assets.

Green pins and green strings of mercerized yarns for GRU officers stationed in the Soviet embassies, consulates, military assistance, and United Nations offices—there were close to one thousand green mercerized yarn strings enveloping the globe. Red pins and yarns indicated fully recruited and documented GRU sources. Yellow pins and yarns were for GRU sleepers, the illegal *Residentura*. The blue pins and strings of mercerized yarn denoted Soviet news correspondents wearing two hats, a *Pravda* or *Izvestia* hat, and a GRU one.

Kasandroff reported that every time Colonel Shobkovskyi stuck a new pin and tied a new string he stepped back and viewed his huge map of his world. Kasandroff wrote, "He seems to grow a few centimeters each time General Fedoroff comes to view the map." On the margin of his drawing Kasandroff had written: "The green, red, yellow and blue strings of this yarns cover the map like a spider net—it is his empire."

Kasandroff s colleagues told him that it had been Colonel Shobkovskyi's wife's idea to use mercerized yarn. She was an avid embroideress, an artistic embroideress, almost a fanatic. There was not a piece of cloth in the colonel's apartment that had not been beautifully embroidered. She needed spools upon spools of yarn of all colors. She had started this hobby while she and the colonel were stationed in Bonn, West Germany—Kasandroff had replaced Shobkovskyi at the Soviet embassy there. In Bonn, Shobkovskyi's wife discovered the varied colored strings of *Perlgarn*. When her husband attained his present position, she nagged him for weeks after she had used the last of the yarn she had brought with her to Moscow. Thus, Kasandroff became the first "clandestine" *Perlgarn* buyer.

Colonel Shobkovskyi convinced him to send spools upon spools of the colored yarns to the Centre; the excuse was the "situation map." However, everyone at Centre knew that it was the colonel's wife who drove the "clandestine" yarn collection. Kasandroff told Hans that at every retirement party of an upper echelon officer, the colonel's wife presented him with a beautifully framed and personalized embroidered memento with a skillfully embroidered GRU emblem, the retiree's name and his dates of service at Centre.

Kasandroff also mentioned that he was not the only one on a procurement mission, and that Colonel Shobkovskyi's request was not totally out of the ordinary. GRU collectors filled diplomatic pouches with every conceivable item; items either difficult or impossible even for the Moscow elite to obtain in the Soviet Union.

GRU Washington had a standing order for Evan Williams, a smooth, easy to drink, single barrel vintage Kentucky straight bourbon whiskey for the chief of the Army Interest Section. GRU London endeared itself to General Fedoroff, director of GRU Centre, by sending a steady supply of Famous Grouse Scotch whisky, the general's favorite drink, and the general's wife favored lingerie from Victoria's Secret. A GRU officer stationed in the Soviet Consulate in Ottawa, Canada, had the dubious, but exclusive, mission to supply Centre female employees and GRU officer wives with Kotex—he shipped large cases of this product every few months—no substitutes acceptable. All that and more came to GRU Centre via diplomatic pouches. Of course, everyone at Centre smoked American cigarettes and Cuban cigars.

During Kasandroff's Moscow assignment Colonel Shobkovskyi received additional accolades for his great visual accomplishment when General Fedoroff brought high-ranking Communist party visitors to show them the map with all the pins and strings. Thereafter, whenever one of these high-ranking party members visited, the general proclaimed, "Comrades, GRU is like a giant spider. We cover the globe to guarantee supremacy of the Soviet Union and to protect Rodina." And Colonel Shobkovskyi stood proudly at the general's side.

CHAPTER 44

While meeting with one of his support agents in Frankfurt-Main, Hans Reiter received a coded message from Room 526 that Kasandroff wanted a Treff in Graz, Austria; Graz, now the capital of Styria, a province founded by the Romans in the year 16 BC.

Hans left his sidearm with the support agent, and flew to Vienna, arriving in the early afternoon two days before the scheduled Treff.

He traveled as Manfred Jaeger, a German resident of Mannheim-on Rhine, his secondary *nom de plume*, because the IC Staff had learned from an Austrian asset that his old cover name, Trenker, had been compromised.

Years earlier, as the man named Trenker, Hans and Horst Niemand, a member of his Special Operations Team, had shot and killed an Austrian police officer who was in the process of delivering to the Soviets a drugged U.S. Army clandestine agent. Hans and Niemand had surprised the officer—long suspected of working for the KGB—as he was dragging the U.S. agent to his police cruiser. When Hans challenged him, the Austrian drew his gun and aimed it at the head of the U.S. agent. Hans and Niemand fired four rounds into the Austrian, then placed the U.S. agent in the Austrian police cruiser and drove three city blocks where they transferred him to their own vehicle.

They brought the U.S. agent to the U.S. Embassy in Vienna. The Marine guard called a physician, an Army lieutenant colonel. The doctor insisted on knowing what had transpired but Hans cut him off with, "Doc, I don't know what happened to him. We just found him and you gotta fix him up so his boss can talk to him." After the physician examined the agent and found him to be in no immediate danger, although he appeared to be drugged, he transferred him to the military hospital in Munich to recover.

Hans thought that he and Niemand had gotten away from the shooting unnoticed, but the IC Staff did not think so—thus the use of his secondary cover identity.

Hans arrived late in the afternoon at the Comfort Hotel Drei Raben on 48 Annenstrasse. He had researched the hotel in *Frommer's*, his favorite tourist guide, and in the Drei Raben, on the eastern bank of the Mur River, he found what he liked. Not a new fancy place, but one that was originally built as an apartment house around 1900, and only later modernized and transformed into a hotel. Another thing he liked was that Graz Old Town was a mere ten-minute walk away. Seven bridges connect the old town on the western bank of the river with the new town on the eastern bank.

The following morning he decided to reconnoiter the Treff area and "walk the land." In a way, he played tourist on Uncle Sam's dollars while noting escape routes; quick exits from buildings, alleys connecting major streets—all the usual and necessary items in clandestine operations. From his hotel he drove across the Mur River and parked his car on a side road leading to the Andreas Hofer Platz. Then he walked along Landhausgasse toward the Treff area, the Landhaus courtyard. Graz's Old Town was ideal for clandestine meetings, but it also gave counterintelligence agents many a nook and cranny for surreptitiously following a subject. According to the message Hans had received, Kasandroff had mailed a postcard with a drawing of the magnificent canopy of the well in the center of the courtyard—the time for the Treff mentioned was "noon." From this Hans assumed that he should be waiting at the canopy of the well to see Kasandroff make his identification pass. They would then follow their usual "dry-cleaning" operation to assure neither he nor Kasandroff had inherited any "keepers."

Hans walked from the Landhaus, through Graz's Old Town, in increasingly larger circles. Only after he felt familiar with the terrain did he return to the Andreas Hofer Platz and his car. Back at the hotel, with a city map at hand, Reiter reviewed the approach and departure from the Treff; he then rewarded himself with a fine Hungarian Goulash dinner at the hotel's dining room.

The following day, about an hour before noon, he drove again to Andreas Hofer Platz and walked along Landhausgasse, a long, straight street, where it was easy to detect surveillance. He saw nothing that could be called a "tail." Just to be sure, he turned left into Herrengasse and walked about half a city block, then turned around, crossed the street as if he had mistakenly walked the wrong way, and walked back toward the Landhaus complex. Now he was certain that no one had followed him.

Arriving at the Landhaus courtyard a few minutes before noon, he walked around the ornate canopy, as would any tourist to admire the finely cast bronze cherubs and women. Then he pulled out his tourist guide, leaned against the well, and pretended to read. At exactly noon Kasandroff walked into the courtyard, paused as if to admire the well and its canopy and then used one of the exits leading into Herrengasse. Since they had been the only ones in the courtyard, Hans waited only briefly before following Kasandroff. Kasandroff had turned left into Herrengasse walking toward Hauptplatz—Hans followed. The crowded street made counter-surveillance difficult. He moved quickly so as not to lose Kasandroff.

Near the Hauptplatz, Kasandroff slowed his walk and entered a small restaurant. Hans joined him at one of the tables; they shook hands. Kasandroff had a look of concern. "I may be getting paranoid but I am almost sure I picked up a tail after I parked my car. Three guys. Don't know if they are from my side, or Austrian. They looked Austrian, but... well, that doesn't mean crap. Just to make sure, during lunch let's play the source / case officer card. You still have your envelope?"

"Yes, and with real documents. But are you sure? I saw no surveillance."

"Well, in that crowd, who could tell?"

"True. Well, you listed that meeting as 'source contact,' didn't you?"

"Oh, yes, it's all on the up and up."

"Good, then there shouldn't be any problem. The envelope I have has some of the stuff you wanted including an updated DIA organization chart, all marked SECRET. Although it's really 'For Official Use Only.'"

Kasandroff seemed to relax. "Doesn't matter, as long as it's official."

Reiter nodded. "That it is. It's the real thing. Okay, let's eat first, then go into our act."

After lunch they exchanged envelopes. Reiter handed his to Kasandroff, adding, "You remember asking about the status of the American titanium submarine?" Without waiting for the answer, he continued, "I had one hell of a time getting the truth. No one in the U.S. Navy wanted to admit it, but it died from lack of funds. I have the details in that envelope, but here is the short story.

"Without assistance from the CIA, the Navy had difficulty surreptitiously acquiring huge amounts of titanium sponge and argon gas. Along the way, there were problems training reliable shipyard workers to work with titanium. In the test lab, they could not solve the problem of shielding with argon gas all functions that involve bending and welding heavy titanium plates. They tried building a large envelope for robot welding; that failed. Then there were difficulties keeping the whole thing secret—keeping it from the Congress and the public. But what eventually killed the project was money. Then, when it became clear that your people succeeded building titanium submarines, no one, especially the U.S. Navy, was willing to admit to the failure. So they buried the whole thing."

Kasandroff shoved the envelope into his breast pocket unopened, replying, "I thought that was only possible in the Soviet Union."

Hans laughed. "I cannot believe myself that this was possible, but bureaucrats can do lots of what seems impossible, when their jobs are at stake." He opened Kasandroff s envelope, looked into it; made it appear as if he was visually counting money, smiled and thanked Kasandroff profusely. Having their ceremony completed, Kasandroff mentioned that he had a number of meetings in Salzburg, and that their next one should be in the city of Wolfgang Amadeus

Mozart fame.

"Ivan Ivanovich, if at all possible," suggested Hans, "make it when there is no holiday, or some other event. The last time we met, I had a hell of a time getting a hotel reservation."

Kasandroff laughed. "I remember. I had the same problem, but in that city, one festival follows another close on its heels."

Hans had promised Kasandroff to check to see if anything looked like surveillance, but in the crowded streets with its noontime traffic, this proved to be impossible. However, he followed Kasandroff along Herrengasse toward the Hauptplatz, but lost sight of him on the busy street. He decided to "clear his own baffles," Navy talk he had learned at NISC, meaning to see if someone was following him. *Am I getting paranoid,* he wondered, *or is it Kasandroff's talk of being followed?* He decided that caution was the better part of valor. During his initial "reconnaissance" he had found a convenient, always busy, escape route through Kastner & Öhler, an interesting department store on Sackstrasse—featured in the tourist information as Kunst Meile, "Artistic Mile." He turned into Sackstrasse and entered the department store. He wandered from one floor to the next, from leather goods to sporting attire.

When he had just about reassured himself that he had not inherited a "keeper," he heard a shrill female voice, "Hans, Hans Reiter. What are you doing here?"

He almost lost his composure. He turned half in shock and saw Margret Johansen, a member of their Alexandria Swimming Pool Association.

He tried to act nonchalant with, "Hello, Margret, what a surprise. What are you doing here?"

"Shopping as usual; with Herman out there on the Stubalpe climbing some dumb mountain."

"Isn't he a little out of shape for mountain climbing?"

"Well, he got an invite from a friend, and he couldn't refuse. I don't think it's too hard a climb, but to each his own. So, you didn't tell me why you are here? Is Susan with you?"

"No, strictly business. I met an associate from the embassy in Vienna who had business here in Graz. I stayed another day to do something touristy."

Trying hard to get out of this uncomfortable situation without further embarrassing himself, he remembered that the department store had a cafe where they could talk quietly and privately. It also occurred to him that if someone were indeed following him, the "keeper" would assume that he had observed an innocent rendezvous.

"Margret, there's a nice cafe in this store where we can sit and talk without blocking the shopping aisles."

Mrs. Johansen thought this a great idea and Hans escorted her into the cafe.

There he told the ever-so-curious lady that he had met in Graz with the U.S. economic attaché to help with interpreting some export-import business and that he just happened to walk into Kastner & Öhler to look at some leather goods. Mrs. Johansen took this uninteresting bit of information as true gospel, and raved about the good prices in this store, and how much she had always wanted to have an original Austrian dirndl dress, and that she had finally found exactly what she wanted.

"Hermann is going to spit when he hears how much this 'reasonably priced' dirndl costs, but he has his fun, and I have mine."

Hans told her that that seemed only fair. He then excused himself with having to catch the next train to Vienna. He paid the bill and left Mrs. Johansen enjoying her *Linzer Torte*.

While he walked hurriedly to Andreas Hofer Platz where he had parked his car, he again tried to "clear his baffles." Back at the hotel he quickly packed his bag, checked out, and drove directly to Vienna Airport's Schengen Area to drop off his rental car. Just to be safe, he wanted to leave Austria as fast a possible. The next flight out was an Alitalia, one leaving in fifteen minutes for Rome. He arrived in Rome in the early evening. There he changed from the German Manfred Jäger into the American Assistant Naval Attaché Lieutenant Commander George Trenker, and booked a seat on another Alitalia to Washington-Dulles International.

At home Hans told Susan about his run-in with Margret Johansen and what his cover story was—should she ever ask.

"What was Margret doing in Graz?"

"Shopping. She bought a very expensive dirndl to punish Hermann for going mountain climbing."

Susan just laughed. "That's going to be a very funny-looking lady at our next pool meeting. I'm sure she will wear that dress."

Hans joined in the laughter, then told Susan of the historic nature of Graz, the marvelous architecture, and the friendly people, and that once he had retired from this crazy job, they would tour Austria so that both could appreciate these places.

While on these "business trips" he could never afford to really look around, to truly enjoy these beautiful landscapes, the quaint places, or delve into the histories of the regions; personnel and personal security made that impossible. Once away from all that "security stuff," he wanted to enjoy and share the beauty of Austria with the woman he loved.

CHAPTER 45

B ack at Room 526 Hans Reiter submitted the information Kasandroff had pro-
duced. Then he called his support agent in Frankfurt-Main and told him to
send the "stuff" he had left with him, including his .38 caliber police special, via
Armed Forces Courier Service, to Washington. During the three years following
Kasandroff's GRU Vienna assignment, he and Hans met in picturesque Austrian
tourist locations. Hans would have preferred meeting in southern Germany, but
Kasandroff did not want the Austrians to know how often he crossed their border;
Germany was the operational area of the Soviet attaché in Bonn.

Although he agreed to the Austrian meetings, Hans requested that they not
meet anywhere near Vienna; that it would be best if they had their Treffs at places
like Innsbruck, a beautiful city just south of the Karwendel Mountains, or Salzburg.

During the previous eight or nine years the information, or misinforma-
tion, Smyth had provided Hans to be passed on to Kasandroff had come from
the, by now long retired, DNIs. The time had now come for Smyth to get additional "trading goods." He approached the director of the IC Staff, the only
one authorized to fill his request. The IC Staff was responsible for screening the
material for accuracy and for ascertaining that no vital information was compromised.

Several months later an Armed Forces Courier Service officer delivered a
large, triple-sealed package of the trading material. The folks in Room 526 now
had enough information—actually disinformation—to slip to the other side for at
least the next two years. They in turn submitted all the information received from
their assets under the reliability indicator "F-6," meaning that the collector could
assure neither the reliability of the asset, nor the accuracy of the information.
Smyth wanted to make sure that just in case they were fed disinformation from
the other side, the information would not enter the intelligence database without
confirmation from other, more reliable sources.

Most of the material Hans and the lads at Room 526 had collected and
disseminated during the past decade was of the counterintelligence nature. It

208

enabled the FBI, the counterintelligence folks at CIA and the Department of Defense to pinpoint almost all major GRU players in the United States, as well as in countries of interest to the United States. The information also permitted security analysts to look inside the GRU, to learn the GRU's major collection requirements—that is, all the information the Soviet Union felt it needed.

Somehow, according to Smyth's friend at the FBI, shortly after Smyth gave the information to the FBI, several of the sleepers fingered by Kasandroff had mysteriously disappeared.

"Hank," exploded Smyth when he heard that, "I told you long ago that there's a skunk at FBI or CIA; looks to me as if it's the FBI." He became beet-red with anger as he continued, "I told Harold—he's FBI Internal Security—I told him, 'You've got a skunk in your outfit,' but he tells me 'impossible.' Thinks it pure coincidence; thinks his boys are true blue. But, Hank, I told him there ain't no such a thing as pure coincidence in this business. I bet that bastard, whoever he is, sold out Misha Kovlosky and Gregory Orloff... the rotten Sonofabitch."

Smyth pounded his desk. "And now those goddamned sleepers." He exploded once more, "I think that SOB informed Centre that their USA sleepers are blown.

"Come to think of it, that could make your operation dicey, and put Kasandroff in big trouble. Next time.... Oh, by the way, you aren't meeting in Austria again, are you?'

Hans thought about this. "Do you think this could have something to do with the Austrian police looking for Trenker?"

"Shit, I never even thought about that. Next time, if you have to meet in Austria, I had better document you as a different naval attaché—can't be too careful."

For some time Smyth sat appearing to be in thought. Then he rose from his chair and started walking back and forth. Hans knew that Smyth did his best brainstorming when pacing between the two windows behind his desk. Finally he faced Hans. "I think we ought to have that Navy fellow, the one you first met at Bonn ... what's his name?"

"Johannes Dreier."

"Yeah, right, Johannes Dreier. I think we ought to have him bird-dog you on the next meetings. He seemed to be a hell of a guy. I'll get the IC Staff to have the DNI assign him to give you security. What do you think?"

"I don't know. Do you really think this is necessary?"

"What are you talking about? If we have skunks in FBI or CIA, they can have the KGB or the GRU tip off the Austrians to have you arrested."

He again started pacing between the windows. "Let's at least do a few of the meetings with Dreier as a backup. If nothing happens—especially after you've warned Kasandroff—maybe we can ease up and have one of our own guys, someone between assignments, do the bird-dogging ... just to be on the safe side. But right now we need a guy who can shoot straight."

Because the IC staff director "encouraged" the DNI to have now Master Sergeant Johannes "John" Dreier assigned to Room 526 for duty as "Personnel Security Expert," he came to Room 526.

On a wet, cold February in 1981, Dreier reported for what was to be a three-month TDY. The doorman at the first floor of the Wisconsin Avenue building called and Hans greeted a surprised Dreier.

"Commander Trenker, what am I doing here?" was the first question Dreier asked while they rode the elevator to the fifth floor.

"Well," replied Hans, "first of all my real name is Hans Reiter. After what we have been through together I consider you my friend; my friends call me Hank; Trenker is my cover name."

"And the assistant Naval attaché thing is also a cover?"

"All as phony as can be ... but backed by the DNI," replied Hans.

Hans introduced the master sergeant to Smyth. Smyth immediately made Dreier feel at home with, "Well, finally I have a man of equal rank in this outfit. I was an Army master sergeant—long ago." Then he explained the security problem they had encountered with a possible leak in either FBI or CIA.

Smyth already had a copy of Dreier's personnel file in front of him when he asked, "Tell me, how comfortable are you with sidearms?"

"Relatively," replied Dreier, "only relatively. I am very comfortable with my issued .45 caliber, less so with .38 caliber pistols and revolvers."

"Okay. Next question: how would you like to attend a Secret Service training course, about three or four weeks, to get to be an expert with .38's; either revolver or pistol?"

"What? Another TDY within a TDY? Is that possible? But, yes, okay."

Smyth laughed. "Sergeant Dreier, anything is possible if you push the right button."

He paused momentarily as if he had lost his train of thought, then, "Oh, by the way. Working here as a military, I owe you around $800 clothing allowance to supplement for wear and tear, care of own civilian clothing, and to purchase additional gear. Working here, you must be prepared for all geographic areas—on a moment's notice. You'll need especially heavy winter clothing, and some kind of workman's wear. We'll have Hank help you in the purchases, because he has the experience."

Three weeks after the interview, Dreier returned with a fancy certificate of Secret Service School completion and a letter from the school's director addressed to Hiram Smyth advising that Master Sergeant Johann Dreier, USMC, had been an exemplary student.

CHAPTER 46

APRIL 1981
BEST WESTERN HOTEL ZUM HIRSCHEN
ST. JULIENSTRASS 21-23
SALZBURG, AUSTRIA

Hans received a postcard with a photo of Atel Hotel Lasserhof in Salzburg Austria. The Treff was scheduled for the first week in April. Hans, this time with Johannes Dreier as backup security, flew into Munich. Both picked up sidearms at the local, recently installed, Room 526 support agent. Dreier rented a Mercedes sedan for the short drive to Salzburg, just across the German-Austrian border. The support agent had reserved two adjoining rooms at the Best Western Hotel Zum Hirschen.

Zum Hirschen was centrally located, between the main train station and Salzburg's Old Town. It even had—unusual for older European hotels—free parking in its own lot. They had a sumptuous meal at the Hirschenwirt, the hotel's restaurant and then walked into the quiet beer-garden to rest up from the trip, and to savor their first Austrian beer.

In late afternoon they decided to reconnoiter the area between their hotel and the Atel Hotel Lasserhof, the Treff area. The hotel, also in the center of Salzburg, was within easy walking distance to all of the historic and interesting points of the city. Hans and Dreier crisscrossed the area walking north on Weiserstrasse, and then returned to the hotel via Auerspergstrasse and Haydnstrasse. Then they checked the entrances and exits of Pasta e Vino, the Atel Hotel Lasserhof restaurant. Reiter told Dreier that they would do the same non-contact security as they had done previously at Königswinter.

"Most probably," he suggested, "Kasandroff will circle the hotel to make sure I am in the area. He will then enter the restaurant and I'll see if he is being followed. If all is clear, I will meet Kasandroff there and we'll take a table and talk and eat lunch."

They agreed that Dreier would follow shortly and ask for a table near the exit to the bar. If everything turned out well, Kasandroff would depart, Hans would follow and they would cover the street—one on each side—and watch Kasandroff entering his automobile.

Shortly before noon the next day Hans and Dreier positioned themselves as agreed. Hans saw Kasandroff walking past the hotel's entrance twice; he signaled that he had spotted Hans and then walked into the hotel. After Hans saw nothing that looked even faintly like surveillance, he too entered the hotel. Kasandroff greeted him in the lobby and they walked into the restaurant. Hans saw Dreier entering the hotel; he walked to a display and appeared to be interested in the tourist pamphlets.

While Hans and Kasandroff perused the menu, Hans mentioned what had happened in Washington; that several of the sleepers he had fingered had mysteriously disappeared shortly after the FBI had received the information; and that Hans's boss suspected a mole in either the FBI or the CIA.

"My boss thinks the mole is in FBI," he confided. "He is terribly concerned for your safety... and for mine. I have with me a non-contact security agent to assure that nothing unforeseen will happen to me, but my boss wanted you to know; wanted you to be especially careful. He told me to assure you that if you suspect danger, to immediately call and disappear in one of our boltholes."

"A mole in the FBI?" asked a shocked Kasandroff. "No one at Centre ever mentioned that." He looked thoughtful, then added, "But, of course, that would have been handled by counterintelligence—different office; even on another floor of the building. Not even that ass-kisser Shobkovskyi had any strings on his stupid map display showing counterintelligence strings."

During dinner Kasandroff reported on happenings in his embassy in Vienna. "I have also another package for you," he said. "Thinking back of what you said about the mole, I must admit I have not seen any change in attitude among my people at the embassy. Usually, any counterintelligence questioning becomes rapidly apparent when each of those questioned tries to distance himself from the presumed suspect. Nothing so far. But I will be alert now that I know there might be a leak." He sipped from his beer. "Does anyone outside your office know my identity?"

"No, we have resisted any attempt to release either the name or the position of our assets. We even split the reports into different categories, and issue them on different dates, with different asset numbers, but... My boss thinks that this not only makes our operation appear more secretive for those who get the information, but it also assures our assets security. However, be alert. We had two cases in the past few years that must have been traced to their source somehow, even though no identifiers were listed. We think it was the quality of the information that blew their cover. That's what worries my boss. That's why he wanted me to caution you."

"Ah," Kasandroff smiled, "I suppose the academician ... what's his name? Gregory Orloff, being one of them?"

"Yes."

"And the sailor in Tokyo?"

"Yes."

"Okay, you tell your boss thank you, and that I will be even more careful than I have been in the past." He paused as if he had forgotten something.

212

"Damn it, I must be getting old. I wanted to tell you that if you don't like to meet in Austria, Centre has given me carte blanche to operate anywhere in northwestern Europe, Germany, Denmark, Holland, wherever."

"Hey, that's great. Let me think." Hans was overjoyed, and mentioned that the best place to meet would be somewhere near Frankfurt-on-Main—it would eliminate changing planes.

"Colonel, have you ever been to Bad Homburg?"

"You mean the place where the Kaiser and the Tsar vacationed?"

"Exactly. You'll love it. It even has a pretty Russian Orthodox chapel in the Kurpark."

"I'll check it out. Next time expect a picture postcard of Bad Homburg." After they had finished their beers they went into the old bit of exchanging information for money.

"I have some interesting items here; straight from Centre," said Kasandroff as they exchanged envelopes. Reiter did his usual play-act as if he was counting the money. They shook hands; Kasandroff clasping both hands over Reiter's.

"And tell your boss that I am especially appreciative that he has shown so much concern for my well-being."

"Colonel, we have been together for a long time. No need to take any chances."

Kasandroff nodded, he then walked away quickly. Dreier had already paid his bill and lingered over an almost empty glass of beer waiting for Reiter to leave. Dreier left first. They followed their agreed security procedure walking on different sides of the street following Kasandroff at a distance. They spotted no surveillance; they saw Kasandroff entering his car and driving east on Lasserstrasse.

CHAPTER 47

Hans Reiter and John Dreier returned to Room 526 and reported that the Treff had proceeded as always—free of surveillance. Hans conveyed Kasandroff s gratitude for Smyth's concerns and that he said he would be twice as careful as before regarding Soviet counterintelligence.

"Well, hell's bells," sputtered Smyth somewhat embarrassed by Kasandroff s gratitude, "after all, he is our bread and butter."

"Hiram, there is more to this than that."

"What are you talking about?"

"Well, let me first tell you that I thought Kasandroff was more than just touched by your concern. But, something else ... I noticed it first when he came back from Moscow. He seemed to be truly glad to get back to Western Europe. When he saw me at Herzo, Kasandroff gave me a big bear hug and said, 'God, it's good to see you.' He seemed to be genuinely glad to see me. I mean," Reiter paused, not quite knowing how to end this story. "But right then it seemed as if everything had just changed. He seemed genuinely glad to see me ... and actually, I too was happy to see him again. We were not quite sure whether he would ever make it back to Western Europe."

"So?" Smyth wondered.

"Well, actually, so was I. I mean, it was a Treff between case officer and asset, but... well, but it was almost like friends who had not seen each other for some time."

"Hank, sit down for a moment. I know exactly what you are trying to say. You wonder whether or not this is an anomaly." He paused, apparently waiting for Hans's acknowledgement. Hans nodded.

"Well," Smyth continued, "It ain't. All that bullshit they tell you at school is exactly that: bullshit. They go by the book—even those who had been street agents at one time or other; they go by the book." Smyth paused. "And I am convinced that book was written by some asshole who had never smelled the streets of Budapest, or Berlin, or Tsingtao. I care about our assets. I do everything to keep them out of harm's way. I love them all, and if they ever disappoint me, I hate their guts forever. Remember Heinz Gerstmann?"

It was rhetorical.

"Remember the Polish security officer you met briefly on the Oder River bridge? Well, we became friends, and I'll do anything, anything, to keep him alive. That's the main reason I get so pissed off when I know that there is a skunk, a mole in CIA or FBI; an American, God damn it to hell."

He heaved himself up and got himself a cup of age-old coffee. "That's one of the reasons I love Kasandroff. He saved the lives of two of our guys. Shit, don't look at them as sources, as assets. Kasandroff and all the others are also men who risk their lives far more than do we. Especially me sitting here in this secure office in Washington, D.C."

He took a deep breath. "Screw what these shitheads at the school teach. You gotta use your nose, what the Germans call *Fingerspitzengefühl*—as the blind man uses Braille to read a book, so must you read the asset."

Hans nodded again. He began to feel better already.

"You are a natural," continued Smyth, "you have this *Fingerspitzengefühl* that every good agent must have to survive. So you and Kasandroff became friends, so what? Keep at it."

Kasandroff s package included detailed information about collection guidance the GRU sent to its collectors—the "where and how" for all important collection targets. This was a treasure trove. It would enable the CI folks to build "walls" to prevent, or at least make it far more difficult, for GRU collectors to succeed.

Smyth reviewed the GRU collection guidance material, then requested a one-on-one meeting with the director of the Intelligence Community Staff to discuss it.

He began the meeting by restating his suspicion of an FBI mole and urging that the GRU collection guidance information be distributed piecemeal—to make it look as if it had come from many different sources: GRU insiders, communications taps, bugs in embassies, the works.

During one of their discussions between Smyth and Reiter, Smyth alluded to violating reporting procedures, "Call me paranoid, but these close calls saving Gregory Orloff and Misha Kovlosky, and some of those Soviet deep cover agents in the U.S. escaping, that can't be just a coincidence. Just so you know, I have Kasandroff reporting sometimes as a 'walk-in' source, other times as a communications intercept, and most often as a 'temporary asset' just to protect him from those SOBs at FBI or CIA." He laughed, "Never got caught in that either, but I just wanted you to know."

In his report, a copy of which Smyth gave the director, Kasandroff had explained in detail—in a rash of different reports from a variety of assets—that Moscow Centre most often told its collectors exactly where they could expect to find requested information—including the street address. He explained that the research bureau at GRU Centre perused all requests to ascertain whether the information was already available, or whether open source research, or overt collectors—attaches, news reporters, "academicians," or business travelers—could produce what analysts needed.

Smyth emphasized to the director that only when no other collection method was available did GRU Centre get the clandestine element involved. Even then, Smyth told him, before GRU Centre launched any collection it reviewed each request to see whether the information requested was of high enough importance to risk a clandestine asset.

Smyth suggested that the CI Staff ought to do likewise.

Although the director expressed concern to Smyth about expanding his staff's workload, he did take the matter up with them. In doing so—so as not to compromise the source—he presented it as his own idea.

Smyth also passed along reports on the more humorous side of the GRU, about which Room 526 received more positive feedback than for all its other intelligence reports.

Kasandroff's shopping tour for the GRU deputy director's wife was one example of GRU's "clandestine" collections.

There were others.

The CI folks in the Washington area were mystified by another shopping tour. The GRU "resident," the chief agent in America, was purchasing nothing but the finest plumbing hardware, faucets, gaskets, toilet bowl items, shower spray nozzles, etc.—plus thousands of fine, double-lined rolls of toilet paper, several cardboard crates at a time.

Smyth explained to them that the general in charge of the GRU had ordered all these items to endear himself to comrades in the upper strata of the party by supplying them with toilet paper.

Carl Simpson, chief of the Washington FBI-CI folks, found this hard to believe. In a conference with Smyth he asked for the names of Room 526's sources; he wanted to talk to them personally. Smyth told him the FBI did not have a high enough security clearance for that, but that his idea that the toilet paper was used to filter highly toxic chemicals was ludicrous.

"Carl," said Smyth, who had known the CI chief for many years, "believe me when I tell you, the Soviets use it to wipe their asses."

He also told Simpson about the purchase—by the GRU "resident" in Ottawa, Canada—of huge quantities of Kotex and other female hygiene goods. Canadian Mounted Police were aware of this and, like Simpson, wondered whether the Kotex was used to filter critical chemicals.

"No," Smyth told Simpson, "it was not.

"This GRU 'resident' was supplying female employees of Moscow GRU Centre with these difficult-to-get items; it was one of the women's employment benefits."

Simpson left the conference room seemingly convinced, but still shaking his head. On the way out he turned and asked, "Are you sure that all that toilet paper is used just to wipe their asses?"

Smyth laughed. "Only the asses of the party high-rankers, Carl, the rest still use *Pravda* or *Izvestia*."

The information in the package Kasandroff gave Hans during that Salzburg Treff rounded out the picture Room 526 had of the GRU and its modus operandi. Sharing this knowledge with intelligence counterparts, Room 526 made it appear that it came from communications intercepts— from bugged telephone lines in various European locations where GRU officers had complained about flawed intelligence assessments. To back up this deception, Smyth invented quotes supposedly made by GRU officers, such as: "We stated clearly, we gave the collectors superb guidance, but GRU is not as great at intelligence collection as we make the Kremlin believe."

The point paper Room 526 put forward was replete with examples of intelligence reports GRU officers had submitted to Centre.

Smyth assured the CI folks that the information in these GRU reports did not come from overt or aggressive clandestine collections but from published sources translated and then submitted as "collected intelligence." "Open sources," i.e., *Aviation Week*—the GRU called it "Aviation Leak"—as well as shipbuilding, transportation, business, scientific and technical journals, military journals, and of late, computer newspapers, provided much of the detailed information GRU case officers used to pad their reports, making it appear that the information came from one-time HUMINT sources with knowledge of upcoming technologies, construction of ships, contracts to build fighter aircraft, bombers, etc.; all of it readily available in the Free World.

According to Kasandroff, one of the more productive duties for Soviet attachés was escorting visiting academicians to trade fairs and technical conferences. Before these academicians returned to the Soviet Union, the attachés debriefed them, and then submitted the information as "attaché collection." Later, GRU Centre debriefed the academicians again in Moscow and compared their information with that submitted by attachés. The two bits of information, coming from two different elements, and reported on two different dates, from two different locations, tended to confirm the veracity of the collections, i.e. "confirmed by multiple sources."

* * * * * *

By the early 1980s Kasandroff and Reiter had traded information for more than a decade. They always played the counter-surveillance card to assure each other's safety. Kasandroff reported at every meeting that the material he received always got the evaluation, "high, and confirmed by other sources." Smyth in turn had learned, and passed to counterintelligence, the whereabouts and the identities of many GRU clandestine officers, changes to the GRU's modus operandi, as well as Centre's collection requirements. After Kasandroff s three-year stint at GRU Centre, Moscow, Smyth knew pretty well all the inside workings, the problems, the internal frictions, the bickering, as well as the personalities that formulated Soviet Military Intelligence collection plans, and he released the information as "snippets" over a period of months.

Without even realizing it Hans and Kasandroff had become something other than two intelligence agents from different sides. They had discovered their various likes and dislikes; they had become concerned with each other's personal security, their survival. It seemed as if they even enjoyed the same foods—Hungarian goulash being one of them—and Warsteiner beer. Reiter wondered, having initially blackmailed Kasandroff into working for Room 526, whether they could ever become friends.

CHAPTER 48

It was high noon. Hans Reiter sat at a little sidewalk cafe in Bad Homburg-vor-der-Höhe waiting for Kasandroff. The arranged Treff was to be at the town's Kurpark, the park surrounding the spa. Bad Homburg, the famous spa just a short drive north from Frankfurt-on-Main, was Reiter's favorite German town. The spa was famous for its many "healing" springs dispersed over beautiful, shady lawns in the Kurpark, the spa's large garden. Central Europeans have an affinity for drinking the most awful-smelling sulfur water, as well as other, mineral-rich, waters; Bad Homburg had them all. Before the big blowout that later became known as "The Great War," or World War I, Bad Homburg was the spa where both the Kaiser and his cousin, Nikolaus II, the Czar of all the Russians, vacationed. Back in the last century, the Russian Orthodox Church was founded and financed by Proworoff, the Russian Imperial Council of State, and designed by Professor Louis Benois. Its cornerstone was laid in October 1896 in the presence of Tsar Nikolaus II and the Tsarina. The church still serves mostly Russian parishioners.

Reiter had known Bad Homburg from the early Cold War days. In those days, his U.S. Army Special Operations Team had inherited an elderly, no longer active, former Kriegsmarine officer living in this quaint spa. The old sailor had good contacts with several Kriegsmarine veterans, or their widows, living along the North and Baltic Sea coasts. For reasons unknown to Hans the old sailor had the code name "the Shepherd." Hans's contact with the Shepherd started out to be a caretaker one, not an operational one. Hans, or one of his lads, would visit the old gentleman once a month, have lunch in one of the fashionable restaurants, and present him with a bottle of bourbon and a box of his favorite hand-rolled cigars; hand-rolled by a little cigar maker in Ybor City, Florida, the home of the finest Cuban cigar-makers in the United States.

Hans never thought he would re-deploy this source, or use him in any of his clandestine operations; it was one of many wrong assessments he had made in this strange profession. The Shepherd became one of his best contact agents. Some of his World War II comrades now captained freighters that plied the Baltic making a round-trip from Lübeck, West Germany, to Gdansk, Poland, and onward to Liepaja, Litovskaya SSR, Tallinn, Estonskaya SSR, Leningrad, USSR, Helsinki, Finland, and Stockholm, Sweden.

The Shepherd had also kept in touch with sources living in the restricted zone along the Baltic Sea where residents had to have two identification cards, one the regular Kennkarte, the other a special photo ID pass. With the Shepherd's help Reiter's team managed to saturate the coastal area with intelligence sources able to report on "Harbors and Landing Beaches," on surface-to-air missile installations, and East German and Soviet naval training areas.

One of the Shepherd's contacts—code-named Lorelei—was the widow of one of his naval academy classmates; she became Hans's most valuable source. Lorelei was an extraordinary lady, an amateur bird-watcher and a photographer of some fame. She photographed every missile site, harbor installation and potential landing beach between Warnemünde, her hometown, and eastward to the island of Rügen. During the middle Cold War days the Pentagon considered this area of "strategic interest."

The Shepherd had long ago entered his final berth, but as Reiter wandered through town he recalled all the wonderful stories he had told of his wartime experiences during both World Wars. During the Great War the Shepherd had served as a lieutenant on the Cruiser Breslau in the Dardanelles and the Black Sea—sailing under Turkish colors. In the second debacle he was one of Admiral Doenitz's aides. He was at the Atlantic submarine base awaiting the return of his only son when a British bomber, coming out of nowhere, dropped a bomb that sank the U-Boat as it entered the channel—there had been no survivors.

It was during that particular 1981 meeting in Bad Homburg when the American Special Operations Officer Reiter and the Soviet GRU Colonel Kasandroff broke the cardinal rule, one all intelligence services have carved in granite, "Never become friends with an asset."

If truth be told, although working on opposite sides, they had become trusted friends long before they had openly admitted it to each other. In Bad Homburg, after the second or third round of Warsteiner beer, Hans thought the time had come to make amends.

"Colonel," he said, "we have been working together for many years. We have shared dangers, dangers others cannot even imagine." Kasandroff looked at him questioningly.

"Colonel, we have become friends, and as your friend I think we should be less formal." Kasandroff nodded in agreement.

"You always call me 'Mr. Trenker,' although I know that you know it is not my real name. You have never asked me what my real name is, but I feel, after all these years, that you should call me by my first name. My friends call me Hank; my full name is Hans Reiter. What say you?"

Kasandroff seemed a little taken aback by this revelation; but then he raised his stein and said, "Hank, my friends call me Ivan Ivanovich." After a deep swig of Warsteiner they shook hands; clasping all four together. In true Russian fashion Hans and Ivan Ivanovich became friends.

CHAPTER 49

DECEMBER 9, 1981
DEFENSE INTELLIGENCE AGENCY
ANALYSIS CENTER
BOLLING AIR FORCE BASE
WASHINGTON, D.C.

On that December date, Rear Admiral Vincence Horstmann, the last surviving DNI involved in the titanium deception operation, attended another of the monthly Joint Services/Defense Intelligence Agency briefings. He finally heard what he had been waiting to hear for many years:

Incredible, extraordinary capital investment in facilities, manpower, talent, and material resource allocation had the Soviet Union hurtling toward financial disaster. The old DNI rose quietly from his seat and left the meeting discreetly. He had just needed to be assured that old Ike, all the Directors of Naval Intelligence, and the OMEGA Team—as the President called them—had been on the right track.

He regretted that he had promised his President never to search for the rest of the OMEGA Team. Now there were so few insiders left. The old President had passed on to the great beyond in 1969; all the DNI's predecessors had entered their final berths. Now only he and the trio the President called the OMEGA Team, people the DNI had never met, were the keepers of the presidential secret—well, also Special Agent Hans Reiter.

All these past years he had been curious about the people who had dreamed up this crazy plot to "bleed the goddamned Commies white." He thought they must have been gifted, brilliant; he regretted never having met them. Of course, he knew the names of two of the operatives, Christian Reiter, the New Yorker, and Karl Cedric "Casey" Miller, the Wizard, and that the elder Reiter was the brother of Special Agent Hans Reiter. He also knew that the New Yorker had some connection with Quadrant Import-Export. In notes kept by Rear Admiral Carl Di Rovalleri, Eisenhower had also frequently mentioned someone called the Philosopher, but the DNI had never picked up any clues to help solve that mystery.

CHAPTER 50

LATE AUTUMN 1982
BAD HOMBURG-VOR-DER-HÖHE
GERMANY

Kasandroff apparently enjoyed his last visit to Bad Homburg so much that he decided to violate the rule of never meeting in the same town twice. On a warm autumn day—the Germans called it Altweibersommer—Indian summer, Hans Reiter watched Kasandroff as he walked from the rear of the Orthodox Church. Kasandroff circled the building, stopping here and there; walking slowly past the front door; wandering tourist like, as if admiring the church's architecture. He then increased his pace and walked into the Kurpark, where he found a secluded bench in the shade of an ancient oak tree.

Hans, after seeing that Kasandroff had not been followed, rose from his chair and leisurely walked into the Kurpark. They greeted each other as old friends do and sat down.

Hans, who knew that Tamara Ivanova, Kasandroff's wife, had visited her mother in Dnepropetrovsk, asked whether she had returned. Kasandroff nodded. "The old woman was ill, but Tamara Ivanova's visit perked her up considerably."

Kasandroff changed the subject. He asked, "Hank, our navy people keep asking whatever happened to the American titanium submarine?"

"Ivan Ivanovich," Hans replied, "you well know that the U.S. Navy had serious plans to build a titanium submarine."

Kasandroff nodded.

"I think you should report that I have questioned Navy people, even some at Naval Intelligence, but no one had ever heard of such a project. But, remember, these are all people who were still in high school or college when these plans were made. Navy old-timers told me that the U.S. Navy did have a titanium submarine project in the 1950s; that it was highly classified at above Top Secret and that the construction was in CIA's Skunk Works. But, as I told you some time ago, the CIA did not support purchasing titanium, and I think that may have killed the project. They told me that no one knew what ever happened to it. Most thought the aircraft carrier people torpedoed it—they were afraid it would cost them a couple of carriers."

Kasandroff shook his head.

"Ivan Ivanovich," Hans concluded, "I also think, from your reportings, that

Gorshkov and his guys know that the U.S. Navy has abandoned building titanium subs—that should be abundantly clear to them by now. My boss, who has high-level contacts, believes—does not know—but believes that either the aircraft carrier people or Hyman Rickover himself may have torpedoed the plan because of the enormous expense. But, for our next Treff, I will get for you the official answer —if I can—to whatever happened to the American titanium submarine.

Kasandroff agreed. "Good, I'll keep your answer in my back pocket, and I'll produce it if they should ask again, but not before."

That matter aside, Hans told him that his "insider" view of Moscow Centre had elated not only his—Hans's—boss, but also a whole chain of folks above his organization.

"Well," responded Kasandroff, "my guys get a good chuckle every time I submit one of your comments about the sniping of the Congressional Intelligence Committee and the Defense Intelligence Agency at the director of the CIA.

"To tell the truth," he continued, "they often do not believe what I tell them until they read a translation from the *Washington Post*. Then I get a *Molodets*—eh, what you call Bravo Zulu."

He paused. "Amazing how different the two opposite intelligence services are, and yet they have so much in common. Each is under the knuckles of politicians—and resents it."

The two decided where the next Treff would be and then retired to the Kurhaus restaurant. As they were eating, Kasandroff mentioned that he was nearing retirement age, and that he planned to accept it if offered.

"What will Tamara Ivanova do?" inquired Reiter

"Hank, I think she will either retire or take a long leave of absence to take care of her mother."

"And what about you?"

"I am not sure. My plans are to retire in warmer climes, you know, the Caribbean—but Tamara Ivanova? She is tied to her family. As long as her mother is alive, I don't think she will be willing to leave Ukraine. I might be able to convince her after her mother's death. What about you, Hank?"

"Thinking. Thinking about it. My boss and I both have talked about it. I mean, we have been in this business a long time; my boss just short of forty years, and I over thirty."

"Hank, an old Russian proverb tells us that 'Lord Time never bows to you; you must always bow to him.' And that's what we must do whenever..."

The two friends agreed to let "Lord Time" take care of this matter.

Only a few months later, in late 1982, Hans and Kasandroff met for the last time. They had both gotten gray and just a little bit heavier, although Kasandroff still looked rugged. He was never exactly handsome; his appearance had always been more on the tougher-than-tough Cossack side. His heavy black mustache had turned a grayish-white, but his eyes could still drill holes through a two-inch plank of Southern yellow pine.

Hans, on the other hand had always been slender; actually, he had always been on the skinny side—he had filled out just a bit. His wavy dark brown hair had turned gray and become less wavy, and he wore it cut shorter than in the olden days. He had also changed from a size 38 suit into size 42.

Once again, their Treff was for high noon at the Russian Orthodox Church in the Kurpark of Bad Homburg. Hans had made himself comfortable on a shaded park bench and watched the chapel. He saw Kasandroff enter the Kurpark. When he spotted Hans, he walked around the chapel into the park. In the meantime Hans surveilled the area—Kasandroff was clean; Hans did not spot any "keepers." He followed Kasandroff, who found a bench in another shady spot and sat down. Hans made his last look around before joining him.

"Ivan Ivanovich, how are you?"

"Not getting any younger, Hank, that's for sure."

"Same here. What is going on?"

"I think I am ready to retire to my Caribbean island," Kasandroff replied.

"Well, Ivan Ivanovich, I knew the day would come. I expected it. To tell you now, I am glad you decided to retire. This gives me a good excuse to put in my papers."

"You are kidding?"

"No, I think the time has come to cut bait."

"Cut bait? Ah, you Americans always amuse me. Another term I had not heard before."

"Cut bait? A fisherman's term; you will hear it often when you get to the islands; they're saturated with American tourists. But tell me, what made you decide?"

"Hank, the only thing that made me stay in the service was my mother. She passed away recently, and now I have no one to hold me back."

"Oh, Ivan Ivanovich, I am so sorry to hear that. Please accept my deepest condolences."

"Thank you, Hank, but it was bound to happen. We all have only a limited time on this earth."

"True, and therefore we must use it to our advantage. I think we both have served in this crazy business long enough. It's time to go."

Kasandroff agreed.

Hans asked if he needed any assistance to reach the island of his choice, or to get into the resettlement program.

Kasandroff laughed, "No, I don't want to become one of your defectors. I just want to fade away."

"Can you do that without endangering yourself?"

Kasandroff said he had all his plans made, all the documentation he needed to make his exit.

"Have you told Tamara Ivanova?"

"Not yet, and I am almost afraid to broach the topic. I mean, you know she does not know about my nefarious activity, or the no-name accounts."

"Of course, it would not have been wise to have told her."

Kasandroff nodded. He was obviously very concerned, but he mentioned that he hoped it would all work out in time. He said that a safe departure would take some time. "Maybe a year or more, but time is all we now have. We must use it wisely."

Hans agreed.

After this revelation Hans suggested they have lunch at the Kurhaus, in the spa's garden restaurant. They selected seats at a table shaded by one of the many large oak trees. As always, they ordered their Warsteiners. They had spent so much time together during the past decades, they ordered the same food; a salad, soup, and a fish dinner, followed by a beautifully constructed "ice cream tower," the restaurant's specialty. During dinner they wondered aloud whether they would ever see each other again.

"It's a small world, Hank," opined Kasandroff.

"Funny you should say that," Reiter countered. "During my early training days as an agent it was my mentor's favorite saying."

Kasandroff nodded. "It was also my mother's."

"So, Ivan Ivanovich, in truth, since we are going to be retired, what are you going to do?"

Ivan Ivanovich laughed. "What is truth? However, to keep the record straight, I will concentrate on two important things. The first, maybe impossible, I will try to convince Tamara Ivanova, my lovely bride, to come to the warmer climes of the Caribbean. As you know, she came from a large family and had strong ties that would not allow her to leave her mother in Ukraine. But now, since her mother passed away, there should not be much to hold her there, and travel into and out of the new Russia has been eased. The second, I will maintain my nefariously gained funds to the best of my knowledge."

Originally, during Kasandroff's tour in Washington, he had done considerable research at the Library of Congress on financial institutions, investment firms and cash handling; it was sort of a hobby with him, since these saving activities were completely alien for any common Soviet.

Also, during the latter stages of his active duty tour, he had looked into identity switching. He had had some knowledge, gained at Olympic Village, the

226

GRU "finishing school," but he wanted to be an expert in identity switch. During an intelligence-gathering visit to Jamaica, at that time as the American Willy Kolbnitz of New York City, Kasandroff had established that identity while investing a part of the Barclays' no-name account in a half-interest in a villa overlooking Port Antonio.

During what was to be their last meeting, Ivan Ivanovich had brought a small artfully crafted wooden box filled with the soil of his homeland. His eyes started to tear. "Hank," he said, "you may think of me as just a sentimental old fool—and I am. But you are my only true friend. I ask one favor. I want you to be the executor of my last will and testament." He handed Reiter the wooden box.

"When I die, I want you to spread this soil on my grave."

Reiter was speechless. After a long pause he said, "Ivan Ivanovich, I am honored. You have my word, that if I outlive you, this shall be done."

"And if you do not," Ivan Ivanovich cocked his head, "maybe your lovely bride, or one of your sons, can do me the honor?" Hans solemnly agreed.

During this, their final Treff, they had not exchanged any information; it was the parting of two friends, each from the other side of a divide. Hans reminded him that the offer of assistance was still valid, that it applied to any matter, security or otherwise.

Kasandroff thanked him.

A sudden thought struck Hans. "Wait, just in case you do need assistance"— he pulled out his business card—"here is my Virginia address. We may be moving to Florida, but until then, you can reach me at this telephone number."

For a moment Kasandroff appeared perplexed. "Damn, Hank, on this last meeting we almost screwed up. I have my own business card here. It's the apartment in the villa overlooking Port Antonio where the Volga-German refugee Andreas Heller will soon live."

With that they shook hands, Kasandroff stepped back, then grabbed Hans and gave him a bear hug that nearly cracked his ribs.

They tried to hide from each other that their eyes were glazed over by tears of sorrow.

CHAPTER 51

When he returned from his Bad Homburg venture Hans told Smyth of Kasandroff's "retirement" plans; that he had given him the routine exit briefing; had voiced the office's concern for his security, and how the offer for assistance was valid for as long as Kasandroff lived, and the rest of the instructions.

Then he took a deep breath and told Smyth of his own plans to retire in the near future.

"My God," Smyth exploded, "Is everybody blowing this joint? Is this some kind of conspiracy? You are the third person on this floor talking retirement. Frank Milushkyi just put in his papers." He gave Reiter his famous Cheshire cat grin. "Frank was first, I'm second, and now you." He pounded his desk. "We can't all leave at once."

"Why not?" Hans was surprised that Smyth had decided to retire.

"Why not? I'll tell you why not, because we gotta have to have a real blow-out party so that these sad sacks on the fifth floor will never forget us."

And what a party it was. After numerous toasts Smyth, Milushkyi and Reiter solemnly swore that they would keep in touch forever and ever. They knew it was partly nostalgia, and partly the good company, and of course the alcohol. They also knew that they had really nothing in common except the job, the dangers they had shared, and the office on Wisconsin Avenue in the northwest part of Washington, D.C.

Deep down they knew that they would go their separate ways, and meet only accidentally—if ever.

CHAPTER 52

Ivan Ivanovich Kasandroff, eh, Walter Kowalski, eh, Willy Kolbnitz, eh, Andreas Heller, came thoroughly prepared for his retirement. Most recently, he had entered Jamaica with three genuine passports. The old one, long expired, from his days as a GRU case officer in Washington, that identified him as the Virginian Walter Kowalski. The second one proved beyond the shadow of a doubt that he was the American Willy Kolbnitz of New York City, and the third, the only one he would keep in his possession, a British passport that identified Kasandroff as the Volga-German refugee Andreas Heller.

The GRU had taught him German, and it has helped him even in retirement. He had picked Jamaica as the best place for a Volga-German to live with a British passport with "refugee status." Also since this was more British than most islands, since it was a large island, and because English of sorts was spoken there, he felt this the best of all choices. Moreover, he had fallen in love with the lush, green mountains, the cascading waters that seem to pour out of every crevice. The waters that turned into cool streams below the falls. However, most of all, he loved Jamaica's white, sandy beaches; its steep scraggy mountains, its dense dark-green jungles, and its charming brightly colored villages. It was all so totally different from the utter drabness of Russian or Ukrainian villages, the unpainted huts, and the deteriorating apartments of Dnepropetrovsk. In a travel brochure he had read that Jamaica was the third-largest island in the Caribbean; had a mixture of industry, farming and tourism; a wealth of resources—bauxite, sugarcane, bananas, citrus, rum, allspice and coffee; all that and tourism had brought a certain measure of wealth, and along with that, stability. He wanted to live on a larger island, one where no one asked questions.

Shortly after his mother had passed away he realized that Rodina, the land of his youth, no longer had a hold on him. The Soviet Empire was changing rapidly and after a few years he slipped the confining environment of the Soviet intelligence service almost unnoticed.

After Kasandroff departed from his homeland for the last time he withdrew the sums Moscow had paid him for recruiting the legendary "naval officer" George Trenker, from the Dresdner Bank in Frankfurt-on-Main. These funds, plus the American payments, he deposited in a no-name account at the Zentral Bank in Liechtenstein, then re-deposited them in an American Express checking account in Bern, Switzerland.

Before his most recent arrival in Jamaica he had emptied his Barclays offshore account at Grand Cayman, where he had long ago deposited the Russian payment he'd received for recruiting Waldo Waldmann in the 1950s. A short time later he sold his part-ownership in the Port Antonio villa to "Willy Kolbnitz" for cash. In a sleight-of-hand, "Willy Kolbnitz" then sold his part-ownership to "Andreas Heller"—once again for cash. Andreas Heller then turned over the business end of management to a broker. He hoped that these cash transactions—not uncommon events in Jamaica—would erase the trail between the former GRU colonel and the Volga-German refugee.

He now resided in that villa, where he rented a two-bedroom apartment with private bath, and a spacious balcony overlooking the waters of the Caribbean. No one there knew, or cared, that he was actually the owner of the villa. His fellow guests knew him as Andreas Heller, a refugee and a former citizen of the Soviet Union. He had thought it best to have this dual East-West background to explain his slightly Russian-accented American English. Should anyone question him—although here in Jamaica no one would—he also spoke a passable Russian-accented German.

As his world, and that of the Soviet Empire, went into free-fall, Andreas Heller enjoyed the fruits of his labor.

When he was in an especially good mood, when the warm breezes of the Caribbean caressed his old body, when he felt that everything is just right, he shouted to no one in particular, "General Fedoroff, eat your heart out.'"

CHAPTER 53

H ans Reiter, as a veteran intelligence officer, was privileged to attend quarterly meetings with other old-timers in an organization that Susan called "Ye Olde Trench-Coat Society." During these gatherings he became acquainted with some of the happenings within the IC, the intelligence community.

Most often the information, told by still active officers, was relatively close to the unclassified level. During one, a Naval Intelligence officer briefed the retirees on the level and state of preparedness of the Soviet Union's submarine fleet. According to this officer, the Soviets had conquered the complexities of shaping and welding titanium in a shipyard atmosphere. They had enveloped the entire submarine, along with the parts to be fitted, in a construction hall filled with argon gas. All the workers wore what looked like space suits while in the workspaces.

The officer told of the enormous expense of producing titanium submarines. However, he implied that titanium, now that they had solved all the welding problems, had become the Soviets favorite metal for submarines.

In a later briefing the same Naval Intelligence officer reported that the entire Soviet submarine fleet was in a deteriorating state because lack of funds prevented required upkeep repairs. He mentioned that from what could be seen— the audience knew it was via satellite photography and infrared sensors—that it looked as if many submarines, including the ALFA Class SSN, had been towed to distant locations in the Severodvinsk yard, seemingly abandoned.

Reiter happened to be sharing a table with Henry Appleton, one of the former "Rickover boys." Appleton leaned over and whispered, "The old man was right fighting the titanium issue." He then elaborated in gloating terms that Admiral Rickover was the man who had torpedoed the U.S. titanium submarine program. He said that the admiral had, and rightfully so, assumed that the cost of one titanium submarine would reduce his submarine fleet by three units; something the U.S. Navy could not afford.

In some ways the gatherings of old spooks was sad. Slowly the hard core of the Cold War Warriors entered their final berths. Reiter lunched with Smyth a few times during these sessions. In the parking lot after one of these briefings he, in his usual diplomatic way, uttered a disgusted, "Hell, Hank, this is like a goddamned old folks home, they walk in, but they come out feet first. This is the last goddamned time you'll see me here." Smyth had a convincing way with these proclamations.

Reiter agreed, and it was right then when he decided that Susan and he should leave the Washington circus. They went on another hunt for a retirement home far away from their beloved Alexandria, Virginia, home. In some respects they hated to leave Washington, the center of what had been their universe for decades, but Susan and he had become tired of the ever-increasing traffic, the cold winters and the heavy Virginia taxes. They decided to look for a place in the sun where they could live comfortably. They had planned to leave for points south—now the time had come.

While still working in the nation's capital city they had bought some property in Palm Coast, Florida, and although they had agreed to never retire in that state, they decided to take "just one last look."

In the world of intelligence this would have been called, "analysis continues," because they found a place that was just a little bit un-Floridaish—if there is such a word. They discovered Amelia Island, bought a house that was not for sale, and did not know how much it cost until the following day when they went to settlement. Their Virginia neighbors, and the Reiters' two sons, thought they had totally lost their collective minds—even Hans wondered whether his neighbors were not entirely incorrect in that assessment.

In a nanosecond they had sold their Virginia home; the place where they had planned to live forever, and moved to the little barrier island.

Every time Susan and Hans wandered along the white, uncluttered beaches of "their" island he would tell her, "Now I know why Ivan Ivanovich so much loves Jamaica." That reminded him to inform his friend Ivan Ivanovich of their Florida's address.

Only twice was their life in paradise interrupted.

CHAPTER 54

1988-1989
THE SOVIET BLOC
EASTERN EUROPE

The Soviet Empire had been on the down-slope for years, but no one had noticed it; not even the CIA. Before the events of 1988 and 1989— later called the "Gorbachev Phenomenon"—shook the Soviet Union and the world, Hans Reiter, and everyone else in the IC, had never in their wildest dreams imagined that the Soviet Union could collapse, collapse so rapidly, and so completely. From his Florida retirement home Hans watched these developments in amazement, and wondered what his former colleges in Room 526 were thinking. Hans knew that the events initiated by Mikhail Sergeyevich Gorbachev left not only the people of the Soviet Union and the rulers of the Soviet satellite nations in a dilemma; he could only imagine the heartburn, extra work, and the confusion that these events caused in the U.S. intelligence circles.

It all started in 1988 with Mikhail Sergeyevich Gorbachev's election to the presidency of the USSR. Suddenly new words appeared in the Soviet vocabulary; words such as Glasnost and Perestroika; alien words in the Communist dictionary; uncomfortable words for those behind the "Iron Curtain."

With great amazement and amusement Hans watched the television broadcast from West Berlin of confused East German Communists. For more than thirty years they had followed Moscow's dictates to the letter.

The leaders of the German Democratic Republic had marched in typical German lockstep fashion behind their Soviet leaders. Now, almost without warning, they received conflicting messages from Comrade Mikhail Sergeyevich Gorbachev, their supreme communist leader.

Long ago, Hans's East German assets had told him repeatedly that most of their countrymen looked at Communism as a theory with no workable solution. They had seen tens of thousands, nay, hundreds of thousands of their countrymen flee East Germany, leave everything they held dear behind, to seek the so elusive, and so difficult to define, concept of "freedom."

In their refugee dictionary, they called defecting to West Germany "voting with your feet."

The wall, built on orders of the rulers of East Germany, was further proof that not only their own system of government, but also that of the Soviet Union and the entire Warsaw Bloc, was destined for bankruptcy. Even without Western propaganda everyone knew that the East German Communist leaders had to build a wall to keep their own people from fleeing; that they had to imprison the entire population.

Finally, on October 18, 1989, the people ousted Erich Honecker, East German leader and head of the Communist regime, and replaced him with Egon Kreuz, another Communist. On November 4, 1989, Hans saw television images he had not seen since the June 17, 1953, riots in Berlin; one million protesters demonstrated against the Communist regime on Berlin's main square, the Alexanderplatz.

In November 1989, the world watched in shock and jubilation as thousands of East Germans, defying their leaders and the armed might of their country, shouted, *"Wir sind das Volk"*—"We are the people"—and with that powerful roar the entire East German Communist apparatus collapsed. News organizations around the world captured footage of celebrating students, workers, and just plain citizens of East Germany and West Berlin scampering along the wall, tearful East-West family reunions, and long lines of East Berliners heading for a look at the "other" Berlin.

One event cascaded over the previous one. Three days after the demonstrations began the East German government and its ruling party resigned. Two days later, the hated Berlin Wall was torn apart and hundreds of thousands of East Germans streamed through the gaps—totally unbelievable.

Hans did not know that this event would get him recalled to do "just one more job" for Room 526; it turned out to be two, because Hiram Smyth encountered a medical problem.

CHAPTER 55

The Canadian tourists had departed Florida. Fernandina Beach, the historic, small town on Amelia Island, once again belonged to the natives. Hans and Susan Reiter, almost natives in their island paradise, had started to enjoy the less crowded beaches. Main Beach, just off Florida State Road A1A, had lost about three feet of sand from a steadily blowing nor'easter, but the old-timers predicted that the next southeasterner would bring it all back. "That's the way of nature," they philosophized, "nothing to worry about."

And so it was. Susan and Hans Reiter were looking toward Christmas only six weeks away, and a family gathering. Hans had not been in contact with his colleagues at Room 526; he thought he would tell them of the wonders of his island paradise in his Christmas letter. But "exigencies of the service" once again proved him wrong and, like an old cavalry horse hearing martial music Reiter reacted, stepping once again into the clandestine world.

Even a retired intelligence officer is duty-bound to respond to these exigencies.

A telephone call from Michael White, Hiram Smyth's successor, requested his presence in Berlin where a man and wife, Heinz and Lieselotte Schwertfeger—not on the new computer printout—claimed to have been "working for the Americans." They remembered two names, Herr Doktor Hermann and Mr. Trenker.

"I think you are their last hope," remarked Michael White, "your old friend 'Fred' Hertzwald having gone to the great beyond. If you could catch a plane tomorrow and fly into Dulles International, I'll have someone meet you there with your old credentials and whatever. What'd you say?"

"Tomorrow? Oh Christ, we are just getting ready for Christmas."

"I know," White sounded sympathetic, "but nobody here can really vouch for them. These goddamned new computers are spitting out all sorts of stuff. We looked into your old reports, we tried 'Landser,' we tried 'Schwert,' we tried 'Schwertfeger,' we tried 'Bolthole.' We're getting all sorts of shit, but nothing that could further ID those folks."

He paused, "Hans, I'm begging you. These are confusing times. We got refugees coming out of the woodworks who claim they were 'working for the

Americans.'"

"Okay, I know those two well. They worked for us for decades. We can't let them just fall through the cracks; they don't deserve this. I'll be there tomorrow. I'll tell you flight and TOA as soon as I have a reservation."

He heard White heave a sigh, "Thanks, Hans. I owe you one. But let me make the reservations and I'll call you back and tell you what flight. That's the least I can do for you."

Susan just shrugged—the normal reaction of a clandestine officer's wife.

Special Agent Frederick Mannheim, one of Room 526 old-timers, met Hans at Dulles International. He handed him the badge and credentials, his old .38 caliber Colt Police Special, and tickets for the connecting flight to Frankfurt-on-Main and Berlin-Tegel International Airport, along with an open-ended return flight ticket.

"We notified Berlin," Mannheim said. "One of our guys will pick you up and drive you to the Refugee Center." He then relayed that Hans had a free hand on how to deal with the Schwertfegers. "They're a bit confused," he said, "you might have to get them settled down and maybe take care of them for a few days. Michael said just to keep it all in the family."

"Fred," Hans complained to his colleague, "I'm getting too old for this shit."

"Hans," Mannheim replied, "be glad you are retired! We've been going like this for the last two months; I mean twenty-four hours a day. And I'm not telling you any news, but this is getting old, too frigging old; even for me."

Mannheim remained and they spoke of the olden days. "I don't know if Hiram has told you, but he has got some kind of prostate problem; might need an operation.

"That serious? I have not talked with him since maybe early this year. I've got to give him a call when I get back from Berlin."

Mannheim shrugged. "He's not complaining. I just heard it accidentally. You know how he is, ornery as always. Love that guy."

And they both laughed.

Hans had not thought about the travel arrangements, but this was a two-day trip. He traveled first class first from Jacksonville to Dulles International, then to New York-Kennedy; then, an early morning arrival at Frankfurt-on-Main, and finally, arriving at Berlin-Tegel in the late afternoon. But the organization was still on the ball. As promised, Chris Tannenberg, one of the junior agents, met Hans at Tegel air terminal and drove him to the Refugee Center. There he introduced him to the center's *Herr Direktor.*

"Yes, Herr Reiter," the *Direktor* spoke fluent English—the King's English, "we have the Schwertfeger couple housed in a private house with an elderly family. Here, I'll get the address. Will you take care of them?" The *Direktor* seemed anxious to be relieved of at least one of his refugee problems—he mentioned that he had thousands of East Germans stashed away in difficult to get private and public accommodations.

"Herr Reiter," he explained as he handed him the address, "there is so much uncertainty at this time. Many of the folks who had come into Berlin right after the wall went down think the East may be closed off again, once the tumultuous times have passed. That is the reason we have exceeded our capacity here at the center, and had to once again depend on the good will of the West Berliners."

Tannenberg drove Hans to an address at Mainzer Strasse in Berlin's Wilmersdorf borough. There they met the utterly surprised Schwertfegers.

"Herr Trenker," Heinz Schwertfeger exclaimed, "not in my wildest dreams..." as he embraced Reiter. "How did you ever find us here? Liesschen just went to buy some groceries. She'll be back in a flash."

After Hans had introduced Tannenberg to Schwertfeger, they met the Schwertfegers' host, who invited them into the living room. Hans had brought a carton of Philip Morris, one of Schwertfeger's favorite cigarettes. "Herr Schwertfeger, are you still fond of Philip Morris?"

"Ah, thank you, Herr Trenker, but I have quit the habit several years ago. But," Schwertfeger pointed at his host, "Herr Fleischmann will be more than happy to take them off your hands."

"So be it." Hans handed over the carton. "Herr Fleischmann, just a little token for being so kind to my friends."

Fleischmann wasted no time in ripping open the carton and extracting a pack of cigarettes. He lit one with obvious pleasure, inhaled, and smiled. "Yes, thank you, Herr Trenker, these are still the best. During the olden days I bought some on the Black Market whenever I could afford it." He took another puff as if to confirm his assessment. "Yes, yes, there is nothing like a good American cigarette."

Liesschen Schwertfeger arrived and nearly dropped her grocery bag when she spotted Hans. "What a surprise, Herr Trenker, what a surprise," she managed to gasp. "What are you doing here?" Then she told Hans that she and her husband had left a month after the country had collapsed within itself. They had locked and left their little apartment near the railroad tracks leading across the Neisse River into Poland, taken a train to East Berlin, and then crossed into West Berlin near the Brandenburger Gate.

"These times are so uncertain," she said. "We thought to get out before something else happens." She said that it was her first time in West Berlin. Initially she was overwhelmed, almost frightened, by the lights, the glitter, the crowds, but most of all by the noise of this vibrant city. They had gratefully received the token handout from the West German government, but were surprised that the Americans had no record of their bolthole operation.

Reiter thought that this was the proper time to explain the purpose of his visit—that he was here to confirm their status with the American authorities. He did not go into details, hoping to elaborate later, during dinner at a local restaurant.

They excused themselves from Schwertfeger's host and walked to the car. Tannenberg suggested that instead of going to a local restaurant, they drive to one of his favorite places on Kurfürstendamm, the Gasthaus-Brauerei Aschinger. "I mean," commented Tannenberg, "as long as we have the car, we might just as well get out of the immediate neighborhood."

Aschinger's was almost filled to capacity, but they managed to get a less noisy corner and settled down to complete the identification formalities.

"Before we do all the formalities for your identification, I should tell you how much my office and my government has appreciated your Görlitz operation. We look at operating a bolthole as one of the very important aspects of clandestine operations—and, as I had indicated when we met in Austria, a relatively dangerous one."

The Schwertfegers looked up in surprise. Hans explained that many aspects of clandestine operations are clouded and complex. That they had always operated in the shadows, and that there was hanging over all of them the threat from the STASI and the GRU, and that U.S. Intelligence had protected the identities of its East German operatives as well as those of the U.S. agents.

He looked at Heinz Schwertfeger. "For example, we never referred to you as Heinz Schwertfeger, only as 'Landser' to protect your identity."

Schwertfeger nodded.

"And," Hans continued, "you have always known me as 'Mr. Trenker,' although you may have guessed that this was a cover name, a nom de plume. So, just to prevent any confusion later, my real name is Reiter, Hans Reiter."

Both Schwertfegers looked surprised. Finally Heinz Schwertfeger stuttered, "Rei... Reiter?"

Hans nodded.

"We come from a small town in Silesia ... from Jauer. We had a neighbor whose great-granduncle had immigrated to America. When I was just a kid I remember him visiting from America. It was a great event in town, and since we were neighbors my family got to meet him. I think he had a business in New York; he was on a buying trip ... or something like that."

Now it was Hans's turn to look surprised.

"Was your neighbor's name August Reiter?"

"Yes, yes, August. I had always wondered ... eh ... when Herr Doktor Hermann had first introduced us; way back in the 1960s, when I first saw you. I almost had a heart attack. You looked like a twin of the young Reiter who was killed on the Eastern Front in '44. It was as if he had risen from his grave."

Now curious, Reiter asked, "Whatever happened to that family? My father had tried to locate them, but was unable to do so."

"I am not sure, but the entire family disappeared during the tumultuous days in February '45 when the Soviets captured the town—they and many others disappeared without a trace. The Soviets transported several hundred in cattle cars to Kandalaksha near the Barents Sea where many died of malnutrition. Those were sad days." Sorrow covered Schwertfeger's face. Hans assumed he recalled the days of horror under Soviet domination, and the years he had suffered as a Soviet POW.

A moment or two later he raised his eyes. "Those were terrible times, but life goes on. We must remember that life goes on. We remember, we honor those lost, but their troubles are over. The Good Lord has taken them home."

Liesschen Schwertfeger patted his arm. "Yes, Heinz, life goes on."

Tannenberg had brought with him several forms—he handled the details. Hans then initialed and signed the forms that would guarantee the Schwertfegers' refugee status. He also gave them written instructions regarding the Liechtenstein's Zentral-Bank no-name account; payments for all the years Schwertferger had worked as American intelligence operatives on the East German-Polish border.

While Tannenberg had filled out the various forms, the waiter served the "Superangebot," Aschinger's daily special, mixed grill—in English no less.

Reiter could not help thinking how times had changed; how Berlin had changed since the 1960s when he operated here as an Army special agent. He thought: *Here we are sitting, totally relaxed and safe; two U.S. intelligence agents, with two former East German bolthole operators. Here we are, instead of eating the customary Knoblauchwurst, Sauerkraut and hot potato salad, we have mixed grill—three pieces of different grilled meats and French fries; written in the menu in English, as if they were German words. What a drastic change.*

Hans then asked the Schwertfegers what their near-term and long-term plans were. In the confusion while leaving East Germany; worrying whether or not they could get through the "wall," and their concerns of living in a totally different environment, they had not really thought about it.

Heinz Schwertfeger looked at Liesschen. She raised her hands indicating that she had no thoughts of her own. "We came here not knowing what would happen in the east," Heinz Schwertfeger admitted. "We just wanted to get the hell out of East Germany."

Hans nodded, "It looks to me as if the break with the East German regime is final. I would suggest that you stay in the West for a while, and when everything has shaken down, you can either stay in the western part, or return to your apart-

239

ment in Görlitz."

The Schwertfegers agreed that this could work to their advantage.

"But," suggested Hans, "right now I would like to take you to Liechtenstein so that you can convert your account to your family name, and draw out money for your stay in the West."

At first the Schwertfegers seemed a little stunned by his suggestion, but then agreed that this would be a good idea.

Tannenberg thought that he could make reservations for a flight to Zurich, Switzerland, where Hans would rent a car for the drive to Vaduz, Liechtenstein.

In Vaduz, Hans preceded the Schwertfegers into the Zentral-Bank and stood, watching the guard of the bank in the Principality of Liechtenstein, as an old, poorly dressed man and an elderly woman—apparently his wife—were coming into the bank. The guard saw the man who appeared to be in his early eighties and his companion, somewhat younger, maybe in her late sixties. The man carried a spiked cane favored by those in this mountainous region between Austria and Switzerland. He walked slightly stooped with a pronounced limp— he seemed to favor his left leg. A felt hat with a feather covered most of his curly, white hair. The feather was fastened by a curious clasp. Of course, the guard did not know that it was a regimental crest, a green oak leaf, and the crest of the German 54th Jäger Regiment of the 100th Jäger Division of long-ago World War II days.

With his deep-set dark eyes Heinz Schwertfeger surveyed the interior of the Zentral-Bank. Schwertfeger noticed an official of the bank looking his way, then, apparently noticing the couple's uncertainty, the official hurried from his alcove and offered his assistance. He spoke fluent German with that wonderful, soft, Austrian inflection. After a brief conversation the official escorted the pair into his office, firmly closing the door behind them. The old man explained that he had never been to Liechtenstein, but believed he had an account at the Zentral-Bank.

Without further explanation the bank officer handed the old man a twelve-centimeter by eight-centimeter blank card. "If you would be so kind, sir, please enter the code name or number." With slight difficulty the old man wrote a curious set of numbers and letters: 54/100. Jäger 337-264027. He handed the card to the bank officer, who bowed and retreated to a back room.

After several minutes he reappeared and handed the old man a printed form. "Sir," he said, "would you please sign this form three times with the counter-signature of 54/100. Jäger 337-264027?"

The old man laboriously wrote the word Feger into the three boxes of the form. Again, the bank officer disappeared into the back room. After several minutes he reappeared with another gentleman.

He smiled. "Herr Feger, may I introduce the vice president for confidential funds, Herr Albert. Herr Albert, Herr Feger," he hesitated momentarily, "and, I presume, Frau Feger?"

Schwertfeger nodded.

Herr Albert extended his hand, "I am so happy to meet you and your wife. If you just follow me, we can complete our transaction."

Liesschen looked somewhat confused, but her husband patted her hand. "Liebchen, it will be all right. These folks here know what they are doing." Heinz Schwertfeger and Lieselotte "Liesschen" Schwertfeger followed Herr Albert into his office.

Almost an hour later the old couple walked out of the Liechtenstein Zentral-Bank with big smiles on their faces, holding hands like young lovers. Reiter met them outside the bank and together they went into a near-by restaurant and ordered dinner. Heinz Schwertfeger raised his Bierstein. "Well, Liebchen, and Mr. Reiter, allow me to give a toast and a thanks of gratitude to the Herr Doktor Hermann and to the man called Trenker."

They sipped their beer. "You know, Liebchen, somehow I knew that those two Americans were honest, God-fearing folk. I would have worked for nothing getting even for what those goddamned Commies did to me, to us, and to our country. Never would I have imagined that the Americans would have deposited that much money into the account."

He looked at Hans and thought for a moment. "You know, I have always had the feeling that I had met the man called Trenker somewhere before, but then I always thought this is impossible. The Herr Doktor Hermann was the first American I ever met, and Mr. Trenker the second. Now we know that this is indeed a small world."

Reiter injected, "That must be an old Silesian saying, 'It's a small world.' I remember it was my grandfather's favorite one."

"Maybe not entirely Silesian," Schwertfeger reminisced, "Herr Doktor Hermann also said it many times, and I still remember it today. Whenever something odd happened he said, 'It's a small world.' Liebchen, we now live in a small world."

"Now that you mention it, yes," remembered Hans, "and he was from Frankfurt-on-Main. God rest his soul."

"Oh, I am so sorry he did not live long enough to see the Communists collapse," Schwertfeger said, "When did he pass into the big beyond?"

"It was in autumn of '75. I attended his funeral."

This seemed to end their reminiscing. The Schwertfegers watched in seeming amazement the many high-priced automobiles passing the bank and the bench on which they were resting.

Lieselotte Schwertfeger still in awe, smiled, "We won't worry about all that now. I am happy that Herr Albert was so understanding, when you told him that your name was not Feger."

Schwertfeger laughed, "Herr Albert was probably better at that than were we."

They talked about these curious circumstances, their good fortune, and the advice Herr Albert had given them to place all the money in an interest-bearing savings/checking account from which both Schwertfegers could write checks.

"Liebchen," Schwertfeger once again touched her hand, "we are now freer than we were ever in our entire life. Let's enjoy these days."

And, they looked into each other's eyes like lovers of old.

CHAPTER 56

A few days after Reiter's return from Liechtenstein, Smyth called. He sounded excited, "Hank, you gotta get to Dresden right away."

"What in hell is going on? I just got back from Germany—had to resettle the Schwertfegers."

"Yeah, I know, sorry about that. I would go myself, but I'm scheduled for surgery next week."

"What the hell is going on? Are you okay?"

"Yeah," he tried to brush off his question lightly, "just a little prostate problem."

He paused. "Cancer." He hesitated again. "But the doc says I'll be all right in a month or so. That's why I called you. You have got to find your Landsmann Heinz Gerstmann. He is retired and lives in Dresden. I think he is in danger. Besides me, you are the only guy he knows—besides, you are his Landsmann. You must get him into the western part of Germany, preferably Frankfurt."

He then told Hans that the boys in Room 526 had asked him to get Gerstmann, but he had to decline and suggested Reiter for the job.

"It's all in the bag. They got your travel orders, money, badge, gun and stuff waiting for you. They'll meet you at Dulles and give you all the stuff you need. There is a guy, he'll meet you at Dulles, he'll go with you and drive you. I'm sorry to rouse you at this time, I know you hate the cold weather, but Heinz may be in danger from East Germans wanting revenge for whatever misdeeds the Communists had done, or out of just plain hate."

He chuckled. "Remember? Last time I sent you into East Germany without a backup. Not this time, old buddy."

When Hans told Susan that she'd have to do the Christmas shopping by herself she shrugged, "So what else is new? I just wonder when all this will stop. I thought you had retired from all that secret agent crap?" But, as always, she prepared him for the trips, packed his leather "grip," and kissed him goodbye.

At the Dulles arrival gate Hans saw a familiar figure, redheaded, freckled-faced, thick neck and broad shoulders, holding a sign that read Trenker.

"John Dreier," Hans shouted excitedly, "what in hell are you doing here?"

Dreier laughed. "I thought you'd get a charge out of this. I am the new

243

Room 526 chief of security. I had planned to go with you like in the olden days, but... got too many balls in the air... juggling. I wanted to meet Hiram's legendary VOPO colonel; you called him 'your *Landsmann,*' did you not? But I got a good man here. Let me introduce you to Gerald Zimmermann. Gerald will be your escort." Dreier handed Hans the old credentials, his badge, and what looked like his old .38-caliber revolver in the spring-loaded holster. He checked it. It was fully loaded—six copper-coated rounds of ball ammunition.

Together they went into the airport security office where they presented their credentials to the airport police; they needed the police escort to get through the new security cordon at Dulles International.

Reiter looked at Zimmermann; he sort of reminded him of when he was young and full of piss and vinegar: six feet tall, skinny, dark-brown wavy hair. The only thing missing, Zimmermann did not have his nose broken in a couple of places.

"Do you speak German?"

"Jawohl," Zimmermann had switched into German immediately, "grew up in a Minnesota-German family. Spoke it as a kid, and improved it at the University of Minnesota."

"See? I told you," interjected Dreier.

"Sounds good to me," Hans replied, "I don't know why you even need me. You could almost pass for a German."

"Almost," Zimmermann switched back into English, "Hiram said 'almost ain't good enough.'"

"Sounds just like that ornery SOB. So what's the drill?"

Dreier then explained that things had gotten out of hand in East Germany, that the CI folks in Room 526 had started pulling out all their East German assets to resettle them in West Germany. He said they had a hard time tracking down "the colonel," that he had moved twice since retiring a few years back, and that Smyth suggested recalling Reiter to make the recognition, the American bona fides, ironclad. Also, Smyth was afraid that if anyone not already known to Gerstmann was sent, he might think a hostile wanted to kidnap him and his wife.

"Hiram said that Herr Gerstmann has a wife, but no other family. So resettling them would not be a problem, only the initial contact."

"Gerald," Hans said, "I hope you have some warm clothes packed. It's colder than a whore's tit out there."

Zimmermann laughed. "All packed and ready to go. I am from Minnesota, remember?"

They took the evening flight to Frankfurt-on-Main, and arrived at Rhine-Main International early in the morning. They stepped out into a freezing rain. The office had reserved a heavy, six-cylinder Opel four-door. Zimmermann loaded the baggage into the trunk; he drove carefully out of the airport onto the

Autobahn. It was his first time in Frankfurt.

Reiter directed him to the eastbound Autobahn to Kassel. "Tell you what," he said, "if you're not too tired from the flight, I'd suggest we get out of the big city and stop along the way. I know of a little place on the way to Dresden where we can rest, eat some good food, and overnight. Tomorrow we'll go the rest of the way. Maybe the weather will clear up a bit."

Zimmermann agreed.

Hans planned to stay in a quaint hotel he remembered in Wertheim on the Main River, a picturesque little town some thirteen kilometers south of the Autobahn, and a little over an hour's drive from Frankfurt. He had the map on his knees and watched for the Dertingen turn-off; he was afraid he might miss it in the lousy weather.

Zimmermann saw the road sign first and turned south into the road to Wertheim. Hans had told him to watch for the massive fortress ruin of Wertheim, but the clouds hung so low they covered all the hills around the area. The clouds were so dense they could not even see the Main River—just steam rising from the waters. Since this was not exactly tourist season, there was no problem getting two rooms on the second floor of the inn.

They agreed to meet at noon in the lobby. Hans wanted to take a shower and sleep at least an hour.

Around noon he walked into the lobby and saw Zimmermann already there reading the local newspaper. The weather being what it was, a light ice-cold drizzle, they decided to eat at the inn.

"Maybe the weather will improve. If it does I'll show you a bit of the town." Hans told him that his niece Eileen, a U.S. Army lieutenant in Hawk missiles, was stationed here during the 1980s and that he and his wife Susan had visited her over Christmas. "It was beautiful, a real fairytale Christmas. The Christmas market was in the town's square. I'll never forget the aroma of roasted sugar almonds ... the lights, and all the music, just great."

"Just like Minnesota, there it's cold and festive, but without all the historic houses in the town's square. I worked in Berlin but only for a little while. The big cities all have a certain likeness, not like these little towns."

They left Wertheim early in the morning. The weather had improved somewhat. Although the sun glimpsed out of the thick clouds only a few times, the road was clear, and the temperature above freezing. Since Zimmermann was interested in history and geography Hans gave the tourist pitch as they went past the various locations. They drove through the Main River wine country, famous for its Frankenwein, the only dry white wine in Germany. From the Autobahn they saw bits and pieces of Würzburg with the Marienberg fortress dominating the view.

As they approached Erlangen, Hans pointed to the right, "I was stationed over there at Herzogenaurach for a couple of years; we called it Herzo Base. That's the home of Adidas shoes."

"You were in the Army?"

"Oh, yes; served twenty plus years."

The road led north of Nürnberg, where they switched Autobahns, turning north to enter East Germany just north of Hof. There they turned northeastward on the Autobahn to Chemnitz—the former Communist East German signs still identified the city as Karl-Marx-Stadt—and arrived in Dresden in the afternoon. The darkness and the wetness made East Germany look even worse than it was. On Zimmermann's map the boys at Room 526 had redlined the road from the Autobahn to the southern part of Dresden. Gerstmann lived on Kesseldorfer Strasse.

The city was the color of gray-on-gray drab, all streets were poorly maintained, and everywhere the houses were shabby and in need of paint and maintenance. Groups of youths loitered here and there; poorly dressed old women carrying shopping bags scurried around puddles of accumulated snow water.

Zimmermann, spotting Gerstmann's apartment house number, made a U-turn and parked in front. As they double-checked the number and the map, a group of youths came stumbling toward the Opel; they stopped. A few smirked. They apparently mistook them for West Germans, "Westies;" it was obvious they were looking for a little "action," having fun with West German visitors apparently was their form of entertainment. One of them, a pale, pimple-faced, longhaired lout, clutching a short club, started tapping on the Opel. Zimmermann got out of the car real slow and deliberate; Hans followed and walked around the back of the car to the sidewalk. The youth, about seventeen or eighteen, the one with the club, said something to Zimmermann that Hans could not hear.

Zimmermann smiled. "Are you all good friends?" he asked in his best German.

"Yeah, any of your business?" replied the punk with the club as he again tapped the Opel.

"Just a friendly question," said Zimmermann as he whipped out his P-38 Walther automatic and grabbed the guy by the throat, sticking his gun under his chin. "Just a friendly question. Because I want your friends to watch the car and make sure nothing happens to it."

Two of the others made a move; it looked as if they tried to get behind Zimmermann.

Hans drew his revolver and asked, "You two assholes trying to commit suicide?"

They apparently thought he was joking and kept moving toward Zimmermann. Hans pulled back the hammer and asked, "Just one more time, who wants to get it first?"

246

The click of the hammer seemed to intimidate them; they froze.

"Wonderful," smiled Zimmermann, "you all are so helpful. Tell you what I'm gonna do. I'll take your buddy along with me into this here house, and if there is even a little scratch on that fucking car when we come back, I'll tear out his fucking guts and you can then pick him up in a hand-basket. Is that clear?"

It seemed to be.

Zimmermann kneed the lout in the groin. The punk reeled up and gasped for air; the club fell to the ground.

"Okay, little boy," Zimmermann said as he propelled him forward, "now let's be nice and easy and nothing will happen to you. Make a wrong move and I'll blow out your fucking lights."

The group stood frozen in space as Hans and Zimmermann walked into the apartment house. Zimmermann said, "I'll take this shit downstairs and you go find your guy."

The young East German started to shake and whimper as Zimmermann pushed him roughly down the stairs. Zimmermann snarled, "Keep you fucking mouth shut. I hate wimps."

Hans found Gerstmann's apartment, knocked several times before a voice—it was Heinz Gerstmann's—asked who was there.

"Trenker, your Landsmann," Hans replied.

Gerstmann carefully opened the door a crack; he still had it secured by a chain. He looked, took a deep breath and shouted, "Hanna, come to the door. We have a visitor." He closed the door, released the chain and opened it wide. "Herr Trenker, I never thought I'd ever see you again."

"Herr Gerstmann," Hans replied, "never say never."

Gerstmann laughed. "That's what Sergeant Smyth used to say." Then he introduced Hans to his wife, Hanna. They went into the small living room. Gerstmann told him that they had been virtual prisoners in their apartment. "Youth gangs are roaming the street. It's terrible. We have a neighbor doing our shopping, what little there is."

Hans explained to the couple the reason for his visit; that he wanted to take them this very afternoon to Frankfurt-on-Main, and set them up in an apartment—all courtesy of the U.S. government. He asked them to pack whatever they wanted, lock up the apartment and come with him.

"For how long?" Hanna asked.

"A few months. Maybe until everything here clears up, or, you can remain in Frankfurt indefinitely. It's your choice." They were in shock. Hans reminded Gerstmann that he had money waiting in a no-name bank account in Liechtenstein whenever he wanted it. This seemed to reassure him that a future in western Germany might not look so bad.

"You can lock the door here, and you can always come back. Or, if you decide to stay in Frankfurt, get a moving company to bring whatever you want to Frankfurt. However, I suggest you tell your neighbors that you are visiting friends, and will be back in a few weeks or so."

Gerstmann turned to Hanna, "Liebchen, what choice do we really have, to live like prisoners in this place, or in a place where no one knows who we are?"

Hanna agreed. She went to tell their next-door neighbors the news. Then they started to pack. It seemed to Hans as if they had all their suitcases and bags in the apartment ready to depart in case of an emergency.

He told them that he had a partner downstairs and a bunch of louts watching the car. Gerstmann looked out of the window. "You have these bums watching your car, Herr Trenker. They are gangsters."

Hans just laughed. "Not this time. Herr Gerstmann, not this time." He walked downstairs and called for Zimmermann to come out of the basement. His "friend" came up first. He was very docile. No wonder, Zimmermann still had his P-38 aimed at the guy's throat.

When they left the apartment house the gang stood around the Opel; it seemed as if they were actually guarding it. When they saw their buddy was still alive they looked relieved. One of the guys actually gave the Americans a friendly wave. After Zimmermann had made a cursory check to see if his car was still as he left it, he turned and snarled as he waved his automatic in their general direction. "Wonderful, you guys can leave now, but don't forget what will happen next time we meet."

The gang stole away like beaten dogs, going faster as the distance between them and Zimmermann increased.

Hans applauded Zimmermann. "You handled that very well."

"Not a problem, Hans, I handled worse assholes than those punks. After college I served three years in the Minneapolis police department... before Room 526 recruited me."

A little later the Gerstmanns joined them carrying several suitcases and bags. Reiter introduced Zimmermann, and then threw the baggage into the trunk. The Gerstmanns sat in the backseat and they drove off, Zimmermann, as usual, driving.

It was still early in the afternoon and Hans suggested that they try to get at least a few miles south of Hof and find a hotel in that area. This time Zimmermann drove fast and they actually made it into Bayreuth. Hans knew of a reasonably priced hotel that also had a restaurant. They stopped at a gas station to fill up and ask directions to Brauerei-Gasthof Goldener Löwe, on Kulmbacher Strasse.

The Goldener Löwe looked unpretentious, but was well managed. It had a friendly, family-like look with window boxes filled with artificial red geraniums. Although Hans and his folks arrived well past normal suppertime, their host served a splendid meal.

It was the Gerstmanns' first visit in western Germany and Hanna especially marveled about everything, the well-kept-up streets and houses, the bountiful food served—their first good meal in a long time, said Heinz Gerstmann. They talked and talked about everything, but the first question Heinz Gerstmann had was, "How is Hiram Smyth?"

Hans was surprised that he knew Smyth's real name and asked, "How well do you know Hiram?"

"Oh, Mr. Trenker. Long ago, since 1953. During the June 17th riots, I tried to defect. Hiram was my interrogator in West Berlin, a master sergeant in the Defector Reception Center. Hiram persuaded me to return to the east and be his agent-in-place. At that time my folks were still alive and Hiram thought it might not be a good thing for a young VOPO captain to leave them behind; he was right. In all the tumult during those trying days in 1953 no one had even noticed that I had disappeared for two days."

Hans thought now was the time to tell Gerstmann his real name, especially since Zimmermann had called him Hans all day. Heinz was not overly surprised; they shook hands and decided that with all that had transpired, they ought to be on a first-name basis. Hans also mentioned that Smyth was going to come instead of himself, but that he was having surgery.

They slept late and it was mid-morning before they left for Frankfurt. The rest of the trip was uneventful, except for Hanna's repeatedly voicing her admiration for the West German scenery, the cleanliness and the many shiny new cars.

Zimmermann stopped off at the I.G. Farben Hochhaus for the addresses of the furnished apartments available, and for 5,000 D-marks in cash for Gerstmann.

Of the two apartments available, the Gerstmanns selected one on Eschersheimer Landstrasse in a building erected during the 1970s—by Frankfurt standards a relatively modern building. When Hanna entered the apartment she was ecstatic. Since Hans had lived in this area off and on for some six years during his Army assignments, he took them on a little shopping trip for the most essential food items. Back in the apartment Hanna made, in her words, "good" coffee, that is with real coffee beans, not roasted barley, and the four of them celebrated the Gerstmanns' arrival in a truly free world.

There were administrative matters to be seen to. The folks in Room 526 still had the responsibility to take care of their assets; one of their agents in Frankfurt would handle the local details. Zimmermann told Gerstmann how to contact the office.

Hans told Gerstmann that Smyth would write after he came home from the hospital, and that he, himself, would report to him that all was okay. Then he asked Gerstmann if he had anything else to be done; he could not think of anything, except to be informed of the outcome of Smyth's surgery and for Hans to convey his gratitude to Smyth for all he had done for them.

They said their goodbyes and after many hugs—Hanna cried a little—Zimmermann and Hans departed for Rhein-Main International for the flight back to Dulles International.

Back in Washington Hans visited Smyth; he was already at home and recuperating. He looked drawn but, aside from that, he was his old exuberant self. He visibly perked up when Hans told him how Gerald Zimmermann had handled the East German louts who had gathered around their car in front of the Gerstmann's apartment. He was happy to hear that the guys in Room 526 had not gotten soft. "You mean that Zimmermann kid actually stuck his automatic under the guy's chin?"

Hans nodded, "Not only that, but when the guy kept holding on to his club, Zimmermann kicked him in the balls. That guy choked and would have fallen down, but Zimmermann had an iron grip on him."

"Way to go," Smyth chuckled, "Way to go." Then he listened to the rest of the report.

"I'm glad that our friend Heinz and Hanna are safe. Maybe in a few months, after it has all shaken down, they can get back to their apartment."

He thought about this for a moment, then remarked, "But, Hank, I think they may even stay in Frankfurt, maybe in a little house in the northern suburbs."

Smyth thought that the office could then take over the apartment and maybe resettle someone else in it. From this Hans assumed that Smyth was on the way to getting back his positive outlook on life.

CHAPTER 57

Vincence Horstmann, the last surviving DNI involved in the OMEGA operation, thought the time had come to do what his wife had wanted to do for some time, to leave the goddamned Washington Circus. It seemed as if they had lived in the greater Washington area forever. They were tired of the ever-increasing traffic, the cold winters, and the heavy taxes. For some time they had planned to leave for points south.

They had traveled cross-country in search of the right retirement location, something near a Naval base, but not too close. They had looked at San Diego where they had lived when the DNI had been a young, recently married, lieutenant, but found it too much of a Navy town. Then, on a fluke, they had discovered Amelia Island, Florida, and fallen immediately in love with it. They left their Maryland home and never regretted the move.

CHAPTER 58

SUMMER 1990
THE RITZ-CARLTON
AMELIA ISLAND, FLORIDA

Christian Reiter, still living in New York, had watched in fascination the collapse of the entire Warsaw Bloc starting with the "Gorbachev Phenomenon" that tore apart the Soviet Union, followed by the fall of the Berlin Wall, and the collapse of the East German Communist apparatus; and, as the western world celebrated these historic events, he decided that, indeed, this was the most appropriate time for the old OMEGA Team to celebrate as well. He wanted it to be something truly special, not just a night on the town. He called the long-retired and widowed Mrs. Clarke at her home and asked if she minded making arrangements for it. He told her he wanted Harold McCurrill and "Casey" Miller, and their spouses or companions—and the widowed Mrs. Clarke herself—to meet at New York's LaGuardia airport where they would board Quadrant Import-Export's executive jet destined for a vacation spot "somewhere" in the South.

After seeing that Mrs. Clarke was quite pleased to be of help and to be asked to go along, Christian then called his brother Hans in Amelia Island to tell him that he, Kjerstine and a bunch of others would visit with Hans and Susan to celebrate an important event.

A few hours after their departure the aircraft started to circle as it prepared to land. The passengers craned their necks. They saw a dark blue ocean, long, white beaches, and lush vegetation. The jet circled twice and finally touched down gently on a small airstrip. "Welcome to Amelia Island. Welcome to paradise," announced the pilot.

At the small terminal a white passenger van awaited the seven vacationers. The driver quickly transferred the luggage, and after a short drive on country roads, the party arrived at the Ritz-Carlton Hotel.

"Good Lord," Casey Miller exclaimed as he walked into the well-appointed lobby, "I feel as if I have just been transplanted to Berlin."

Hans and Susan were waiting to finally meet the group that had thought up how "to bleed the goddamned Commies white."

"Why are you smiling?" Susan asked.

"I was just thinking Christian and the others have no idea our guys in Room 526 carried out what Ike had requested."

"Are you going to tell Christian?"

"Not yet. I'll wait for the right moment."

Susan laughed. "You are so terrible, so devious."

"C'est moi," Hans said, chuckling.

As the Reiter families, and the former OMEGA group members and their families, concluded their late dinner, Kjerstine became concerned that the aged Mrs. Clarke needed to get to bed after the day's excitement. Mrs. Clarke did not protest.

"Come on, girls," Kjerstine yawned, "let's drop Mrs. Clarke off for the evening, and then do some catching-up in our room. If I know these men," she said as she pointed toward the two Reiters and Miller and McCurrill, "they will be up all night going over old times. Let's leave them to their entertainment, shall we? I, for one, would rather be up at the crack of dawn to walk the beach. I'm sure that I'll meet Christian on his way to bed at that time." She winked at her husband, who gave her a smile of gratitude. At the elevator the men said goodnight to their wives and then headed for the hotel bar.

The bar, adjacent to the lobby, faced the Atlantic Ocean. It was a cool, moonlit evening, and the rustle of palm fronds masked the conversations of the other patrons. After they had settled down with drinks, Christian raised his glass, "Gentlemen. Let us remember and toast once again those who have gone before us. First, a toast to the Old General." They toasted Eisenhower with a hearty "hear, hear."

McCurrill stood, raised his glass, and in a voice just a tad too loud boomed, "And here is a toast to the success of the OMEGA Solution, the Old General's wisdom, and to the craftiness of the DNIs."

Christian Reiter and Miller gleefully pulled a slightly tipsy McCurrill back into his chair. The atmosphere became electrified, joyfully electrified, as they all tried to talk at once. McCurrill and Miller jostled each as they playfully fought over who would make the next toast. Miller won and almost shouted, "I raise my glass to toast the innovative Old General and the brilliance of my good friends and colleagues, Christian and Harold, and here is a toast to 'bleeding the god-damned Commies white.'"

"Hear, hear," all four shouted in unison, as other patrons raised their eyebrows at the rowdy group.

As they formulated their next toast, a dapper elderly gentleman rose from a nearby table, excused himself from his companion, and walked toward the merrymakers. In contrast to most of the vacationers at the hotel he wore a dark blue suit, gleaming white shirt and a gold and blue tie. He approached Christian Reiter.

"Excuse me, gentlemen," he said. "Have I heard correctly? Did you mention OMEGA Solution? Are you based in New York City?"

Christian gasped. He and his group were momentarily dumbfounded. Then, almost in unison, they shouted, "The DNI!"

The old gentleman chuckled and nodded. The members of the OMEGA Team shook hands vigorously, and clapped him on his back.

"Finally," said Rear Admiral Vincence Horstmann, the former DNI, with a twinkle in his eye, "finally, after all these years, I get to meet the rest of the illustrious OMEGA Team. Let me see." He looked from McCurrill to Miller and back. Pointing to Miller, "Now, if I remember correctly, you are the Wizard?"

Casey Miller nodded smiling.

Horstmann pointed at McCurrill, "And you, sir, must be the dreamer—oh, yes, the President said 'the Philosopher.'" He looked around. "That leaves only one other, the New Yorker." Pointing at Christian he proclaimed, "Christian Reiter, of Quadrant Import-Export and the leader of the OMEGA Team."

This time, the entire OMEGA Team gasped. Christian laughed, then exclaimed; "Now I know why the Navy made you the DNI."

"I never thought I'd live long enough to meet you." The admiral smiled. "Would you mind very much if I introduced you to my wife?" He motioned for his wife to join them. His spouse stared at them in wonder. "Are these old Navy friends of yours, dear?" she asked her husband quietly, as Christian ordered another round of drinks.

The DNI leaned closely toward his wife and in a low voice said, "Remember OMEGA?"

A look of revelation transformed his wife's countenance, as she broke out into a wide smile. "Well, I never..." she began, as Christian Reiter handed her a flute of champagne.

The surprise meeting turned into a long, joyous evening. It seemed as if thousands of questions demanded answers.

Christian asked, "How did you happen to be here?"

"I... we live on the island," was Horstmann's reply. "We live almost directly across the street from the Ritz, at Summer Beach. We could almost walk here, and we come to the Ritz almost every Friday for an evening of elegance. Of course, that might be a bit easier if I knew everyone's name."

Christian turned to the DNI and his wife with, "I am Christian Reiter, and the man you called the Philosopher is indeed the cerebral Harold McCurrill. The Wizard is Karl Cedric 'Casey' Miller, he once was the creator of ingenious, explosive, operational equipment, and—" Christian waved to his brother.

The admiral interrupted Christian, "No need, I have known Special Agent Hans Reiter for many years."

The three OMEGA members looked perplexed, as the DNI continued, "Hans Reiter led your plan to its final conclusion."

Hans bowed in mock innocence and grinned. *"C'est moi."*

"Oh, no, Mr. Reiter, you don't get off the hook that easily." The admiral laughed. "We, almost outsiders, would like to hear how it all played out. The OMEGA team has been out of touch for decades, and I for a good few years. Tell us the rest of the story."

The New Yorker, the Philosopher and the Wizard agreed.

"That's going to be a long night," Hans said.

The DNI asked: "What about the GRU officer, Kasandroff, what happened to him?"

"Kasandroff? Well, aside from our primary mission, the OMEGA Deception, he gave the Intelligence Community a never before archived, unparalleled look, into the function, capability, and weaknesses of GRU Centre in Moscow."

Hans paused collecting his thoughts, "Kasandroff's emergency code word was 'Iron Horse'. And, as the only one here knows, Kasandroff also saved the lives of two of our most valuable assets, Soviet Navy Warrant Officer Misha Kovlosky, and the academician Gregory Orloff."

Hans then told about the hair-raising ride through East Germany with Heinz Gerstmann his *Landsmann*, the VOPO colonel, to rescue Orloff. He the reminisced about his trip to Japan with Special Agent Frank Milushkyi, and Kovlosky's the fake suicide of in Japan.

The admiral lifted his hand signaling that he remembered.

Hans reminded the admiral that both these assets had been betrayed by someone high up in U.S. Intelligence, someone with high clearances."

Hans Reiter squirmed a bit, thinking, *Should I tell them of the breach of the cardinal rule?*

"Ivan Ivanovich Kasandroff, that's his full name, and I worked together almost two decades. Together we faced extreme difficulties. There were times when we were in extreme danger. Both of us."

"There is an iron rule in the clandestine services: Never become friends with your asset. I accepted this rule for a long time. But Ivan Ivanovich and I had been through too much. Too much danger. Together. Ivan Ivanovich had spent a couple of years at the Moscow Centre. We met in Herzogenaurach after that assignment. He seemed to be a different person. He gave me a bear hug, and said, 'God, it's good to see you.' That's when I admitted it. That's when he admitted it. We were friends."

The audience showed no visible surprise. "So," asked the DNI, "are you now finally retired?"

"Admiral, intelligence officers are like military horses, when the regimental band strikes up, it or he falls in and marches in step."

"Admittedly," the admiral concluded, "Hans Reiter, you have had one hell of a ride."

Reiter grinned. *"C'est moi."*

POSTSCRIPT: LAST THOUGHTS

*R*oom 526 is fiction based upon fact. The Soviet Projekt 705 was real. An explosion ended the trial run of the project's first titanium hull submarine, but, once its nuclear pressure container was strengthened, this submarine was the world's smallest, fastest, and deepest diving. Six were built. This was all top secret for the Soviets but, as recounted in *Room 526*, US Naval Intelligence and the CIA were able to penetrate the secrecy and keep abreast of all the Soviets were doing, including mothballing of the titanium fleet forced by the Soviet Union's bankruptcy.

The U. S. designation for the Projekt 705 subs was: ALFA Class SSN.

On 19 January 1979, the commander of the US Naval Sea Systems Command wrote Naval Intelligence that CIA'S extraordinary collection and Naval Intelligence's timely analysis of the ALFA Class SSN threat had saved the Navy $325,000,000 in new torpedo designs. I believe this may have been the first time in history that a U.S. Department of Defense organization had officially credited an intelligence collection and analysis with saving such a large sum of money.

The savings was for the Advanced Lightweight Torpedo (ALWT) that was to be modified to go beyond the original designed crush depth. Our findings were submitted just before the ALWT was to go into production

*B*y its very nature, an intelligence operation is hidden from all except those directly involved. This vital security measure is called "compartmentation." Compartmentation limits knowledge of operations to those few who have, in intelligence jargon, "the need to know." A leak would not only endanger the operatives and their "assets," it would also cause the loss of huge amounts of tax dollars. Worse yet, it would have certain residents of Capitol Hill clamor for investigations to show the folks back home that they are valiant guardians of the people's money. Last, but not least, it would destroy the careers or lives of intrepid men and women. Pervasive secrecy is what gives espionage that certain mystique, that aura of mystery that surrounds those in the cloak and dagger profession.

Even with today's sophisticated means of intelligence collection, the human agent continues to be the most important key to meet a nation's intelligence needs. Only with a human agent can an intelligence service reach deep inside the opponent's apparatus. Only the human agent can provide answers to specific questions. Only the human agent can voice opinions and provide assessments from the opponent's "the inner circle." Only the human agent can—wittingly or unwittingly—insert "hard copy" deception material into that inner circle.

Deception operations must meet all the criteria of other intelligence operations except one: secrecy. The secrecy of deception operations is feigned.

To trick the Soviets into overextending their resources by building titanium hull submarines, the lure was secretiveness. For a deception to succeed, the bait must be offered, and the bait must be taken. As Sun Tzu, the Chinese philosopher and guru of the intelligence world, wrote 2,500 years ago in *The Art of War:* "The enemy is deceived by creating shapes." The shape the Director of Naval Intelligence created to deceive the Soviets was the design of a fully functional, totally credible, submarine from which any naval design bureau engineer could build a nuclear-powered, titanium attack submarine. With this set of blueprints, which the Soviets were allowed to purloin, the DNI managed to mislead the Soviet Naval Staff. Counting on Soviet Russian paranoia, the DNI created a conceivable threat to the Soviet Navy, a valid reason for the Soviets to counter this threat.

A succession of DNIs, akin to experienced fly-fishermen, dangled the bait ever so cunningly before the GRU collectors. The DNIs' bait was total secrecy; intelligence operatives everywhere hoped that their operation would run its course unnoticed; that it would flow silently past the rocks and shallows, and that their operation would pass others silently, unnoticed, like ships at night in bygone days. The essence of a successful operation is normality—total normality. The operation must follow a logical sequence. If it does not, someone may wonder the lack of a logical sequence of events—and question it; then the entire plan could become unraveled.

During the many years most of the men, and the very few women in Room 526 on Wisconsin Avenue in Washington lived in this world of shadows, smoke, and mirrors. They would not have been surprised that the folks at Room 526, including Hiram Smyth, Hans Reiter, as well as Reiter's old friend Ivan Ivanovich Kasandroff, had all been "pawns in a bigger game."

So says the Pointman.
Fernandina Beach, Florida,
October 17, 2015

CPSIA information can be obtained
at www.ICGtesting.com
Printed in the USA
LVOW01s2341100316

478680LV00015B/120/P

9 780996 523516